who is my shelter?

To Rachel Joy
My daughter
My friend

Other Novels by Neta Jackson

The Yada Yada Prayer Group Series

The Yada Yada Prayer Group

The Yada Yada Prayer Group Gets Down

The Yada Yada Prayer Group Gets Real

The Yada Yada Prayer Group Gets Tough

The Yada Yada Prayer Group Gets Caught

The Yada Yada Prayer Group Gets Rolling

The Yada Yada Prayer Group Gets Decked Out

The Yada Yada House of Hope Series

Where Do I Go?

Who Do I Talk To?

Who Do I Lean On?

who is my shelter?

BOOK 4

A
yada yada
HOUSE *of* HOPE
Novel

NETA JACKSON

THOMAS NELSON
Since 1798

Published in Nashville, Tennessee, by Thomas Nelson. Thomas Nelson is a registered trademark of Thomas Nelson, Inc.

Published in association with the literary agency of Alive Communications, Inc., 7680 Goddard Street, Suite 200, Colorado Springs, CO 80920.

Thomas Nelson, Inc., titles may be purchased in bulk for educational, business, fund-raising, or sales promotional use. For information, e-mail SpecialMarkets@ThomasNelson.com.

Scripture quotations are taken from the following: HOLY BIBLE, NEW INTERNATIONAL VERSION®, NIV®. © 1973, 1978, 1984 by Biblica, Inc.™ Used by permission of Zondervan. All rights reserved worldwide. www.zondervan.com.

Holy Bible, New Living Translation. © 1996. Used by permission of Tyndale House Publishers, Inc., Wheaton, Illinois 60189. All rights reserved.

THE NEW KING JAMES VERSION. © 1982 by Thomas Nelson, Inc. Used by permission. All rights reserved.

REVISED STANDARD VERSION of the Bible. © 1946, 1952, 1971, 1973 by the Division of Christian Education of the National Council of the Churches of Christ in the U.S.A. Used by permission.

"I Go to the Rock," words and music by Dottie Rambo. © 1977 New Spring, Inc. (ASCAP). Administered by Brentwood-Benson Music Publishing, Inc. Used by permission.

4618 1821 6/11

Publisher's Note: This novel is a work of fiction. Any references to real events, businesses, organizations, and locales are intended only to give the fiction a sense of reality and authenticity. Any resemblance to actual persons, living or dead, is entirely coincidental.

Library of Congress Cataloging-in-Publication Data

Jackson, Neta.
  Who is my shelter? / Neta Jackson.
    p. cm. -- (A yada yada house of hope novel ; bk. 4)
  ISBN 978-1-59554-863-4 (pbk.)
  1. Christian women--Fiction. 2. Shelters for the homeless--Fiction. 3. Chicago (Ill.)--Fiction. I. Title.
  PS3560.A2415W49 2011
  813'.54--dc22

2010046481

prologue

The face in the mirror was barely recognizable. Philip Fairbanks winced at the black-and-blue mask that spread like a handprint over his broken nose and encompassed both eyes like tattooed sunglasses. Most of the swelling had gone down—it'd been almost a week since those thugs had attacked him—but he still looked like the poster boy for a horror flick. The forty stitches that started on his forehead and ran in a jagged path along the right side of his head didn't help, especially since they'd shaved his entire scalp to avoid leaving him with a bald spot on only one side.

"Don't you worry, honey," the plump nurse's aide—they called them "Patient Care Technicians" now—had chirped cheerfully as she'd shaved away his fifty-dollar haircut. *"Hair always grows back. And bald heads are rad now, verrry sexy."*

Yeah, right.

"I can't go to the office looking like this!" he growled to his reflection. He was on enough shaky ground with his business partner at Fairbanks and Fenchel without also freaking out their clients. What in the world was he going to do?

He had to do something. Before Henry made good on his threat to sue him for the money missing from their account.

Tentatively opening his mouth—*Uhnn*, that hurt—Philip inserted the hospital-issue toothbrush and carefully waggled it around his teeth. If he was going to be discharged today, he had to clean up. But brushing hurt. Chewing hurt. Talking hurt. Blowing his nose hurt. And that was only his head! His broken right arm and the three broken ribs where he'd been kicked repeatedly meant that almost every movement hurt, even breathing. Especially breathing. The sharp pains in his gut still made him grit his teeth when he took the required daily walks around the nursing floor, even though none of the x-rays or blood tests had turned up any definitive internal injuries.

Probably just bruising on his organs, the internist had said. But they'd kept doing tests since he still had pain. Seemed like something would've shown up by now.

Coming out of the bathroom of the private hospital room, Philip saw that his breakfast tray had been taken away, and some-one—probably one of those "senior volunteers" who roamed the place—had laid today's *Tribune* on his bed. He was tempted to settle into the recliner and read the paper until housekeeping had changed the bed and cleaned the bathroom, but it was such an ordeal to get comfortable and then struggle to get up again, he might as well get the morning walk out of the way since he was already upright. At least they'd unhooked him from the IV pole and let him eat real food—if you could call Jell-O and Cream of Wheat and lukewarm chicken broth "real food."

Reaching for the brown terry bathrobe Gabby had brought him, he pulled it over his shoulders with his one good hand and started for the hall. He couldn't remember who'd loaned it to him, maybe that tall Baxter kid, the young one who'd moved into Gabby's building to be the property manager or something. He didn't like wearing someone else's robe, but at least it covered the yawning gaps in the back of the faded hospital gown.

Walking was tedious. Past the room with the old man who always seemed to be asleep with his mouth hanging open . . . past the room that always had at least three or more visitors yakking it up . . . past the room full of flowers and balloons, and the room that had none . . . thirty-seven steps to the nurses' station, situated so the staff could keep an eye on the comings and goings of visitors and patients and the call lights outside each room. Philip stopped. "Excuse me, nurse? When is Dr. Yin coming around? He said I might be discharged today, and I'd like to get out of here sooner rather than—"

"He'll be here, Mr. Fairbanks." The closest nurse didn't even look up from the computer where she was typing in notes. "Just be patient. Glad to see you walking . . . that's good. You got somebody to pick you up?"

Philip didn't answer. No, he didn't have anybody coming to pick him up—though he supposed Gabby would if he called her and let her know what time he was getting released. Today was Saturday—she'd said something about P.J.'s cross country meet in the morning and a dedication thing at that shelter where she worked, then she'd bring the boys to see him.

The boys. Philip grimaced as he turned into the next hall. He wished she wouldn't bring P.J. and Paul. He hated having his sons see him like this. They were both good sports but—*wait.* He sniffed. Smelled like fresh coffee. Oh! What he wouldn't give for a good cup of hot coffee. *But where . . . ?*

Philip glanced down the hallway. It was deserted except for a young man, maybe college age, leaning against the wall outside one of the patient rooms holding two tall Starbucks cups with molded plastic lids, sipping from one of them. Drawn by the fragrant aroma, he approached the young man who was wearing faded jeans, gym shoes, and a thin jacket over a white T-shirt. He had longish, sandy hair escaping from beneath a baseball cap and a backpack slung over one shoulder.

"Uh, say, sorry to bother you, but where'd you get the Starbucks? Do they have a café here in the hospital?" Philip winced, hearing his words mushing together.

The kid looked up, his eyebrows shooting skyward as he took in Philip's arm cast and battered face. "Whoa, dude! What's the other guy look like?"

Great. A smart aleck. "Never mind." Philip started to walk away.

"Hey, wait! Didn't mean to be rude—you just took me by surprise. Uh, yeah, sure, there's a nice place on the first floor. They sell Starbucks. You want somethin'?"

Philip hesitated. "Well, yeah. Could use a cup of good coffee. But . . ." He held out both hands as far as his sling would allow to indicate his stocking feet and hospital gown. "Not exactly dressed for public viewing."

The kid chuckled. "No problem. I'll get it for you. What d'ya want? Oh, hey. Why don't you just take this?" He thrust out the second cup of coffee he was holding. "Brought it up for my nana"—he tipped his head to indicate the patient room behind him—"but she zonked out. Snoring happily. It'll be cold by the time she wakes up. Go ahead, take it." He held it out farther. "Just black, nothin' in it—but I got some creamers and sugar packets in my pocket somewhere."

"Black's fine. You sure? I'll pay you for it. Wallet's in my room."

A shrug. "Whatever. I'll carry it back for you. Where's your room? Looks like you could use another hand anyway."

Philip had meant he'd go back and get his wallet, but the kid was already starting to walk alongside as he headed back the way he'd come. It meant cutting his walk short, but . . . so what? The coffee wouldn't stay hot indefinitely.

Back in his room, Philip opened the narrow closet storing the jogging clothes he'd been wearing when he'd been attacked and rummaged in the duffel bag Gabrielle had brought him that held a clean set of clothes, his keys, and wallet. Fishing a few bucks out with his good hand, he turned around to see that his benefactor had moved the rolling table next to the recliner, set the second paper cup on it, and settled into the other visitor chair.

Looked like he had company, whether he wanted it or not.

Philip handed the dollar bills to his visitor, then lowered himself gingerly into the recliner. Reaching for the coffee, he sipped carefully. *Mmm. Still hot. Perfect.* "Thanks. Appreciate the coffee." He studied the young man slouched in the other chair, nursing his own cup. "I'm Philip Fairbanks. You are . . . ?"

"Oh yeah." The kid laughed. "Forgot my manners. Nana would box my ears. I'm Will Nissan—yeah, like the car. What happened to you? Car accident?"

The kid sure was nosy! But for some reason, Philip found Will's straightforward friendliness refreshing. Somebody who wasn't ticked at him like his father was for messing up his life. Somebody who wasn't being nice to him—like his wife—in spite of how he'd treated her, making him feel like a snake in the grass.

Somebody who wasn't out to get him, like those thugs, trying to squeeze him for the money he owed their boss.

Philip shrugged. "Actually, I got mugged."

Will Nissan's eyes widened with ill-concealed delight. "You gotta be kidding!"

"Nope. Truth." But that's all he was going to say. Philip didn't want to think about those thugs who'd worked him over. Or the fact that they were still out there and knew where he lived. "What about your grandmother . . . she going to be all right?"

Will shrugged. "Probably. Nothing seems to keep her down long, though she gets this bronchitis stuff easily and her doc's worried about pneumonia. But, nah, Nana ain't gonna die until she finishes her mission in life."

"Her . . . what?"

"Her mission in life!" Will chuckled and leaned forward. "See, Nana's big sister ran away from home when she was sixteen—oh, it's gotta be sixty-plus years ago now. Nana's seventy-seven at last count and Cindy was a couple of years older. Anyway, last they heard from her, big sister was working in Chicago, but nobody's seen her since. My Nana got married, raised a family in Detroit—I was born and raised there too—but she never gave up looking for her sister. When Gramps died a few years back, she moved here so she could keep looking for her."

Philip shook his head. "It's been over sixty years? She could be anywhere! People move all the time. Or she might be dead. Sixty years is a long time."

"Try telling that to Nana! 'I know she's alive!' she says. 'Can feel it in my bones.'" Will shrugged and leaned back in the chair. "My folks think Nana's crazy, but I don't mind. I'm staying with her now while I'm going to UIC, and I've been helping her do all these Internet searches. Kind of like detective work."

"Any luck?"

"Nah, not really. We did find somebody with a similar name who worked as a hotel maid way back when, but that was decades ago. Not much since then—oh." Will jumped up as the door opened and a thirty-something Asian man strolled in wearing a tan corduroy sport coat and black slacks, an ID tag and a stethoscope sticking out of one coat pocket identifying him as medical personnel.

Philip nodded. "Dr. Yin."

"Good morning." The doctor glanced at Will, a pleasant smile creasing his smooth face. "I see you have company. Your son taking you home?"

"Nah. We just met actually." Will grabbed his backpack. "Gotta go see if Nana's awake." He held out his hand to Philip. "Good luck, Mr. Fairbanks. Better stay away from the prize ring, though. Don't think boxing's your thing." The young man's hazel eyes crinkled merrily as they shook hands.

Philip smiled at the joke, sorry to see him go. "What's the name of your missing relative? Never know who I might run into."

Will grinned. "Yeah, you never know. Lucinda. 'Great-Aunt Cindy,' we always called her. The myth, the legend! We kids always imagined she became some famous movie star. If so, she's probably sipping daiquiris in a swanky nursing home in Hollywood." The young man sidled toward the door. "But, hey, if you do need a ride home, just let me know. I've got Nana's car, I'd be happy to drop you off."

With a cheerful wave Will Nissan was gone.

Dr. Yin pulled out his stethoscope. "So, Mr. Fairbanks. They tell me you want to go home." He nodded thoughtfully. "Might let you do that. But I wouldn't go back to work yet if I were you. A few more days rest—even a week—would be smart. You've still got some healing to do. Tell them 'Doctor's orders.'" He stuck the earpieces in his ears and placed the stethoscope on Philip's back. "Deep breath now . . ."

chapter 1

The Good Shepherd painted on the wall of the Manna House Women's Shelter seemed to hover over the crowd in the multi-purpose room, as if the babble of street talk, Jamaican *patois*, and bits of Spanish swirling around me was an extension of the motley herd of sheep in the mural itself.

Standing in front of the mural holding a plastic cup of red, watery punch, I savored the unusual painting once more. The pictures of the biblical Good Shepherd I'd seen as a kid always had a flock of clean, white, woolly sheep looking up at the shepherd adoringly. But the sheep on the wall were all different shades of white, black, brown, and tan, some with scraggly, dirty wool, some scrawny and hungry looking, others with bloody or bandaged wounds. But the thing about the mural that never failed to grab me was the Shepherd's face as He coaxed the bedraggled sheep into the pen where they would be safe and warm.

A look of sheer love.

I dabbed at my eyes with a wadded-up tissue. How I wished

my mother—Martha Shepherd—could see this beautiful mural and be here for the dedication of the room that had been named after her: Shepherd's Fold.

"Gabby Fairbanks! You blubbering again, girl? Here." Precious McGill, on-again, off-again resident of Manna House, took the plastic cup out of my hand and replaced it with a mug of steaming coffee. "You need somethin' stronger than Hawaiian Punch to prop you up today. I know, I know, we all feelin' sad that Gramma Shep be gone. But it's all good. It's all good."

I took a swallow of the hot liquid. "Mmm. Good coffee. And just enough cream. Thanks."

The thirty-year-old single mom—soon to become a grandmother herself—craned her neck, checking out the crowd. "So where's this famous artist we s'posed to meet today? Ain't he gonna show up for the dedication? I thought that's what today was all about."

I took the arm of my friend and turned away from the mural. "I'm sure he'll be here. And he's not famous *yet*—he's still an art student at Columbia College. I don't see his parents or the Baxters yet, so I imagine they're all still on the way." Now it was my turn to case the room. "But I don't see Lucy either. *She* better show up. This whole dedication thing was her idea."

Precious snorted. "Yeah, but you know Lucy. Never can tell when she gonna show up—or not. Uh-oh, gotta go. Estelle's givin' me the Evil Eye 'cause I abandoned my post. Ya gonna take your boys to the Lock-In tonight up at SouledOut? Sabrina wants to go—which I think is crazy, her bein' six months pregnant an' all." Without waiting for an answer, Precious scooted through the crowd and a moment later I saw her head full of wiry twists pop up behind the snack table where Estelle Williams, the shelter's cook, was busy setting out hot wings and fresh veggies.

I groaned to myself. Why did the church schedule a youth group Lock-In the same day as the dedication here at Manna House? Josh Baxter was involved in both—a volunteer here at the shelter as well as one of the youth leaders at SouledOut Community Church. So what if he was only twenty-something. He should know better.

Guess I'm showing my age. All-nighters of *any* variety were definitely a thing of my past.

But the Lock-In had put a crunch on other things as well. I still needed to take my boys to see their dad in the hospital this afternoon—but there wouldn't be a lot of time after the Shepherd's Fold dedication if P.J. and Paul had to be at the church by six o'clock. And, darn it, I'd been hoping to have a potluck or something this weekend to celebrate our first week at the House of Hope, our experiment in "second-stage housing" for homeless single moms—moms like Precious McGill and her daughter, Sabrina, who'd moved in a week ago across the hall from me.

But that was a wash now. Not with the Lock-In tonight, which took out my boys *and* Sabrina. Not to mention Josh and his wife, Edesa, too. The young couple had moved into the House of Hope last week after Josh had agreed to be the property manager for the six-flat. Josh and Edesa definitely needed to be at any "festivity" we had to celebrate this new beginning.

A commotion at the double doors leading into the large multi-purpose room shook me out of my thoughts. *Oh, Gabby, quit complaining*, I told myself, seeing Josh's parents and their friends, the Hickmans, arriving with a young man I presumed was our guest of honor. As usual when I got an idea—like this potluck, which I was already envisioning as a once-a-month get together for the residents and staff of the new House of Hope—I wanted it to happen *now*. But who said the potluck had to happen on the first weekend of the month? Having another week to plan wouldn't hurt either.

Huh. God seemed to think patience was a virtue I still needed to practice. On a daily basis, no less.

Making my way to the knot of people greeting each other by the double doors, I hesitated, suddenly feeling shy. What in the world was I going to say to the young man who'd painted the awesome Good Shepherd mural? I didn't have words.

I recognized his mother, Florida Hickman, one of the Yada Yada Prayer Group sisters, and I'd seen her husband, Carl, a couple of times. The story was, their son Chris had been a teenage "tagger," illegally decorating garage doors and El underpasses with his cans of spray paint. Until somebody recognized that the kid had real talent—

"Gabby Fairbanks!" hissed a familiar voice in my ear. "Where've you been? I want you to meet Chris!" Jodi Baxter—Josh's mother and one of my best friends—grabbed my arm and dragged me right into the middle of the group of people clustered around the young artist. "Chris, this is Mrs. Fairbanks, the program director here at Manna House. She's—"

"I know. Gramma Shep was her mama." The young black man's soft voice surprised me, and I was completely dazzled by his beautiful grin. He shook my hand, a nice, firm grip. "My pleasure, Miz Fairbanks. Saw you across the room and knew who you were." He pointed to my hair and grinned even wider. "The Orphan Annie hair, like the movie, know what I'm sayin'?"

I had to laugh. "I know. Dead giveaway." I took a deep breath. "I'm so happy to finally meet you, Chris. I've been wanting to thank you. The mural—" Darn it if those rogue tears didn't come rushing to the surface and I had to fish for another tissue. "Um, sorry. It's just that the mural is . . . is . . . so meaningful. So perfect for Manna House and the lost sheep who come here." Uhh, that sounded lame. I could feel the tips of my ears turning red. "Oh! Here are my boys."

Jodi had managed to pry my young teenagers away from the hot wings at the snack table and was herding them toward us. "P.J., Paul, this is Chris Hickman, the artist who painted the mural over there."

P.J. nodded in greeting and awkwardly bumped fists with the older teenager. But Paul's eyes widened in twelve-year-old awe. "You did that? Man, I thought you'd be a lot—you know—older."

Chris started to say something when we were interrupted by Estelle banging on the bottom of a pot, followed by the voice of Mabel Turner, the director of Manna House. "Everyone, please find a seat and let's get started. We have a short program of dedication for the naming of our multipurpose room, and we also want to introduce the young artist who . . ."

Mabel continued her introductions as the crowd—current residents of the shelter, members of the board of directors, volunteers, staff, and "friends of the shelter"—obediently began finding seats in the rows of folding chairs facing the mural. Leading Chris toward the front row, I whispered, "Thanks again, Chris. I only wish my mom could see it."

"Yeah, me too," he whispered back. "Wish I could've met her. Whole time I was paintin' that mural, folks here at Manna

House came by wantin' to tell me stories about Gramma Shep. She must've been quite a lady."

That made me smile. "Actually," I murmured as we found seats, "she was just an ordinary woman with ordinary gifts. But that was her strength. She didn't see herself as anything special, which made everyone feel comfortable around her. She loved people and treated everyone like her best friend."

Everyone, I mused, as Mabel opened the dedication service with a prayer—even Lucy Tucker, the seventy-something "bag lady" who'd been my introduction to Manna House six months ago. My mom and Lucy had bonded in a strange, sweet way the last few weeks of my mother's life—partially because my mother could no longer take her yellow mutt, Dandy, for walks here in the unfamiliar city, and streetwise Lucy had risen to the occasion. Which was why I'd given the dog to Lucy when my mother died two months ago.

It was Lucy who'd made a fuss that Manna House didn't have a proper memorial for "Gramma Shep." Lucy who first raised the idea of renaming the multipurpose room, and who kept fussing until a brass plaque with "Shepherd's Fold—Dedicated to Martha Shepherd" had been engraved.

I twisted in my seat and gave the room another cursory glance. So why was Lucy missing now?

To my disappointment, Lucy and Dandy never did show. I would have liked to stay to visit with all the other friends, staff, and former residents who'd shown up for the dedication, but once the board chairman delivered the final "Amen," I had to slip out with P.J. and Paul and head straight to Weiss Memorial Hospital where my estranged husband had been admitted a week ago after a vicious beating.

When we got off the elevator on the patient floor, Paul darted ahead of us and into his dad's hospital room—but he came right back out. "He's not there!" Sure enough, the hospital bed laid flat, side rails down, clean sheets tucked and military taut, pillow stiff and undented. The monitoring machines were gone—no beeps, no blips, no drips—as if the room had never been occupied. "Philip?" I called, peeking into the bathroom, which was silly because the room was obviously empty.

"Mom?" Paul's voice wavered. "Dad isn't . . . he didn't . . . you know . . ."

"No, no, honey!" I put an arm around my youngest in a quick hug. "They either moved him to another room or he's been discharged. Come on, we'll find out."

I hustled both boys out of the room and down the hall to the nurses' station. "Can you tell me if Philip Fairbanks has been moved to another room?"

The light-skinned African American woman at the desk—her ID tag said Floor Manager—held up a finger, then typed something into her computer. "Let's see. Pretty sure he was discharged this morning—yes. Here's the discharge order from Dr. Yin."

"Already? He was still having a lot of pain. And he can't drive with just one arm—"

"Taxi, Mom," drawled fourteen-year-old P.J. in his *parents-can-be-so-dumb* tone of voice.

The woman behind the desk smiled. "Yes. But I think he got a ride. A young man met up with him when they brought the wheel-chair for your husband, said something about getting his car from the parking garage. Nice-looking young man, sandy hair, maybe nineteen or twenty . . . not your son?"

I shook my head. Did I look old enough to have a twenty-year-old? I thanked her, and the boys and I headed for the elevator. Who in the world came to pick him up? Sandy hair, college age—almost sounded like Josh Baxter. But he'd been at the dedication the past couple hours. So who?

The elevator doors pinged open and we crowded on with an empty gurney, a transport tech, and two women in housekeeping tunics talking to each other in rapid Spanish. I looked at my watch. Already past four thirty. I had to get P.J. and Paul to SouledOut by six. Did we have time to stop by Richmond Towers and make sure their dad had gotten back to the penthouse safely and had everything he needed? Prescriptions? Food in the house? Laundry done?

Cool it, Gabby, I told myself. *You're not his mother.* Not even his wife exactly. We'd been separated for more than three months—under ugly circumstances. But Philip had been so different the past few weeks . . . well, halfway decent, anyway. He didn't fight me for temporary custody of the boys, and we'd worked out a reasonable weekly visitation when the boys slept over at the penthouse. But his gambling losses . . . *whew*. Philip's addiction to the poker table had turned his well-planned world inside out, and I couldn't turn my back on him when some loan shark sent his hooligans to "persuade" Philip to pay up.

"So what do you guys want to do?" I asked the boys as we located our second-hand Subaru in the parking garage and climbed in. "We could go to Richmond Towers and try to see your dad now. Or we could go tomorrow after church when there won't be any rush."

"I wanna go see Dad now," Paul piped up from the back seat.

"You sure? We won't have much time to visit if you guys still want to go to the Lock-In. And what if he asks you to stay overnight? You missed your overnight with him last weekend when he ended up in the hospital."

"He just got out, Mom." P.J. sounded ticked off. "It's not like we'd be able to *do* anything together."

"I wanna go now," Paul repeated.

I backed out of the parking spot and headed down the multi-level ramp toward the exit. "Okay. Now it is." Maybe just as well. We'd have a natural leave time since I had to get the boys to the Lock-In.

I handed four bucks and my parking ticket to the attendant at the exit, and within minutes we were heading north on Sheridan Road toward the luxury high-rise I'd once shared with my husband.

chapter 2

I pulled the Subaru into a Visitor Parking space on the narrow access road between Richmond Towers and the park that ran along Lake Shore Drive in the distance. The trees in the park were still full and green this first weekend of October since the weather was fairly warm. But I imagined the park would be dressed in beautiful reds and golds in a few weeks . . . before the lakefront turned to ice and the Windy City lived up to its name during a sharp, biting Chicago winter.

And what would Lucy and Dandy do then?

Following my boys toward Philip's building, I glanced back over my shoulder on the off chance I might see my bag lady friend and the yellow dog she'd adopted after my mom died. This park was one of Lucy's favorite hangouts and where I'd run into her the first time we'd "met" last spring. Didn't see either of them . . . but I did catch a glimpse of the opening to the pedestrian tunnel that ran beneath Lake Shore Drive, allowing dog walkers and joggers access to the shores of Lake Michigan on the other side.

The tunnel where Philip had been viciously attacked and beaten a week ago today while out jogging.

A cold shudder ran down my spine as the boys and I pushed through the revolving door into the lobby of Richmond Towers. Lucy had seen some suspicious characters hanging around the luxury high-rise for several days before the beating took place. Since the attackers hadn't taken his watch or anything valuable, it looked like a "warning" from the loan shark who'd been threatening Philip.

Those brutes obviously knew where Philip lived. Was he safe coming back here?

Using the key card I still had in my purse, I swiped the security pad that let residents into the small elevator lobby. A few minutes later the boys and I stepped out of the elevator into the marble foyer of the thirty-second floor. The penthouse was the only living unit on this floor. Even though I still had a key, I pushed the doorbell. No way was I going to walk in if Philip was already there.

The door opened. But it wasn't Philip framed in the doorway. A young man stood in the gallery, sandy hair sticking out from under a Cubs baseball cap, a curious grin on his face. "Hi!" he said. "You looking for Mr. Fairbanks? C'mon in. He's in the living room. Guess that's what you call it. Wow! Never seen such a view."

P.J. and Paul both stared at the stranger, then Paul ran inside. "Dad? Dad! You okay?" P.J. and I followed.

Philip was sitting in his recliner, facing the floor-to-ceiling glass windows that wrapped around one corner of the large room. He turned his head as the boys came close. "Hey, guys," he said, wincing as though the movement took too much effort.

Even though I'd been at the hospital at least once a day since the beating, it was still a shock to see Philip's shaved head—that beautiful head of dark brown hair, always so carefully groomed— with the ugly red gash on the right side held together by a railroad track of stitches. The bruises from his broken nose were still spreading and now filled his eyes, giving him a brooding look. His broken right arm in its cast and sling rested on the arm of the recliner, but he managed to give both boys an awkward hug with the other arm.

"Hey," I said, standing a few feet away. "You okay? We got to the hospital and you weren't there."

"Yeah. Doc said I could heal just as well at home." He barely moved his mouth as he talked, as if his jaw hurt to move it.

"Yes, but—" I was wondering how he was going to cook his meals and dress himself with only one arm and those broken ribs.

But Philip interrupted. "So you met Will here?" He tipped his head toward the young man who'd opened the door and had followed us back into the living room. "He brought me home from the hospital."

"Not officially." I politely held out my hand. "Hi, Will. I'm Gabby Fairbanks. This is P.J. and Paul." I wasn't giving up any more until I had a better idea who this "Will" person was.

"My pleasure." He shook my hand with a nice grip and grinned at the boys. "I just met Mr. Fairbanks this morning at the hospital. I was visiting my grandmother on the same floor and we got to talking just before the doc discharged him. Didn't look like he had a way home and I had Nana's car . . . and here we are." He shrugged. "But now that your family's here"—he directed this comment at Philip—"maybe I should hustle on out of here."

In spite of myself, I liked this guy. "No, that's okay. We can't stay long. Just wanted to check on the boys' dad, make sure he's all right." I turned back to Philip. "Do you have any prescriptions that need picking up? And I can check the cupboards, make sure you have enough food—"

"Oh, we got it covered," Will said. "Stopped at Dominick's on the way here to get his meds filled and we picked up some frozen dinners—easy stuff—ought to keep him for a few days anyway."

Who *was* this Good Samaritan? "Oh. Well, uh, that's good. Thanks." If I was honest with myself, my nose felt a tad out of joint. After stepping up to the plate to make sure my husband was going to make it through this ordeal, I suddenly felt "kicked to the curb," as the kids liked to say. But maybe it was a good thing. I mean, did I really want Philip depending on me right now? It complicated our relationship, made it hard to figure out what was real and what was just . . . necessary. We still hadn't talked after Philip had begged me to forgive him for his despicable behavior—my words, not his—saying he wanted to try to patch together the broken pieces of our marriage.

That was after he'd landed in the hospital. I knew better than to respond to something that emotional in the middle of a crisis.

"Will's a college student at UIC," Philip was saying, but it was hard to hear him. The boys had turned on the flat-screen TV—three times as big as the old standby at my apartment—and were watching some nature program about alligators and other slimy reptiles.

"Hey, turn it down, guys," I said, then turned to Will. "What are you studying?"

"Architecture. And business. Not sure what I want to do."

I smiled. "Well, Philip's your man. He works with architects all the time. He's got his own commercial development business."

Will nodded eagerly. "Yeah, I know. He was telling me. I think I was wearing him out when you guys showed up. But I'd like to come back when you feel better, Mr. Fairbanks, and pick your brain . . . if you wouldn't mind. I've got a major project I have to do for school—it'd be great to have your input. Thanks for your business card."

"Yeah, yeah, sure." Philip did seem tired. Exhausted, really. But he murmured, "You're a good kid, Will. Hope you find your Great-Aunt Cindy."

Will laughed. "*Then* what would keep Nana occupied? It's the Grand Search that keeps her busy. Otherwise she'd be all in *my* business."

Philip grunted and shut his eyes wearily.

What was *that* all about? It was obvious it was time to go. "Come on, boys." I picked up the remote and clicked Off.

"Aww, can't we just finish this?" Paul grabbed unsuccessfully for the remote.

"Nope. Gotta get you to the Lock-In, remember? Say good-bye to your dad."

"Bye, Dad." Both boys gave their father another awkward hug, then headed for the front door.

I started to follow, but heard Philip mumble my name. "Gabby? Can . . . you come back? Maybe stay?"

I hesitated. I *was* worried how well he was going to manage on his own. But stay? It was one thing to stay with him the first couple of nights at the hospital when he was in crisis. But now that he was home . . .

"I don't think that's a good idea, Philip. But I'll come back tomorrow to see how you're doing. After church. Is that okay?"

His eyes flickered open. He seemed agitated for some reason. But then his eyes closed and he turned his head away. "Yeah, yeah. That's okay. Just call from the desk downstairs before you come up so I'll know it's you."

Well, fine. Whatever. I touched Philip's arm to let him know I was leaving, then picked up my purse and followed Will and the boys out into the marble foyer.

"What's this about a missing aunt?" I asked Philip's new friend as we waited for the elevator to arrive.

"Oh, that. I'm staying with my grandmother since I started UIC. Nana moved to Chicago to look for her sister who went missing when she was a teenager. Ran away, actually. Last they heard from her, she was here in Chicago, but it's been, like, sixty years. Nana still thinks she'll be found one of these days."

The elevator dinged and the doors slid open. P.J. and Paul hustled inside. This was interesting. For once I barely noticed as the elevator sank rapidly down all thirty-two floors.

"You're worried about her?"

"Who? Great-Aunt Cindy?" Will shrugged. "Not really. Never met her or anything. Mostly I'm just humoring my grandmother. But I don't mind."

As we got off the elevator, the boys and I headed for the main lobby, but Will turned toward the door that led to the parking garage. "Will? This way. That's for residents only."

He looked sheepish. "I know, but I'm parked in the garage. Actually . . ." He looked beyond my shoulder and saw that the boys were already out in the lobby. "Actually it was kind of weird. I pulled up outside the revolving door, was just going to let him out, you know. But then Mr. Fairbanks saw these two guys sitting on a bench in the park, kinda facing the building. Not homeless guys or anything. In fact, one of the guys was wearing a suit. But when Mr. Fairbanks saw them, he slid down in the seat and said, 'Go! Go!' and made me pull into the parking garage for the residents. He had a key card in his wallet—he was so nervous I had to find it for him. Once we got in, he asked if I'd bring his stuff up to the penthouse. Which was no problem. In fact, we got to talking about architecture and stuff. Before you came, I mean."

My mind was spinning as Will talked. Could the men they'd seen be the same guys who'd beaten him up? Philip said he hadn't gotten a good look at them—they wore hooded sweatshirts that hid their faces. But still.

"Do you think you could identify the men on the bench?" I asked Will.

He shrugged. "Maybe. Why? Who are they?"

I hesitated to mention my suspicions. "I'm not sure. But they obviously upset him. Do you mind giving me your phone number in case I need to contact you?"

"I guess."

I scribbled the phone number he gave me on a scrap of paper from my purse. But as we went our different ways, a lightbulb flicked on in my head.

Now I knew why Philip wanted me to stay.

He was afraid.

chapter 3

My cell phone rang somewhere in the depths of my purse as I got back in the Subaru after dropping off the boys and their overnight gear at SouledOut Community Church. The large storefront church in the busy shopping center was brightly lit and crawling with kids. I shuddered. Couldn't think of anything worse than an all-night Lock-In with a herd of teenagers high on hormones and pizza.

I caught a glimpse of Sabrina McGill—still a teenager, even if she was "great with child"—laughing with some other girls, and sighed with relief. *Well, good.* I'd left Manna House without offering her a ride to the Lock-In because of going to the hospital, but I'd felt slightly guilty since her mom didn't have a car, and now we all lived in the same building. But she either got a ride with someone or she'd taken the El. Easy enough. The Red Line ran like an arrow between the Wrigleyville neighborhood where Manna House was located and the Howard Street El Station next to the shopping center.

But I guess that separated true Chicagoans from transplants

like me. I still wasn't used to thinking "public transportation" when it came to getting from A to B. Or letting my young teenage sons ride around the city on their own. No way. I wanted to be sure they *got* to wherever they were headed.

My cell was still ringing. Digging out the phone, I looked at the caller ID: *Estelle Williams. Uh-oh.* Was she going to get on my case because I ducked out of cleanup after the dedication?

"Gabby? Where are you? You comin' back here to Manna House by any chance?"

"Uhh . . . hadn't planned on it. Had to take the boys to see their dad." I groaned silently. "But if you still need help with cleanup, I can—"

"Lucy's here lookin' for you. She's all upset about somethin'. Right now she's talkin' to Harry."

"Lucy showed up? Is she okay? Has something happened to Dandy?"

I heard a snort in my ear. "Hero Dog is currently helping himself to as many chicken bones as he can snitch out of the garbage. Whether he'll be fine by the time you get here is another question—"

"I'll be there in fifteen minutes! Tell Lucy to wait."

Quickly sticking the key in the ignition, I threaded my way out of the busy parking lot, and fifteen minutes later backed into a tight parking space half a block from the women's shelter. Estelle said Lucy was upset—what was going on?

Several of the shelter residents were sitting outside smoking on the steps of the shelter, bundled in jackets and sweatshirts against the cool October evening. The original shelter, housed in an old church that used to stand on that spot, had burned down, I'd been told, and the new building still resembled a church—because it was a "sanctuary," people said.

"Hey, Miss Gabby!" a young woman called out to me, blowing a smoke ring into the air. "That was a nice dedication for Gramma Shep."

"Thanks, Hannah. I thought so too." But as I passed her I murmured in her ear, "Don't tell me you've started smoking. You've got good things going for you!"

Hannah shrugged me off. "Aw, it's just somethin' to get me by. Least I ain't doin' no drugs."

"I know. I'm proud of the way you've hung on to the job at Adele's Hair and Nails too. I just hate to see you start a bad habit now."

Hannah rolled her eyes and took another drag on the cigarette, so I dropped it and used my key to let me into the Manna House foyer. The reception cubby on the right was dark and empty and Mabel's office door on the left was shut, no light under the door. But beyond the double doors leading into the main room, I saw lights and heard voices.

"What took ya so long?" Lucy Tucker demanded as I came into the large room dominated by the Good Shepherd mural. The old lady was wearing a purple crocheted hat crammed down on her head, topping her usual mishmash of blouses, sweaters, cotton sweatpants, and mismatched socks. Dandy made a beeline for me, wriggling all over.

"Could ask you the same thing," I said, feeling annoyed. I bent down and scratched Dandy's rump. "You missed the dedication of the mural, and if I remember right, it was your idea . . . okay, okay, Dandy, I love you too." I pushed the dog away and straightened up.

"Sorry 'bout that, but I was takin' care of business—*your* business, Fuzz Top. I think your maw will forgive me fer that." Lucy turned away in a huff. "Tell her, Mister Harry."

Puzzled, I looked at the other faces gathering around Lucy and me: Harry Bentley, Estelle Williams's "special friend," looking more like himself—smooth brown dome and trim gray beard outlining his jaw—now that his eye surgeries were over and he'd gotten rid of his pirate's patch. Estelle herself, our own staff "diva," swathed in one of her voluminous handmade caftans. Jodi and Denny Baxter, a white couple who were not only Josh Baxter's parents and "friends of the shelter" but my friends too. And Precious, who might as well be "staff" as much time as she put in helping out at the shelter. They must have all stayed to help with cleanup after the mural dedication.

My gaze went back to Harry. "What's going on, Mr. B?"

Harry held up his hand. "Just a minute . . . hey, DaShawn! Take this dog downstairs and play ball with him or somethin'."

Harry's ten-year-old grandson popped up from the nearest couch. "Can I? Cool. Come on, Dandy."

"Just stay out of the kitchen!" Estelle yelled after him as boy and dog disappeared down the stairs to the shelter's lower level, which housed the kitchen, dining room, and a rec room for kids, not to mention my "office," which used to be a large broom closet.

"That okay, Lucy? The kid has big ears."

"Yeah, yeah. Just tell Miss Gabby here what's goin' on."

Harry Bentley ran a hand over his shaved head. "Well, according to Lucy, those same two characters who'd been hanging around Richmond Towers before the attack on your, uh, husband showed up again today—"

"An' lights came on up in that penthouse," Lucy butted back in, "makin' me think your man is outta the hospital an' back home. But I'm tellin' ya, Fuzz Top, it ain't safe for him ta be there—not if he don't want another muggin' first time he step outta the building."

A headache started at the back of my head. "Well, that makes the second time I've heard about suspicious characters hanging around Richmond Towers today. And you're right, Lucy, Philip did get discharged today." I told the others about the young man who gave Philip a ride home from the hospital, and his story about Philip getting upset seeing a couple of guys sitting in the park and asking him to park in the residential parking garage. "Seemed like a nice kid. He picked up Philip's meds and some groceries on the way home, and even saw that Philip got safely up to the penthouse."

I turned back to Harry, retired cop and former doorman at Richmond Towers, who'd been my first real friend when we moved to Chicago last spring. "What do you think, Mr. B? Is Philip in danger?"

Harry shrugged. "Depends. The building itself is pretty secure, and the street out front is busy most of the day. But I wouldn't recommend any more jogs in the park or late-night strolls around the neighborhood, at least not until Philip can get Fagan's boys off his back by paying off his loan, or until they slap Fagan in jail for extortion. Though even that's no guarantee his thugs won't stay on Philip's tail 'til he pays up."

Denny Baxter frowned, his face sober in spite of the two big dimples in his cheeks that gave the high school coach a perpetual boyish look. "If Philip's gambling debts have piled up like you say, Gabby, he'd be smart to give up the penthouse and rent something cheaper. But if Harry and Lucy are right about this rogue cop—or loan shark, whatever this Fagan is—using violence to put the squeeze on Philip, that might be another reason he should relocate somewhere else."

I sank into the closest chair. "But you don't make a move like that overnight! He'd have to find an apartment and sublet the penthouse—'cause I'm sure Philip can't afford two places right now. Besides, I don't think he'd listen to me, telling him he's got to move—"

"Hey!" Precious interrupted. "Ain't any of you just a tiny bit suspicious of a total stranger showin' up to take Philip home from the hospital? Gettin' himself into the parking garage for residents only? Ends up inside Philip's penthouse? Huh? Maybe that Fagan guy is using the kid to get to Philip. Ever think o' that?"

I stared at Precious. *What?* No, no. Will Nissan had seemed like an ordinary college kid who just happened to hit it off with Philip. A talker. Open. Friendly.

Too open? Too friendly?

Now I really did have a headache. "Harry? Denny? Could she be right?"

Harry scratched his beard. "Not Fagan's usual style. Too subtle. But you might want to check out the kid's story. Said he's living with his grandmother? A student at Circle Campus? Ought to be able to check that out."

I sighed. When was I going to have time to do *that*?

Precious wasn't through. "As for your man movin' someplace else? Just be a matter of time 'til those goons find him again. Then it's the same story if he livin' all by himself. He should be around *people* who're lookin' out for him."

Harry snorted. "Huh. You can't put the Secret Service on him to guard him day and night. No man wants a bunch of babysitters taggin' after him."

"Men!" Estelle muttered, wagging her silver-streaked mane. "What's wrong with people lookin' out for each other?"

"I'm tellin' ya," Lucy tossed in, "those no-good characters mean some business."

I grabbed a handful of snarly curls on either side of my head. "Arrrrgh! I don't need this right now! What can *I* do about it?" Suddenly I had a panicked thought and glanced at the faces standing around me, trying to read them. "Wait a minute. If anybody's thinking I ought to let Philip move in with *me* . . . uh-uh. No way. We are definitely *not* there."

"Calm down, Gabby girl. Ain't nobody sayin' that . . . wait." Estelle stiffened. "Is that DaShawn?"

Then we all heard a boyish voice from below. "No! Stop it, Dandy! Drop it! Drop it! Estelle gonna kill ya!"

Estelle moved like greased lightning toward the stairs in spite of being a plus-size woman. "That dog better not be in my kitchen! I got chicken coolin' on the counter—Harry! Come on! You the one sent them down there!"

Rolling his eyes, a reluctant Harry followed. As they disappeared, I saw Denny Baxter whispering to his wife. Then Denny cleared his throat. "Jodi and I haven't had a chance to talk this over yet, but what if Philip came to stay with us for a few days? It'd give him some time to think about what he wants to do."

I gaped at the Baxters. "You're kidding. Stay at your—you'd do that for *Philip*? Jodi, are you sure? After everything he's done?"

Jodi shrugged ruefully. "Yeah, well, can't say he's a candidate for sainthood. But he seemed like a broken man when we visited him in the hospital."

Denny nodded. "Yeah. Maybe God wants us to show him—not just tell him—that God's people haven't given up on him."

I sat there, stunned. Then I slowly shook my head. "Can't imagine Philip agreeing to something like that. He'd never believe you'd offer, for one thing. For another, he'd probably be too uncomfortable living with people he's only met a couple times." *That* was an understatement. The casual Baxter family, whom I loved dearly, would probably drive Philip nuts. They were definitely *not* upper crust.

"Yeah, well, I know it's a long shot." Denny put a reassuring arm around Jodi, who seemed to be seriously considering her husband's crazy idea. "That's why I should probably go with you and invite him myself. Let me know when's a good time."

chapter 4

I gave Precious a ride back to the six-flat I'd bought several weeks ago, but I wasn't much company. This complication with Philip was *not* what I wanted to be thinking about right now! As I pulled up in front of the three-story building, my eyes lingered on the large wooden sign over the doorway, just barely lit by the closest streetlight:

HOUSE OF HOPE

The sign still excited me—a visible reminder that my dream for second-stage housing for homeless single moms was starting to become a reality. Two of the old tenants had already moved out, and the apartment on the third floor, 3E, now housed Jodi and Denny's son, Josh, his wife, Edesa, and their soon-to-be adopted toddler, Gracie. Asking Josh to be the property manager for the House of Hope in exchange for reduced rent had been an idea straight from God, providing an affordable apartment for them, since they were both still in school, and a "man about the place" for me. Precious and her daughter, Sabrina, along with Tanya—another single mom from Manna House—and Sammy, her eight-year-old son, had moved into the other apartment, 1E, right across the hall from me on the first floor.

"So, you gonna sit out here all by yourself and sog, or you wanna talk? Make up your mind, 'cause I'm gettin' cold."

I jumped, almost forgetting Precious in the seat beside me. "I'm sorry." I quickly unbuckled my seat belt and opened the door. "Yeah, we'd better go in."

Hurrying up the broad steps of the six-flat and through the foyer with the mailboxes and buzzers, three sets on each side, I unlocked the door into the main stairwell, aware that Precious was two steps behind me. I didn't stop to get the mail, wanting to duck into my apartment, get into my jammies, and turn on the TV so I wouldn't have to think about this crazy mess with Philip.

But I'd no sooner gotten inside my apartment and headed for the kitchen at the back of the apartment when I heard a loud knock at my front door. *Knock?* Had to be someone in the building already, or it'd be the buzzer. I turned the heat on under the teakettle and groaned as I hurried back down the hall, hoping it wasn't one of the three tenants I'd inherited with the building, complaining about a clogged toilet or something.

"Yes?" I said through the door.

"It's Precious. Open up."

I took off the chain and unlocked the two bolts. The lean black woman walked in clutching two mugs, a box of herbal tea bags, and a plastic Honey Bear. "Knowin' you, you got the hot water goin' already. But you need somebody to listen to what's goin' on inside that mop-head o' yours, or you gonna be up all night stewin' 'bout stuff. Now go sit on the sun porch. Light a candle or somethin'." Precious marched out of sight down my long hallway and five minutes later was back carrying two mugs of steaming tea into the sun porch where I sat curled up on the window seat, hugging a throw pillow. Candles flickered on the sill in their little glass jars.

She handed me a mug. "Okay, spill it. Your noggin, I mean. Not the tea."

I sighed and took a sip of the hot sweet tea. *Peppermint. Mmm.* "Well, you heard that whole thing about Philip. They discharged him from the hospital, but he's in no shape to go back to work." I heaved a big sigh and sipped my tea thoughtfully. "I don't know, Precious. It was easier relating to him when he was stuck in the hospital, trying to recover from that beating. But now—"

I suddenly turned to her. "Okay, you want to know the truth? I resent having to worry about Philip right now. I mean, look at us! You and me and Tanya, here we are, out of the shelter and living in real apartments! And Josh and Edesa and little Gracie have a real apartment now too—not that two-room shoebox they were crunched into. God did it! The House of Hope is a reality! We should celebrate! But instead"—I threw the pillow across the room—"I've been going back and forth to the hospital all week, with no time to plan anything!"

"Hey, hey. Slow down, girl. Life happens. But we can still do something. How about next weekend? How you wanna celebrate? A house blessing?"

"A house blessing? That's a great idea!" A lot better than just having a potluck. "Except . . ." I stared into my mug, my mind tumbling. It'd been a big deal getting Manna House and the City of

Chicago to work out our three-way partnership for second-stage housing for homeless single moms, once my offer on the building had been accepted. Manna House would provide social services to the single moms who lived here, the city would provide rent subsidies from the Low Income Housing Trust Fund, and our first two moms had moved in. So, yeah, we should celebrate, but . . .

"Except what?" Precious prodded.

I eyed my friend sideways. "After the house blessing, then what? To be honest, we don't—okay, *I* don't—really know what I'm doing!"

Precious snorted and rolled her eyes. "Now she tells us."

I couldn't help it. I laughed. "Yeah, well, 'Leap before you look.' That's been my motto my whole life. But I'm trying to change, really I am. I don't want another whole week to go by before we figure out some of the nitty gritties, like, well, you know—"

"You mean, like, who do we call, Josh or you, when somebody drops a box of tampons in the toilet? Or who's supposed to wash all those cute little square windows in the foyer door? What if Tanya and I get in a big fight and she punches me in the nose? What if I don't wanna sort out recycle stuff from my trash and I just throw all of it in the dumpster? Can we have men stay overnight? What if—"

I gaped at her. "Men? *Men?* Overnight?!"

"Okay, I'm kidding. Actually, I'm not. You've got"—she counted on her fingers—"four apartments, not counting the ones you and the Baby Baxters are livin' in. By the time you put two moms in each one, that'll be eight single women when you've got a full house. An' you think *men* sleepin' over ain't gonna be an issue?"

I gulped. "Yikes. I never thought of that." Then I giggled. "The Baby Baxters? That's what you call Josh and Edesa?"

Precious simpered at me. "Look. I'm messin' with ya. I'm just agreein' that there's a lot of things to talk about. So the first thing ya gotta do is call a house meeting and decide how often we gonna meet—like we did at the shelter—to talk over problems and expectations and stuff like that."

"See? That's what I'm talking about! That's the kind of stuff I need to be thinking about, not . . . not worrying about whether my 'ex' is going to get beat up again by some loan shark and his henchmen. I mean, he's the one who kept going to the casino when he was drowning in debt. What can I do about *that*?"

Precious looked at me for a long moment, then slowly shook her head. "Ain't got no idea. All I know is, those boys of yours likely to be mighty worried if they knew their dad was still in danger. So if I was you, I'd put Philip back on the radar. You let me work on settin' up our first house meeting."

The apartment was deliciously quiet the next morning with the boys still at the Lock-In. Supposedly the youth were planning something special for the Sunday service that morning, then the parents would take their sleep-deprived kids home to recover for the rest of the day.

I curled up on the window seat with a mug of coffee and my Bible, grateful to see some blue sky peeking through the clouds. This was my first fall in Chicago and I wasn't sure what to expect. I'd loved fall in Virginia, the gently rolling hills outside

Petersburg blanketed with brilliant yellows, reds, and oranges, like a multicolored afghan. Would the trees turn color here? Or did the weather jump from muggy summer to deep-freeze winter?

I opened my Bible to the chapter I'd been reading in the gospel of Luke, but I had a hard time concentrating. Precious's comment last night about putting Philip "back on my radar" for the boys' sake niggled at me. *Is that what I'm supposed to do, God? I don't know how to help him right now! Even if I did, how does that fit with starting up the House of Hope? I mean, this whole idea was impossible, but You kept opening up doors, gave us favor with the city, favor with the Manna House board—even provided the money from my mom's life insurance so I could make the down payment on this building! But now that we've started, I want to do this right. Not be distracted by Philip's problems.*

A chorus of birds in the trees outside the bay windows of the little sunroom interrupted my thought-prayer. I opened one of the windows a couple of inches so I could hear the singing—one of the gifts of living in this apartment. Something I'd missed terribly the few months I'd lived in the penthouse—thirty-two stories up, way above the treetops—and the windows didn't open either.

Maybe I should get a bird feeder and a bird book.

I closed the window. Talk about distractions. I was supposed to be spending time "reading the Word" and "listening to God"—a commitment I'd made when I'd decided to renew my faith in front of the church a few weeks ago. Trouble was, there were times I didn't particularly want to know God's thoughts about something. Not if what He wanted to say might conflict with what I wanted to hear.

Some Christian I was.

Sighing, I closed my Bible and pulled one of my mom's old

afghans around me. It wasn't just Philip's safety that was distracting me. It was what he'd said in the hospital the morning after he'd been attacked. I could still hear the words, hear the pain in his voice.

"Gabby, I've messed everything up so bad. I don't know what to do! You . . . you were the best thing that ever happened to me, and I . . . I drove you away. Please . . . please, don't leave me. You have every right to . . . to walk out of here, but . . . can you forgive me? I'm begging you! Please . . ."

I shuddered. Lee Boyer—my lawyer friend, who'd started to become "something more"—had shown up at the hospital right then. Told me what Philip was saying was a load of crap. Practically made me choose then and there. Either stand by Philip—in a crisis of his own making, Lee reminded me—or come away with him. Choose?! How could I choose! Lee had become a real friend, the kind of guy I should have married—down to earth, casual, fun, kind. Except he wasn't interested in God or church or faith. And all that "religious stuff," as he called it, had once again become very important to me.

Something deep down—God?—wouldn't let me walk away from my husband right then, even though months earlier Philip had thrown me out of the penthouse, left me homeless and penniless, and taken our sons back to Virginia to stay with their grandparents without telling me. Even though it hurt like hell to see Lee walk away that day in the hospital. But I'd told Philip I couldn't answer his question right then either.

I needed time.

That was a week ago. A week ago today. And he hadn't brought it up again.

Oh God, what am I supposed to do?

Arrgh. I needed more coffee. Knowing I was procrastinating, I threw off the afghan and took my empty coffee mug back to the kitchen for a refill. As I grabbed the coffee pot, I glanced up at the card I'd taped to the cupboard with the scripture Jodi Baxter had given me back when she first agreed to be my prayer partner. I'd been obsessing about whether my House of Hope idea would ever get off the ground. There it was, the verse from the book of Proverbs that had sustained and guided me through the whole House of Hope process.

"Trust in the Lord with all your heart and don't lean on your own understanding. In all your ways acknowledge Him, and He will direct your paths."

In all my ways.

Including the next steps for the House of Hope? Hadn't God been faithful so far? Couldn't I still trust Him?

In all my ways.

Including my relationship with Philip? Hadn't God picked me up, dried my tears, given me hope when it looked as if my entire life had fallen apart? Could I still trust God about Philip?

Acknowledge Him, and He will direct my paths . . .

Forgetting my coffee, I sank down into a chair at the kitchen table and put my head in my hands. "Jesus, I'm so sorry," I murmured. "Sorry that I take my eyes off You so easily. I want to trust You—I *do* trust You! Just . . . show me the way to go. Show me the next steps for the House of Hope. Show me if I should take Philip's plea to forgive him seriously. Because, okay, I admit it, I'm scared. What would it mean to forgive him? I don't know! And . . . I'm scared to find out. And show me—"

Loud knocking at my front door jerked my head up just as I

was going to pray about whether I should encourage Philip to get out of the penthouse or not, and my eyes caught the hands on the wall clock.

Ten minutes to nine!

Worship at SouledOut started at nine thirty. And Precious said she wanted to go with me since Josh had recruited Sabrina and some of her friends for the Lock-In. But I hadn't showered or gotten dressed or anything!

chapter 5

Precious and I were a few minutes late arriving at SouledOut Community Church, but I needn't have worried. Chairs were still being set out, replacing the sleeping bags that had been rolled up and stacked around the edges of the large room that functioned as the sanctuary. I didn't see many of the teenagers, but I heard music coming from the back rooms and a rhythmic thumping. Working on their "special presentation," no doubt.

When the service was finally ready to start—only fifteen minutes late—Avis Douglass announced the call to worship from Psalm 73. The fifty-something African American woman was my favorite worship leader at SouledOut, though I wished I knew her better. I'd first met her at the shelter—she was the wife of Peter Douglass, the Manna House board chair—and at first I was intimidated by her serene presence. Then I found out she was also the no-nonsense principal at Bethune Elementary where Jodi Baxter taught third grade *and* she led Jodi's Yada Yada Prayer Group, which I'd visited a few times. Avis had prayed a few passionate prayers on my behalf in the group, which had touched me deeply. Still, I had yet to have a personal conversation with her.

"'. . . is what the wicked are like,'" Avis was reading, "'always carefree, they increase in wealth. Surely in vain have I kept my heart pure . . .'"

I quickly flipped pages in my Bible to find Psalm 73. Kind of a strange call to worship.

"'When I tried to understand all this,'" she read, "'it was oppressive to me'"—here Avis paused dramatically, lifting her chin—"'until I entered the sanctuary of God.'"

"Oh yes!" someone shouted from the congregation. "That's right" . . . "Thank You, Jesus!"

Avis continued, "'Then I understood their final destiny. Surely you place them on slippery ground; you cast them down to ruin.'"

"That's right, that's right!" . . . "Lord, have mercy!" The comments and affirmations from the congregation almost drowned out Avis's voice as she continued to read the doom and judgment that was going to happen to the wicked.

But then she paused, waiting for the room to quiet before she read the last few verses. "'Whom have I in heaven but you, Lord? Earth has nothing I desire beside you! My flesh and my heart may fail, but God is the strength of my heart and my portion forever!'"

"Hallelujah!" . . . "Praise the Lord!" . . . "Oh, thank You, Jesus!"

Two members of the praise band with violin and keyboard played a short introduction and then the praise team began to sing a hymn lifted straight from that psalm: *Whom have I in heaven but Thee? My flesh and my heart faileth, but God is the strength of my life . . .*"

Wow, I thought, when we finally sat down. That psalm felt as if it had lifted thoughts and feelings out of my own experience the past few months—except the psalmist had written them centuries ago. Guess King David knew what it was like to be down-and-out, too, with nowhere to go but to God.

Pastor Joe Cobbs bounced up onto the low platform, grinning from ear to ear. He was a short, sturdy black man—and seemed even shorter when he stood next to his copastor, Hubert Clark, an older white man with whom he shared the pulpit since their churches merged a few years ago. Today I noticed that Pastor Clark seemed paler than usual and stayed seated even when the rest of the congregation stood, though he seemed fully engaged, smiling and nodding.

"Praise God, church!" Pastor Cobbs said. "Our service will be a little different today, as you've probably already guessed by the special decorations around the room." People laughed as he swung an arm to indicate the piles of sleeping bags and duffels piled against the walls. "Praise God, this room was full of young men and women last night—our own teenagers and youth we invited from the neighborhoods here in Rogers Park—having a Lock-In. And if your kids were here, you *know* they weren't hanging out on some street corner last night, gangbangin' or doin' drugs, praise God."

Laughter swept the room and some people clapped. Which felt odd to me, since my boys wouldn't be out "gangbanging" or "doing drugs," whether they were at the Lock-In or not. Probably talking about the non-church kids they'd invited.

"Well, you know they made a lot of noise, ate a lot of pizza, played some crazy games, and listened to music that would bust our ears." Pastor Cobbs stuck a finger in his ear and wiggled it. "Mine anyway." Which got another laugh. "But they also got into the Word—and I believe they have something to share with us this morning. Brothers and sisters, the SouledOut Steppers!"

Heads turned and necks craned as the double doors at the far end of the room opened and two lines of teenagers walked in, both boys and girls, and even a couple of the youth leaders—Josh Baxter and another guy whose name I didn't know—all wearing black T-shirts. As the congregation murmured and threw out smiles to their kids, the teenagers lined themselves up at the front of the room two deep, some on the six-inch-high wooden platform, the rest on either side. I tried to catch the eye of my sons—P.J. was in the group on the left, Paul on the right—but both of them avoided looking at me.

"Where's Sabrina?" Precious whispered, scanning the group. "That girl better not be tryin' no steppin', not in her condition!"

"There," I whispered, pointing to where Edesa Baxter stood off to the side holding little Gracie, Sabrina by her side. The pretty girl looked as if she'd been crying. Poor thing. The reality of being a teenage mom-to-be was hitting home.

A good-looking young man I hadn't seen before—he looked college age, not high school—took the mike. "Thank you, Pastor Cobbs. Good morning, church. My name is Omari Randall. I'm a junior at Northwestern University, majoring in African American studies. Some of you may have heard about our gospel choir at NU, and we've expanded our repertoire a bit."

"All right now!" The mood in the room was definitely going up.

"I was invited by your pastor to come to the Lock-In, and I gotta say—you folks here at SouledOut have some great youth leaders and a great group of kids. Let's give it up for these folks!" Omari Randall led all of us in giving the youth and leaders a standing ovation—which was funny in a way, since they hadn't done anything yet.

But as soon as we all sat down, a CD began to play through the sound system, more of a beat than actual music, and suddenly the kids on the "stage" began to clap in rhythm . . . slapping their chests, their arms, their thighs . . . then clapping their hands under one leg, then another. After a noisy prelude, Omari started to rap into the mike as the kids clapped, stomped, turned, and slapped in rhythm.

> Gettin' down an' gettin' dirty (*clap, slap, stomp*)
> Not knowin' what we missin' (*slap, slap, stomp, stomp*)
> Smokin' hash an' talkin' trash (*clap, slap, stomp*)
> But it was God we was dissin' (*stomp, stomp, clap-clap-clap*) . . .

The grin on my face was replicated on nearly every face in the room. A few people stood up, calling out encouragement as the "Steppers" performed. The teens on the wooden platform in the center were obviously the most experienced, doing more complex rhythms while the two groups on either side kept it simple. I caught enough of Omari's rap to appreciate his straightforward gospel message. And then with a final *stomp!* in unison, they were done.

Now the room *did* give them a standing ovation. I grinned until my face hurt. Never in my life had I imagined P.J. and Paul—two white boys from Virginia—would be doing a Chicago-style "stepping" performance. In church, no less. Giving honor to Jesus.

The service was shorter than usual, probably in deference to the kids and leaders who hadn't had much sleep the night before.

"Come *on*, Mom, let's go," P.J. said for the third time, holding his sleeping bag, duffel slung over one shoulder.

"Hang on a couple minutes, kiddo. I have to talk to somebody. Look, here're my keys. You and Paul go wait in the car." I craned my neck, trying to find Denny Baxter in the crowd around the coffee pot. Not there. If he really wanted to go with me to talk to Philip, we needed to make plans—oh, there he was, talking to Harry Bentley over by the front windows. I threaded my way past the coffee klatch and headed their direction, hoping the men wouldn't mind an interruption. I did need to get the boys home. Precious and Sabrina too.

"Look, it's just a bad idea," Mr. B was saying as I came up to them.

"Yeah, yeah, see what you mean." Denny shook his head. "I just think we—oh, hey, Gabby."

"Hi, guys. Sorry to interrupt, but can I talk to you for a minute, Denny? I'm going to go see Philip this afternoon, and last night you said—" Denny and Harry exchanged glances. "What?"

"That's just what we were talking about," Denny said. "Harry, here, reminded me that Matty Fagan—the rogue cop we all presume is behind this attack on your husband—lives here in Rogers Park. In fact, just one street over from our house. He's just across the alley and one house down."

"Fagan lives near *you*?" I frowned at Harry. "How do you know this?"

"Look, I worked with him on the force. I've been at his house before." Harry looked uncomfortable. "It's a long story. Tell you another time. But the fact is, Denny's bright idea to move Philip in with him and Jodi would put Philip in Fagan's backyard. Literally."

"Oh." For some reason I felt relieved. Bringing Denny Baxter with me to talk to Philip this afternoon had promised to be awkward at best. "Guess that puts the kibosh on—oh, sorry. That's my cell." I dug in my purse for the phone. If P.J. was calling from the car to bug me, I was going to—

The caller ID said *Philip Fairbanks*.

Startled, I looked at Harry, then Denny. "It's Philip. Excuse me a minute." I walked a few paces away, flipping the phone open. "Hello? Hello?"

I could hear voices on the other end, but they were in the background. Sticking a finger in my other ear, I said hello again, then strained to listen.

"—not smart, Fairbanks." A voice I didn't recognize. Who had Philip's phone?

"Uhhh." It sounded like a groan. "Look—Fagan. You'll get your money, just call off your hooligans . . ." Philip's voice! But not talking to me. He'd said Fagan! Turning toward my friends by the window, I tried to catch their eye.

"*Fagan!*" I mouthed at Harry, pointing frantically to the phone. Harry frowned and moved toward me. I pressed the phone to my ear, trying to hear the distant voices.

"You bet I will." A sneering laugh.

A gasp from Philip. "Can't if you shoot me. Please—put that gun away."

My heart leaped into my throat. Pressing the mute button, I hissed at Harry, "He's got a gun!"

"Oh, I won't kill you, Fairbanks," I heard in my ear. "But you won't be much good if I shoot out both your knees—"

Harry snatched the phone and put it to his own ear. "*Is it muted?"* he mouthed at me. I nodded, aware that my heart was hammering triple time. Frowning in concentration, Harry pushed through the double doors to get outside, away from the noisy room.

"Gabby!" Denny grabbed my arm. "What's going on?"

"I don't know! The phone rang, it was Philip's ID, but he wasn't talking to me—I think he's talking to that Fagan guy in the background. And I heard Fagan say he was going to shoot Philip in the knees." Suddenly my own knees felt weak and I groped for the nearest chair.

"What?!" Denny spun toward the wide windows, where we could see Harry pacing back and forth outside, my phone still to his ear. Through the windows we saw him suddenly pull his own cell out of his jacket pocket, punch in a number, then hold the second phone to his other ear. A moment later he was talking rapidly into the phone.

"What's going on, Denny? What's Harry doing?"

Denny shook his head. "Not sure—I think he's calling for help."

I felt faint. *Oh God, oh God! Don't let that mad man shoot Philip! Please, please.*

That's all I could think to pray.

chapter 6

Five minutes ticked by. Harry was still outside, pacing back and forth with my phone. I looked beyond him to the red Subaru in the parking lot. The car door on the driver's side stood open and P.J. was sitting glumly behind the wheel, as if toying with the idea of driving away. Paul was leaning against the back of the small SUV, talking to Sabrina and Precious, who cast impatient looks in our direction.

I glanced back at Harry, who was yelling into the phone. Yelling at who? Fagan? Somebody else on the other phone? What was happening?

I suddenly gasped for air, realizing I'd been holding my breath. Standing up shakily, I started for the door. I had to know what was going on! Denny put a hand on my arm. "Don't, Gabby. Let Harry handle it. He knows what he's doing."

But I pulled my arm away and marched outside. "Harry, what—?!"

Harry waved me off and turned his back. "The alley!" he said into his phone. "Behind the store . . . Yeah, yeah, the guy with the gun . . . he's going to tell you he's a cop and give you a cock-and-bull story about the other guy . . . just arrest him! . . . Yeah, Matty Fagan . . . Yeah, he *is* a cop, but he's on suspension . . . Okay, I'm still on . . ."

I backed off a few steps, hesitated, then headed for the Subaru. "Finally!" P.J. moaned, climbing out of the driver's seat. "Can we go now?"

"Sorry, guys. Uh . . ." *What should I say?* "We can't leave just yet. Mr. Bentley has an emergency and had to borrow my phone. Just be patient. It won't be long."

I started back toward the church and then realized Precious had run to catch up. "Emergency? What up? Ain't DaShawn, is it? Gotta be Harry's mother."

I shook my head and kept walking. "Just stay with the kids, okay, Precious? I'll tell you later."

Harry still had both phones, one to each ear, so I went back inside. Estelle and Jodi had joined Denny and the three were talking in low intense tones, but I didn't want to talk. I wanted to pray! I found a chair off to the side where I could keep an eye on Mr. Bentley. *Dear God, I don't know what's happening. But please protect Philip. The boys need their dad! And I haven't . . . we haven't . . .* I stopped. I didn't know how to pray. I just knew that Philip and I had unfinished business and we needed more time. Lots more time.

The glass doors opened and closed as the large room emptied of SouledOut worshipers. But finally Harry Bentley came back inside and handed me my phone. Sweat glistened on his shaved head and trickled down the side of his face. He looked exhausted. I stood up as Denny, Jodi, and Estelle quickly joined us, and the four of us stared at him expectantly.

"It's over. I called for a squad car and they've arrested Fagan and another guy with him, but . . ." Harry sank into a chair, pulled out a handkerchief, and mopped his face. "I need to go down to the station to make sure the arrest sticks."

"But what about Philip?" I asked anxiously. "Is he all right? Did they hurt him?"

"I think he's all right. At least he wouldn't let the officer call an ambulance. So they're taking him down to the station to make a statement and then they'll drive him home."

"But—where was he? When I saw him yesterday, he could barely walk! He shouldn't have even been out!"

Harry shrugged. "Don't know how he got there or why, but they were in the alley near the Dominick's store on Sheridan."

"How—?!" sputtered Denny.

"How did I know that?" Harry allowed a tired grin. "I heard a bus in the background announcing the stop at Sheridan and Berwyn. That's when I called for a squad car. Turned out I was right."

"Amazing," Denny muttered in disbelief. "Absolutely un-believable."

"But . . . but Philip's phone. Did he call me? I don't understand."

Harry shrugged. "You'll have to ask Philip. They'll take him to the police station to make a statement—might take awhile. But my guess is that the phone was in one of his pockets and somehow got turned on in their confrontation. Does he have your number on a speed dial? That might explain it."

I threw my hands open. "I have no idea. But I've got to go. Got to get the boys home, go see Philip as soon as he's done at the station." I gathered up my coat, purse, and Bible and started for the door.

"Wait, Gabby," Denny said. "Do you still want me to go with you?"

I turned back. "I don't know. If Fagan got arrested, maybe there's no danger now. I don't know what to *think*, I don't know what to *do* . . ." To my embarrassment, I started to cry and a moment later felt Jodi's arms around me.

"It's okay, Gabby. We don't have to do anything right now. Go pull yourself together, go check on Philip if that feels right to you. We can talk about this other stuff another time."

I took the tissue she handed me and blew my nose. "Thanks, Jodi. I'll . . . I'll call you later." Out of the corner of my eye I saw Harry stand up and realized I'd forgotten something. I scurried over and gave him a hug. "Thanks, Mr. B," I whispered in his ear. "Don't know what magic you worked with those two cell phones, but thank you. You probably saved Philip's life. He owes you big time."

He awkwardly unhooked my arms from around his neck. "Just doin' my job, Firecracker. Once a cop, always a cop. Didn't you say you had to get those boys home? Go on, go on now. I gotta get down to the station and make sure Fagan doesn't weasel out of this one. This oughta keep him behind bars till his trial."

I quickly pecked him on the cheek and headed again for the door, but not before I heard Estelle say, "I'm going with you to the station, Harry."

"No, no, better if I go alone."

"Did you hear me, Harry Bentley? I'm going with you."

"And *I* said you're not. Now listen to me, Estelle Williams . . ."

The door closed behind me, but by now I was chuckling. Those two were starting to sound like an old married couple. Why in the world didn't he just up and marry her?

"Mr. Gomez!" It was comforting to see a familiar face at the lobby desk when I came through the revolving doors of Richmond Towers a few hours later. "I wasn't sure if you were still working here since Mr. Bentley quit the job. Don't have my 'inside informant' anymore." I tried to laugh lightly.

"*Sí, sí, Señora* Fairbanks! Working overtime now. It is good to see you too. How is my man Harry? He doesn't come by much anymore now that he's raising that *muchacho*."

"They're both good, Mr. Gomez. I'll tell Mr. B you asked about him. Um, could you ring Mr. Fairbanks in the penthouse and tell him that I'm coming up? He wanted to know when I got here."

"Oh, *sí*, Mrs. Fairbanks. Very sorry to hear what happened to your husband." The doorman reached for the desk phone as I headed for the security door leading into the elevator lobby and swiped my card through the keypad.

As the elevator rose floor after floor, I closed my eyes, took a deep breath, and blew it out slowly. *Oh God, I don't know what to expect when I see Philip . . . just help me say the right things.* I hadn't told the boys what happened to their father—both because I didn't really know what had happened, and because I didn't want to upset them—though I'd been tempted to dump it on them to shut up their complaints about me taking so long to leave church. But I chalked up their crabbiness to a night without much sleep and swung through a McDonald's drive-through to get hamburgers and shakes for everyone.

Precious, on the other hand, hadn't been as easy to brush off. "You gonna tell me what's goin' on, Gabby Fairbanks?" she'd hissed at me when I finally pulled up in front of the six-flat and the kids had piled out.

"I will, Precious. Just not now." The all-too-familiar head-ache had started again at the back of my head. "I've got to get the boys settled, then I have to check on Philip, but we'll talk later. I promise."

"*Humph*. Okay, you do that. I'm gonna talk to the Baby Baxters and Tanya to see when we can have a house meeting this week. Any nights better for you?"

"Uh, Monday, Tuesday . . . any day is okay." At the moment I couldn't remember whether I had anything on my calendar that week or not. "Just try for early in the week. Then we might have time to plan a house blessing for next Saturday—"

"I know, I know. I'm on it." But the look she gave me let me know she was going to hold me to my promise to tell her what went down back at the church.

With lunch eaten in the car, both boys crashed on their beds before we'd been home even ten minutes, but not before I made it clear they had to do their homework before turning on the TV or playing any video games later on. And, I'd told them, hopefully I'd be home in an hour or so.

The elevator door slid open. For a moment my feet wouldn't move. This was the first time I'd been back to the penthouse with-out someone else with me. Maybe I should've had Denny come with me . . . or Jodi . . . or the boys. Of course, the boys! I could've waited until they'd had a nap and come later. What had I been thinking?

But here I was. *Trust in the Lord . . . don't lean on my own understanding.*

I kept that verse running through my head as I crossed the marble foyer and pushed the doorbell, which chimed on the other side. Somewhere inside I heard Philip's muffled voice call out, "It's open!"

Sure enough, the door was unlocked. I stepped inside the cool gallery and walked slowly toward the bright living room. Through the floor-to-ceiling windows at the far end, I could see patches of blue sky between the migrating clouds and sunlight sparkling on the wide expanse of Lake Michigan. *Beautiful*—as long as I didn't get too close to the windows and look straight down.

Caught up by the view, it took me a moment to realize the room was empty. "Philip?" I called.

"In here."

I followed his voice into the wood-paneled study, which was just off the living room. He sat at his desk, half leaning sideways in his chair, his free hand manipulating the mouse as he shut down his computer. Then he turned—and I was taken aback by the lines of pain in his face.

"Philip, what—? You're hurting!" I hustled to his side as he struggled to get out of the chair, trying to push up on the armrest with his broken arm as his other hand clutched his gut. But he waved me off.

"I'm . . . okay. Once I get up." He finally stood, slowly straightened, and took a few shallow breaths. Then he headed slowly for the living room and sank into the recliner. "Thanks for coming. Wasn't sure if you would."

An irritated retort sprang to my lips, but I bit it back. Pulling the hassock closer to the recliner, I sat down and leaned forward. "Philip. What happened this morning? My cell phone rang, the caller ID flashed your name, but all I heard was you and this Fagan person arguing. He threatened to shoot you!"

Philip looked at me strangely. "Your phone rang? You heard all that?" He looked dazed. "But I didn't call you. I don't know how . . ." His eyes left mine and he stared out the window for a long moment. "Must've been when that thug who was with him slugged me in the stomach. I had the phone here." He patted his chest. "In the inside pocket of my sport coat."

"He *slugged* you? Is that why you're hurting? Why didn't you go to the ER and get checked out?"

Philip shook his head. "Don't want to go back to the hospital. I'll be all right."

I felt exasperated. "But, Philip. What were you doing out there anyway? You just got out of the hospital! If you needed something, I was coming back this afternoon and could have gotten it for you."

He winced slightly and tried to smile. "Just needed to get out, get some coffee and a paper. Don't want to be cooped up here like a prisoner. Thought I could walk down to the grocery store if I took it slow." The smile disappeared. "Didn't know Fagan's goons were still out there watching for me. They must've called him when I first came out, because when I got near the store, he drove up and cut me off at the alley. If those cops hadn't come—" Philip suddenly looked at me strangely. "You said you could hear us talking? Did *you* call the cops?"

"Not me. Harry did."

"Harry?"

"Harry Bentley. Our former doorman, Philip. He's a retired Chicago cop—I *told* you."

"Yeah, yeah, right. I forgot. But—" Philip looked totally confused. "How did he know where to find us? I thought those squad cars just happened to come by that alley and saw what was going down. Decided I was one lucky guy."

I shook my head. "Not luck, Philip. God was protecting you. Mr. B stayed on the phone—two phones, actually, mine and his—for maybe fifteen minutes, telling the police where to find you."

Philip stared at me. He seemed stunned.

I watched him as he sat there. He was still hurting, I could tell. His ragged breathing, the way he winced whenever he moved, his good hand holding his stomach. "Philip, you said one of those guys slugged you, and maybe that's what turned the phone on. You need to see a doctor, go to the ER, something! Please, I'll take you. You're obviously in pain. You need to get it checked out."

There was no way he could deny it. Still, he shook his head. "I'll be all right."

"You're not all right! Please. I said I'll take you." Then I added, "For the boys."

He considered that. Finally he nodded. "Okay, okay. I'm supposed to make an appointment with my doctor this week anyway. If I can get in tomorrow, I'll call you, tell you when."

Tomorrow! I'd meant today. Now. This afternoon. But tomorrow was Monday. I had to work! Maybe I should tell him to call a cab.

No, I'd promised. If I took him, then I'd know a doctor actually saw him. Well, all right. I'd take time off and take Philip to his stupid doctor, wherever that was.

I stood up. "I better go. Is there anything you want me to do before I leave?"

He closed his eyes, seemingly drained. But he gestured to a pile of his stuff on another chair. "Yeah. Take that robe back to whoever loaned it to me. And tell 'em thanks. But I didn't get it washed. Would you—?"

I picked up the brown robe. "Sure. It was Josh Baxter. He's the one who loaned it to you. I'll tell him."

I turned to go.

"And, Gabby?"

"Yes?"

The muscles in Philip's face twitched, as if he was trying to control his emotions. "Tell Bentley thanks too. I think . . . he may have saved my life."

chapter 7

The boys got off to school in decent time the next morning—P.J. was still riding the city bus—and I came in to work a few minutes early, knowing I'd have to take some time off later in the day if Philip got an appointment. Even then the coffee pot in the kitchen was down to the dregs, and I had to make a fresh pot before I could settle down to work.

I turned on my computer and squinted at the computer calendar. Second week of October. I typed in *8:30 p.m. House Mtg* on Tuesday, thanks to Precious. She'd left a note taped to my apartment door last night saying Josh, Edesa, and Tanya had agreed to eight thirty Tuesday evening for a meeting if we could meet in 3A so Edesa could put Gracie to bed first. *What about the other kids?* she'd written. *Maybe they should be there too. They need to know the rules. I'll see you then. My cousin's in town from South Carolina and I'm going to hang with her tonight, maybe tomorrow too. Sabrina's going with me. Ciao!* Then she'd added, *P.S. So what happened at church today?*

I was just as glad she was "hanging" with her cousin for a couple of days. If and when I talked to Precious about Philip's run-in with Fagan in that alley, I didn't want the boys around to overhear.

What else was happening this week? Last week had been a blur with Philip in the hospital and the boys wanting to go see their dad every day after school. His parents had flown in from Virginia and hovered in the hospital room a few days, which was awkward for everyone. We were all relieved when Mike Fairbanks had gone back to work and took Philip's smother-mother with him.

But in spite of all the hurly burly, there had been one huge, silent void.

Lee Boyer hadn't called me. Not once.

My head sank into my hands. What did I expect? He'd wanted me to declare it was over with Philip, to let my husband mop up his own mess. But I couldn't. Not right then. Not when Philip had just been worked over by some thugs and my sons were terrified for their father's life.

I squeezed back tears. Had I done the right thing to stand by Philip? *Yes*. Except I didn't know I'd miss Lee this much. Had I fallen in love with him without knowing it?

Raising my head, I let out a long sigh. *Okay, Gabby, suck it up. You'll never get anything done today if you start second-guessing about Lee.* I blew my nose and focused on the computer calendar once again. *Monday—staff meeting at ten.* Hopefully Carolyn would show up and give a report on the afterschool program, which I thought was going well. Considering. We still had to decide whether to open it up to neighborhood kids whose parents had asked for the extra tutoring help. And it was time to talk about adding a GED program here at Manna House for our residents who still needed to complete their high school education.

I continued to review the regular weekly activities we had scheduled: Estelle's sewing class this afternoon, still working on their apron project. The ESL class on Tuesday, which was about to lose its volunteer teacher because Tina, our Puerto Rican resident who spoke both Spanish and English fluently, didn't feel qualified to teach the formal written stuff. Cooking and nutrition on Thursday, Estelle again, no worries there. Jodi Baxter's typing class on Saturday.

Jotting a note to myself about calling some local schools that trained ESL teachers, I turned my attention to the list of new activities I wanted to add here at Manna House. *"One at a time, Gabby, one at a time,"* Mabel had warned me. *"We've got to make budget, remember?"*

I grinned at the item at the top of my "proposed" list: a "Fall Getaway" weekend for some of the residents who'd never been out of the city, to see the fall colors and enjoy a bit of nature. But it was already October! If that was going to happen, I needed to get it on the calendar pronto. Maybe the last weekend of this month?

Philip still hadn't called by the time I gathered up my papers and headed for staff meeting at ten. I was tempted to phone and bug him about calling his doctor but talked myself out of it. Wasn't I always running ahead of God and trying to *make* things happen? Okay, I was even going to turn off my cell phone during the meeting.

I tried to catch Estelle after the staff meeting to find out what happened when Mr. Bentley went down to the police station yesterday, but she zipped out of the room without so much as a nod in my direction. What was she in such a hurry about?

But there was one new voice mail when I turned my cell phone back on. *"Gabby, it's Philip. I've got a two o'clock with Dr. Gordon. Can you pick me up at one?"*

One o'clock? Why did he need a whole hour to get to his doctor? *Whatever.* I sent a text back to him—"OK 1:00"—and made a detour to Mabel's office to tell her I needed a couple hours for a doctor's appointment.

I pulled into the Visitor Parking space outside Richmond Towers right at one. Philip was already downstairs in the lobby waiting for me. He didn't say much as he lowered himself gingerly into the front passenger seat of my Subaru, just "Thanks for the ride. Here's the address." He handed me a slip of paper. "Take Lake Shore Drive to the Randolph Street exit and I can direct you from there."

Randolph Street? Philip's office was in the AON Center on East Randolph right downtown. Was his doctor in the same building?

Turned out he wasn't, but the building was right around the corner on North Michigan Avenue. I let Philip out as close as I could to the front door of the office building while I looked for a parking garage. After circling the block, I ended up in the AON Center parking garage after all and walked to the building where I'd let him out.

The receptionist in Dr. Gordon's office said Philip was already in with the doctor, so I leafed through a copy of *Money* magazine. The other options weren't much better. *Business Week* . . . *Harvard Business Review* . . . *Forbes* . . . Good grief. Didn't anybody besides CEOs come to this doctor? "Excuse me." I waggled a hand at the receptionist. "Do you have *Good Housekeeping* or *National Geographic* or something?"

"Sorry," she said. "Those are the doctor's personal subscriptions. We just put out the old copies."

Humph. I should've brought a book.

Philip came out half an hour later, looking a bit ashen. "Doctor wants me to get a CAT scan of my midsection," he said as we rode the elevator down. "I think I can get it done at Weiss Memorial, but . . ." He swore under his breath. "Blast that Fagan. I don't have time for this!"

I kept my mouth shut. Philip wouldn't even *know* Matty Fagan if he hadn't tried to pay off his gambling debts with a shady deal.

"You want me to go get the car so you don't have to walk?"

"Where are you parked?"

"The AON Center garage."

A strange light went on in Philip's eyes. "No, no, that's good. I need to stop by the office anyway. Only take a few minutes."

A few minutes? Not likely. *I* was the one driving, and I needed to get back to work! But Philip had already started out the automatic door as if the prospect of going to the office had given him an energy boost.

Don't be a wimp, Gabby, I told myself. *If he takes more than fifteen minutes, just tell him to take a cab home.*

By the time we got off the elevator on the sixty-second floor of the AON Center, tiny beads of sweat lined his forehead and he kept his right forearm pressed against his middle. I should have insisted on taking him home. But here we were—might as well see it through.

As we approached the door with a sign that read Fairbanks and Fenchel Development Corp., Philip hesitated. "Uh, Gabby, do me a favor. Would you go in and make sure Henry's not meeting with anyone? I don't want to meet any of our clients looking like . . . well, you know."

I studied him for a moment. Why should I do that? It wasn't my idea to come up here to his office! And he'd been calling me Gabby lately instead of Gabrielle . . . what did that mean? He was acting as if we were on buddy-buddy terms.

But I had to admit he did look messed up, even though he was wearing a hat and wraparound shades that covered the jagged stitches and the bruises around his eyes. I couldn't blame him for not wanting to run into any business clients with his arm in a cast and his sport coat sagging off his left shoulder.

"Okay. Give me a minute." I pushed open the door. The waiting room was empty. I approached the reception desk—rats, I couldn't remember the name of the receptionist—and tried to sound businesslike. "Hello. Is Henry Fenchel in?"

The receptionist looked startled. "Oh . . . hello, Mrs. Fairbanks. I'll, um, see if he's available." She picked up the phone.

Ah, my clue. She wouldn't say that if he were meeting with a client. I smiled benignly. "Just tell him Gabby Fairbanks is here to see him."

The girl seemed competent—short brunette hair in an attractive style but nothing gorgeous, reading glasses, gray suit jacket. I politely stepped away from the desk, pretending to look at a decorator print on the wall until I heard her say, "Mrs. Fairbanks? He'll be with you in a moment."

I stepped into the hallway and motioned to Philip. He came into the waiting room just as Henry Fenchel stepped out of his office.

The moment seemed to freeze in time. The two men looked

at each other behind blank masks, as the young receptionist stared wide-eyed at Philip. And then Henry Fenchel said crisply, "Philip. You're out of the hospital. It's, uh, good to see you, Gabby. Let's go into my office. Judy, hold my calls."

Later I wondered why Philip didn't just go into *his* office and do whatever he came there to do. Henry would have surely followed him in and the conversation would have been on Philip's turf. Or why I didn't bow out of the scene and just find a comfy seat and a magazine in the waiting room. At least Fairbanks and Fenchel had *Newsweek* and *Sierra Magazine* besides *Architectural Digest*.

But the next thing I knew I was seated in a padded chair in Henry's office. Philip stood at the tall window, looking north over the city, and Henry ensconced himself behind his desk, eyes shifting back and forth between Philip and me. "Surprised to see you both here. You two back together?"

Neither of us answered. The silence hung heavy in the room.

"You look awful, Fairbanks," Henry finally snapped. "What am I supposed to tell people?"

"I had an accident."

"It's not that easy. You missed a couple important meetings last week. Had to make some decisions without you."

"I know. We can review—"

"And what about the meeting with the county board you missed the week before that, the one we scheduled early Monday morning, but, no, you weren't back from Indiana yet."

"We already talked about that, Henry. It won't happen again."

"You bet it won't!" Henry sucked in a breath. "I asked for an audit."

"You *what*?" Philip turned from the window and stared at his partner. I saw his left eye had started twitching.

"Asked for an audit. Look, Fairbanks." Henry stabbed his finger at Philip. "I know what you've been doing. Making withdrawals from the business account to cover your little jaunts to the Horseshoe—"

"I covered that withdrawal!"

"Yeah, yeah. That last one. But how do I know you haven't been leaching funds from the business for who-knows-what monkey business?"

Philip drew himself up as best he could, given his injuries. "I'm *half owner* of this company, Fenchel. So what if I was short of cash and needed a personal loan? I'm good for it. Every penny."

"Is that right?" Henry snorted. "Well, let me tell you something. If this audit turns up any irregularities—any at all, Fairbanks! Even one dime!—I'm going to sue you for fraud, for embezzlement, for—"

"Henry. Wait." Philip shook his head back and forth. "Look, I admit, I've made some mistakes. You don't think I know that? But I've got a lot invested in this company. I'm trying to get things straightened out. I just . . . I need some time."

"Time? We don't have time! The county board wants to meet again tomorrow with prospective developers about that new construction project. It's critical. We're up against two other companies. You gonna be there?"

Philip seemed to sway slightly and put his hand on the window to steady himself. He had to be exhausted. I spoke up. "The doctor doesn't want him back at work for at least another week. In fact, we should go. Philip? Maybe you two can talk on the phone about that meeting tomorrow."

Philip didn't look at me, but I knew I'd probably get it for poking my nose into their business. Henry pushed his desk chair back with unnecessary force as he stood up and then leaned forward, stiff armed, knuckles on the desktop. "Tell you what, Fairbanks. There's another option here. I won't sue and you can take all the time you need."

Philip turned, eyes narrowed, and focused on his partner. "And what's that?"

A small smile tipped the corner of Henry Fenchel's mouth. "A buy-out. I'll buy out your interest in this company. That should give you enough money to take care of whatever you've got going on. Give you time to get things 'straightened out,' as you say. But it'd be hands off, Philip. Hands off. Starting today."

My mouth nearly dropped open. I saw Philip's features go hard. "Never!" he hissed between clenched teeth. "I started this company and you are *not* going to grab it away from me." He pushed away from the window and strode with effort for the door. Then he turned back and stabbed a finger in Henry's direction. "I'll be at that meeting tomorrow, Fenchel. Put *that* in the bank. Come on, Gabby."

I followed him out the door, but behind us Henry yelled, "Get some help, Fairbanks!"

chapter 8

Philip and I barely spoke on the way home. But as I turned off Lake Shore Drive and onto the frontage road toward the curving glass and steel edifice that was Richmond Towers, I broke the silence.

"Philip, don't go back to work. Henry's bluffing. He's got to be. But you need to get that CAT scan like the doctor said. Something's wrong—you're still in pain. I can tell. Nothing's going to get better until *you* get better."

To my surprise, Philip didn't reply. He didn't yell at me for speaking up in Henry's office either. I pulled the Subaru to the curb in front of the revolving door on the backside of the luxury building but left the motor running. "I should get back to work," I said. "Are you going to be all right getting up to the penthouse?"

Philip nodded and reached for the door handle. But something—someone—caught his eye across the frontage road in the park. I followed his eyes and saw a man sitting on one of the park benches, arms resting along the back of the bench, ankle balanced on one knee. Seeing us, a slow grin spread across his face and he gave a thumbs-up signal in our direction. Then the man got up and sauntered off down the path.

I felt Philip slump back against the passenger seat. My heart started to race. "Was that one of the men who's been stalking you?" I didn't wait for an answer but turned off the motor. "I'm coming up with you."

Philip shook his head. "No . . . no, it's okay. You go back to work." He glanced over at me. "Thanks for taking me to the doctor, Gabby. I appreciate it." He pulled the door handle and opened the door, then hesitated and turned back. "Do you pray, Gabby?"

His question caught me off guard. But I tried to keep my voice steady as I said, "Yes. Yes, I do pray. All the time lately."

"Then maybe you could send up a prayer for me. I . . ." He looked away. "I don't know what to do."

It was four o'clock by the time I got back to Manna House. Paul was there already per our afterschool arrangement, walking Keisha and Sammy back to the shelter from Sunnyside Magnet School. Even though Sammy's mom had moved to the House of Hope, Tanya was trying to find a job and wanted Sammy to be in the afterschool program at the shelter. I'd agreed to bring Sammy home along with Paul when I got off at five.

I was half hoping Estelle would still be there, but her sewing class was over and the dining room where they met was dark and empty—at least until the volunteer group who was scheduled to bring that Monday night's dinner would arrive at five thirty or six. I breathed a brief "Thank You, God" that I wasn't the one who had to schedule supper volunteers seven days a week, week after week. What a job!

But maybe it was just as well Estelle was gone. I needed some time alone in my office to process what happened that afternoon. Philip had asked me to *pray* for him? And that man on the bench— was Philip still in danger from Fagan's cronies? Things between Philip and Henry were certainly a mess. Like the rest of Philip's life right now.

Leaning my elbows on the desk, I rested my head in my hands and squeezed my eyes shut. "Oh God," I breathed. "How do I pray for Philip? He's got himself in such a mess! And it's all so complicated! But You know all about it, Jesus, and in his own way he seems to be asking for Your help, so please . . ."

I meant to spend only five or ten minutes praying and was surprised when I looked up and saw I'd been crying out to God for half an hour! But one thing led to another and I'd found myself praying about our broken marriage, and my dicey relationship with Lee Boyer, and how to manage this tiger I had by the tail that we were calling the House of Hope. But when I was done I felt a certain peace leaving all my worries in God's lap.

I'd call Jodi Baxter tonight and ask her to pray for Philip too. She probably had no idea how much I was going to dump on her when she'd agreed to be my prayer partner!

The boys asked about going to see their dad that night, but I told them he'd had an exhausting day and it'd be better to wait a day or two. Wednesday for sure. By then I hoped he'd have followed through on getting that CAT scan and we'd know if he was on the mend or needed more medical intervention. None of which I mentioned to the boys.

Philip did not call me for a ride. Was that good or bad? Either he didn't make an appointment to get the scan, or if he did, he called a cab. Hopefully he didn't try to make that meeting with the Cook County Board. As for Henry Fenchel's outrageous offer to buy out Philip's share in the business—that one had me down on my knees a few times on Tuesday.

Still, I was looking forward to our first-ever house meeting Tuesday evening. We decided to not include the kids the first time and left them on the first floor doing their homework while Tanya, Precious, and I climbed the stairs to the third floor and tiptoed quietly into Josh and Edesa's apartment so as not to wake little Gracie, who'd just fallen asleep.

"I brought Josh's bathrobe back," I said, handing it to Edesa. "Philip said to tell him thanks for the loan—oh, wow, your apartment looks great!" The living room of apartment 3A mirrored my own structurally—but there the similarities ended. I'd painted mine in subdued neutral colors, but Edesa and Josh's walls boasted what she called "hacienda colors" of rusty orange and green trim, with a warm, bright yellow in the adjoining sunroom. Several pottery vases and small woven baskets that looked South American in origin lined the mantel of the gas fireplace. Their furniture was sparse—they'd been in a tiny two-room apartment above the Hickmans—but the couch was covered by a brightly woven throw with Aztec-type designs, and live plants hung in the windows of the sunroom.

"*Gracias*, Sister Gabby. It's wonderful to have so much room!"

Edesa whirled around on the bare floor, brown arms outstretched, her full skirt twirling like a little girl's. A moment later she plopped down on a floor pillow beside Precious. Even though both women were considered black—one African American, the other African Honduran—their skin tones were distinctly different. Precious was darker, like rich dark chocolate, while Edesa had mahogany skin with gold highlights. And Tanya, who was also African American, had her own lighter caramel skin.

Josh appeared from the hall lugging a couple of straight-back chairs. "'Desa, honey, you want that salsa you made out here? Couldn't bring it and the chairs too."

"I'll get it," Tanya offered and returned with a bag of tortilla chips and a bowl of homemade salsa *verde* with green tomatillos and avocados, which rapidly disappeared. Tasted nothing like the stuff that came in a jar from the store! But finally I asked Josh to start our meeting with a prayer.

"Me?" He shrugged an okay. "Well, Lord, I want to thank You for this House of Hope, for giving all of us a home here. And I pray for the other single moms and kids You want to bring here. Even if we don't know who they are yet, we know You do and that they are part of Your good plan for this place. Bless Mrs. Fairbanks for her vision, and help us as we work out the nitty-gritties of living together. Oh, and it'd be great if You could keep the furnace and water pipes and everything working this winter. Amen."

We all opened our eyes, grinning a little at Josh's "guy prayer." I leaned toward him and stage whispered, "But remember, you can call me Gabby like everyone else."

Edesa's husband rolled his eyes and turned red. "I know, I

know! It's just—maybe I should call you Miss Gabby like the kids do, or Sister Gabby, like my wife."

"Whatever, Josh." I shook my head and chuckled. "Okay, thanks, everybody, for getting together for our first-ever house meeting. I thought it'd be a good idea to have a regular time when we can work out the 'nitty-gritties,' as Josh called them, of living together in this building. To be honest, this is all new to me—"

"Tell me about it," Precious snickered. "Ain't none of us done this before."

"Exactly. Which is why it might be good to have a meeting once a week for a while to take care of things right away. Is everyone okay with that? Is Tuesday evening good for everyone?"

"Uhh, not really," Josh said. "I could do it on Tuesday one more week because Mr. Douglass is out of town on a business trip, but usually I go to the men's Bible study that he and my dad are part of on Tuesday nights. Wednesdays would be better."

"Okay. Tuesday next week, after that—Wednesdays okay for the rest of you?"

Precious snorted. "Ain't like we all got those little black books with lots of appointments in 'em. Tuesday . . . Wednesday . . . don't make no difference to me."

That settled, we moved on to making a list of things to talk about. A laundry schedule for using the battered washer and dryer in the basement . . . the best way to leave messages for Josh if something needed fixing . . . rules for the kids, like cutting off loud music after ten p.m. and not running or yelling in the stairwell.

"But what about the other tenants who still live in the building?" Tanya huffed. "The guy who lives above us had *his* music on till one o'clock the other night! I banged on the ceiling with the broom handle, but it didn't change nothin'. And sometimes they be yellin' at each other like they was at a dogfight or somethin'."

The other tenants—that was going to be tricky, since three units were still occupied. I'd met them all briefly when I'd delivered my "I'm the new owner" letter, explaining that we were turning the building into second-stage housing for homeless single moms and would not be renewing their leases. They weren't happy about it, though I'd tried to sweeten the deal by saying if they found another place before their lease was up, they could move out without any penalties. "Maybe we need a tenants' meeting of everybody," I said, thinking out loud.

"Or maybe *you* could just tell them what's what, since you the landlady." Tanya folded her arms across her small chest. "*I* don't see no need to meet with them other folks."

I eyed Josh. "Okay, okay . . . but, Josh, since you're the property manager for the building, maybe you and I could do it together?" Hated to admit it, but I might get a better hearing with some of these tenants if a man backed me up. And Josh spoke fair Spanish too.

Josh nodded, a bit reluctantly. "Well, yeah, sure, but I couldn't do it till Saturday. I've got midterms this week. Speaking of which, are we almost done? I still need to study tonight. Edesa, too, right, honey? While Gracie's asleep, you know."

I still had a few more items on my agenda. But we'd said an hour, so better keep it. "Okay, guess anything else can wait till next week. Just one more thing. Precious suggested we have a house blessing this weekend. Maybe invite Manna House staff and volunteers to come pray. Would Saturday evening be okay? Should we make it a pot—"

I was drowned out by voices yelling out in the stairwell, accompanied by loud crashes as if somebody was throwing things. "An' *stay out*, you creep!" a woman screamed, followed by the slam of a door that rattled my teeth.

"You can't kick me out, woman!" A man's voice. Pounding on the door. "Unlock the door this minute, you—!" A string of nasty words ran up and down the stairwell.

Edesa's eyes went big. "Oh no, Gracie will wake up!"

Tanya rolled her eyes. "What'd I tell ya?"

Josh leaped to his feet and strode to the door. "I'll take care of it," he muttered.

Guess some things couldn't wait till Saturday.

chapter 9

The next thing we heard, the irate tenant from 2A was yelling at Josh that it was none of his *blankety-blank* business. That's when the rest of us stuck our noses in his business. As we piled into the hall, I leaned over the railing and saw P.J., Paul, Sabrina, and Sammy craning their necks from below, listening to the whole mess.

Okay, that's IT!

I don't know if it was me reminding the young man—he had Mediterranean good looks, olive skin, dark hair and eyes, maybe Italian?—that I was the owner of the building, that I lived on the premises, and I was ready to call the police if he and his "woman" didn't quit disturbing the peace, or whether it was being surrounded by the whole motley crew of us from 3A, 1A, and 1B, but the young man suddenly swore, thundered down the stairs, and disappeared out the front door.

Peace settled on the stairwell like pixie dust. We all looked at one another. The kids started to snicker from below.

"You hush!" Precious hissed over the banister. "That young

man don't need us to laugh at him. He needs some serious prayer. Her too." She jerked a thumb at the door of 2A.

"*Sí,*" Edesa agreed. "Right now." And she sat down on the stairs, motioning the rest of us to gather around. To my astonishment, she closed her eyes and began to pour out a prayer on behalf of the couple in 2A. I noticed that the door across the hall to apartment 2B opened a crack, then quietly shut again.

On Wednesday the clouds finally unloaded and the wind off the lake spun the rain around like tiny whiplashes, so I gave both boys and Sammy a ride to school, though I felt awkward not offering a ride to Sabrina, whose high school was in a different direction. I learned later she took one look at the weather and stayed home.

I half expected to see Lucy and Dandy when I finally blew into Manna House at nine, shaking rain off my umbrella. But when I signed in, Angela said she hadn't seen her. However, more residents than usual seemed to be hanging around Shepherd's Fold this morning, talking, playing cards, or just sitting. Even the TV room was crowded. The weather had put a damper on making the effort to show up at the employment office, social security, or public aid—at least until the rain stopped. So where was Lucy? Funny how I seemed to worry more about her in weather like this now that she had my mother's dog than I did before.

Delores Enriquez and Estelle Williams were already setting up the portable nursing station in the dining room as I walked through to my office. Still hadn't found out what happened last Sunday when Harry Bentley went to the police station after Matty

Fagan's arrest, but Estelle was busy taking names to see the nurse and setting out skeins of yarn on one of the tables for her knitting club, so I'd have to catch her later.

Somehow the dampness had chilled me to the bone, and I had a hard time staying warm in my office. After several futile phone calls trying to find a retreat center within a couple hours drive of Chicago where I could take some of the residents for a Fall Getaway, I headed for the kitchen to make some hot tea with lemon—hoping to ward off a cold—and ran into Estelle spooning sugar into her coffee. Although with Estelle, it was more like adding coffee to her sugar.

"Hey, Estelle." I turned on the gas under the teakettle. "You know of any retreat centers or cabins on a lake somewhere close, maybe even southern Wisconsin, where I could take some of the ladies for a little getaway this fall? You know, see the fall colors, enjoy nature, stuff like that."

Estelle raised an eyebrow. "Your latest brain child?"

"Well, sure. People do that all the time in Virginia to see the leaves turning color. Why not here?"

"Uh-huh. Good luck."

"What do you mean?"

"A lot of folks who grow up in the city ain't that comfortable gettin' too close to nature."

"But maybe that's just because they don't have the opportunity! That's part of my job as program director, don't you think? To give our residents life skills and new opportunities?"

Estelle chuckled. "Well, like I said, good luck! Especially if you get wet weather like this."

I was not going to let Estelle rain on my idea. "Then we'll just cozy up to a roaring fire in a big stone fireplace and play charades or something. It'll still be fun." The teakettle whistled so I poured boiling water over a tea bag and scrounged in the big industrial-size refrigerator for a bottle of lemon juice. "Hey, got two more things I want to ask you. Got a minute?"

Estelle glanced over the counter at the three women laboring over their knitting needles while waiting for the nurse. "If you mean 'a minute' like sixty seconds."

I'd think she was just being feisty, except she seemed to be wearing a perpetual grin this morning. What was up with her? But if she was only going to give me sixty seconds . . . "Can you and Harry come to a house blessing at the House of Hope this Saturday? You know, pray over it, like an official dedication. DaShawn's welcome, too, for that matter. And second—"

"A house blessing?" Her eyes lit up. "Is that like a party, except to bless the building and the people? Who else you invitin'?"

"Well, I'm not sure who all. Manna House staff for sure, hopefully someone from the board, and folks like you and Harry and the Baxters who've been supporting this idea. It's going to be a potluck, too, so can you bring a dish?"

Now Estelle was chuckling again, almost to herself. "Uh-huh, that's it. That's the perfect time, all the right people . . ." She looked at me almost as an afterthought. "Yep, yep, we'll be there. I'll bring some food too. Uh-huh, couldn't be better . . . okay, okay, I see ya wavin' at me, Bertie! I'm comin'." And Estelle scooted out of the kitchen with her coffee cup toward the table of knitters.

Rats. Didn't get to ask her what happened last Sunday! Maybe I should just give Mr. B a call and ask him.

When I got home from work, I called Philip and said the boys would like to visit him that evening if he wasn't too tired. "Tired? Why would I be tired? Just sitting here when I should be working." He sounded frustrated. "Sure, sure, bring the boys. I'll be glad to see them. Just an hour, though, okay?"

I'd boiled a chicken the night before, so I made a pot of chicken noodle soup for the boys and at the last minute packed up the leftover soup to take to Philip. I pushed aside the incongruity of taking chicken soup to my estranged husband. It couldn't be easy cooking for himself with one arm in a cast. I'd do the same thing for Mr. B or anyone else who was laid up, wouldn't I? It didn't have to mean anything.

The rain had let up and the last few rays of sunset poked through the patchy clouds. The boys and I showed up at the penthouse shortly after seven and had a moment of déjà vu when Will Nissan opened the door, wearing the same faded jeans, gym shoes, and baseball cap as if he hadn't taken them off since the last time we saw him. "Hey, Mrs. Fairbanks. Mr. Philip said you guys were coming over. How ya doin', P.J.? Hey, Paul." The young man grinned as if genuinely glad to see us.

Couldn't say the feeling was mutual. Will had been here the last time my sons had come to see their dad. Couldn't they spend some time with their father without having to share him with some eager-beaver college kid who was probably just using Philip to get an internship or something? And I noticed it was "Mr. Philip" now instead of "Mr. Fairbanks."

But Paul, ever Mr. Friendly, gave the young man a high five and said, "Hey, Will! Find your missing aunt yet?" Even P.J. nodded a greeting before heading for the living room.

"Haven't been looking!" Will called after them. "Pretty much a lost cause, I think," he muttered to me under his breath. But he must have picked up on my reticence. "Sorry if I'm intruding. I was in the neighborhood to see Nana, she's still in the hospital, and thought I'd drop by to see how Mr. Philip was doing, see if he wanted to play cards or something. But, uh, since you guys are here . . ."

He left his comment hanging, as if waiting for me to give him a thumbs-up or thumbs-down. *That's right. Make me the bad guy.* On the other hand—why was I worried about him being here, anyway? The boys didn't seem to mind. Might even help Philip and me avoid any awkward conversations. Let Philip make the call if he wanted to spend time alone with the boys.

Which is what I said to Will. "Philip might want to spend some time with the boys—but that's up to him." I smiled sweetly. "Would you tell him I'm heating up some chicken noodle soup? How about you, would you like some?"

"Oh, man! Is it homemade? Sure, if you've got enough." He grinned self-consciously. "Tell you the truth, my Nana is a great lady, but her culinary expertise extends to meatloaf and Stouffer's frozen lasagna. Anyway, I'll tell him." He headed for the living room at a trot.

The kitchen was a mess. Dishes in the sink. Peanut butter jar open on the counter, knife stuck in it. Half-eaten frozen food entrees in the fridge—uncovered. What was the matter with Philip? He was normally so fastidious. Was it that hard to do things one-handed?

After starting the soup reheating on the stove, I tried to tear off some plastic wrap from the box in the drawer and stretch it over some of the leftovers in the fridge—and decided that, yes, the job needed two hands.

Oh Lord, I groaned, half thought, half prayer. *How's he going to manage for the next six weeks? I can't be over here mothering him every day.*

By the time I'd washed the dishes in the sink and cleared off the counter, the soup was steaming. I served up two big bowls, found some crackers, and carried them out to the living room on a tray, where Will, P.J., and Paul were sitting on the floor beside Philip's recliner playing Uno, snickering because P.J. had played a Draw Four card on his dad.

"Ah, saved by the soup!" Philip said, giving up his cards as I set a soup bowl on the wooden TV tray by his chair. "Smells good, Gabby. Thanks."

Will and the boys scooted over to the floor near the glass-topped coffee table so Will could eat his soup and keep playing.

I pulled the hassock near Philip's recliner. "What happened with the CAT scan?" It was the first time I'd taken a good look at my husband since we'd arrived, and I realized the bruises around his nose and eyes were starting to fade and a dark shadow covered his head. New hair.

"Had an appointment today, took a cab over to Weiss Memorial." He leaned forward to spoon the hot soup into his mouth, dribbling some on the arm of the leather recliner. Frustrated, he dropped his spoon and swiped at the spill with a paper napkin. "Doc has to read it, I guess. Maybe he'll call tomorrow. But the pain is better—except for my ribs. Supposed to take deep breaths with that thing"—Philip pointed to the plastic spirometer they'd given him in the hospital—"but the ribs . . . uh-uh."

I retrieved the spoon. "And the meeting with the county board yesterday? You didn't try to go, I hope." I knew I was pushing it, asking questions that were none of my business. But, hey, bringing the soup should give me some leverage for snooping.

"Said I'd be there, so you bet I showed up. If Henry thinks he's getting rid of me, he's got another think coming." Philip managed a couple of spoonfuls of soup without spilling, then muttered, almost to himself, "But probably a mistake. I was a distraction, looking like this. Did everybody a favor by leaving early."

He leaned back in the recliner, the soup only half gone. After a long minute he spoke again. "Henry called later. Said he salvaged the deal, no thanks to me. Told me to keep my butt at home."

"I'm sorry, Philip." I was too. Seemed like Henry Fenchel was kicking Philip while he was down. Though I had to admit his partner had good reason to be upset, the way Philip had been "playing loose" with the accounts.

"Ha! I win!" Will laughed. The card players broke up. "The soup's good, Mrs. Fairbanks. Thanks." The young man turned his full attention to the bowl on the coffee table while P.J. put the cards away and Paul wandered over to the bank of curved, floor-to-ceiling glass windows along the outside wall. No one had pulled the drapes, so the ribbon of lights along Lake Shore Drive splayed out below, like a rippling border on the edge of Lake Michigan, which lay beyond the lights like a thick, dark blanket.

"Hey, Mom, come here!" Paul called. "I think I see Lucy and Dandy in the park."

I joined my youngest at the window, trying not to give in to the queasy feeling in my stomach as I looked downward where he pointed. The narrow park below, which lay between Richmond

Towers and Lake Shore Drive, was lit by sporadic streetlights along its jogging paths, as well as the lights falling from the luxury buildings and the bright lights from the Drive. Still, the distance from the high-rise along with the shadows from trees and bushes made it difficult to identify the half-dozen people walking the paths, a few with dogs. But one lone figure sat on a bench across from Richmond Towers. Couldn't make out the person's features from above, but the wire cart parked at the end of the bench and the light-colored dog cavorting nearby gave her away.

I gave Paul a squeeze. "Think you're right."

"Who's Lucy and Dandy?" Will had joined us at the window.

"Homeless ol' bag lady," P.J. snorted from the couch. "She spies on us."

"Dandy's my grandma's dog," Paul added. "Or was."

"A friend of mine," I murmured.

"Yeah! She's the one who found my dad when he got beat up."

Oversharing, Paul.

Will laughed. "Whoa. Sounds like a story there. I'd like to meet her."

But when we looked again, the bench was empty.

chapter 10

The topic of Lucy had always been a bone-in-the-craw as far as Philip was concerned. Glancing uneasily toward the recliner, I saw he was dozing. "Maybe another time, Will. I think we better go. Come on, boys. Philip? Philip, we're leaving."

Philip shook himself awake and, to my surprise, asked if the boys could sleep over this Friday night as usual, though I'd have to bring them. "If they get too bored, I'll send them home in a taxi," he said.

P.J. looked at me. "Uh, I dunno, Dad. I've still got cross country meets. City championships are this Saturday, and regionals the following week. After that"—he shrugged—"depends on whether we qualify for sectionals and state."

"I can come, Dad," Paul chirped. "I'll bring a movie and we can make popcorn."

I was encouraged. If Philip was feeling good enough to have the boys on his own, he must be feeling better. "We'll see what we can work out about getting P.J. to his meet. But you might want to wait till you know what the doctor says about your CAT scan. Call me when you get the results, okay?"

Will left at the same time we did and we rode down the elevator together. I was tempted to ask if he'd seen either of the two
suspicious characters around when he came this time, but figured
he would've mentioned it if he had. One of them might've been
arrested last Sunday with that Fagan person—Mr. B had said there
were two guys who'd cornered Philip in that alley—so maybe
they only worked in pairs. If so, Philip might be safe from another
attack.

Wished I knew for sure.

We waved good-bye to Will as we climbed into our respective cars. "Hope your grandmother gets better soon," I called after
him.

"Oh yeah. I think she's coming home this weekend. She's
bossing everybody on the floor. I'm sure the nurses will be glad
to discharge her!" He laughed and climbed into the old Ford. "See
ya around!"

The next few days flew by too quickly. Besides working with
Carolyn on a proposal for expanding the afterschool program
and trying to line up my weekend getaway for the Manna House
ladies—I did find a good-sized retreat house for rent near Devil's
Lake State Park in Wisconsin—I made up a list of folks to invite
to the house blessing at the House of Hope this weekend. The list
got kind of long: House of Hope residents, which was ten of us
right there, Manna House staff and volunteers, board members,
plus friends who'd been supportive.

I finally threw myself on Mabel's mercy. "Help! I don't want to leave anybody out who's involved in the House of Hope, but I've got too many. And I can't invite the residents here at Manna House—where would I stop? Except Lucy. I'd like to invite her, but I haven't seen her all week."

Mabel looked at me, completely unruffled. "Let me see your list."

I handed it over. She took a pen and started circling names. "You don't have to invite the whole board. Invite Peter Douglass and his wife—he's board chair. And why do you need all these names under Yada Yada?"

I tried to explain that the prayer group Edesa and Estelle and Jodi Baxter were part of had been praying for me and the House of Hope. "Peter Douglass's wife, Avis, is part of it too."

"Fine. They can represent the group." My boss crossed out and circled and crossed out, then handed back the list. "Your idea for starting with a potluck is nice, but it's a little late to organize a big party, don't you think? Why don't you have a meal with the people living in the House of Hope, and the rest of us will show up afterward for the house blessing."

Amazing. The whole thing suddenly seemed manageable. I wanted to kiss her. "Did I ever tell you I want to be just like you when I grow up?"

The director waved me out the door. "Get on the phone and make your calls. I've got work to do." And wonder of wonders, she didn't call me back two seconds later with her usual, "Oh, and one more thing, Gabby . . ."

There was one more person I thought about inviting to the house blessing. After all, he'd been the one who found the building in the first place, had helped me rent an apartment there so I could get my sons back, then walked me through the process of buying the building even though he had doubts about the wisdom of such a large purchase. He'd even gone along with my giddy desire to fly a kite to celebrate when I'd signed the purchase contract.

Lee Boyer. My Legal Aid lawyer.

But I hadn't heard from Lee since the day we'd faced each other outside Philip's hospital room. Not since he'd blurted, *"I love you, Gabby. Don't you know that?"* Not since I'd had to leave him standing there and go back into that room to sit with the man who'd rejected me and kicked me out. I knew I couldn't turn my back on Philip. Not right then. Not when the father of my sons was broken and hurting and needed me most.

But maybe Lee didn't mean it when he'd said I had to choose: *"Now or never."* Maybe he regretted speaking so recklessly. Maybe he was waiting . . . hoping to hear from me.

We could still be friends. Couldn't we?

When I got back to my office, I shut the door, took a deep breath, and picked up the phone.

Disappointed that I didn't get a response from Lee to my invitation— his voice mail had picked up and I'd had to leave a message—I almost forgot that I'd asked Philip to call me with the results of his CAT scan. But when I hadn't heard by Friday afternoon, I finally called the penthouse. "Oh yeah, sorry I didn't call," he said. "The doctor thinks I might have a small tear in my spleen that's gotten infected, so I had to go back for another blood test. He wants to try treating it with antibiotics, see if it heals on its own. But I'm doing okay. Boys coming?"

I drove both boys to Philip's apartment that evening, along with a deep-dish pizza we picked up from Giordano's and a rented copy of the last *Star Wars* movie. Josh Baxter had offered to pick up P.J. in the morning and get him over to Lane Tech in time to catch the team bus. When I told Philip, he said, "That the same kid who loaned me his bathrobe?"

"Not exactly a kid. He's married and has a little girl."

"Yeah, I know who he is." Philip scratched his chin with his good hand. "Guess I owe him a thing or two."

I was sure Josh wasn't thinking Philip owed him anything, but I didn't say as much. I was eager to get back to the six-flat and put my head together with Florida, Tanya, and Edesa about our house blessing the next day. But when I let myself into my apartment, the light was blinking on the answering machine. With a strange flutter of excitement, I pressed the button.

"Gabby, I'm glad to hear from you"—Lee!—*"and I'd be honored to attend the open house Saturday night. See you at seven thirty."*

I sank down onto the floor, right there beside the telephone table. Lee was coming. Oh help! I wanted so much to see him— but what kind of message was I giving him by inviting him? This was a man who'd said he loved me, but couldn't understand why I didn't drop everything and go away with him in the middle of a family crisis. And it was obvious he didn't share my journey back to faith—we'd talked about it that night in the hospital.

Still, I didn't realize how much I would miss his comforting presence in my life.

He'd called it an "open house." Maybe he had no idea what a house blessing was. No big deal . . . but I wondered what other people would think when he showed up. I'd told Jodi Baxter about our confrontation in the hospital and cried on her shoulder about how confusing it all was. She'd encouraged me that I'd done the right thing and prayed that God would give me wisdom to sort through my natural feelings and be able to make wise decisions. Estelle had probably figured out what happened, even if I hadn't told her the details—she always seemed to be able to read me like a book. I could count on getting a few looks from her tomorrow night, if not outright questions.

Well, he was coming. And I was glad. It didn't have to mean anything, did it? It would've been a slight to leave him out, since he'd been so instrumental in getting the building in the first place. That's all I needed to say.

But I knew if I was honest, that wasn't "all."

Saturday was a full day. After Josh deposited P.J. at the high school early that morning, he and I visited each of the original tenants still in the building when ownership changed hands. First stop was apartment 2A, the scene of all the yelling Tuesday evening. The young woman who opened the door was as olive-skinned and dark-eyed as the young man who'd left in a huff, her thick, tousled hair gathered into a haphazard knot at the back of her head. Bassi was the name on the lease. Hers? Sounded Italian. When she saw us, she shrugged and opened the door for us to come in.

Boxes littered the front room. "*Sì*, I'm getting out of here," she said, her voice flat. "You gave us a letter saying we could move out before our lease was up, right? Well, I'm leaving that no-good jerk, going back to *la mia famiglia*. As soon as he's tired of that *puttanella* he's been seeing behind my back, he'll show up and sweet-talk me into letting him come back. But he stepped out on me one too many times. I'm through."

"I'm so sorry, Miss, uh . . ." I said, not knowing what else to say.

"Zia Bassi. Actually, it's Fabrizia Bassi, but I go by Zia."

I smiled. "Pretty name." I felt sorry for her, because I knew what it felt like to be abandoned by the one who was supposed to love you.

"—anything we can do?" Josh was saying kindly. "When are you planning to leave? Do you need help with the move?"

I looked at him, wide-eyed. Letting tenants leave early with no penalty was one thing. Helping them move was beyond our resources. Moving trucks could be expensive!

And then I realized he meant actual physical help. Like carrying boxes down the stairs. That was so like Josh. What a prince.

Well, our little talk about rules and responsibilities wasn't needed here. Zia said she planned to be out by the following weekend. We wished her well and moved across the hall and knocked on 2B. I looked at the names on the lease. Freddie and Bertha Hill. I had only a vague memory of a middle-aged white couple and two or three younger adults—their grown children? relatives?—going in and out of that apartment. I'd heard them from time to time—heavy footsteps in the hallway over my head, occasional noisy music, loud conversations—but nothing to complain about. We got no answer to our knocks.

Next stop, 3B, across from Josh and Edesa's apartment. Maddox Campbell, a friendly Jamaican man I'd met earlier, came to the door, his "dreads" tucked into a roomy knitted cap in green, yellow, and black layers—Jamaican flag colors. "Ah ha! De poodle lady!" he teased—a reference to my curly hair. "And de new neighbors 'cross de hall wit dat cute baybee." He shook hands with Josh. "What mi can do you for?"

I felt almost silly handing Mr. Campbell the sheet of paper on which I'd printed out the rules for the building—which included a number of obvious things such as proper use of the trash and recycling bins. The tall, thin man frowned. "You tink we be cause of dese problems?"

"No, no, Mr. Campbell. There have been a few complaints about the other tenants, so we decided to just give this list to everyone. Josh Baxter, here, is our new property manager, so if you have any problems in your apartment, you contact him, all right?"

Maddox Campbell's face relaxed into a wide smile, showing good teeth. "Ah, den. Irie, mon."

Maddox Cambell was a likable guy. Almost wished he didn't have to move. I hoped he'd be able to find a good living situation, but decided not to ask how the search was going. Didn't want to pressure the guy. Besides, the day was slipping away and I was expecting a conference call with my two sisters at noon, not to mention I had to cook something for our potluck tonight and clean my apartment if I was going to host all those folks for the house blessing!

P.J. took a city bus after the cross country team got back and was home by five o'clock. "We came in second, Mom!" he crowed, dumping his duffel bag and leaving a trail of sweaty green-and-gold sportswear on his way to the shower.

"Congrats!" I yelled through the bathroom door. "But I just cleaned that bathroom and it better be clean when you come out—and hang up your wet towel too!" *Boys*.

But Paul still hadn't showed when Tanya and Sammy tromped in at quarter to six, carrying a hot dish for our in-house potluck. Was Philip waiting for me to pick him up? I thought he was going to send Paul home by taxi. I'd better check.

Sammy scurried to the front window to watch for Paul, and I grabbed the phone as I followed Tanya down the long hall to the dining room. I lifted a corner of aluminum foil on Tanya's dish. "Smells yummy. What is it?"

"Mac-an-cheese, of course." The young mom looked at me scornfully. "Can't have a potluck without mac-an-cheese. Kids hardly eat anything else. What'd you make?"

"Scalloped potatoes and ham and a fruit salad—where're Precious and Sabrina?"

"She tol' me to tell you she'd be a few minutes late. Sabrina, she snuck out to see that deadbeat dude who knocked her up an' Precious be havin' a cow."

"Paul's back!" Sammy yelled, clear from the front of the house. "Some other guys are with him!"

I hustled down the hall toward the front door, a sense of foreboding growing in my gut. On the way, I passed little Gracie Baxter, toddling as fast as her tiny legs would go, followed by Edesa carrying a hot dish. "Just put it on the dining room table!"

I called over my shoulder as I darted into the foyer—only to run into Estelle Williams, Harry Bentley, and his grandson, DaShawn, standing on the other side of the glass-paneled door.

Ohmigosh. I'd forgotten to tell Estelle we'd changed the pot-luck to be for House of Hope residents only! And here she was, big as life, dressed in a shimmery caftan and headdress, carrying a big pot—probably her famous greens or something. Even Harry had on a suit and tie, his hands full with a large Tupperware container.

I pulled open the door and put on a smile. "Come in, come in. You guys look ready to party! Take that on back to the dining room . . . Hi, DaShawn! Sammy's in the sunroom. You're looking good, Mr. B . . ."

But my smile faded as the trio passed me and another trio appeared, framed in the doorway of the outer door.

Paul. And Philip. And Will Nissan.

chapter 11

As Paul pushed the outer door open and led the trio inside the foyer, I heard footsteps thudding down the stairs. Josh Baxter loomed up beside me. "Hey there, Paul. Hi, Mr. Fairbanks. Good to see you out and about. And who's this?" He thrust a hand out toward Will Nissan. "I'm Josh Baxter. Live up on third. You all here for the potluck?" He laughed. "Save me from being the lone male in a pack of females—oh, except for Paul and P.J. of course." He gave Paul a teasing poke with his elbow.

I gritted my teeth. Did Josh have to be so doggone friendly?

"This is Will, Mr. Josh. He's my dad's friend. They met at the hospital."

Will shook hands with Josh. "You look familiar—haven't I seen you on Circle Campus? It's my first year, but I remember faces."

Josh shrugged. "Could be. I'm taking classes there. Maybe I've seen you around." He sidled toward my open apartment door. "Well, my wife wanted me to hurry up with these tortillas. I'm not late, am I, Miss Gabby?"

I shook my head and forced a smile. "Not yet. Just waiting for

Paul here. Uh, thanks for bringing him home, Will . . . I see your grandmother's car out there."

"Yeah, I thought she was getting discharged today, but now they're saying they want to wait till Monday, so I dropped in to see Mr. Philip. He was just about to send Paul home in a taxi, but I said, hey, no problem, I can give him a ride—then we're going to go out for a bite to eat. Between you and me, Mrs. Fairbanks, I don't think he's had a decent meal since you brought that soup a few days ago."

Paul tugged on my arm. "Why don't they just stay for our potluck, Mom? There's always lots of food at these things."

I started to shake my head, ready to protest that it was just for House of Hope residents—except that wasn't exactly true, since Estelle and Harry had shown up—when P.J. poked his head out the door. "Hey, Dad! Guess what! I beat my best time at the city championships today and Lane Tech came in second. Regionals next week . . . oh, hi, Will. You two coming to the potluck? That'd be cool."

"Can they stay? Please, Mom." Paul hopped up and down. "I told Will about the House of Hope we started here, and he said he'd like to know more about it."

Oh, right. Of *course* he would. Will wanted to know everything about everything. I felt outnumbered. Philip and Will had been invited to stay three times now. "I . . . well, it's our first time eating together as residents, and others will be coming later for a house blessing. I don't know if you'd be interested—"

"Sounds great, Mrs. Fairbanks—if you don't mind. That okay with you, Mr. Philip?"

Philip had the grace to say, "It's up to Gabrielle. It's her party."

I wasn't sure whether to laugh or cry. Why did all of my plans seem to skid off the runway, no matter how organized I was? I shrugged and nodded. *Wimp,* I told myself.

Gleefully, the boys pulled both Philip and Will into the apartment. I followed, fuming, realizing I needed to have a talk with both Philip and the boys about respecting boundaries and not putting me on the spot—and stopped short by the telephone table.

That message, still on the answering machine.

Philip was here, in the house—and *Lee* was coming!

Paul was right about one thing: we had plenty of food. Precious showed up with enough wings to feed the Cubs and the White Sox—though I don't think she realized just how much "heat" she'd put in the sauce, probably while she was fussing at Sabrina. The girl wore an attitude as obvious as her burgeoning tummy, parking herself in my mom's wingback rocker with a magazine and refusing to eat. "Ignore her," Precious hissed in my ear, piling her plate with hot wings, mac-an-cheese, Estelle's smoky greens, Edesa's tasty tamales and deep-fried plantains, and even my not-so-exciting fruit salad and scalloped potatoes. Everyone else followed suit—though my stomach was in such a knot, I wasn't sure I could eat. How was Philip going to manage a potluck with one arm in a cast and sling? I didn't want to hover over him, serving up his plate—besides, I was still irked that he was even *here*—but I noticed Will Nissan had no compunction about loading a plate for him and getting him set up with a TV tray in the living room.

I was both relieved and annoyed. The kid unknowingly let me

off the hook, but it bothered me the way he was weaseling himself
into Philip's life. And now he was here in *my* house having an ani-
mated conversation with Edesa about ethnic foods from her native
Honduras. Didn't the kid have a life?

Estelle bumped my ruminations off center stage by herding me
into the kitchen. "Where is everybody?" She did not look happy. "I
thought Mabel an' the Baxters an' some of the Yada sisters were
comin' to this party. And you *didn't* mention you were invitin' your
ex and his new sidekick. What's with *that*, Gabby girl?"

Didn't know why it should be a big deal to Estelle, but I tried
to reassure her. "The others are coming at seven thirty for the
house blessing. We decided to do potluck just for the House of
Hope folks and I forgot to tell you about the change in plans—but
I'm glad you came," I hastened to add, "because I didn't invite
Philip and Will. They just showed up, and the boys . . . well, you
know. Still trying to get us back together, I think. Hopefully they'll
leave before the house blessing." *And before Lee gets here. Yes, yes, oh
please, God. Yes!*

Estelle's face relaxed. "Well. That's okay then." She grabbed one
of my dish towels, covered the large Tupperware container Harry
had brought in, said, "Don't touch those brownies, they're for later!"
and sailed out of the kitchen like the HMS *Queen Elizabeth*, leaving
me staring at her back. *Humph.* Estelle was acting weird.

But a few quiet moments in the kitchen helped clear my
head. I needed to be proactive. Refilling the pitcher of lemonade,
I marched down the hall toward the living room. I'd refill people's
drinks—a friendly gesture—and matter-of-factly tell Philip and
Will that more people would be arriving soon for a work-related
event, thanks for coming, good-bye.

But before I could get around the room with my pitcher, I noticed that Will hopped up, dug his cell phone out of his pocket, and walked out into the foyer to answer it. When he came back, he headed over to me. "I'm sorry, Mrs. Fairbanks, but I've gotta run. That was my grandmother—she wants me to stop back by the hospital before visiting hours are over." He grinned indulgently. "She's got a whole list of stuff she wants me to bring so she can be decent when she gets discharged on Monday. I'd wait until tomorrow, but I need to spend the day on campus in the library. I was wondering . . . could somebody else give Mr. Philip a ride home?"

"Don't worry about it, Will," Philip growled. "I can take a taxi."

Josh butted in, "My dad can take him home. They go up that way. Nice to meet you, Will. Maybe I'll see you around on campus."

Several people joined in, saying it was nice to meet him and good luck finding Great-Aunt Cindy. Good grief, did everybody know Will and his grandmother were doggedly pursuing their cold case for a person missing sixty-plus years? Well, at least one uninvited guest was out the door, one to go. I walked Will out to the foyer and held the door open. "Hope everything goes well with your grandmother, Will." I shook his hand. "Best wishes."

The young man gave a quick grin, then ran down the steps toward his car.

"Hey!" yelled a raspy voice from down the sidewalk. "Hold that door."

I turned my head to see a familiar dumpy figure pulling a wire cart and jerking on a leather leash. At the end of the leash, a yellow dog was stopping to sniff at every tree along the sidewalk. For the first time that evening, a happy grin bubbled up from my spirit and spread out on my face.

"Hey there, Lucy. I see you got wind of my invitation!"

So many people started to arrive that I finally parked myself by the foyer door to welcome them and guide them into my apartment, where we were going to start before moving on to bless the other apartments. Lee arrived with a clump of other people, including Mabel Turner and her nephew, Jermaine, and she acted as if it was perfectly natural that I'd invited the Legal Aid lawyer who'd often done work for the shelter . . . though the bouquet of flowers he handed me felt a little awkward. He'd dressed for the occasion, trading in his signature jeans for khaki slacks and a nice pullover sweater.

"Thanks for coming, Lee." I gave him a warm smile, took the flowers without comment, and turned to the two couples just arriving. "Welcome to the House of Hope, Peter and Avis. Hey, thanks for agreeing to emcee on short notice . . . Hi, Denny! Hi, Jodi! What's this?" Jodi was carrying a large basket filled with breads fresh from the bakery. "You weren't supposed to bring gifts!"

"House blessing, house warming—why not?" Jodi gave me a quick hug and whispered in my ear, "Did you think we'd ever see this day? Seems like forever ago when we talked about it while driving Moby Van to North Dakota last summer!" She laughed and joined the growing crowd in my living room.

The Baxters weren't the only ones to arrive bearing gifts,

so Lee's flowers just became part of the "blessings" people had brought. Breathing a sigh of relief, I finally slipped inside the apartment and whispered to Peter Douglass, "Guess we're all here."

The chairman of the Manna House board called for everyone's attention and the room quieted. Peter presented a dignified picture of a middle-aged African American businessman—close-cropped salt-and-pepper hair, neatly pressed pants, sport coat over an open-necked dress shirt. "Most everyone here probably knows the history of the House of Hope—"

"Pretty short history," Precious cracked, sparking chuckles around the room.

"—but I'm going to ask Gabby Fairbanks, our program director at Manna House, to give us a brief review. Gabby?"

I could feel my face turning red as heads turned my direction. And I suddenly remembered that Philip was still here! How could I tell the history of the House of Hope without telling how my own experience of finding myself homeless and unable to have my children with me helped me understand how desperately homeless moms needed a place to call home? Tearing up, I shook my head and croaked, "Sorry. Can't. Mabel?"

My boss, bless her, gave a brief "Manna House version" of how I'd come to her with the idea for second-stage housing, which had seemed rather grandiose at first, but with a lot of prayer God had brought all the pieces together. He'd provided a building and the means to buy it, rent support from the Chicago Low Income Housing Trust Fund, and Manna House to supply social services to the women who would live here. "But we have Gabby to thank for her vision and her persistence in believing this was God's idea and God's timing . . . and here we are today, to ask God's blessing on the House of Hope."

"Hallelujah for God and Gabby!" Precious cheered, and the room erupted in a hearty round of clapping. Now my face really was burning and tears threatened to open a floodgate. Jodi slipped me some tissues, but not before I saw Lee across the room giving me a private smile as he joined the clapping. I couldn't see Philip . . . had he left after all? That, or he was sitting down someplace behind folks who were standing.

As the clapping died down, Avis Douglass opened her Bible. "As we bless this house, I want to read a scripture from Hebrews that has the House of Hope written all over it. 'Do not neglect to show hospitality to strangers, for thereby some have entertained angels unawares.' Chapter thirteen, verse two."

"Did she say *angels* gonna live here?" Sammy piped up. More laughter.

Tanya clamped a hand over her son's mouth. "She didn't mean *you*, pipsqueak."

"Oh, but I did." Avis smiled at the third grader. "Each mother and child who will live in the House of Hope may be a stranger before they walk in the door, but some may be God's angels disguised as the homeless to bless this house."

"*Sí, sí!* Amen! Right, Gracie?" Edesa nuzzled the little girl in her arms, making her laugh.

Peter Douglass cleared his throat. "Well said. Why don't we pray a blessing over this apartment, then do the same in the other apartments—"

"I got a prayer," Lucy announced.

Everyone stared as the old woman pushed her way into the

middle of the room. Dandy started to follow, probably thinking his new mistress was getting ready to leave, but Paul pulled the dog back and made him stay.

It was all I could do to keep my jaw from dropping. Lucy wanted to *pray*?

chapter 12

Without further ado, Lucy clasped her big-knuckled hands together, squeezed her eyes shut, and boomed in her raspy voice, "Bless this house, oh Lord, we pray. Make it safe by night an' day. Bless these walls, so firm and stout, keepin' want and trouble out . . ."

I smiled to myself. The prayer was obviously a poem of some sort she'd memorized.

". . . Bless the roof and chimney tall, let Thy peace lie over all. Bless the door that it may prove, ever open to joy and love. Bless these windows, shinin' bright, lettin' in God's heavenly light. Bless the folks who dwell within, keep them pure and free from sin. Bless us that we'll dwell one day, oh Lord with Thee." Lucy opened her eyes and grinned. "Amen. The end."

Murmurs of appreciation circled the room. "Where'd you get that prayer, Lucy?" Estelle asked.

Lucy shrugged. "Dunno. Learned it as a kid. My mama used to pray it ever' time we moved to new digs—which was ever' couple months, seems like. Followin' the crops, ya know. Seemed like it fit this here new House of Hope."

My ears perked up. Lucy rarely, if *ever*, shared information about her former life.

"*Sí, mi amiga*," Edesa said warmly. "And I want you to pray it again when we get up to our apartment, okay? Shall we go?"

"Our apartment first!" Tanya said. "Sammy, go open the door."

I glanced at Peter Douglass. He'd been usurped. But the unflappable businessman gave me a wink and nodded. "Let the Spirit move," he murmured as he followed the crowd across the hall and into apartment 1A.

I waited until the room cleared and approached Philip, who had been sitting on the window seat in the sunroom, his broken arm resting on a stack of throw pillows. "You go on," he said. "I don't do stairs too well."

"Do you want me to call a taxi?"

"Just . . . go, Gabby. I'm sure they're waiting for you."

Fine. I left the apartment, but the only person waiting for me in the hall was Lee. He was frowning.

"What's he doing here, Gabby? Have you two patched it up?"

I felt a flicker of annoyance. After our confrontation at the hospital, Lee didn't exactly have any claim on what I did or didn't do as far as Philip was concerned. At the same time, I wanted him to understand. "I didn't invite him, if that's what you mean. He brought Paul home, and Paul begged me to let him stay. That's all."

Lee's face softened. He nodded and glanced at his watch. "Wish I could stay, but I've got some research to do for a case I'm arguing Monday. But this house warming—"

"House *blessing*," I corrected.

"Right. House blessing. Anyway, it was very nice. I'm . . ." He reached out a hand and gently touched my cheek. "I'm proud of you, Gabby. What you've done here. You're quite a woman."

"Now can we serve your brownies?" I asked Estelle as our little throng returned to the first floor after blessing the other two apartments. I'd noticed that Avis had also quietly anointed the doors of the three apartments still occupied by other tenants.

Estelle smiled coyly. "As long as you stay out of the kitchen. Harry an' I've got it covered. Right, Harry?" I caught a wink passing between the two of them. *Hm.* What were those two up to?

"Don't anyone leave," I announced. "We still have dessert and coffee." I saw Denny Baxter in the sunroom talking to Philip. Probably offering to give him a ride back to the penthouse. Well, Philip and Lee had been here in the same room and the roof hadn't caved in. I started to relax for the first time that evening. *Thank You, God, for pouring Your peace over our house blessing.* I didn't think anyone had seen Lee touch my cheek out in the hall, even though I could still feel the exact spot on my skin.

After what seemed longer than necessary to set out a pan of brownies, Harry Bentley appeared in the doorway of the living room. "Dessert is served. This way, ladies and gentlemen." He offered his arm to me. "May I escort you, Firecracker?"

"You're being so formal," I teased. "Except for that 'Firecracker' bit."

We all forged our way down the long hall, past the boys' bedrooms and bathroom to the dining room at the rear of the apartment. To my surprise, the makeshift plywood table had been cleared of my everyday tablecloth and the potluck dishes, and it now boasted a white damask tablecloth and elegant silver candlesticks. Tall white candles flickered cheerfully. On one end sat a silver coffee service with a silver creamer and sugar bowl and, on the other, china dessert plates and silver forks. All this for brownies and coffee?

I groaned silently. I *really* needed to get a decent table.

"Come in, come in, make room for everybody . . ." Mr. B glanced over the faces bunching into the room, whispered something to Paul, and a minute later my youngest reappeared with his father.

"Is it my mom's birthday?" Paul asked, obviously as confused as the rest of us. "I thought it wasn't till next weekend."

Oh no. Harry and Estelle didn't go to all this trouble for—

"No, son. Matter of fact, didn't know your mom had a birthday comin' up." Harry winked at me. "But it *is* an important occasion. Just wanted all you folks to know . . ." Harry reached for Estelle's right hand and pulled her close to him. "Show 'em, babe."

Eyes shining, Estelle raised her left hand and turned it in the candlelight so we could all see the exquisite diamond ring sparkling on her third finger.

For a nanosecond, the whole room seemed to gasp . . . and then whoops, hollers, and "hallelujahs" broke out as if Harry Bentley had just scored the winning home run that gave the Cubs a pennant. Sensing *something* exciting was happening, even Dandy offered several joyous barks, and I was grinning so hard my cheeks hurt.

"Yep!" Harry beamed. "Last weekend I asked Miss Estelle Williams to marry me—and she said yes."

"'Bout time!" Precious snorted. Even moody Sabrina was

smiling and clapping. The cheering hiked up another couple deci-
bels when the ex-Chicago cop pulled his ladylove into a clinch and
gave her a long, sensuous kiss.

And then we were all over both of them, giving them hugs,
congratulations, and slaps on the back—well, the guys slapped
Harry. "Oh, Mr. B," I breathed into his ear when I finally got my
turn for congratulations. "I am *so* happy for you. So . . . happy."
The lump in my throat cut off the rest of what I wanted to say, and
I just hugged him hard.

Harry and Estelle insisted on serving the coffee and brownies to us all—"Estelle's Double-Rich Double-Fudge recipe," Harry
bragged—as everyone started begging for details. "Where'd he
pop the question, Estelle?" . . . "Did you have to twist her arm,
Harry?" . . . "Do you guys have a wedding date yet?"

As my teeth sank into a second piece of Estelle's brownies, I
suddenly realized Harry said he'd asked Estelle to marry him *last
weekend*—the same weekend he'd saved Philip from another serious attack by that terrible Fagan person. I started to ask Harry if
he'd asked Estelle before or after that traumatic event, but held back
because I saw Philip gingerly make his way through the crowded
room and extend his good hand to Harry. "Congratulations,
Bentley. Happy for you. And I hear I've got you to thank for saving
my skin last Sunday. Don't know how you sent those cops to the
right alley, but—thanks."

Harry pursed his lips a moment and then nodded thoughtfully as he slowly shook Philip's offered hand. "Glad you're okay,
Fairbanks." He looked hard at Philip. "But the one you should
really thank is the Man Upstairs. Might not have sent those cops to
the right place if God hadn't let me go through hell."

Philip seemed taken aback. "What do you mean?"

"My eyes. God allowed my sight to give out on me not long ago, real scary time. But I learned to use my other senses a lot more, 'specially my hearing. It was the things I *heard* over your phone—the buses goin' by, other sounds—that told me where that shakedown was happenin'. Learned somethin' the hard way— God can use *anything*, even the pain in our lives, to do some good."

I was so astonished by their interaction, I had to slip away into the bathroom to gather my wits around me. I was glad Philip took the opportunity to thank Mr. B for coming to his rescue last weekend. Maybe . . . maybe that was even the reason God allowed him to end up here at the house blessing tonight. I held on to the sink, my shoulders slumping. *Oh God, I'm sorry—sorry all I was thinking about was me and my feelings. Maybe you wanted Philip to be here tonight, to talk to Harry, or just to witness a group of people giving You the glory for putting the House of Hope together.*

Harry's words just a few moments before suddenly echoed in my head. *"God can use anything, even the pain in our lives, to do some good."* The comment hit me with such force, I had to sit down on the toilet seat. It was true. God had caused a lot of good to come out of my pain! It didn't excuse what Philip had done, but tonight's house blessing for the House of Hope would never have happened if I hadn't ended up homeless and close to losing my sons—

Knock! Knock! "Sister Gabby, are you in there?" Edesa's voice. "People are getting ready to go home, but the Douglasses want to have one last prayer."

"Uh . . . coming! Give me a sec." I took several deep breaths, patted a wet washcloth on my face, and finger-combed my frowzy curls before opening the door. The group had gathered back in the living room, forming a haphazard circle. I slipped in between Jodi and Denny and took their hands.

"Ah, there you are, Gabby," Peter Douglass said. "Just wanted to ask what's next for the House of Hope so we can commit the next steps to prayer before we leave."

On the spot again! I thought fast. "Well, actually Josh and I found out today that the tenant in 2A is moving out next weekend—which is good, as it frees up another apartment for the House of Hope. But that's sooner than we thought, so we need God's guidance in selecting our next residents. Same for the other two apartments, of course—and also pray that the tenants who move out would find good places to go."

Peter Douglass nodded, closing with a simple prayer asking for guidance and wisdom in filling the House of Hope with the people God would bring. And then there was a flurry of good-byes, more congratulations for Harry and Estelle, reclaiming of coats and food dishes. Jodi had been helping with the cleanup, so she and Denny and Philip were some of the last to leave. We were saying good-bye when I felt an urgent tug on my arm.

"Mom? Mom!" Paul darted eager looks between Philip and me. "If that apartment on the second floor is gonna be empty, why doesn't Dad just move in there? Then we could see him more often and not hafta wait till Fridays!"

chapter 13

I could have throttled Paul Michael Fairbanks, then and there. No way was I going to stand there in front of Philip, P.J., and the Baxters and explain to my youngest why his father was *not* going to move into that apartment.

"Another conversation, another day," I quipped, giving Paul the Evil Eye. Quickly leading the way into the hall, I opened the door into the outer foyer. "Thanks for the basket of yummy breads, Jodi. I'll make sure the other residents get some. Glad to see those bruises are almost gone, Philip. But take care, don't overdo it. Thanks for giving him a ride home, Denny. Thanks for coming, y'all! Bye! Bye!"

The moment the foyer door wheezed shut, I turned on Paul and P.J. "Inside. Family meeting—*now*."

I marched both boys into the sunroom and pointed to the window seat. "Sit."

They sat, looking up at me sullenly. I folded my arms across my chest, breathing heavily. It was all I could do to not tap my foot too.

"Look," I said, "we need to have a clear understanding. Your dad and I are separated. Which means we need *space* from each other. And we don't do everything together either. So no more putting me on the spot in front of him—or even worse, in front of *other people*—by begging for him to stay for dinner or a party or something else that's happening here. And, Paul, you were *way* out of line harping about him moving into one of the apartments here—"

"But, Mom! He—"

"Quiet! *I'm* talking here and I want you to listen, young man. This is not an apartment building where just anybody can move in! I'm working with Manna House and the City of Chicago to provide housing for homeless single moms. So every apartment that becomes available is earmarked for moms from Manna House, until they get on their feet and can get their own house or apartment. Manna House staff will decide who lives here—not you." I glared first at one son, then the other. "Do you understand? *Do not* ambush me in front of your dad or other people."

Both boys pouted. Then P.J. muttered, "The Baxters moved in here, and *they* weren't homeless. Not a single mom either."

"That's different. I hired Josh to be the property manager for the House of Hope and it's helpful if he lives on the premises. Edesa's also a Manna House volunteer. Living here, she's like support staff for the House of Hope, same as me."

"But, Mom . . ." Paul's lip was quivering. He grabbed his T-shirt and rubbed it across his eyes.

My resolve to be hard-nosed started to dissolve. I dropped my arms and sank down on the window seat beside him. "Look, honey. I know our separation is hard on you. Hard for both of you. And I'm sorry. Really sorry." I reached out and touched P.J. gently, then put an arm around Paul. "If you want your dad to do something—come to your birthday party or whatever—or if you have questions about what's happening with your dad and me, just talk to me in private first. That's all I'm asking. Okay?"

"Guess so," P.J. muttered.

Paul sniffed. "But—"

"But what, honey?"

"What if it's an emergency? Couldn't Dad move in here then?"

"What do you mean?"

"Because I saw him again."

"Saw who again?"

"That man. The one who sits on the park bench and watches for Dad. I saw him today, just before we came over here. He went like this . . ." Paul cocked his hand like a pistol and pretended to shoot.

I cornered Harry Bentley at SouledOut the next morning after the worship service. "Mr. B, what happened last Sunday when you went to the police station? You know—after the police picked up Fagan and his crony. Are they both locked up? Off the street?"

Mr. Bentley scratched his chin, covered by the gray beard that ran ear to ear along his jawline. "Far as I know. Fagan was caught in the act of committing a felony after being indicted on previous felony charges. That's a bail violation. The responding police took Mr. Fairbanks to the station where he signed a statement about what happened, and I backed him up based on what I heard over the phone. I'm pretty sure they'll keep Fagan in the county jail now until his trial's over. Both he and the other cop—"

"The other *cop*?" I squeaked.

Mr. Bentley's generous mouth twisted in a cynical smile. "Yeah. Unfortunately, several of Chicago's finest have gotten sucked into Fagan's little gang of rogue cops. We just don't have enough evidence against them to make charges stick. Yet." He tipped his head and looked at me with concern. "What's this about, Firecracker?"

I told him about the man Paul had seen watching Richmond Towers and making threatening gestures. "It sounds like the same man I saw in the park last week when I brought Philip back from a doctor's appointment. Paul's scared for his dad, wants him to move out of the penthouse. *Is* Philip still in danger, Mr. B?"

My friend didn't answer for a moment. A hubbub of people talking and laughing around the coffee urns, kids darting here and there, and people leaving through the double glass doors filled the space around us until he spoke. "Don't know, Firecracker. Wish I could say for sure he wasn't, but knowing Fagan, he's gonna make sure he gets his money back—somehow. Fairbanks's best bet is to pay back that loan. But how that's gonna happen . . ." Harry shrugged.

I sighed. "Yeah. A lot of problems would be solved if Philip would—could—pay off his gambling debts. Well, thanks." Then I eyed him slyly. "So. Who won the argument last Sunday? Did Estelle go to the station with you or not? Had you already given her the ring?"

Harry threw back his head and laughed. "She did *not* go with me to the station. Fact is, I was going to pop the question that afternoon, until that mess with Fagan came up. So I had to do some mighty fast juggling." Still chuckling, he glanced across the room to where Estelle was holding court around the coffee urn, showing off her engagement ring to a gaggle of eager females. "But as you can see, we got it done. Oh yeah—hee, hee—we got it done."

Staff meeting at Manna House ran overtime the next morning due to the influx of new names on the bed list. Even though daytime temperatures still played tag in the fifties, nighttime temps had been falling below freezing, bringing more of the homeless indoors. I jiggled impatiently, eager to talk privately with Mabel about who might be our next candidates for the House of Hope.

Leafing through the stack of intake forms, Mabel sighed. "We need more case managers. Any suggestions?" She glanced around the circle of volunteers and paid staff. "Any of you want to get certified? And yes, I'm serious."

"I think Gabby would make a great case manager." Edesa flashed a grin at me. She and Josh tried to take turns making staff meeting on Monday mornings when they could juggle their class schedules at Circle Campus. One-year-old Gracie was no doubt the center of attention out in Shepherd's Fold at the moment. A few residents had been at Manna House long enough to remember when the tiny girl had shown up at the shelter in the arms of her drug-addicted—and now dead—Latina mother. Gracie certainly had no shortage of adoring "aunties" willing to babysit during staff meeting.

Mabel lifted an eyebrow and smiled. "Good suggestion. But I'm guessing Gabby has enough on her plate right now getting the House of Hope up and running. Anyone else?"

No one else volunteered, and it went on the list of prayer

needs. I felt torn. I'd already been wondering what it'd take to qualify as a case manager—a role that would give me more opportunity to help some of the young women like Naomi Jackson, who'd managed to work her way into my heart. Even though the young drug addict had kind of latched on to me, I felt helpless to know how to help her.

But Mabel was probably right. *One thing at a time, Gabby.* Like the weekend getaway I had put on the agenda for today. I not only needed final approval from Mabel in order to reserve the retreat house—a *yes* there, hallelujah—but I needed a couple of staff willing to go along. *Huh.* I already knew Estelle wouldn't volunteer. But to my relief, Angela Kwon and Edesa Baxter both said they were interested. All I had to do now was determine how many residents could sign up.

After staff meeting I tagged along on Mabel's heels. "Got a minute to talk about the House of Hope?" I asked hopefully as she stopped by the reception cubby where Angela had just relieved the resident who'd covered for her.

"Mm," the director said absently, glancing through the phone messages Angela handed her. "A few minutes. What's up?"

I followed her into her office and sank into a chair. "The second-floor apartment that'll be vacant next weekend. It'll need to be patched and painted, I'm sure—but knowing how hard Josh works, it could probably be ready two weeks after that, which is the first weekend in November. We need a list of viable candidates and to get them started on their applications—because hopefully the other two apartments will be vacant by the end of the year."

Mabel Turner nodded thoughtfully. "All right. The obvious

candidates are the moms whose children are here at the shelter right now. Who are . . . ?"

"Well, Cordelia Soto comes to mind. She has two—Rufino and Trina."

"Except it's my understanding she's hoping to move to Little Village where she has family."

I snorted. "Yeah, I'll believe it when I see it. Her brother's been stringing her along with empty promises for months. Cordelia's so sweet. They should be falling all over themselves to make room for her."

"So who else? Celia Jones has her granddaughter with her. How old is Keisha?"

"Ten. I think those two—Celia and Cordelia—would make perfect housemates. Cordelia's kids already relate to Celia like a surrogate grandmother."

"But if Cordelia's not a candidate, next on the list would be . . ."

I grimaced. "Shawanda Dixon. The two babies are hers—Dessa and Bam-Bam. But I don't know, Mabel. She's a tough cookie. And the kids have no discipline."

"Maybe an older woman like Celia is just what she needs."

"*Humph*. What she *needs* is an apartment by herself."

Mabel shrugged. "So assign her to 2A by herself. The board decided three should be the minimum number for a three-bedroom with subsidized rent, so she'd fall within the guidelines."

I fell silent, my thoughts tumbling. I was hoping for a few more *likable* residents at the House of Hope before we took on a hard case like Shawanda. "I'm going to ask Cordelia and Celia first," I said stubbornly. "That would give us a more stable quorum in the building before adding Shawanda to the mix."

Mabel nodded slowly. "All right. But if Cordelia takes herself off the list, you'll need to find someone else to share the apartment since it'd just be Celia and her granddaughter in a three-bedroom."

I was going to hope for the best. "Who else should go on the list? Any moms like me, who need second-stage housing so they can get their kids back?"

"Well, there's Sunny Davis. She's got four kids farmed out to various relatives. Court won't give her custody until she has a place to live."

I could hardly wait to ask Celia and Cordelia if they wanted to apply for the vacant apartment at the House of Hope. Celia's dark eyes filled with tears when I invited the middle-aged grandmother to my office and told her we'd have a vacancy at the House of Hope by the first of November.

"Oh, Gabby, honey. These old bones would be grateful to sleep in my own bed instead of a bottom bunk with Keisha over-head! That girl flops more'n a fish in the bottom of a rowboat."

"Old bones, my foot," I teased. "You can't be a day over fifty." I was guessing. Celia's acorn-brown face was smooth and unlined, though her close-cropped nappy hair was salt-and-pepper already. But I realized I knew very little about Celia's story—only that her daughter was strung out on drugs, leaving Celia to raise her granddaughter. And something about losing her apartment when her husband died and she could no longer afford the rent.

"Close. I'm fifty-two. But feels like I've lived double that. Lord have mercy, the things I've seen, mm-hm, help us!" She waved a thin hand in the air, and for a minute I thought she was going to "have church" right then and there. But she regained her composure and asked, "What do I have to do?"

I explained the application process the city required and left her in my office to fill out the forms while I went hunting for Cordelia.

"Haven't seen her," Angela Kwon informed me at the reception desk. She ran a finger down the sign-out page. "But she hasn't signed out, so she should be around. Oh! This message came for you awhile ago, but you didn't answer your office phone. Somebody from Wisconsin wanting to know if you still want the retreat house the weekend of the twenty-eighth. Guess they've got another request for the same dates."

I snatched the note. "Yikes. Yes, we want it!" I scurried back to my office to return the call. Finding Cordelia would have to wait.

chapter 14

"The good news," I told Mabel Turner the next day, "is that we've got that retreat house in Wisconsin for the last weekend in October. Are you sure you don't want to come?"

She eyed me with the same *"Are you kidding?"* look Estelle had given me. "And the bad news is—?"

I sighed. "Cordelia Soto says she and her kids are moving in with her cousin around the first of November. At least that's the plan."

"But that's good news, Gabby. They'll be with family. Cordelia's been here over three months. She lost her job, then her apartment, and hasn't been able to find another job. We're not set up for long-term shelter, as you well know."

"I know." I made a face. "I'm being selfish. The bad news is, that puts Shawanda and her kids next on the list for the House of Hope."

The Manna House director made a tent with her fingers, letting my words hang in the air a few moments. I could feel a lecture coming.

"Gabby. You know as well as I do a lot of different women come through that front door. Some are cooperative and likable, some need a whole lot of help, and some, I admit, are a pain in the you-know-what. But every woman has God-given potential within her, some just need more help than others to develop that potential. Including Shawanda. She's prickly—but she's managed to not get kicked out of the shelter. The important thing is to be clear about the rules and expectations."

I suddenly had a brilliant idea. "We made a list of house rules last week. But that was basically for the current tenants. Maybe you could come to our next house meeting and help us create an appropriate list for the House of Hope."

Mabel turned to her computer and called up her calendar. "Which is . . . ?"

"Tonight. We're changing to Wednesday next week though."

"Tonight! I'm not sure I can on such short notice. Unless— could I bring Jermaine with me? Let him hang out with Paul for an hour?"

"I'm sure Paul would love it." *P.J. might be another story.* It was one thing to include Mabel's nephew in a large group, like the house blessing, where P.J. could ignore him. Another to leave the three boys alone together, especially since P.J. had been less than friendly to the kid he'd labeled a sissy. Even though P.J. and Jermaine were both freshmen at Lane Tech, it was Paul and Jermaine who had developed a friendship around their love for creating music.

But having Mabel come to our house meeting would be a big help. I couldn't let P.J.'s attitude toward Jermaine dictate what happened. And he'd been warned.

"Thanks, Mabel. Guess I better talk to Celia, see if she's

willing to share an apartment with Shawanda." Though what we were going to do if she didn't want to, I had no idea. And I still had to double-check with Josh. "See you at eight thirty, okay?"

I brought Paul's keyboard home from the shelter, where he'd been keeping it so he could practice after school, figuring there was a good chance he and Jermaine would want to do music. But P.J. threw a fit. "Don't tell me I'm gonna have to listen to the Dorky Duo play their stupid music for a whole hour! How am I s'posed to get my homework done with that racket?"

"You can hole up in my bedroom in the back, and I'll tell them to keep the volume down. Plug yourself into your iPod. Besides, it's only an hour, P.J."

"Why does Ms. Turner have to bring him anyway? You let me stay home by myself, and he's the same age I am." P.J. snorted. "The big baby."

I'd wondered the same thing, but Mabel was protective of her nephew, who'd once tried to commit suicide because of all the torment he got from other kids. If bringing him with her made her feel better, I wasn't going to question it.

Mabel and Jermaine were a few minutes late that evening, so I waited till they arrived, left the boys with popcorn and soft drinks at opposite ends of the apartment, and hustled up to the third floor after Mabel. Edesa was still trying to put Gracie to sleep and Josh was on the phone—*"My grandparents,"* he mouthed to us when he opened the door, phone cradled between shoulder and ear—so we started without them. Tanya said things had been a lot quieter since Zia Bassi had kicked her boyfriend out. I reported that Celia Jones had applied for that apartment when Zia moved, and she and her granddaughter would probably be sharing it with Shawanda Dixon and her two kids.

"Celia and Shawanda!" Precious scowled. "Thought maybe Tanya or me could move in there. Each havin' our own apartment, like you said at first, 'fore the Baby Baxters moved in."

I saw Mabel hide a smile at the tag Precious had bestowed on the younger Baxters before she said, "I'm sure that would be nice. Except the board drew up some guidelines for residence in the House of Hope and determined at least three persons need to occupy a three-bedroom since we're asking the city for subsidized rent."

"Well then. Me an' Sabrina *gonna* be three people when she drop that baby." Precious was working up quite a snit.

Tanya looked hurt. "I thought you an' me decided we liked the idea of sharin' an apartment. Good for Sabrina to have the baby in her room an' all that. Ain't you happy with how things been goin'?"

"Yeah, yeah, it's not that." Precious scowled again as Josh and Edesa joined us in the front room, and kept scowling as we brought the young couple up to speed. But when we mentioned Shawanda as a probable resident, she popped in again. "Okay, *that's* what stickin' me in the butt. That Shawanda—she 'bout as easy to get along with as one o' them pit bulls. Miss Celia and Keisha? They be fine. But Bam-Bam an' Dessa gonna be runnin' they itty-bitty legs off over our heads an' Shawanda ain't gonna do a thang. Can't tell her *nothin'* 'bout carin' for them kids or she up in your face havin' a screamin' fit."

"Which is why it's important to have rules for living here at the House of Hope," Mabel said. "This isn't a personality contest, but we *can* have clear expectations for cooperation and reasonable behavior. So let's talk. Some of the best rules come from the residents themselves. Gabby, you said you'd already come up with some basic rules last week. Let's start there and fill them out . . . do you want to take notes?"

I was so grateful Mabel had come to the house meeting. She had much more experience than I had setting rules and limits for the residents at Manna House—and yet she had a heart of compassion for even difficult cases like Shawanda. And how often had she been willing to bend those rules for me during my sojourn as a resident at Manna House? She'd treated me like a person, not just another homeless blight on society. And it was obvious she wanted us to treat Shawanda that way too.

By the end of the hour, we had a decent list of rules and expectations, which I planned to type up and have in hand when I talked to Shawanda tomorrow. "But what we gonna do when somebody breaks one o' them rules?" Tanya wanted to know. She might just as well have said "Shawanda" as "somebody."

Josh nodded. "Right. We still need to talk about the process we follow when someone has a complaint or something happens we didn't anticipate."

Edesa giggled. "'*Process*.' That's such a white-guy word, Josh."

He made a face. "So? I am a white guy, if you haven't noticed."

The rest of us cracked up. Even got a smile from Mabel. "Next time," she said. "I'll be glad to come the next few weeks until you all feel the House of Hope is on solid ground. Then maybe I could meet with you all on a monthly basis." Heads were nodding all around. "Edesa, why don't you wrap up this discussion with a prayer for God's wisdom and guidance? We don't want to be like that foolish man in the Bible who built his house on loose sand. There's only one foundation that will sustain the House of Hope—and that's Christ the Solid Rock."

For some reason, Mabel's comment at the meeting burrowed into my mind and dug up the old gospel hymn we used to sing at Minot Evangelical Church when I was growing up: *On Christ the solid Rock I stand, all other ground is sinking sand . . .* The song played around in my head all night, even though the only words I could actually remember were in the refrain. I'd have to look it up in a hymnal.

I was curious. Was that old hymn the inspiration for the more recent gospel song that had sustained me again and again the past few months? The CD was in my car, so on the way to work the next morning I punched the Play button and the familiar words filled the car.

Where do I go . . . when the storms of life are raging?
Who do I talk to . . . when nobody wants to listen?
Who do I lean on . . . when there's no foundation stable?

And then the "answer" boomed out at me:

I go to the Rock—I know that He's able, I go to the Rock!

By this time, I was bouncing in my seat and thumping the steering wheel as I sang along with the gospel beat.

I go to the Rock of my salvation!
Go to the Stone that the builders rejected!
Run to the Mountain and the Mountain stands by me-e-e!

The female driver in the car next to me at a stoplight looked at me strangely. But I didn't care. Because all of a sudden, there it was, and I hollered it out:

The earth all around me is sinking sand
On Christ the solid Rock I stand
When I need a shelter, when I need a friend
I go to the Rock—

Beeeep! Beeeep! The guy behind me was leaning on his horn to tell me the light had changed. I waved an "Excuse me!" at him but I was grinning. How about that! Both gospel songs used the phrase "On Christ the Solid Rock I stand . . ." *Hm.* As soon as I got to work, I was going to make a little sign and tape it to my computer. Usually when the phrase of a song imprinted itself on my brain, God had a purpose for putting it there.

Something told me I was going to need it.

As far as I could tell, the boys had managed to coexist in our apartment without incident last evening. Maybe my strategy of not making too big a deal of the whole situation—continuing to include Jermaine in our lives in a normal way but not expecting P.J. to be his best friend—was paying off. But the difference in personality between Paul and P.J. often perplexed me. Paul was easygoing, outgoing, friendly, easy to love—not to mention his hair and complexion took after my natural reddish curls and freckles—while P.J. had the dark good looks of his father and some of his surly attitudes too. I had to be careful not to play favorites, to give P.J. as much unconditional love as I gave Paul.

Help me know how to love my boys, dear God, I prayed, threading my way through the usual Wednesday morning here-to-see-the-nurse crowd in the dining room and shutting my office door on the hubbub. I reached for my Bible. *And I could use some help with my attitude when I talk to Shawanda today. Help me to see the God-given potential You see in her, Lord.*

When I finally felt fortified with some Bible reading and prayer, I settled down to my first task: typing up the list of rules and expectations we'd come up with at the house meeting last night. Printing out a "Letter of Understanding" that would need to be signed by each resident, I pulled open my office door to go find Shawanda—and ran smack dab into Lucy Tucker, nearly knocking her down.

"Hey!" she growled. "You always got ta be in such a hurry, Fuzz Top?" A couple of raspy coughs punctuated her fuss.

The scarf tied around her head—one of my mother's, given as a memento—was damp, as was the sweater she had pulled over several other layers of clothing. The weeklong on-again, off-again October drizzle must have started up again. "Hi, Lucy. I'm glad to see you too." I grinned at her. "Hope you're here to check out that cough. You don't want to get bronchitis again like last spring."

Lucy glared at me. "Don' remember askin' you ta be my mother. I'm twice as old as you, missy, and still livin' an' breathin' ta tell about it."

I had no idea how old Lucy was in actual years, but I came back at her. "You can't be *twice* as old as me. I'm turning forty on Friday."

The old woman looked me up and down. "*Humph.* Forty, eh? Ya still wet behind th' ears." She shouldered past me into my office. "What I come for is to fill up my bucket with more dog food. Gotta put some fat on Dandy, get him ready for winter."

That alarmed me. "Lucy, you're not planning on you and Dandy spending the winter outside, are you?" What had I been thinking, giving my mother's dog to an elderly bag lady who dragged all her worldly possessions around in a wire cart and spent more time on the streets than in a shelter? "You need—"

Lucy hummed loudly as she filled her plastic bucket from one of the twenty-five-pound bags of dog food that had been donated to the shelter after Dandy's heroic routing of a nighttime burglar. *Fine.* She wasn't going to listen to me. I flounced out the door and resumed my original errand to hunt up Shawanda.

But one of these days—soon—we needed to have a sit-down about how Lucy and Dandy were going to survive this winter.

chapter 15

I found Shawanda sprawled in a beanbag chair in the playroom on the main floor, idly leafing through a magazine and chewing gum while two-year-old Bam-Bam pulled toys off the shelves, scattering the pieces of Legos and puzzles, then moving on to the next shelf. Three-year-old Dessa was tugging on her mother's leg, whining about something, and being ignored.

Gotta help me here, Lord. "Shawanda? Got a minute?"

The young black woman, her long legs encased in skinny jeans, hair gelled and coiled tight to her head, shrugged. "Sure. Whatchu want?"

I tested my weight on one of the small wooden tables and sat while I explained the concept of second-stage housing, then said we might have space in a shared apartment for her and her kids.

The magazine slipped to the floor and her face perked up. "For real? Ya mean me an' the kids can get outta this dump into a real apartment? Who else be in the apartment?"

"Celia Jones and her granddau—"

"Well then, that's cool. Celia's all right. So when can we move in?"

"First of next month, if all goes well. You would need to fill out an application, because the House of Hope partners with the city, which would subsidize your rent. And you would still work with your case manager here at Manna House on finishing your GED and—"

"GED! That schoolin' be such a joke. What I *want* is daycare for these babies so I can get me a *job*. How'm I s'posed ta find a job with these two hangin' 'round my neck all day?" A wail erupted from across the room. "Bam-Bam! Quit hittin' on your sister. Don't make me come over there." Shawanda balled her fist in a threatening gesture, then turned back to me and wiggled her shoulders in a little joy-dance. "Oh *yeah*. I'll be glad to get out from under all the *rules* they got in this place. Gotta sign out ever' time I leave, gotta be in by eight at night, gotta do those dumb chores. What a load of—"

"Shawanda!" My voice was sharper than I intended, so I took a deep breath, then continued. "You need to understand that the House of Hope is affiliated with Manna House and we also have rules. Here." I handed her the sheet I'd typed up from our meeting last night. "Look that over. If you can sign this agreement to abide by these rules and expectations, then let's talk. If not—well, there are others waiting in line for the House of Hope."

I managed to get out the door without giving Shawanda a *real* piece of my mind. Who did the girl think she was? Frankly, I hoped she'd read the rules and flip off the opportunity. Good riddance.

But back in my office, Mabel's compassionate words fought with my attitude. *"Every woman has God-given potential within her, some just need more help than others to develop that potential. Including Shawanda."*

I groaned and put my head in my hands. *Okay, Lord. I'm going to have to trust You with this one. If she signs the agreement—well, guess we'll take her and hold her to it. But if Shawanda has some God-given potential You want developed at the House of Hope, You're going to have to reveal it, because it sure isn't obvious to me!*

Opening my eyes, I saw the card on which I'd written the phrase from those gospel songs: *"On Christ the Solid Rock I Stand!"* I smiled ruefully. Guess we'd find out soon enough whether the House of Hope was being built on "sinking sand" or Solid Rock.

The drizzles stopped and the sun came out Thursday. "Looks like it's going to be a nice weekend for my birthday," I told the boys, who had the TV on when the weather guy popped up on the evening news. "Almost sixty degrees on Saturday! Hey, we haven't ridden the bike trail along Lake Michigan yet. This might be our last chance before winter. Whaddya say?"

"Uh, Mom, hello. The cross country team has regional meets this Saturday. I *told* you." P.J. rolled his eyes. "Besides, you left your bike in Virginia, remember?"

"Aren't we staying with Dad Friday night and Saturday?" Paul added.

I made a face. "Details. I could probably borrow a bike from Edesa. She and Josh have bikes in the basement. What time will your regionals be over? If you're done by, say, two o'clock, I'll ask your dad if I can borrow you a couple hours early. Or we could go Sunday afternoon. Come on . . . let's do it!"

P.J. shrugged. "I guess. If I'm not pooped after running all morning."

Paul pulled a puppy-dog face. "It doesn't seem right to leave you tomorrow night on your birthday, Mom. Maybe we should skip going to Dad's this weekend."

I tousled his chestnut head, which insisted on curling even though it was cut short. "Aw, that's sweet of you, hon. But the actual day isn't that important. How about if we declare the whole weekend 'Mom's birthday'? That way you have to be extra nice to me for three whole days!" I laughed as I headed back toward the kitchen. "Starting tomorrow morning—better yet, starting *tonight*. Which means you guys get to do the dishes."

"Use paper plates, then!" P.J. yelled after me.

"Can't!" I hollered back. "We're having chili!"

But as cheerful as I tried to be about the boys going to their dad's on Friday, I dreaded spending my birthday evening alone. If things hadn't changed between Lee and me, he'd probably take me out to a fancy restaurant and we'd have a great time talking and laughing.

For that matter, I told myself as I drove to work the next morning, if things hadn't changed between Philip and me in the first place, I'd be spending my birthday with my husband and kids, blowing out forty candles—and Philip would get all forty on the cake, I was sure of that. He used to be quite the romantic, getting me a dozen red roses every birthday, and another dozen for our anniversary . . .

I blinked back tears of self-pity as I parked the car near the shelter. No roses this year. Wasn't even sure if anyone at Manna House knew it was my birthday.

But I did have a surprise waiting for me in my cubbyhole office. A sheet of paper had been shoved under the door. I flicked on the light and picked up the "Letter of Understanding" I'd given to Shawanda—with her signature scrawled across the bottom.

I spent the morning making plans for the first annual Manna House Fall Getaway, only a week away now. So far eleven residents had signed up, plus me, Angela Kwon, and Edesa Baxter, who would function as staff. We could take one more and still fit into Moby Van without needing extra transportation. But we still needed to plan meals and shop for food. This was a do-it-yourself retreat house, one reason we were able to get it for a reasonable price. Maybe Angela could help with food, and I was counting on Edesa to lead a prayer and devotion time on Saturday and Sunday mornings.

Which reminded me—could I sneak into Edesa's Bible study in Shepherd's Fold this morning? I wondered if she was still doing the *Bad Girls of the Bible* studies, which had gotten a better-than-usual turnout from the residents. But a quick glance at the clock told me it was almost over. Where had the time gone this morning? It was nearly time for lunch.

Whatever Estelle was making, it smelled wonderful. As soon as I heard the lunch bell, I joined the residents and staff lining up along the far wall of the dining room as Estelle and her lunch crew set out the final dishes on the open counter separating kitchen and eating space. "Gabby Fairbanks!" Estelle called out from the kitchen. "I don't see Mabel yet. Would you bless the food so we can feed these folks?"

I still wasn't comfortable praying out loud in front of people. On the other hand, it was easy to thank God for Estelle's good cooking, so I did. ". . . And we also thank You, gracious God, for the beautiful day outside today, for sunshine and warmth and beautiful leaves on trees." Once I started, my heart seemed to swell with gratefulness. "And for each precious sister You have brought here to live or work, and for the good plans You have for each one—"

"An' hallelujah, thank You, Jesus, an' all that, amen. Let's eat!" interrupted a raspy voice, which was greeted by a whole lot of other "Amens" and snickers.

Lucy.

"Okay, okay." I grinned as she joined me in the line. "What brings you here today? Let's see, you already got dog food earlier this week. And last time I looked, it wasn't raining—yes, yes, hello to you, too, Dandy." I gave the Manna House mascot a scratch on the rump.

"I got reasons. Fer one thing, came to sign up fer that little trip ya got goin' next weekend. Kinda liked that trip you an' me took out west to bury your ma, but it was real long, ya know? A weekend sounds more ta my likin'. Be good to get off these streets a few days. Where ya goin' again?"

"Really?" I hadn't expected Lucy to sign up. But we did have one more seat on the van. "Well, that's great. We're going up to Devil's Lake State Park in Wisconsin to see the fall colors. But this place we're renting doesn't allow pets. What about Dandy?"

"Been thinkin' 'bout that. Thought maybe that boy of yours

might want a four-legged visitor over the weekend. Whatcha think?"

Huh. Good question. Paul would be delighted. But the boys would be with their dad Friday night and Saturday. I'd even thought of asking Philip if they could stay the whole weekend since I'd be gone, but I was sure he wouldn't want the dog in the penthouse—he'd made *that* clear enough. If the boys didn't stay the whole weekend with Philip, I'd been planning to ask Josh Baxter to look after the boys till we got back Sunday evening. Josh wouldn't mind the dog, but—

Snap, snap. Lucy snapped her fingers in front of my face. "You still in there, Fuzz Top? When ya done thinkin', let me know. I'm gonna get somethin' ta eat 'fore mold grows on it. C'mon, Dandy." Lucy flounced off.

I followed in her wake, loaded my tray with a bowl of Estelle's homemade beef-barley vegetable soup and crusty garlic bread—day-old but still good from a nearby bakery—and rejoined Lucy at one of the tables. "Sorry, Lucy. I'll ask about Dandy, but there are a few wrinkles I've got to iron out."

Shawanda Dixon plonked Bam-Bam and Dessa into a couple of booster seats across the table from us. "Didja get that paper I stuck under your door, Miss Gabby? An' I signed up for that get-away weekend too. Miss Celia said she'd keep my kids if I wanted to go. Hey—can you watch these two while I get their food?" Without waiting for an answer, she was back at the counter loading up a tray of food for the three of them.

Lucy slurped away, totally ignoring the two wriggling toddlers grabbing for the salt and pepper and anything else within reach. As I tried to keep them in their seats, I had an unnerving vision of what life might be like at the House of Hope in a few weeks. I certainly hoped Celia Jones knew what she was getting into.

Shawanda finally returned and I had a chance to eat my own lukewarm soup while she busied herself trying to get more soup into the toddlers' mouths than on their clothes and the table as they wriggled and banged spoons. Suddenly Dessa yelled, "Gotta pee, Mama!" Shawanda grabbed both kids and stalked off toward the bathroom.

Ah. Peace.

Lucy was well into her second bowl of soup. Half in jest, I resumed our interrupted conversation. "So, Lucy. You said the *first* reason you came today was to sign up for the Fall Getaway. What's your other reason?"

The old lady snickered. "That."

"That? What do you mean?"

"*That.*" She jerked her head over her shoulder.

I turned—and saw Estelle standing behind me holding a large sheet cake lined with flaming candles around the edges. Only then did I realize the room had hushed a few moments earlier, which I'd presumed was because Shawanda had taken her kids out, but now the residents and staff broke into laughter, clapping and hooting as Estelle set the cake in front of me. Someone began a raggedy version of "Happy birthday to youuuu . . ."

I'm sure I turned beet red—which always clashed with my hair. I even got teary, not realizing how much I'd been hoping *somebody* would remember it was my birthday.

"Blow out them forty candles!" Lucy cackled. "Betcha can't."

I did—though it took three tries. The cake boasted delicate yellow frosting with orange, red, and yellow marzipan leaves all around the edge. Scrawled across the cake in orange frosting, it said, "HAPPY BIRTHDAY, GABBY!" and "OUR FAVORITE FUZZ TOP," which I read aloud.

"I tol' em to put that on there," Lucy snickered.

Estelle handed me a knife. I eyed her suspiciously. "This better not be a foam-rubber cake like the one Harry had decorated for you."

"*Humph. He* better watch out when he goes to cut our wedding cake."

"Estelle! You wouldn't!" I sputtered, laughing.

"Wouldn't I?" She patted me on the shoulder. "But yours is safe, Gabby girl. Lucy tried to get me to make it banana-nut, swore it was your favorite. But I know you and chocolate—*ha.*"

"Oh, she did, did she? Don't think I've ever had banana cake." I cut into the moist, crumbly cake—fudge chocolate and definitely not foam rubber—and started handing out pieces left and right. I finally took a bite of my own piece. "Mmm. Yummy." I nudged Lucy. "So why'd you tell Estelle banana was my favorite? Just a guess?"

She grinned, her mouth full of cake. "Nah. But it's *my* favorite, so I figgered you might like it too. My ma used ta make it . . ." Her voice drifted, and for several moments her mind seemed to wander. She finally shrugged. "That was a long time ago. But that chocolate ain't bad." She held out her paper plate. "Gimme another piece there."

Banana cake. Her mom used to make it. When? For her birthday when she was a kid? Which made me wonder—had Lucy had a birthday cake since she was a kid? Did any of us even know when her birthday was?

Mabel clapped her hands for attention. "And this is for you, Gabby. From all the residents." She handed me a fat envelope.

I took it and peered inside. A whole lot of one-dollar bills. "Count it!" Lucy demanded. So I did. Exactly forty.

My eyes teared up again. For some of these women, giving up a dollar for my fortieth birthday was a real sacrifice. "Thank you, everybody. I'll . . . I'll do something really special with this."

I went around the room, giving out hugs, but as the dining room finally cleared I took the last of the cake up to the counter. "Can I take this home for the boys? Don't think they're going to bake me a cake."

"Sure, sure. Take it. But hold on a minute." Estelle leaned across the counter and lowered her voice. "Harry told me to tell you Fagan's trial started yesterday. They're gonna be callin' Harry to testify, since he's the one who blew the whistle on his crooked boss in the first place. For your man's sake—and Harry's too—we need to pray that thug in a uniform gets put away for a long time. I'm just sayin'."

chapter 16

Philip still wasn't supposed to drive, so I dropped the boys off at Richmond Towers at six for their overnight with their dad. I almost went up to the penthouse with them, since I hadn't heard much from Philip this past week. Was Henry Fenchel still threatening to sue him? Philip's partner had made it abundantly clear he didn't want Philip in the office looking all beat up, and Philip had said something to me about working from home.

I also wondered if Fagan's henchman was still hanging around Richmond Towers. Didn't see anybody when I pulled into the visitor parking area on the frontage road. But I had no idea what Philip was doing to get rid of the debts hanging over his head. To tell the truth, I agreed with Henry's parting words that day Philip and I were at the office: *"Philip needed help."* I should ask if he'd contacted Gamblers Anonymous yet.

But—not today. I didn't want to go up there and risk the possibility that Philip had totally forgotten it was my birthday. The Big Four-O at that. Or if he remembered, deliberately "forget" to say anything to me. No use rubbing salt in my wounded spirit.

"I'll pick you up tomorrow morning at seven thirty," I reminded P.J. as he got out of the car. The cross country teams were meeting at Harms Woods, one of Chicago's large forest preserves, for the regionals.

"Okay. Thanks." P.J. leaned back into the open window. "Sorry about tonight, Mom. But we're gonna surprise you with something soon."

"Yeah," Paul echoed, scrambling out of the car. "Something big!"

Sweet. I watched both boys disappear through the revolving door with their backpacks before heading back out onto Sheridan Road. On the way home I made a few stops, and when I got back to the six-flat, I showed up at the door across the hall with a couple videos I'd rented, a large bag of Chinese takeout in paper cartons, and Estelle's leftover fudge-chocolate cake.

"It's my birthday," I blurted when Precious opened the door. "And I refuse to sit home sogging in self-pity all by myself. You guys want to party?"

Precious threw the door wide open. "Girl, I don't need an excuse, but your birthday is good as any! Sabrina!" she yelled over her shoulder. "Take that leftover spaghetti off the stove! We got us fancy food!"

The egg rolls and Crab Rangoon disappeared before the movie previews were even finished—though Sammy and Sabrina took one look at the "weird" takeout and opted for the leftover spaghetti. We tackled the cardboard cartons of General Tsao's chicken, sweet-and-sour pork, and shrimp fried rice while watching *The Chronicles of Narnia*. Sammy loved all the talking animals and Aslan the Lion, but Sabrina—bored out of her mind (her words) by the "kiddie movie"—holed up in the bedroom with her cell phone, and when the credits rolled, Sammy was sent off to bed with a piece of birthday cake.

Once the kids were out of the way, I popped in the second video and Tanya, Precious, and I blubbered our way through *Message in a Bottle* while finishing off the rest of Estelle's cake.

Well, P.J. and Paul didn't have to know about the cake.

"Thanks, guys," I sniffed as I left about eleven thirty. "Not a bad birthday. I'm trying to sneak past forty anyway." It did seem strange that I hadn't heard from Jodi Baxter, who was practically my best friend, or anyone in my family—though my sisters were probably waiting until our regular Saturday conference call tomorrow.

But when I let myself into my apartment, the answering machine light was blinking. Three calls. I punched the Play button. *Beeeep. "Hi, honey! It's Aunt Mercy. Was hoping to catch you to wish you a happy birthday. Should've known you'd be out celebrating. I'll try again tomorrow. Love you, sweetheart."* Click.

Beeeep. "Hi, Gabby! It's Jodi, calling from Indiana to wish you a happy fortieth—Denny, stop it! Honestly. He's hobbling around making like you're turning a hundred. Sheesh, he should talk. He's gonna be forty-eight next April. Anyway, hope you remembered that we planned a trip for this weekend to see U of I women's volleyball play Purdue. Amanda made the team! And they'll be playing the Hoosiers tomorrow in Bloomington . . . Denny, Denny! There she is! Do you see her? Number eleven! . . . Sorry, Gabby. Gotta go. Game's gonna start. Talk to you when we get back!" Click.

Remember? I was sure Jodi had *not* told me they were going out of town. Oh well. Sweet of her to call.

Final beep. *"Hey, Gabby. Lee here."* Lee? My skin prickled. *"Wanted to wish you a happy birthday but guess you're not home. I have something for you, but maybe I can drop it off tomorrow. Hope you're out celebrating."* The message clicked off.

Lee remembered? I didn't think he even knew it was my birthday. What did he mean he was going to drop off something tomorrow?

Well, guess I'd see. But I went to bed grinning to myself in the dark.

I woke the next morning to thumps and bumps out back. I peeked through my bedroom blinds. A couple of burly guys were lugging Zia's couch down the outside stairs to an orange U-Haul waiting in the alley. Moving day for Fabrizia Bassi. Starting kind of early, weren't they?

I glanced at my bedside clock. Seven—yikes! I told P.J. I'd be there to pick him up at seven thirty! Throwing on a pair of sweats and a sweatshirt, I ran out to the Subaru and headed for Sheridan Road, feeling gritty and unprepared. No shower, no mouthwash, not even my usual cup of coffee.

But I got P.J. to the forest preserve about the same time the team bus from Lane Tech pulled into the parking lot at eight-fifteen. "Do you know what time your race will be?" I asked my eldest. Maybe I should stay and watch him run. It might be my last opportunity since I was going to be gone next weekend. After that, winning teams went downstate.

P.J. shook his head. "Naw. It's okay, Mom. It'll just be a lot of hanging around. Besides, you need to be home today in case something gets delivered." He ran off, joining the rest of the green-and-gold-clad cross country team piling off the bus.

In case . . . what? Maybe the boys had pooled their allowance and sent me flowers. *Roses?* A lump formed in my throat. Were they trying to fill the gap their dad had left in our family life? I brushed away another doggone tear. Well, I'd act surprised when they came home.

I wouldn't have minded staying at the meet if I'd had my shower, coffee, and something to eat. Should've set my alarm. Except—maybe just as well I didn't stay. Lee said he was going to drop something by today. I didn't want to miss him again.

Back home—showered, toasted English muffin and hot coffee in hand—I curled up on the window seat in the sunroom and opened my prayer notebook, trying to shut out the noise of movers going up and down the stairwell. My prayer list kept getting longer and longer! Who should be the next residents at the House of Hope was only the most recent addition. I was trying to pray regularly for my sons, my two sisters in California and Alaska, the staff at Manna House, stuff brought up in staff meeting, and the current residents of the House of Hope—not just when there was an emergency. I'd added Harry Bentley's eyes after all those surgeries last month, and Estelle's schizophrenic son, Leroy, who'd been in the burn unit at the county hospital since he'd burned his own house down. Poor Estelle didn't want to put him in a mental health facility, but what else could she do?

And Philip. Jodi had encouraged me to pray *for* Philip, not just *about* him.

Oh God, I groaned. *I don't really know how to pray for Philip right now. His injuries seem to be healing—thank You, God, for that. And Fagan is out of the picture, I hope. But as far as I know, Philip's still got all that gambling debt hanging over his head and the threat of a lawsuit from Henry Fenchel. Just . . . please, God, help him get his act together. For P.J.'s and Paul's sakes, if nothing else. And—*

My prayer stopped short. I still hadn't responded to Philip's tearful plea in the hospital to forgive him. It was hard to know how to pray about it. He hadn't brought it up again. Was he waiting for an answer? Or had he forgotten that he'd asked for my forgiveness? Maybe it was just the trauma of the moment.

Oh God, what do you want me to do? I don't even know how I feel about Philip right now—

A knock at my front door jerked me out of my thought-prayers. I peeked out the sunroom windows but didn't see Lee's Prius. *Silly,* I scolded myself on the way to the door. I'd hear the buzzer if it was Lee.

Zia Bassi stood in the hallway, Josh Baxter behind her. "I'm all moved out, Mrs. Fairbanks, thanks to the help of Josh here," the young woman said. "Do you want to do an inspection so I can get my deposit back?"

"Now? Uh . . . all right. Be up in a minute. Josh, can I see you a sec?"

When Zia had run back up the stairs, I pulled Josh into my apartment. "I have no idea what to look for! Do you have a list or something?"

"Should be with the rental contract."

Which was precisely where it was. Good grief, I was such an amateur at building ownership! But together Josh and I took a tour of 2A, which seemed in remarkably good condition to me.

All kitchen appliances accounted for and clean—check. No broken fixtures or mirrors in the bathroom—check. Blinds still in decent condition—check. The only "damage" was a few scratches on the wood floor in the bedrooms and living room from moving furniture and small holes in the walls where pictures had hung. Josh eyed me whether I wanted to deduct anything for that, but I gave a brief shake of my head.

"Seems in good order, Ms. Bassi. If you'll give me your new address, I'll mail your deposit back first thing Monday." The security deposits for remaining tenants had been included in the final deal with the former owner.

Zia's face fell. "Uh, I was hoping I could have my deposit back today. I really need the money."

I saw Josh give a slight shake of his head. The rental contract said the landlord had thirty days to return the deposit. "I'm sorry." *Keep it professional, Gabby.* "I'll be sure to get it in the mail first thing Monday." Even that would be doing her a favor.

Once Zia was gone, Josh and I talked a good while about what needed to be done to prepare the apartment for the next House of Hope residents—mostly spackling those holes, a coat of varnish on the wood floors, and painting the walls in all the rooms. I was going with neutral colors this time. Letting Precious and Tanya pick their colors had been too much of a headache.

"That's your buzzer, I think," Josh said, poking his head into the kitchen pantry and testing which shelves might need replacing.

Buzzer. I ran down the stairs but didn't recognize the stocky man in jeans and sweatshirt out in the foyer. "Fairbanks? Apartment 1B?" he said when I pulled open the glass-paneled door. "Got a delivery. Where do you want it?"

"Uh . . . what is it?" He had a clipboard. No flowers. A truck stood out by the curb that said E-Z MOVERS along the side.

The man was already halfway out the front door. "Table and chairs. We'll bring them in. Just tell us where you want them."

My mouth hung open. I hadn't ordered any table and chairs, though I kept meaning to. But a few minutes later two men came in carrying a large flat piece of furniture between them, not in a box, but wrapped and strapped in movers blankets. Still perplexed, I led them down the hall to the dining room. The legs came next, each wrapped individually in a blanket. Then chairs—eight of them, wrapped in bubble wrap.

I recognized the chairs even before the blankets came off the table.

The Belfort Signature dining room set from the penthouse.

The two men—obviously local movers-for-hire—removed their straps and blankets, asked me to sign the form on the clipboard, and were gone.

An envelope was taped to the underside of the table. With shaking fingers, I took out a simple note card. *"Happy Birthday, Gabby"* it said on the outside. On the inside, in Philip's distinctive script, I read, *"You need this more than I do. Whatever happens between us, it's yours."* It was signed, *"Philip."*

chapter 17

I simply stared at the gleaming mahogany tabletop leaning against the wall. The table and chairs had beautiful lines, decorated with vine-and-leaf scrolls and claw feet. The chair backs were softly curved, the seats padded with patterned gold velour. The dining set seemed far too elegant for the other furniture in my patched-together apartment, but that wasn't what astonished me.

Philip had sent me *our table* from the penthouse. As a gift. A birthday gift. He knew I needed a table and sent this one, leaving the dining room in the penthouse empty.

What did it mean? I hardly knew what to think!

Josh Baxter came down with his tools, bolted the curved, hand-carved legs onto the table, and helped me set it in place. Then he graciously took my make-do table—the sheet of plywood and sawhorses that had been hiding under one of my mother's table-cloths—down to the basement, never asking a single question.

The telephone rang at noon. Both of my sisters were on the line, warbling an off-key version of "Happy Birthday" and making

148

jokes about being "forty and fit" or "forty and fat," which was it? I let them prattle and didn't tell them about the table, knowing I'd get an earful of disparate opinions—Celeste's no-nonsense, practical Alaskan self usually took hot issue with Honor's airy, California-dreaming flights of fancy.

I didn't need that right now.

Saved by the buzzer. "Gotta go! Someone at the door! Love you both!" I smooched kisses into the phone as I hung up and scrunched my curls into a semblance of good behavior before dashing out into the hall.

Lee Boyer stood on the other side of the glass-paneled door with—a bicycle?

"Happy birthday, Gabby!" He grinned as I pulled open the door. He was wearing biking shorts, a lightweight white-and-blue windbreaker, and sunglasses, his hand resting lightly on the handlebars of a sleek, red women's hybrid bike. A wide, white ribbon had been tied into a bow on the narrow padded seat.

"What?" I laughed. "What's this?"

"Hm. Seem to remember you made a big deal of getting the boys' bikes from Virginia so you could ride the bike trails along the lakefront, but you don't have one of your own. So now you do!"

I lusted after that bicycle. It was everything I'd ever wanted in a bike—trim lines, flat handlebars, multiple gears, and candy-apple red. Even a neat leather pouch behind the seat to hold stuff.

But I slowly shook my head. "I . . . can't accept it, Lee. It's too much. You and me, we're not . . . you know."

"Now wait a minute, Gabby Fairbanks. Can I come in? Or are you going to make me stand here in the foyer like the mailman?"

I reddened. "Sorry. Of course. Come in." I led the way into the living room of my apartment and sank into my mother's rocker. Lee followed, wheeling the bike inside.

"Now look," he protested. "First off, I didn't spend any money on this bike. It belonged to my sister, who thought she was going to take up cycling. Then she got married to a New York actor and left town. She gave the bike to me and told me I could do 'whatever' with it. That was three years ago! It's just been taking up room in my storage locker. Might as well get used."

"Still—"

"Okay, Miss Stubborn. Consider it a loan then. You need a bike. The bike needs a rider. Seems like a match made in heaven, if you ask me."

I relented with a smile. "All right. A loan. Thanks, Lee. It's very sweet of you to think of me for your sister's bike."

He'd taken off his sunglasses and replaced them with his usual wire rims. His voice got gentle. "Think of you? Gabby, I think of you all the ti—"

"Don't. Please." I held up a hand. For some reason my emotions felt all in a jumble and I was afraid I might cry any moment. "Not now."

He backed up. "All right. Would you like to take a spin? I've got my bike on the car."

I peeked out the sunroom windows. Sure enough, another bike was mounted on a bike rack on the back of Lee's Prius.

"But I don't have a helmet—"

"Comes with the bike. Used to be my sister's, remember? It's in the car."

I'd run out of excuses. The boys wouldn't be home till five at least. "Well . . . all right. Sure, I'd like that. I'll get my jacket."

The lakefront was less than a mile away, but I wasn't eager to ride city streets until I got used to the bike with its zillion possible gears, so Lee put it back on the bike rack and drove to an accessible point. But once on the bike trail that wound its way through Lincoln Park, I soon found a comfortable gear and relaxed, following Lee's windbreaker as he dodged dog-walkers, couples out for a stroll, and runners plugged into their iPods who stubbornly ran on the bike trail instead of the jogging path.

With temps in the fifties and low-hanging clouds covering the sun, I was glad I'd layered up under my windbreaker and worn my jeans. Even then my ears and nose still got nippy.

We rode south as far as the Lincoln Park Zoo, where I called out to Lee to turn around. "Guess I'm out of condition," I gasped, laughing and pulling off the path.

Lee rode a few circles around me. "Yeah, sometimes I forget to go only as far as a decent halfway point, because you always have to ride back the same distance!" He nodded toward a nearby bench. "Want to rest awhile before heading back?"

I shook my head. "I'm good." I could've used a break, but resting would mean conversation, and conversation might lead to talking about *us*. Frankly, I'd been grateful for the single-file bike ride that left me alone with my thoughts and confused emotions. Here I was out again with the man who'd said, *"I love you, don't you know that?"* just before he'd given me an ultimatum: leave Philip's hospital bedside or call it quits. I wheeled my bike onto the path. "I should get home. It's getting colder too."

Forty-five minutes later we pulled up in front of the six-flat and Lee unloaded the red bicycle. "Thanks, Lee. The ride was fun." More than fun. I loved it. But what now? He started to walk the bike up to the door, but I said, "Oh, that's okay, I can get it inside." I gave him a grateful smile—but I was walking a tightrope here. A month ago I would have thrown my arms around him and given him a big hug. Instead I said, "I really appreciate you loaning me your sister's bike. The helmet too. I promise to take good care of them."

Lee caught my messages: I wasn't inviting him in, and I was accepting the bike as a loan, not a gift.

"Sure." For a moment he seemed at a loss for words. "Uh, you should probably get a good lock for that before you go for another ride." I could feel his eyes on my back as I wheeled the bike up the walk, carried it up the steps, and pushed open the outside door. Then he called after me, "Happy birthday, Gabby! Maybe we can do this again—"

A distant rumble of thunder caught away his last words. I gave him a final wave. "Looks like we got back just in time! Thanks again!"

Just in time was right. For a second there, I'd been ready to take it all back, invite him inside, tell him I loved his birthday gift, tell him . . . what?

Once inside the foyer I fumbled with my keys. Where was I going to keep the bike? I didn't want to put it in the basement until I got a good lock. Finally unlocking my apartment door, I pushed it open with the front wheel—and nearly fell over when the door suddenly swung wide.

"Happy birthday, Mom!" P.J., Paul, and Philip stood just inside, grins plastered on all three faces. Philip's arm was still in its cast, but the bruises on his face had faded to a pasty yellow, and his dark hair was starting to grow over the long scar on his skull.

"Wha—what are you guys doing here already?" Had they seen

me drive up with Lee Boyer? I busied myself taking off the bike helmet, feeling my face flush.

The boys talked at the same time. "We wanted to celebrate your birthday!" . . . "Did you like Dad's surprise?" . . . "Come see what we got you!" . . . "Where'd you get the bike? Is it yours?"

The thunder was getting louder. My mind scrambled. *Play down the bike, Gabby.* "Yes, I got your surprise! Couldn't imagine *what* it was when that delivery truck pulled up this morning. But the Belfort Signature table? Oh my, it's so beautiful! Did you see it set up in the dining room?" I leaned the bike against the closest wall and headed down the hallway, talking all the while, leading the entourage. "I was so surprised! We certainly need a table, but I never imagined getting one this elegant. You can be sure I got rid of that old makeshift table we've been using quicker than—oh my, what's this?"

We'd arrived in the dining room where the table and chairs stood in all their glory, and in the center of the table on a cut-glass pedestal cake server—one of our wedding presents, used only for special occasions—stood an elegant bakery cake. Three layers at least. "Double fudge with almond icing," Philip murmured, a smile playing at the corners of his mouth. "Your favorite."

He remembered.

Several wrapped birthday gifts surrounded the cake. "And we ordered Gino's pizza!" Paul broke in. "You shouldn't have to cook on your birthday, right, Dad?"

"Absolutely not," he agreed. "I wanted to order Chinese, but I was outvoted."

I almost laughed aloud. Good thing. I wasn't sure I could eat Chinese takeout two nights in a row.

"But where'd you get the bike, Mom?" P.J. insisted. He was frowning and exchanging looks with his father.

"It's on loan from a friend until I can get one of my own. Remember, I said I wanted to go for a bike ride with you guys before the weather gets too cold."

"Looks new, though." P.J.'s tone was just this side of challenging. "How did that lawyer guy have a brand-new bike to loan you?"

So they *had* seen me drive up with Lee. "Belonged to his sister, but she moved out of state and left the bike with him. I'm just borrowing it." I laughed it off and clapped my hands. "How about if we get this table set with Grandma's china before that pizza gets here. Or can we have dessert first and open those presents now?" I tousled Paul's hair and headed for the china cupboard in the kitchen.

The rain finally arrived, complete with lightning and thunder, but we hardly noticed it in the back of the apartment. And when all was said and done, I realized I'd had the best fortieth birthday party I could have wished for, but hadn't even considered was possible: supper around the same table with my family. Just the four of us. I tried to enjoy it simply for what it was, pushing aside awkward thoughts about Philip giving me such an expensive gift and *being* there, given the dubious nature of our current relationship.

At their request, I did indeed open the boys' presents first, which turned out to be scented pillar candles in different sizes and a couple of decorative candles in jars. "We know how much you like candles, Mom," Paul blurted. "We actually wanted to—ow!"

He glared at his brother, whom I surmised had kicked him under the table. What was *that* about?

Let it go, Gabby. I lit all the candles and turned out the lights, bathing the room in candlelight, then cut the cake, finishing up with Gino's stuffed pizza when it arrived. P.J. told us all about the regional meet that day—both the boys' and girls' cross country teams at Lane Tech had qualified for the sectional meet next weekend—and I mentioned that Lucy Tucker wanted to go on the Manna House Fall Getaway the following weekend and might need someone to look after Dandy.

"I will! That'd be cool," Paul said, mouth full of pizza.

"Well, we'll see," I said. "Have to work out what you'll be doing next weekend."

Philip finally pulled out his keys and said he'd better get home. "Wait a doggone minute!" I said. "How'd you guys get here? Philip Fairbanks, don't tell me you *drove*."

He shrugged. "I did all right, didn't I, boys? Had to start sometime."

Shaking my head, I walked him out to the foyer. He declined my offer of an umbrella. "Thanks again for the table, Philip. I mean that. You didn't have to do it, you know. What are you going to do for a dining room table now, anyway?"

Philip's eyes shifted to the dripping trees outside along the sidewalk. "Don't need a table like that for just me, do I? And I'm thinking of getting out of the penthouse anyway, Gabby. Can't really afford it right now."

Gabby. He'd been calling me that a lot lately instead of Gabrielle.

"I'm sorry about that, Philip." Not knowing what else to say, I took a chance on bringing up the next weekend. "Say, I'm wondering if next week you could keep the boys all weekend? I'll be gone until Sunday on this Fall Getaway. Of course, they'll be with you half the time anyway, so I was just wondering . . ."

He didn't answer immediately.

"Don't worry about the dog," I hastened to add. "If the boys stay with you, I'm sure Lucy can find someone else to look after Dandy—maybe even someone here in the building. Edesa Baxter is going, but Josh will be here." That was fairly presumptuous, since Josh would also be taking care of little Gracie all weekend, but I didn't say so.

"Can I get back to you? It might work out, but let me think about it."

"Sure, of course. If it's too much, you know, while you're still on the mend, just say so. Uh-oh. It's still raining. Are you sure you don't want the umbrella?"

Philip didn't seem to hear. Turning to me he said, "Thought you might want to know the boys really wanted to get you a bicycle for your birthday. They even pooled their allowance but came up short. They asked me to help them out, but . . ." He almost seemed to wince. "I had to tell them I couldn't. I've been advised to cut up my credit cards so I wouldn't be tempted to use them until I get my finances straightened out. P.J. got pretty mad about it, reamed me out about gambling myself into a hole." His mouth twisted sardonically. "Nothing like having your own kid give you a lecture. But he's right, of course."

I was too startled by Philip's honesty to say anything.

"So maybe you can understand why P.J. got upset when that Boyer fellow drove up with you and unloaded that fancy bike.

Have to admit, I felt like a heel that I wasn't able to help the boys get a bike for you—but *he* was."

My throat caught, realizing the boys had wanted to do something special for me.

"It's just a loan—" Philip held up his good hand to stop me.

"I know. You said. But what I'd like to know, Gabby . . . is Lee Boyer the reason you haven't been able to forgive me and talk about mending our relationship?"

chapter 18

The usual before-service hubbub swirled around me as I sat by myself in one of the folding chairs at SouledOut Community Church the next morning waiting for worship to begin. But I barely noticed. My mind was still wrestling with Philip's startling question the night before. It was the first time the subject had come up again since he broke down in the hospital and begged me to forgive him for how he'd messed everything up.

When I finally got my tongue untangled, I'd said something lame, like, *"It's more complicated than that, Philip."* I could tell he was frustrated, but he didn't say any more, just pulled his London Fog over his head and injured arm and made a dash for his car.

I'd slept badly, confused by my own feelings. Lying in the dark, I'd tried to remember Lee's gentle kiss that day in the car after the closing on the six-flat and the teasing as we'd splashed in the fountain at Millennium Park. But as I fell asleep, it was Philip in my dreams, twirling me in the rain beside the Fountain of Three Graces where we'd first met in Montpellier, France.

But by the light of day, my head cleared by two cups of strong coffee, I knew it wasn't just my feelings for Lee that kept me from being able to say "I forgive you" to Philip. I wanted more from him than just "I messed up." I wanted him to admit he'd been *wrong* to not welcome my mother into our home, *wrong* to lock me out of the house, *wrong* to cut off my phone and credit cards, *wrong* to disappear with our boys without telling me where they'd gone. Frankly, I wanted him to grovel.

"Gabby! Happy belated birthday, girl!" Jodi Baxter plonked herself down in the chair beside me and gave me a quick hug. "You got my message, right? So sorry I wasn't here to help celebrate your birthday. I'd love to take you out for lunch, just you and me. I know it's kind of last minute but—" Jodi stopped and frowned at me. "Are you okay, Gabby? Don't tell me you had a rotten birthday."

I made a face. "I didn't have a rotten birthday, but I'm not okay." The praise team looked as if they were just about ready to start. "Can't talk now."

The sax player, a fine-looking young black man with a trace of a Jamaican accent, spoke into his mike. "Praise the Lord, church. Can we all find our seats? Except don't sit down yet, because we're getting ready to praise the Lord! Most of you know this song by Percy Gray, and if you don't know it, you should! Ready, one, two . . ."

As the keyboard, drums, sax, and electric bass launched into the first praise song, Jodi grabbed me and pulled my ear close to her mouth. "Then we are definitely going out to lunch together, no excuses."

I let it go till later. I'd made a big deal with the boys about going for a bike ride this afternoon, now that I'd "borrowed" a bike, but the thunderstorm last night had left a light drizzle in its wake this morning. If the rain stopped . . .

The words to the gospel song began to work their way into my thoughts. *When trouble's around me, I can go to the Rock* . . . The sax was wailing lustily and the praise team headed into the vamp: *"Jesus, my waymaker . . . strong tower . . . heart fixer . . . I can go to the Rock!"* Again and again we sang, *"I can go to the Rock!"*

I had to smile. Nothing like God confirming what He'd been trying to tell me about building on Christ the Solid Rock.

The sax player—his name, Jodi whispered, was Oscar Frost—then read the morning scripture in his slight Jamaican accent. "From Psalm 91 . . . 'He who dwells in the shelter of the Most High will rest in the shadow of the Almighty. I will say to the Lord, He is my refuge and my fortress, my God, in whom I trust.'" Oscar laid aside his Bible. "Are you trusting Him, church? Are you resting in His shadow? Are you living in His shelter?" He adjusted his saxophone and nodded to the woman at the keyboard, launching into another song.

"God is my everything! . . . A shelter in the time of storm! . . . God is . . ."

A shelter. The word flashed like a neon light inside my head. I'd been glad to get *out* of the Manna House women's shelter when I'd finally found a place of my own. But there was something about that word that touched a tender place in my spirit. I still needed a shelter, a safe place for my broken heart to be mended. The scripture and the songs were obviously talking about finding shelter in God, the Solid Rock Who cannot be moved. *And I am drawing closer to You, aren't I, Lord?*

But if I was honest with myself, what I truly missed was that safe place of having a man's arms around me, my knight in shining armor, making me feel he would protect me from any storm or dragon or danger or evil that threatened to snatch me away.

The way Philip used to make me feel.

The way Lee wanted me to feel—if I'd let him.

But something was holding me back. That Voice in my spirit. *Wait. Wait, Gabby. Let Me be your everything.*

The boys were not interested in riding bikes in the drizzle, which looked like it might keep up all day. So I sent them home with Josh and Edesa and met Jodi at The Common Cup coffee shop on Morse Avenue near the church.

The coffee shop was typical—small tables that wiggled, customers sitting by twos or alone working on their computers or reading, a tiny library of books in a back corner with a couple of overstuffed chairs. We each ordered a large, fresh bagel and cream cheese with our coffee and found a free table near the front window.

Jodi had brought me a birthday gift—a beautiful leather-bound journal. "To write your prayers in," she said, smiling. "I don't know about you, but I often write my prayers to keep my mind from wandering and making to-do lists!" She made a face as if embarrassed. I envied the way her medium-length bob swept her shoulders. Jodi had soft brunette hair, bangs that brushed to one side, and warm brown eyes—the kind of pretty teacher I imagined third-grade students would all be in love with.

I opened the journal reverently. "Write my prayers in *this*? My prayers are way too discombobulated for such a nice book. Right now all I've got is a scribbled prayer list."

Jodi laughed at my big word. "Doesn't matter. Write your prayers anyway, they don't have to be fancy. It's a good thing to do because later you can go back and see all the prayers God has answered. Try it. I double-dog dare you!"

We both laughed at the childlike "dare." But two bites into our bagels, I was telling Jodi about my triple birthday surprise yesterday—first the table Philip had sent me from the penthouse, then the nearly new Schwinn Lee Boyer had tried to give me and that I'd finally accepted as a loan, followed by Philip and the boys showing up with my favorite double-fudge birthday cake and eating pizza "as a family."

"Wow," she said. "That's . . ." She seemed at a loss for words.

"Exactly." I rolled my eyes. "Really nice. Really, *really* nice. Except, given the fact that I'm separated from Mr. Husband, and Mr. Lawyer washed his hands of me when I wouldn't leave said husband for him in the middle of a crisis, and both of them are jealous of each other—all this birthday niceness is killing me!"

"They're fighting over you, that's what."

I snorted. "You think? Now that I'm forty? *That's* a laugh."

Jodi leaned forward and laid a hand on my arm. "Gabby, what do you think about Philip asking for forgiveness? Are you—can you—I mean, do you see *any* hope of restoring your marriage?"

I breathed out a long sigh. "I don't know. Is he truly sorry? Or just sorry things got so messy for *him*. Would anything be different? He's . . . well, he *has* been different since that beating. Maybe it made him think about how self-centered he was, how stupid he's been! But I don't know. It would take a *lot* of work to rebuild trust again."

"And Lee?" Jodi was probing. "Are you in love with him?"

I hesitated. "I don't know. I like him a lot. He's kind and sweet and, have to admit, it's very nice to have someone treat you like you're the best thing that's ever walked the planet, especially when you've just been rejected by someone else. But"—I toyed with my half-eaten bagel—"he's not interested in talking about God or coming to church. Treats my faith like a quaint hobby or something." I eyed her sideways. "Tell me, Jodi. Did you get the last man on earth who loves you *and* loves God?"

"Oh, Gabby."

Unbidden, tears welled up in my eyes. I pressed a napkin to my face. "I'm so confused, Jodi. Last night in bed, I was thinking about Lee, remembering the time he first kissed me." Had I told Jodi about that? I was glad the napkin was pressed to my eyes so I couldn't see her reaction. "But when I fell asleep, all my dreams were about Philip. The way it was before. When we were in love."

I was glad Jodi hadn't tried to tell me what to do—or feel. Instead, she'd just prayed with me right there in the coffee shop, never mind the weird looks we got from other customers, and encouraged me to trust God to make things clear. "Keep reading the Word, Gabby. Keep praying. I really believe God will show you the way through all this in His own good time."

Kind of the same thing I'd sensed God telling me in worship that morning. *Wait. Wait, Gabby. Let Me be your everything.*

But as I'd driven home from The Common Cup, I had a moment of doubt. What if letting God be "everything" meant just that? Neither Philip *nor* Lee in my life? No knight in shining armor? No man to make me feel complete and loved and protected?

That thought was still hanging over my head as I signed in at Manna House the next morning and headed for my office. But I soon got busy making a list of everything that needed to get done before taking off next Friday for our Fall Getaway. Then I reviewed the proposal Carolyn had written up about expanding our after-school program to include neighborhood kids, tweaking it here and there so I could hand it to Mabel Turner at the staff meeting, which started at ten.

Mabel glanced at the proposal and said she'd get back to us with any questions. Next step would be submitting it to the board for their October meeting. We spent most of the staff meeting reviewing the current list of residents—who was new, who still needed a case manager, and the status of residents who were supposedly still working on getting proper IDs, finishing up their GEDs, and diligently getting their names on lists at different sites that offered long-term housing. As usual, some residents were motivated and had something new to check off at each meeting with their case manager, while others just had a long list of excuses.

"And we're still looking to hire more case managers," Mabel said. "Keep praying."

I was eager to get back to work, but Estelle pulled me aside as staff meeting broke up. "Gabby girl. Don't know what your schedule is like this week, honey, but I've got a big favor to ask."

"Sure, Estelle, if I can."

"I need someone to go with me when I see Leroy tomorrow. They're ready to discharge my boy, but he don't have any place to go. The house, it's gone. And besides, I wouldn't let him go back there anyway, not after those gangbangers took him for a chump and made it into a drug house."

I stared at her, my mouth dropping. "A . . . *what*? What are you talking about, Estelle?"

She shook her head. "Long story, don't got time for it now. What I'm needin' is someone to go with me, be a second pair of ears when they tell me what he's gonna need, given his mental history and the burns an' all—you know."

Well, yeah, I did, sort of. Obviously there'd been a lot more going on with Estelle's adult son than I knew about.

"Harry usually goes with me," she went on, "but he's gotta testify at Fagan's trial this week. They want him in court every day. So I'm needing a good friend to go with me, thought of you."

A warm feeling bubbled up inside. Estelle had called me a good friend. She was certainly that to *me*, but I'd never thought of *her* feeling that way about me.

"I'll be glad to, Estelle. Let me check with Mabel, see if I can get the time off. When do you need to go?"

chapter 19

I was nervous when we stepped off the elevator at Stroger Hospital the following afternoon. I'd never met Leroy, hadn't even known Estelle *had* a son until the fire that put him in the burn unit two months ago. What would he look like? The burns had covered thirty percent of his body, and he'd had to undergo some excruciating treatments.

Estelle led the way, turning this way and that through the maze of hallways, finally stopping at the closed door of a patient's room. She took a deep breath, as if preparing herself, then tapped on the door and opened it. "Hello, son." Her voice was cheery. "How ya doing today?"

A thin, dark-skinned man somewhere in his thirties was sitting in a high-backed, padded chair, facing the window. He didn't turn around. "Okay, I guess."

Estelle motioned me to move into eyeball range. "Leroy, my friend Gabby came with me today to see you. Can you say hello?"

Leroy didn't look at me but mumbled, "Hello."

"I'm happy to meet you, Leroy." I wished I'd brought

something, flowers maybe, but since he was getting discharged, it had seemed a bit silly. I moved to the window. "You've got quite a view here." Mostly other buildings in the huge medical complex, but at least the sun was peeking through.

"You come to take me home, Maw?" For the first time, Leroy turned his head slowly and looked up at his mother.

Estelle shook her head. "The house burned down, baby. Remember that? Nothin' there now. But we're goin' to talk to the doctor today 'bout what you need when you leave here. Tell me how you're feelin', son."

Turning from the window, I got my first good look at Leroy. I could see the family resemblance. His skin was several shades darker than Estelle's caramel coloring, but he had the same wide-set eyes and broad forehead. Not a bad-looking young man—except for the puckered, shiny skin along the left side of his neck that continued up along the side of his face. I noticed he still had a pressure bandage on his left arm—and, I presumed, around his chest and left leg under the hospital gown.

I shuddered involuntarily. Couldn't even imagine the pain and skin grafting that he'd had to go through to come this far.

"Ah. Ms. Williams, you're here. Good, good." Two doctors entered the room, one male, one female, both wearing white coats and name badges. "I think we're ready to talk about discharging our patient in a few days. He's making excellent progress!"

Estelle made introductions, but I just smiled and stepped aside as they began talking about continuing outpatient treatment. I picked up that Dr. Jameson was a burn specialist, and his associate, Dr. Alena Sanchez, specialized in nutrition and aftercare for burn patients. I tried to pay attention as they talked over Leroy's head about "decreased sensation" in the burned areas, the importance of keeping the areas moist with skin lotion, regular exercise so the skin didn't atrophy, how long he'd need to wear the pressure garments, and watching carefully for any signs of infection.

"You'll be taking him home, Ms. Williams?" Dr. Sanchez asked, her tone kind and concerned. "He'll need a caregiver for several months, maybe a year. Good nutrition and adequate hydration will be very important for his full recovery."

Estelle looked distressed and motioned the doctors and me out into the hall. "Look here. I'd take care of Michael Leroy twenty-four-seven if I could, but my housemate and I don't have any extra room in our apartment. And"—she made sure the door to Leroy's room was shut—"he needs more care than I can give him. For his mental issues, you know."

Dr. Jameson frowned. "But I thought he was basically living on his own and taking care of himself before the incident."

Estelle's distress was becoming more acute. "He was, he was— but, Lord help me, he probably shouldn't have been. I didn't want to put him into an institution, you see, but I never thought . . ." Estelle's hand went to her mouth, and I could see she was trying hard to stay in control. I moved close to her and took her other hand in mine. She gripped it tightly.

Dr. Jameson pursed his lips. "I see. If he can't go home with you, we need someone from social services to sit down with us. We may be talking about a psychiatric nursing facility for a while, if we can find an available bed. Dr. Sanchez, could you see what you can set up?"

Estelle walked away as the nutritionist pulled out her cell phone and turned aside, talking rapidly in Spanish for a few minutes. I followed Estelle, just to let her know I was near. Why was she having such a hard time with this? A facility would be a good thing for Leroy, wouldn't it? He'd be taken care of, get the kind of help he needed, and would no longer be a danger to himself or others. Wasn't that why Estelle had moved out of the family home to begin with? Because Leroy had "gotten physical" with her during one of his schizoid episodes? Though it was hard to imagine. The man in there seemed as meek as a kitten.

"Ms. Williams?" Dr. Sanchez was calling us back. "We can meet with social services on Thursday at ten. Is that all right with you?"

Estelle was quiet on the way home, her head turned toward the passenger-side window, and I didn't pry. Hopefully she'd tell me what was going on when she was ready. I dropped her off in front of Jodi and Denny's two-flat in the Rogers Park neighborhood, where she shared the second-floor apartment with Leslie Stuart. "'Preciate it, Gabby," was all she said before she walked slowly up the steps to the front porch, shoulders slumped, and let herself in.

We had our third house meeting at the House of Hope that week, which we moved to Wednesday night in deference to Josh, since Tuesday conflicted with the men's Bible study that met at Peter Douglass's home. "They've stolen our name," Jodi once complained to me. "Calling themselves the Yada Yada Brothers." Both names sounded kind of silly to me—I mean, *yada yada*?—and I'd told Jodi as much. After which I got a five minute etymology of the word *yada,* which supposedly was a Hebrew word that appeared in the Old Testament hundreds of times and meant something like "to know and be known intimately."

Who would've thunk it?

Mabel met with us again, but we spent most of the time listening to Precious moan and groan about Sabrina sneaking off to see the Big Bad Dude who got her pregnant in the first place. "I'm 'bout ready to call the po-lice and get him arrested for statutory rape," she fussed. "She still a minor and he twenty if he a day! But she say if I do, she jus' gonna run off again with him, like she did before."

"Oh, Precious." Edesa moved from a chair to the floor beside Precious and put an arm around her. "Have you tried talking to this young man? He *is* your grandbaby's daddy. Maybe he's afraid of you, but if you were willing to talk—"

"He got reason to be scared a' Precious." Tanya nodded knowingly. "She sweet as sugar long as you on her good side. But mess with Sabrina? Uh-uh. She like a she-bear!"

We couldn't help chuckling. But Edesa said she was serious about talking to the young man. Precious kept shaking her head but finally threw up her hands. "Okay, okay. I'll pray about it. If God tell me to jump into the lions' den, I'll jump. Not before."

We moved on to other House of Hope business. Tanya pointed out that next week was Halloween, what were we going to do with trick-or-treaters? We certainly didn't want them traipsing up and down the inside stairs. I finally asked if she and Sammy would be willing to pass out candy in the foyer on behalf of the whole building. Her eyes lit up. "We'll dress up! It'll be fun."

Josh reported on how work was progressing in apartment 2A—slowly, since he was doing most of it himself after classes and at night—and I reported that Celia Jones and Shawanda Dixon had agreed to share the apartment, and their applications for assistance were in process with the city. Before we ended I was able to squeeze in my requests about needing somebody to look after Dandy this weekend so Lucy could go on the Fall Getaway, as well as needing backup for the boys if Philip couldn't take them the whole weekend.

Tanya offered to take care of Dandy. "He a sweet dog. Sammy will like that."

And Josh agreed to look after the boys if Philip couldn't keep them the whole weekend. "But he's their dad, Gabby. Why wouldn't he take them for the weekend?"

Humph. Good question. Why hadn't he called me with his answer either?

I found out when I got back to my apartment after saying good-bye to Mabel and Jermaine, who'd come to hang out with Paul again. "Mom?" P.J. came out of his room. "Dad called while you were upstairs. Wants you to call him back soon as you got done with your meeting."

About time. "Your homework done?"

"Mom! Like, he wants you to call him back *right away!*"

"Fine. I'll call him. Go finish your homework." I picked up the handset and walked toward the kitchen to make myself some tea, pushing the speed dial for the penthouse.

"Philip? P.J. said you called."

"Yes. Uh . . . Gabby, I can't take the boys this weekend—"

My dander flared up. "Why not? It's just another twenty-four hours, Philip." After Josh's comment, I'd decided to push if Philip seemed reluctant. "You *are* their fa—"

"Listen to me, Gabby. I mean I can't take them *at all* this weekend. Something happened."

Now I was getting mad. *Something happened?* Yeah, right. Sounded like the excuses he'd give me when he had the Horseshoe Casino on the brain. "What are you talking about, Philip? You can't take them *at all*? I'm not going to be here this weekend! I need you to—"

"I *know*. I know that. Please, just listen a minute. I can't take the boys because it's not safe here. Someone—I can guess who—left an anonymous note with the doorman tonight, threatening me with physical harm if I didn't pay Matty Fagan what I owe him by this weekend. I can't take a chance on the boys being here if something should happen to me."

My anger dissolved into a puddle of outright fear. "Oh, Philip!" I took the phone into my bedroom and shut the door. Couldn't chance the boys overhearing. "I'm so sorry. What are you going to do? What about you? It's not safe for you either!"

There was a pause. "I don't know, Gabby. I can't stay here. I'll probably be okay tonight, but I need to get a hotel or something until I can figure out what to do. I just want to keep the boys out of this."

My heart was tripping all over itself. "All right. I understand. Just . . . just keep me posted where you're going to be. Call me tomorrow, all right? I'm going to have to tell the boys something."

Like what? I clicked the phone off and sank onto my bed. What in the world was I going to do? Philip was in danger . . . I

was going out of town . . . I couldn't leave the boys here by themselves . . . But I didn't feel comfortable asking Josh to look after
them *all* weekend when he was doing the solo-parent thing with
Gracie too.

Arrrgh! I flopped backward onto the bed. Maybe I should cancel the weekend, forget the whole thing!

chapter 20

I felt slightly panicked as I arrived at work Thursday morning. I'd told Estelle I'd go with her this morning to the hospital meeting about Leroy if she needed me, but I *had* to decide something—quick!—about the Fall Getaway. Especially if I needed to cancel. We were supposed to leave right after lunch tomorrow, trying to miss traffic. But no way could I leave town if I didn't have someone to look after my boys.

I need some help here, Lord. I glanced at Mabel's closed office door as I came into the Manna House foyer. *Should I ask Mabel if the boys could—?* I immediately tossed out that idea. Wouldn't work. Not for P.J., anyway. Maybe for Paul. Should I separate the boys, find different places for them? Whoever P.J. stayed with would have to get him to his cross country meet on Saturday—

"Gabby? Message for you." Angela Kwon waved a piece of paper at me. "Hope you know what it means." She grabbed the phone, which was ringing for the third time. "I wrote what she told me. Hello, Manna House Women's Shelter . . . Who?"

Unfolding the note, I read it as I headed for the stairs to the lower level. *"Jury's out. Harry has day off, going with me to hospital* meeting. Pray. Please check if Mabel able to find someone to make lunch. If not, leftovers in freezer. Take your pick. Estelle."

A wave of relief calmed my jitters. Now I'd have time to figure out what to do about the weekend—but not if I had to rustle up lunch. Hopefully Mabel had found a replacement to cook lunch, and not leftovers either. Ugh.

I stopped at the coffee urns to get a cup of coffee, rereading the note. Good news—I hoped—about the jury being out, which meant Fagan's trial was almost over. But Estelle had said accusations against a police officer were never a slam-dunk. They might be deliberating for days. Probably why she wrote *"Pray."* Or did she mean pray for her meeting at the hospital?

Stupid question, Gabby. Both, obviously—

"Miss Gabby? Miss Gabby!"

I looked up and saw Naomi Jackson waving at me across Shepherd's Fold. The young girl looked a lot better these days, her blond-streaked brown hair washed and pulled back into a ponytail, her face not so pinched and pale. She met me halfway across the room.

"What time we leavin' tomorrow, Miss Gabby? For the getaway, I mean." She smiled shyly. "I ain't ever been to Wisconsin before. I'm real excited about it."

"Right after lunch. That's the plan anyway." I hoped I sounded more confident than I felt. "We've got a few glitches to work out, though. Do you pray, Naomi?"

"Well, sure, sometimes. Ain't too good at it, though. Why you askin'?"

"We could use some prayer about working out those glitches. We don't want to have to cancel the trip."

"Cancel the trip?" Her gray eyes widened. "No way! If prayin' can help, I'm gonna start right now!" She started off, then turned back. "Would prayin' in the chapel make it more, like, legit?"

I shook my head, smiling now. "You can pray anywhere, Naomi, and God will hear you. But it's quiet in the chapel"—a tiny prayer room, really, tucked away on the main level behind Shepherd's Fold—"real nice if you want to get away for some special prayer time, just you and God."

"Then I'm gonna pray there." Naomi marched off and disappeared into the back hallway.

I watched her go. *Take your own advice, Gabby*, I told myself. God had already answered my first prayer, giving me some time this morning to work on alternative plans for the weekend. A good reminder to pray about the rest of the mess Philip's phone call had stirred up. I wished I could call Jodi Baxter and ask her to pray with me, but she didn't get home from school until three o'clock. Estelle wouldn't be back until . . . who knew when. So I shut my office door and prayed by myself.

Then I talked to Mabel, who was encouraging as usual. "Canceling the weekend should definitely be a last resort, Gabby. I'm sure something will work out for your boys. Paul can spend the weekend with Jermaine and me if that'll help. Why don't you explain the situation to Josh Baxter and see what he says? P.J.'s fourteen, could pretty much take care of himself if he has someone who knows his comings and goings. Call me tonight, let me know, all right?"

"Thanks, Mabel." She made it sound so reasonable. I got up to go.

"Oh, one more thing." She laughed as I gave her a look. "Some very sweet ladies from Chicago Tabernacle are coming to make lunch today. You're off the hook with the leftovers."

Paul showed up at the shelter after school as usual since he could walk from Sunnyside, got some help from Carolyn in the schoolroom on his math homework, then holed up in the rec room with Jermaine, who also came to the shelter after school on Tuesdays and Thursdays. The two of them were working on a jazz number they were creating together. I'd decided not to say anything to Paul *or* P.J. about the situation with their dad and the weekend until I had my ducks lined up for both boys.

But my supposedly reasonable intentions were shot to pieces the moment Paul and I walked into the apartment at five fifteen. "Mom!" P.J. met us five steps inside the door. "Why didn't you tell us we can't go to Dad's this weekend? What's going on? I asked him and he said you'd tell us. But you haven't!"

"We can't go to Dad's?" Paul echoed. "I thought you were going on that getaway thingy this weekend, Mom."

"You talked to Dad?" I stalled, hanging my jacket in the hall closet.

"Yeah, just called him. I wanted to ask if he'd come see me run in the sectionals on Saturday. Might be my last race this fall if we don't go to State. But he said he didn't even know where he'd be this weekend. What's that mean? What's going on?"

I sighed. There was no avoiding laying it out for the boys. I ushered them into the sunroom—a misnomer today, which was again gray and drizzly—and we curled up on the window seats for a talk. As simply as I could, I said the same people who had attacked their dad before were threatening him again, and he was concerned it wasn't safe for the boys to come there this weekend. So I was looking for someone else they could stay with while I was gone.

"But what about Dad? He shouldn't stay there either!" P.J. spouted.

"True. He'll probably go to a hotel or—"

"Why doesn't he just stay here?" Paul asked. "You're gonna be gone."

I opened my mouth to protest, but P.J. jumped in. "Sure! Then we could just stay here and wouldn't have to go anywhere. And we'd be with Dad for the weekend, like usual."

The trouble was, it made sense—from the boys' point of view. How could I tell them I didn't even want them around Philip until that whole mess got straightened out? "I don't think—"

"And then I could take care of Dandy!" Paul grinned. "You said Lucy wanted to go on your trip and needed someplace for Dandy to stay."

My boys were two steps ahead of me, ironing out all my problems. But would they be safe? I needed time to think! Besides, all I could think of in the moment was whether Philip would sleep in my bed, the twin I'd brought from my childhood home when my mother died. The thought unnerved me. I wasn't ready for Philip to share my bed, even if I wasn't here!

"Let me think about this, boys. I need to make supper and we can talk later, okay?"

I fed the boys tuna sandwiches, chips, and applesauce—the easiest thing I could throw together without having to think about it. My mind was a whirling dervish. It was already six o'clock on Thursday night, and I was supposed to leave town in less than twenty-four hours. Paul's idea was tempting. It would solve all the glitches in one fell swoop! The boys would get to spend time with their dad after all. Paul could take care of Dandy. I could pack and get ready for *my* weekend instead of spending all evening trying to patch things together. And Philip would get away from the penthouse—and not have to pay for a hotel room with money he should be using to get himself out of debt, which was no small thing.

Except . . . Philip in *my* space for a whole weekend? Would it be harder to keep the boundaries I'd established since I got back on my feet? And what would he do when I got home on Sunday? The danger at the penthouse would still be there—until he paid off his debt to Fagan, anyway.

I needed to talk to somebody.

I dialed Jodi Baxter.

When she answered, I spilled out the whole complicated mess with hardly a pause for breath. "So what do you think?"

"Whoa. Slow down, Gabby. You've got several things going on here. Philip's being threatened again? I thought that went away when Fagan got arrested. Isn't his trial this week?"

"Yes. It went to the jury today. But apparently he's still got his goons on Philip's tail, trying to get his money back."

"So what is Philip doing about it? Paying the money back, I mean. They're obviously not going to leave him alone until—"

"I don't *know*, Jodi! That's not my business. Right now I'm just trying to get things covered for the boys while I'm gone this weekend. And they want to stay with their dad—rather, they want their dad to stay with them. I've got to decide something tonight, or cancel the whole thing."

A pause. "You're right. I'm sorry. Okay, what do I think about Philip staying at your place this weekend . . . basically sounds like a good idea, works out for everybody all around—if the boys would be safe, that is. But, Gabby, what I think isn't important. *You* need to feel at peace about it. You know, the whole boundaries thing you mentioned. Why don't we pray about it? There's a scripture in Philippians that says something like, '. . . let your requests be made known to God, and the peace of God that goes beyond under-standing will guard your heart and your mind.' Fourth chapter, I think. You need that peace, no matter what you decide. So . . . okay to pray?"

Which she did. But right in the middle of her prayer, I butted in. "Jodi! Pray for Philip's safety too. Frankly, after what's happened already—the horrible beating he got that put him in the hospital and then Fagan threatening to shoot his knees out—I don't blame him for taking it seriously. I've been so focused on my plans for the boys falling through this weekend that I haven't been concerned enough about the reason for it."

"Of course," she said, and added impassioned prayers for Philip's safety. But she was quiet for several moments after she said, "Amen." Then . . . "You know what, Gabby? All of us ought to take this threat seriously. I'm going to talk to Denny and see if he and maybe some of the other guys could hang out with Philip and the boys this weekend—just so he's not alone with them. I mean, if he's not at the penthouse or hanging around there, he'll probably be okay. But like you said, their threats need to be taken seriously."

"Oh, Jodi, do you think . . . I mean, would Denny do that?

I wonder what Philip would think about that. He hasn't exactly been Mr. Sociable, if you know what I mean. I mean, he *can* be— he used to be Prince Charming, you know. But he doesn't know Denny or Josh *that* well, and to tell the truth, I think he's kind of embarrassed by all this. You know, the gambling debt and threats and everything."

"Well, let me talk to Denny anyway. You need to decide what you want to do about Philip staying with the boys at your place. Just one thought: We prayed over that building, remember? Not just the building but all the people in it. At some point, Gabby, you've got to let go and trust God for your family."

I surprised myself by inviting Philip to stay with the boys in our apartment at the House of Hope—and by feeling it was the right thing to do. I was also surprised how quickly he accepted. "That's generous of you, Gabby. Are you sure?"

When Josh heard about the plans, he got the brainy idea of leaving little Gracie with Grandma Jodi on Saturday so "all the guys"—Josh and his dad and Philip and Paul—could go see P.J. run with the Lane Tech cross country team. "Then we could grill steaks in my folks' backyard or something." That got the boys excited—how could Philip say no? And so it was decided.

Sammy was disappointed that he wasn't needed to take care of Dandy for the weekend, but since he and his mom lived right across the hall, Paul said he could help take Dandy for walks, which seemed to satisfy the little boy.

I decided to leave my Subaru with Josh while I was gone—

much better than leaving it parked all weekend near Manna House—in exchange for a lift to work the next morning with my suitcase, as well as picking up Dandy and taking him back to my apartment. That gave Josh an idea. "After the boys get home from school, we could use the Subaru to pick up their dad and bring him here. If Mr. Fairbanks leaves his car at Richmond Towers, that'll confuse anyone who might be on the lookout for his car leaving the parking garage."

Even Philip thought that was a smart idea.

With the whole Baxter family covering my family—God's peace in skin is what it felt like—I was able to concentrate Friday morning on last-minute details for our trip to Wisconsin. Estelle was back and helped Angela Kwon pack up the food for the weekend while Edesa led her regular Friday-morning Bible study, then Edesa and I checked with all the ladies who were going, to be sure they had adequate sweatshirts, socks, and other warm clothes in case the weather got cold. Once again I had to tell Lucy she could *not* take her wire cart in the van—there was just no room. For a few minutes I thought she might back out of the trip altogether rather than part with all her worldly goods, but she finally agreed to store her cart in my office, taking what she needed in a pillowcase.

I was able to catch a few minutes alone with Estelle in the kitchen while everyone was eating lunch. "How did the meeting about Leroy go yesterday? Did social services find a place for him?"

She nodded but kept on scrubbing a pan with baked-on cheese in the sink.

"Are you feeling good about that?"

No answer. *Scrub, scrub, scrub.*

"Estelle, don't make me guess what you're thinking. I care about you! Did something happen in the meeting to upset you?"

The scrubbing stopped. "Oh, the meeting was fine. They found a psychiatric facility for Leroy with a nursing unit. The doctors are happy. Harry's happy. 'Now you don't have to worry about him, Estelle,' he says. And that was that." She glowered. "*That's* the problem."

She tackled the scrubbing again. "He's my *son*, Gabby. Can't just wash my hands of him like I done before."

"Like you . . . whatever do you mean, Estelle?"

"When I moved out and let him stay in the house. I shoulda known them drug dealers in the neighborhood would take advantage of him. They just moved in, made *my* house a drug house, Gabby, and threatened to hurt Leroy if he said anything about it! That wouldn't have happened if I'd stayed with him, now, would it?"

"But you can't blame yourself, Estelle. You moved out because it wasn't safe for you—*he* wasn't safe. Look at what happened with the fire! Bad enough that he set the fire and got burned. But what if you'd been there? You could have been seriously hurt."

"Wasn't the way it was."

I blinked. "What? But you told me earlier—"

"Harry's been doing some sleuthin'—he an' that former partner of his, Cindy. The day before the fire, I was worried 'cause Leroy wouldn't answer his phone. I couldn't go down to the house, so Harry said he'd check up on Leroy for me. That's when he discovered all them druggies had moved in. Harry didn't tell me, didn't want to upset me. Just ordered them drug dealers to move out—or else. Now we findin' out the fire was set in retaliation, made it look like Leroy did it."

My eyes widened in shock.

"An' you know what's worse?" Estelle shook a spatula in my face. "Them drug dealers are sayin' that Officer Fagan put them up to it, else he'd take away the 'protection' he'd been givin' them."

"Oh, Estelle." Unbelievable! I hoped the jury would put that evil man away for a long time. Made me shudder, all the harm he'd done hiding behind his blue uniform. "I'm so sorry. But . . . isn't it good that Leroy will be in a safe place now, can't be taken advantage of?"

"Maybe. Maybe not. Lets me off the hook now, don't it?"

"But what else could you do?"

"Nothin' today. Ain't got no place to take care of him. But I been thinkin' . . . maybe when the insurance money for the house comes through, I could buy me a little Chicago bungalow. Except . . ." Estelle's shoulders sagged and she leaned against one of the big counters. "Except, Harry an' me, we're engaged now. Supposed to get married. But he got DaShawn. No way he gonna agree to take Leroy in too. I dunno, Gabby. Maybe I should give Harry's ring back, set him free." Her eyes teared up. "Do my duty as a mama and take care of my boy."

chapter 21

By two o'clock that afternoon Moby Van was crammed to the gills with fifteen bodies, two big coolers, several grocery bags of food, and assorted bags of clothes and personal items stuffed under seats, under feet, and anywhere else that didn't block my view of the road in four directions.

It wasn't exactly a peaceful send-off. Shawanda's kids screamed bloody murder when their mom climbed into the van, and Celia Jones and her granddaughter, Keisha, had to carry them kicking and bawling back inside. Poor Dandy didn't understand why he couldn't go along—and I could tell Lucy was having a hard time leaving him. She climbed into the front passenger seat, slammed the door, and stared straight ahead, even when Dandy jumped up against the side of the van barking for her attention. Josh Baxter, who'd stopped by the shelter with Gracie to say good-bye to Edesa and pick up Dandy, held tight to the dog's leash so he wouldn't run after us.

But several staff and residents gathered on the steps to see us off. Estelle had exchanged her white kitchen hairnet and apron for one of her handmade caftans and head wraps, a gorgeous purple print, because Harry was picking her up for an early dinner date. "Oh, Estelle!" I whispered in her ear when I hugged her good-bye. "You aren't *really* thinking about breaking your engagement, are you? Don't do anything rash—promise me!"

"I'm just thinkin', not doin'," she huffed. "You can pray about it, though, 'cause it's weighin' heavy on my heart. Now go on! Git! Stop hangin' on my neck or you gonna break it."

We finally pulled away from Manna House at two thirty. "Good-bye!" . . . "Good-bye!" . . . "Call when you get there!" But we still got caught in early traffic heading out of the city for the northern suburbs. Lucy got tired of watching trucks roar past us on the highway and dozed off while I tried to keep an eye out for signs to Route 12, which would take us off the tollway and cut northwest toward Madison, Wisconsin. *Huh*. So much for someone riding up front who could help me navigate. But at least her snoring kept me awake, along with the excited chatter of the "city girls" behind me.

Glancing in my rearview, I saw the younger set—Naomi Jackson, Tawny James, Aida Menendez, and Hannah Something-or-Other, who ranged in age from eighteen to twenty—had commandeered the far rear seat, giggling and gossiping like typical teenagers. Tawny and Aida had been dropped from the foster-care system when they turned eighteen but had somehow managed to avoid the trap of easy drugs and living on the street. Naomi, on the other hand, was just two eyewinks on the other side of kicking her early drug habit and needed a lot of support, while Hannah . . . *hm*. What did I know about Hannah's story? Not much.

The girl had bugged me to death when she first came to the

shelter, as lazy as an old dog lying in the sun, interested only in painting her nails and doing hair. But the part-time job I'd found for her at Adele's Hair and Nails had done wonders to help her straighten up and find some purpose. Or maybe the miracle-worker was Adele herself, who could straighten *my* hair just by giving me The Eye.

My other passengers were mostly in their thirties or early forties—except Shawanda, who, at twenty-five-with-two-kids, fell between the two groups. And Lucy, of course, still kicking at seventy-something. A few I knew pretty well, like Tina Torres and Wanda Smith. But several of my passengers were fairly new at the shelter, and I was doing well just to remember first names: Monique . . . Kikki . . . Sunny . . . Bertie. Of those four, Sunny was white, but I knew better than to assume the others were all African American just because of their brown skin. Heinz 57 Varieties had nothing on the ethnic variations in Chicago. Haitian . . . Jamaican . . . Nigerian . . . Ugandan . . . even South American. Look at Edesa Reyes Baxter. African Honduran to be precise.

But that was one of the reasons for this little trip, I told myself, finally flicking my turn signal and taking the exit for Route 12. By the end of the weekend, we'd probably all know each other a little more, for better or worse.

Uh . . . maybe for worse. Monique turned out to be a fountain of religious clichés, which she threw about Moby Van like holy water. "Girl, I'm too blessed to be stressed . . . Didn't say being homeless was a blessin'. This just a test. No test, no *testi*mony! . . . God ain't through with me yet. I *know* I'm blessed and highly favored, oh glory! . . ."

I slid a CD into the player and turned it up. Loud.

Two hours into our trip—we'd crossed the Wisconsin border awhile back—I stopped at a gas station to fill up the van and let my passengers use the facilities. Didn't realize it'd take half an hour. Angela and Edesa hung around the Mini-Mart inside the station to make sure we had no shoplifting incidents. When we finally got everyone rounded up, I talked Lucy into trading seats with Angela Kwon so the Manna House receptionist could help me with directions.

"I met a guy," Angela murmured to me out of the blue as the boring miles passed.

"What?" My eyes swung off the road to glance at the beautiful young woman, her silky black hair falling coyly over one eye. "Who? Where?"

"At church." She giggled. "He's a doctoral student from Korea. His name is Jin."

"Jin? That's a nice name. So he's a Christian?"

"Yes. Well, I think so. I met him at church."

"Yeah, well, I met my first husband at church and he dumped me after two years," I muttered, then realized Angela was looking at me, wide-eyed. "Sorry. Just—be sure. You're so special, Angela." I gave her a smile and then turned my attention back to the road. "You deserve the best."

"Are we almost there yet? I'm hungry," Shawanda whined from the middle seat.

"Nope! Just halfway," Angela said cheerfully. "But we've got snacks. Coming up!" She dug into one of the coolers wedged between the front seats and passed around soft drinks, chips, and raw veggies. The soft drinks and chips went fast, but the bag of veggies came back nearly full.

"Give me those," I said, grabbing some raw carrots. "I need help staying awake." Wasn't sure why I was so tired. Maybe it was all the emotional stress of the past week. Feeling anxious about Shawanda moving into the House of Hope . . . Philip getting that threatening note, then saying he couldn't keep the boys this weekend . . . the Baxters coming to the rescue at the last minute. And Estelle! That woman nearly tied my nerves in a knot, talking about giving Harry's ring back.

We were deep in the countryside now, and the turning leaves lay like a colorful afghan over the hillsides. Angela gave me directions as we got close to Devil's Lake State Park, and I turned onto a narrow, two-lane paved road. The retreat house we'd rented was on a tiny private lake just outside the park.

I glanced at my watch as the sun disappeared behind the wooded hills and twilight began to settle. *Almost six. Josh and the boys should be picking up Philip about now. What were they going to do this evening? Would Philip drive the Subaru to P.J.'s cross country meet in the morning or would Josh? Maybe I should call, see how it's going—*

"That was it, Gabby!" Angela pointed at a narrow dirt driveway we'd just passed, leading into the trees. With my Subaru I would have just made a U-turn, but with the fifteen-passenger van I had to wait for another driveway and turn around.

There. A painted sign beside the driveway said, "Pine Tree Retreat." We bumped along the winding driveway and pulled up in front of a rustic, two-story log house, nearly hidden under the towering pine trees. Well, we'd unload and then I'd call home, just to check that everyone got connected.

But a quick glance at my cell phone killed that idea. No signal.

I stifled a laugh. *Okay, God, I get it. Trust You—and keep out of it.*

Angela and Edesa set out a quick supper of cold fried chicken and potato salad while the women chose beds—two to a room—and I carried in wood from the shed next to the house and tried to get a fire started in the big stone fireplace. The wood was damp and smoked a lot at first, but I finally got it going. I smiled smugly. Hadn't lost my North Dakota genes after all.

"Now tha's nice." Lucy sank into a padded chair, kicking off her worn shoes.

"Why's it so dark outside?" Hannah wrapped a blanket around her shoulders and huddled close to the fireplace.

"Because it's night?" I teased.

Hannah frowned. "But it ain't this dark at night back in Chicago."

"That's just because of all the city lights. Actually, let me show you something I bet you've never seen in Chicago. Anyone else want to come?" I shrugged into my jacket and stood by the glass sliding doors that faced the nearly invisible lake.

"Whatchu gonna show us?"

"Can't see nothin' in the dark!"

"I ain't goin' out there! There's bugs and wild animals and stuff out there."

Even Edesa and Angela seemed a little dubious about going outside at night.

"Come on, people! It will be spectacular, I promise! That's what this weekend's all about, to experience some of God's beautiful natural world. So who's coming?"

Half the group wouldn't budge, including Lucy, who muttered she knew good and well what "outside" looked like at night. But Edesa said she'd come, along with Tina, Monique, Aida, Tawny, and even Naomi, who held on to my hand in a death grip. At the last minute Kikki yelled, "Hey, wait for me!" and hustled after us, but seeing her stop to light a cigarette, I figured it was mostly an excuse to get a smoke than anything else.

Monique clucked at Kikki in disapproval. "God ain't gonna bless no mess," she muttered to the rest of us. I decided to ignore her.

As our eyes adjusted to the sliver of moonlight, I led the way down the solid wood stairs built into the sloping hill leading to the lake. The quarter moon in the clear sky shone bright enough to guide us out onto the modest pier at the edge of the lake, though Aida and Naomi squealed and clung to each other as if they were walking a tightrope over Niagara Falls.

But once at the end of the short pier, which broadened into a square float, I swept my hand at the sky. "Look."

Heads gradually took eyes off their feet and turned upward. Then I heard first one gasp, then another as we drank in the thick carpet of stars above.

"Are all them *stars*? How come there's so many more up here than back home?"

I had fun explaining that these same stars hung over Chicago, too, but the light pollution from all the city lights hid them from us.

"Oh, *El Señor*," Edesa breathed. "What an amazing world You have created!" Then a moment later, "We used to see stars like this in my village in Honduras . . . but I'd almost forgotten."

The hoot of an owl floated out of the woods. Naomi screamed. "What's that?!"

"Oh! Oh! Let's go back!" Aida had heard it too.

I tried to explain it was just an owl that slept during the day and came out to hunt mice at night, but the frightened girls practically stampeded back to the log house and its glowing windows. The rest followed, shuffling through the pine needles, picking their way around fallen branches and up the wooden stairs.

I brought up the rear reluctantly and turned back for a last look before going inside. Seeing the sky crowded with ancient stars, so majestic, always there, even if hidden behind clouds or city lights, filled my spirit with a deep peace I hadn't felt for a long time. *God* had flung those stars into space. God was a *big God*! Made my problems seem puny. Or at least not insurmountable.

I finally rejoined the Manna House ladies in the cozy log house with its crackling fire. We stayed up late playing Whist and Rummy and a loud game of Trivial Pursuit—all except Lucy, who managed to get a room to herself where she could snore to her heart's content. The house finally quieted around midnight. Only when I crawled into bed in the room I was sharing with Edesa did I allow my mind to drift back to the realities I'd left behind.

If only I could hold on to that sense of *God's-in-control* and let God worry about getting Philip out of the mess he was in—a mess that bothered me more than I liked to admit. His gambling debts and the very real threats from Matty Fagan's cronies—and from his business partner, too, for that matter—complicated our already stressed relationship. Could I forgive him? He seemed to be trying. God had forgiven me and taken me back, after running from Him for so long. But even if I did forgive Philip, what did it mean? Could we ever be a family again?

A family.

Philip and our boys were together at *my* apartment. And he

was probably asleep—in my bed. Was he bare-chested, wearing only a pair of silk shorts, his usual sleepwear? Smelling faintly of the last remnants of his Armani aftershave?

No, no. Couldn't go there!

But as I drifted off to sleep, I had one last thought. Where did Lee Boyer fit into this fuzzy picture . . . ?

"Miss Gabby! Miss Gabby! Wake up!"

I felt someone shaking me. "*Uhhh* . . . what?" I mumbled.

"That noise? Did you hear it—there it is again! Oh, Miss Gabby, what is it? I'm scared!" Fingernails dug into my arm.

Now fully awake, I pried the fingernails off my arm and sat up. The shadowy figure trembling on her knees beside my cot took the shape of Naomi Jackson. *Figured.*

"*Shh.* Don't wake Miss Edesa. I don't hear anything . . . oh." Something metal was rattling and scraping near the house. "Oh, that. Don't worry, Naomi. Probably just a raccoon getting into the garbage can." *Drat.* I knew better than to put those chicken bones out there.

"A raccoon!? But, but . . . what if it's a *bear*! Oh, Miss Gabby, can I sleep with you? I don't want to go back to my room by myself." Without waiting for an answer, Naomi dove under my covers, nearly pushing me out the other side of the narrow cot.

I groaned and mumbled, "*Oof* . . . okay, okay, just for a few minutes."

It was going to be a long weekend.

chapter 22

Sometime during the night I managed to get Naomi back into her own bed and get a few hours of uninterrupted sleep. We'd decided to let the ladies sleep in until eight as a small luxury, since the schedule at Manna House got them up at six o'clock every morning in order to get showers, breakfast, and chores out of the way before their appointments for the day.

So the log house was fairly quiet as Edesa and I crept down the rustic stairs at seven to make coffee and plan the day. The small lake below us sparkled in the new-day sun and birds chirped merrily, promising a good day weather-wise, even though the air was a bit nippy. As we prayed together, I was impressed that my Honduran friend wanted to pray for each woman by name, which took some time, but it did help me focus on God's purpose for bringing each woman there that weekend.

After our "Amen," Edesa said Jodi Baxter had given her an idea: to pray a blessing for each woman based on the meaning of her name. "Sister Jodi does that for her students at school, and she's done it for the Yada Yada *amigas* too." Beaming her generous smile, the vivacious black woman waved a thick paperback. "She loaned me her baby name book. I'm just getting started. Do you want to help? Maybe we can find them all by tomorrow morning, *sí*?"

An hour later, yawning women started to wander downstairs looking for breakfast, which we'd set out on the counter for do-it-yourself: cold cereal, bananas, bagels, and OJ. And by ten o'clock everyone had gotten showered and dressed—even Lucy, after I offered to help wash her hair in the sink—and we gathered in the main room overlooking the lake for a short Bible-and-prayer time before heading out to see the sights.

Edesa read the story of Hagar from Genesis, chapter sixteen—which was also the story of the childless Sarai, who gave her servant to Abraham as a second wife so he could have an heir. But when Hagar got pregnant, the servant girl couldn't help feeling superior to her barren mistress, which made Sarai so furious she threw Hagar out of the household. "Now she was homeless," Edesa said. "Nowhere to go. Pregnant and abandoned."

I noticed all the women were listening intently. "Know 'xactly how she feel!" Shawanda spouted. "This dude got me pregnant—*bam-bam, thank you ma'am*—then threw me out for a slut who had more booty than me. How you think I ended up at the shelter anyway?"

Oh dear. I'd wondered where the name Bam-Bam had come from.

"But notice what God did," Edesa urged, rereading several of the verses. "God sent an angel to her, who called her *by her name*. Isn't that amazing? God knew the name of this unappreciated servant girl! And the angel asked her, 'Hagar, where have you come from? And where are you going?' The angel of the Lord was asking her to tell her story! Hagar was so amazed by this encounter that she gave God a name: *El Roi*, the God Who Sees Me."

Edesa let that sink in for a moment. Then she said softly, "Did you ever think of that, *mi amigas*? That God is interested in *your story*? That God sees *you*?" The room was so quiet, all we heard were the whistles and chirps of the sparrows, wrens, and juncos flitting in the trees outside. Then suddenly several women wanted to talk at once and tell their stories.

"I'm from Cleveland, see," Kikki said, twisting a strand of dark blond hair around a finger. "Got two kids back there living with my folks 'cause I was all strung out on drugs. My parents wanted to get me away from my old crew, so they brought me to Chicago six months ago, stuck me in a residential rehab center—but I got kicked out of the program. I just couldn't stay clean." The blue eyes teared up. "I been clean again almost four weeks . . . but sometimes I'm scared I won't ever get to be with my kids again."

Several women murmured sympathy. But not Bertie. "Ain't seen *my* kids in ten years." The woman's hard features matched her tone. "State stole 'em. Nothin' I do seem to work out. Nobody want to listen to me. So I just end up not carin' anymore."

"Leastways you had kids," Hannah said, her voice quivering. "I got pregnant when I was fifteen, knew I couldn't take care of no kid—so I got an abortion. My boyfriend even paid for it. But somethin' went wrong, and now they tell me I can't have no kids." The girl I'd so easily nicknamed "Hannah-the-Bored" started to cry.

Wanda put a big arm around our would-be manicurist and murmured in her Jamaican *patois*, "Aw, gal, it goin' fe be ah-rite, it goin' fe be ah-rite."

We heard a few more stories that morning. I was familiar with

Wanda's story, who'd come to the States from Jamaica as a temporary resident three years ago, but lost all her ID when her purse was stolen. The process of applying for new ID was held up until her elderly mother in Kingston sent a copy of her birth certificate. "But it been t'ree months an' I hear not'ing. Dey gon' ship me back home if it don't come soon."

But I knew nothing about Sunny Davis, a sad-faced white woman with bad teeth, which seemed to mock her name. Her story came out in bits and pieces: bounced around from relative to relative growing up, no one seemed to want her, no one cared when she dropped out of school. Unable to hold down a job, she was finally trying to complete her GED—at age forty. "But learnin' don't come easy for me." She shrugged. "Feel like givin' up most days."

"Nah, nah, don't give up," several encouraged. "Ask Carolyn to help you! She real smart. Teaches the kids in the afterschool program."

Finally Edesa asked everyone to hold hands while she thanked God for knowing each woman by name and caring about her story. I had to drop the hands I was holding to fish for a tissue halfway through her prayer. Her words touched me. *God knows my name—Gabrielle Shepherd Fairbanks. And He cares about my story too.*

We spent the rest of the day sightseeing around Devil's Lake State Park and Baraboo, the closest town. The fall colors were as spectacular as I'd hoped—brilliant yellows and reds sparking from among several shades of greens. But some of the women got bored just driving around, so we found a couple of picnic tables and pulled out the cooler, which we'd packed with sandwiches—each woman had made her own—as well as cans of pop, apples, cookies, and the not-so-popular raw veggies. Angela Kwon led a group along a short hiking trail and came back with tales of purple and blue and pink wildflowers still poking their noses through the blanket of leaves that had fallen to the ground.

But even in the sun, the air was chilly, so we piled back in the van and headed for Baraboo. There were several signs for the Circus World Museum, but Tina Torres got all excited when she saw a sign for the Ho-Chunk Casino featuring . . . bingo? "Hey, bingo! I love bingo!"

Huh. Didn't know casinos offered bingo. *Yeah, right.* Probably the come-on to lure tourists to the slot machines and blackjack tables. I was about to deliver a three-point sermon about the evils of gambling when Angela piped up. "I saw a kids' bingo game back at the retreat house. We can play for chocolate kisses tonight if you want."

The ladies all laughed. "'At's more my speed," Lucy muttered.

As we drove through Baraboo—a tourist town if I ever saw one—someone spied a Sweet Shoppe and yelled, "Ice-cream!" As our motley crew of black, tan, and white faces piled out of the van and filled up the tiny store, a few of the customers pulled their children close and left quickly after getting their ice-cream cones. I bit my tongue before I said something I'd regret and caught Edesa's eye.

She just patted my arm and smiled gently in a *don't-let-it-bother-you* way.

I sighed. Sure hoped I could be like Edesa when I grew up.

"Can't they spell in Wisconsin?" Shawanda snickered in a loud voice. "Everybody knows ya don't spell *shop* S-H-O-P-P-E."

The woman behind the counter rolled her eyes, but customers were customers and I was paying with real dollar bills, so twenty minutes later we walked out with fifteen assorted ice-cream cones, though most of the ladies elected to eat them in the warm van instead of the outdoor tables with the red-and-yellow striped umbrellas.

As we headed out of town back toward Devil's Lake State Park, we saw more signs for Circus World. "Pull in, pull in," Angela begged. "Wouldn't that be fun? Maybe it won't cost anything."

Well, she was right. It didn't cost anything because the season was over. We got out of the van and looked around, but the museum was closed. The signs indicated there were circus performances and animal acts daily from May through September, and that this was the original site of the old Ringling Bros. Circus winter quarters. It gave me an idea. What if we scheduled our Fall Getaway next year in September? I'd call and see if Circus World had special group rates. Maybe we should even bring the kids.

"Who needs a circus?" Tawny James teased. "I can stand on my hands." Which the pretty girl with the creamy caramel skin and dark, tiny ringlets proceeded to do in a grassy patch just beyond the parking lot.

"Huh. That's nothin'. I can do a flip," snorted Shawanda. And she did. Not just one, but two.

The ladies laughed and clapped. Getting in the mood, some of the others tried to outdo each other. "I can touch my nose with my tongue!" . . . "Can you make yourself into a human knot?" I grinned at Angela and Edesa. Who knew what other "talents" this group possessed?

"Well, watch *me*. I can walk a tightrope." Lucy's raspy voice took me by surprise—even more so when she hauled herself up on one of the park benches scattered around the site and, holding out her hefty arms to either side, pretended to be walking a narrow tightrope. Now the younger women were cheering her on. I couldn't help but laugh. This was good. Getting away from the everyday stresses of being homeless in the city or housed in a shelter, letting down their hair, even getting silly.

Until Lucy came to the end of the bench, that is. "No, Lucy!" I cried, seeing that she was about to step off.

I was too late. With a flourish, the old lady stepped off—but the step was too high. Her left foot twisted as it hit the ground and she went headlong into the hard dirt.

"*Humph*," Monique sniffed. "'Pride goeth before a fall.'"

"Shut up, Monique," I hissed, as half a dozen of us rushed to Lucy, whose face, covered in dirt, was twisted in pain.

But after getting the old woman up and back into the van, Lucy refused to let me take her to the hospital, even if I knew where one was, which I didn't. "Jus' a few scratches, that's all. Don't be such a fussbudget." Angela and Edesa got the bleeding stopped on her scraped face and hands with some disinfectant wipes from the van's small medical kit while I drove, my hands sweating on the wheel. But by the time we got back to the Pine Tree Retreat house, her left ankle had swollen to softball size, and it took three of us to get her inside and lowered onto the couch.

Angela eased off Lucy's shoe and worn sock while Edesa propped up her foot and emptied ice cubes from the freezer to make plastic-bag ice packs. My anxiety level was about to go through the log roof. "You should see a doctor, Lucy. It could be broken!"

"It ain't broke. Don'tcha think I never sprained my ankle b'fore? Just get one o' them elastic things and wrap it 'round."

Fortunately, the retreat house had a cupboard of basic medical supplies, including elastic bandages. "Here, let me do that." Tina Torres elbowed the rest of us out of the way and deftly wrapped Lucy's ankle, ignoring the old lady's complaints that it was too tight. "Shut up, Lucy," the large Puerto Rican ordered. "You one *loco* old woman, you know that? Doing something *estúpido* like that! Here, take this." She handed Lucy a couple of pain relievers and a glass of water.

"Praise your way through it, sister Lucy!" Monique admonished and would have kept preaching if I hadn't pulled her away with a reminder that she was on supper duty with Kikki and me. I kept the two newbies scurrying like squirrels as I banged pots around and tossed out orders. Forty-five minutes later we set out a big bowl of spaghetti on the long wooden table, along with a simple tossed salad and loaf of hot garlic bread.

A round of cheers greeted Angela's announcement at supper that Daylight Saving Time ended that night, so we'd all get to sleep in *another* hour the next morning. Well, she should know, given her job as receptionist and timekeeper at Manna House.

Lucy seemed to enjoy bossing the rest of us around as we waited on her hand and foot—literally—the rest of the evening. I'd had visions of building a bonfire in the fire ring down by the lake and introducing these city girls to the joys of roasting marshmallows and making s'mores with the chocolate bars and graham crackers we'd brought along. But Lucy's sprained ankle and temperatures dipping into the thirties as the sun set kept us in the log house around the stone fireplace, and I decided I didn't want to deal with hot, gooey marshmallows on the carpet and furniture. So I offered the chocolate bars and marshmallows straight from the bag as prizes for the hot bingo game that lasted for at least two hours after supper.

Not exactly my cup of tea, but I shrugged and took three bingo cards and even won two marshmallows. Nobody would trade me for chocolate.

It wasn't until much later, as I covered a sleeping Lucy with several blankets and turned out the house lights, that I realized I'd totally missed my chance while in town to make a quick call back home to see how the "guy weekend" was faring. While getting ready for bed, Edesa caught me checking my cell phone to see if I had any voice mail or text messages. She eyed me quizzically. I shook my head. Nothing.

Edesa laughed and gave me a sweet-smelling hug. "Don't worry, *mi amiga*. I am sure *El Señor* is capable of working out His own purpose for this weekend."

But as I slid under the covers, I thought, *Yeah, but the least God could do is tell me what He's up to.*

chapter 23

Hallelujah! No raccoons, tipped-over trash cans, or frightened girls shaking me awake in the middle of the night. But I did get up to investigate a grunting noise at one point and discovered Lucy crawling over the floor to the bathroom.

"Oh, Lucy, let me help you! You need some crutches as soon as we get back to Manna House today."

Lucy pushed me away as I tried to get her up. "I'm doin' jus' fine, Fuzz Top. Now git. Go back to bed, will ya?"

Huh. Who was calling whom Fuzz Top? I'd just washed her frowzy gray hair yesterday morning, but it already looked like a bird's nest in the dim glow from the nightlights plugged into sockets around the log house.

I went back to bed.

The end of Daylight Saving Time meant nothing to my body clock, which woke me up at the usual time. My glow-in-the-dark watch said six thirty, which meant it was only five thirty new time. Too early to get up. But I didn't go back to sleep. My mind was awake and already tumbling.

Sunday . . . will Philip take the boys to church? Probably not. Maybe Josh will take them . . . unless Philip thinks up something to do with the boys, which would be hard for them to resist. After all, going to church every Sunday is a new routine for the boys since they came back from Virginia. Oh well . . . it isn't the end of the world if the boys miss one Sunday, I guess.

I finally gave up trying to fall sleep and got up at six, pulled on a pair of leggings, added a sweater over my sleepshirt, and crept quietly down the stairs to the first floor. The sun wasn't up yet, but the first light of dawn etched the tops of the trees in stark relief to the brightening sky. Lucy was still snoring on the couch, so I slid quietly past to the kitchen, made a pot of coffee, and then sat at the kitchen counter with Jodi Baxter's baby-names book and started looking up the meanings of names.

Edesa found me still at the counter an hour later. "Why did you not wake me?" she scolded in a whisper. "I wanted to help with the names!"

"Well, you can help now," I murmured. "I found what their names mean—but how to make a *blessing* out of some of them is beyond me! Want some coffee?"

Putting our heads together—Edesa's tiny black corkscrew ringlets next to my messy curls—we went over the list:

Angela—*"Angelic messenger."* Edesa grinned. "Seems appropriate for someone who answers the phone all day. Who's next?"

Naomi—*"Pleasant."*

Tawny—*"Golden-brown color."* "What can we do with that?" I wondered aloud.

Aida—Swahili: *"An advantage or reward."* "Hm. The name is Swahili—but Aida's Latina," Edesa said. "That's interesting."

Hannah—Hebrew, biblical: "Grace" or "Favor."

Shawanda—"Closest I could find was 'Shawana,' which means 'graceful,'" I said. "Kind of nice."

I pointed at Kikki's name. "Couldn't find hers. Maybe a nickname?"

Edesa grew thoughtful. "I heard her tell someone her real name is Kiersten, but her baby sister couldn't say it, so she called her Kikki. Look up *Kiersten*."

I flipped to the *K*s. "Whoa—it means 'Follower of Christ.'"

"Gloria a Dios!" Edesa breathed. "That will make a wonderful blessing. Okay, who's next?"

Monique—Latin: "Advisor." Oh, Monique was going to love that.

Wanda—"Wanderer." "That's true enough," I murmured. "She's not really at home here *or* back in Kingston."

Bertie—"Bright." I made a face. "*That's* a misnomer. Her spirit seems so dark. And Sunny. Her name means 'Filled with Sunshine,' but she's the saddest-looking woman here. And Lucy? Look at that. Her name means 'Light.' Go figure."

Edesa was thoughtful a moment. "You know, when prophets speak they say what God sees, not necessarily what we see. These names may be prophetic—our Father God speaking what He saw when He created each woman. Don't you think He wants to change Sunny—wants to give her a bright sunny spirit, full of light?"

I leaned over and gave the young woman a hug. "You always think the best of people."

She seemed embarrassed. "That's because *Jesuchristo* thinks the best of us, and I want to be more like *Him*. But don't be fooled." She made a face. "I have my moments. Just ask Josh!"

Humph. Hard to imagine. When Josh looked at Edesa, he still seemed starstruck.

I'd changed my watch to the new time, which now said seven thirty. We'd announced that breakfast would be at eight thirty. "We better get started on these blessings before people get up."

"Wait. Do you remember the meaning of *your* name, Gabrielle?"

I nodded. How could I forget? When Philip first kicked me out of the penthouse and my life was falling apart like so many broken shards, Edesa had encouraged me to "live into your name," which she said meant "strong woman of God."

"It was the first time I ever thought of myself that way," I murmured, "and it's made a big difference in my life." I picked up the paperback book. "But this says my name also means, 'God is my strength'—which I also like, because I don't always feel like a strong woman of God!"

Edesa giggled. "Nor do I. Reminds me of this song . . ." She hummed a few notes that sounded vaguely familiar. "It's from Psalm 73," she said. "'God is the strength of my life, and my portion forever.'" She let the words sit in the air for a moment or two, then pulled a handful of colorful note cards out of her tote bag. "Okay, let's do this."

For the next half hour we worked on writing a blessing for each woman in the house. Finally we heard people moving about upstairs and showers running. "Guess we should get breakfast started." I sighed and started to gather the cards when we heard *thump . . . thump . . . thump* and looked up.

"Oh, *buenos días*, Lucy!" Edesa cried. "How are you feeling this morning?"

The old woman was a sight. The scrapes on her face made her

look like she'd been in a fight—and lost. She was hopping on one foot, balancing herself in the doorway. "What's a body gotta do ta get some food 'round here?" she growled. "Sun been up a couple hours aw'ready."

Breakfast, cleanup, and packing took the better part of the morning, so it was almost eleven by the time we gathered for our final worship time. The temperature was edging toward the fifties, but it still felt too cool to sit outside, so once more we gathered in the living room of the log house with its large windows overlooking the tranquil lake.

Lucy and her sprained ankle—which was starting to turn an ugly black and blue—took up the whole couch, so we had to hunt up a few more floor pillows, but finally all fifteen of us were seated around the fireplace, where I'd built a cozy fire. Angela, who let it slip that she sang in the choir at her Korean American church, led us in some simple choruses such as "This Little Light of Mine" and "O, How I Love Jesus," ending with the soulful "Amazing Grace."

At least I thought we were ending, until Edesa began singing the last song again, this time in Spanish. *"Sublime gracia del Señor . . ."* To my delight, Aida Menendez and Tina Torres—one Mexican, the other Puerto Rican—joined in. But the biggest surprise was Kikki—a.k.a. Kiersten from Cleveland, as white-girl as they come—who also sang along with perfect Spanish. "Took four years in high school," she confessed shyly at the end of the song.

The things we learn about each other when we spend time together, I thought in amazement. I wished the whole staff of Manna House had come along to see another side of these homeless women.

Opening her Bible, Edesa picked up where she'd left off the day before about God knowing each of us by name, and read several Bible stories about blessing people based on the meaning of their names. Isaac blessed his twin sons, Esau and Jacob. Moses blessed each tribe according to their name. John the Baptist was named John, meaning "God is gracious," instead of being named Zacharias Junior after his father. Even the Messiah—the angel said He should be named Jesus, because the name means "Savior."

"So," Edesa said, pulling out the colorful note cards, "we want to bless each of you according to your name."

By the looks on their faces, the circle of women didn't know what to make of this. But they listened intently as Edesa picked a card, knelt in front of Naomi Jackson, and took her hand. "Naomi, your name means 'Pleasant,' and even though your teen years have been rough, God wants to bless you with pleasant years ahead, which can be yours if you let God be your guide."

Naomi threw her arms around Edesa and started to cry. "Oh, thank you!"

My turn. I picked a card, gulped a little when I read the name, and knelt down beside the woman who was always spouting platitudes at people. "Monique, your name means 'Advisor.' God invites you to fill your heart and your mind with *His* wisdom, which is found in His Word—not on the Internet—so that you can encourage others with His promises."

Monique took the card, beaming. "Amen! Amen! I like that!" I knew she would. I just hoped she wouldn't take it as permission to preach at everybody.

Back and forth, Edesa and I read the cards, holding the hand of the woman who was being blessed.

"Bertie, things may look dark today, but God wants to brighten your heart with the light of Christ, as your name implies!"

"Kikki, your real name, Kiersten, means 'Follower of God.' If you truly follow Him, He *will* restore your relationship with your children and your parents."

"Shawanda, your name means 'Graceful.' As you let God fill you with His grace, you will grow more *graceful* in your speech, in your actions, and in your relationship with your young children."

I knew Shawanda's blessing sounded a little preachy—I wrote it—but she seemed to like the meaning of her name. "Graceful— how 'bout that," she mused.

Soon everyone had their blessing card—even Lucy, whose card said, "Lucy, your name means 'Light,' and you do light up a room whenever you enter!" Chuckles circled the room and even made Lucy smile as the card was read aloud. We'd added, "Let God shine His light into every dark corner of your life so that you are free to be who He created you to be."

I half expected Lucy to protest that she was already a free woman, or that she didn't have any "dark corners," but she just snatched the card and stowed it somewhere in a pocket of her multilayered clothes.

To close, Edesa prayed a prayer of blessing over the group, thanking God for each woman and praising God that He was still "working His purpose out" in their lives. But when she said, "Amen," hardly anyone moved. Several read and reread their cards to themselves, and a box of tissues got passed from hand to hand.

But we finally did get all our gear cleared out of the log house, did a final inspection, and managed to get Lucy into the second seat of the van with her leg propped up on one of the coolers. We planned to stop along the way and get sandwiches or something for lunch rather than mess up the kitchen again.

But as the van bumped along the dirt road toward the highway, I started to worry. How in the world was Lucy going to manage when we got back? Even if she stayed at Manna House, the bunk rooms were on the second floor. If we could convince her to use the service elevator—big IF—she might be able to get up there that way.

And what if her ankle was broken? If she didn't get decent medical care, it might never heal properly! But even if it was only a bad sprain, it was going to be a couple of weeks before she was on her feet again.

What were we going to do about Dandy?

As soon as I was able to get a cell phone signal, I told myself it was totally appropriate to call home to the apartment and let Philip and the boys know we'd arrive back at Manna House by four thirty or so and I'd be home soon after. And there was one thing we hadn't talked about: what Philip was going to do once I got home. Go back to the penthouse? Get a hotel room? Hunt for another apartment?

But no one answered, so I left a message. *Where were they?*

As it turned out, it took longer than I'd anticipated stopping for lunch—especially getting Lucy in and out of the van—and we ran into stop-and-go weekend traffic crawling back into Chicago.

When we finally arrived at Manna House, we had to unload every-thing, put away the food and coolers, and sweep out the van—not to mention getting Lucy situated on a couch in Shepherd's Fold on the main floor and talking Sarge, the night manager, into letting her sleep there for one night until we figured out what to do.

"Where's Dandy?" Lucy fussed. "Wanna see my dog."

I shook my head emphatically. "Not tonight, Lucy. Not till we figure out what we're going to do with you."

"Dagnabit!" The old lady glowered at me. "When did you get so bossy?"

Thankfully, Edesa and I were outside still cleaning the van when Josh Baxter arrived in my Subaru with Gracie in her car seat and Dandy in the way back. "Leave him there!" I called out before he let the dog out. "He's coming back home with me."

Josh shrugged and wrapped his arms around Edesa, giving her a long, amorous kiss. *Must be nice*, I thought, taking my time locking up the van. But then Josh handed me the Subaru keys and folded his long legs into the front passenger seat while Edesa climbed in the back with Gracie.

"Thanks, Josh," I said, starting the car and noticing that the gas gauge said Full. "Uh . . . is Philip still at the apartment with the boys?"

"Actually, no. We were at my folks' for lunch, and Harry and Estelle joined us. Mr. Philip knew you were getting home soon and decided to go back to his place, so Harry Bentley offered to give him a ride to Richmond Towers." Josh glanced at me with a conspiratorial grin. "I'm sure part of it was to make sure Mr. Philip got up to the penthouse safely, though Mr. Harry didn't come right out and say so. Anyway, I brought the boys and Dandy back to the House of Hope with me and Gracie. I left them at your place doing their homework—supposedly." The young man winked knowingly.

"Philip and the boys had lunch with you and your folks? How did that happen?"

"Well, we were already at church—"

"The boys went to church? Did you take them?"

Josh nodded. "Yep. And Mr. Philip too."

I nearly ran a stop sign. "*Philip*? Went to *church* at SouledOut?!"

Josh chuckled. In the back seat I heard Edesa murmur, "*Gloria a Dios!*"

A zillion questions flooded my brain, but to tell the truth, I was in a state of shock. Like the world had turned upside down. Next thing I knew, the morning papers were going to say Mayor Richard Daley had suddenly given up politics for belly dancing.

chapter 24

The boys were playing a video game on their Xbox when I hauled my suitcase in the front door with one hand, holding Dandy's leash with the other. Behind me in the hallway, Josh and Edesa were tromping up the stairs to the third floor with Gracie.

"I'm home!" I called out, which was totally unnecessary because Dandy bounced in like he hadn't seen Paul in a month of Sundays instead of just half an hour.

"Dandy! You're back!" Paul dropped his game controller and rolled on the living room floor with the yellow dog. "Hey, Mom, how come you brought Dandy back?"

"Well, hello to you, too, kiddo. C'mon, give me a hug and then I'll tell you. You, too, P.J.! I've missed you guys!" I stole hugs from both boys and dropped into the rocking chair. "Lucy sprained her ankle so I said we'd keep Dandy for another day or so. Josh said he left you two doing your homework. Did you—?"

"Done!" the boys chimed in unison, grabbing up their controllers and sending their cursors flying on the TV screen. Dandy flopped on the floor beside Paul, panting happily.

"How was your weekend? Did you have fun with your dad?"

"Uh-huh . . ." *Zap! Zap! Zing!* "Got him!"

"Yeah, it was good . . . Argh! Where'd those robots come from?" *Zing! Pow! Pow!*

O-kaaay. Maybe later. I got up and pulled my suitcase down the hall to unpack and think about supper. I was suddenly ravenous. What could I make fast . . . quesadillas?

I stopped in the doorway of my bedroom. Philip's leather overnight bag sat on the floor beside the bed. I gulped. He had slept in my room. We'd never talked about where he would sleep. I should have! Paul had a bunk bed. He could've slept there.

A wave of annoyance lapped at my senses. Why did he leave his bag here? Was he leaving me a message, like I did the time I left a lipstick smudge on a glass in the penthouse kitchen after he'd kicked me out? *"You-know-who was here . . ."*

I picked up his bag and set it out in the dining room. *Okay, Gabby, don't do the knee-jerk thing.* After all, Josh said they went to church—don't forget *that*—then to his parents' house for lunch, and then Mr. B took him home. Philip probably didn't realize he'd been gone all day.

Besides, it gave me a good excuse to call him and get Philip's version of the weekend.

I cradled the phone in the crook of my shoulder as I coated a frying pan with cooking spray and tossed in a tortilla, covered it with grated cheese, and topped it with another tortilla. After a few rings, the phone picked up on the other end. "Philip? Hi, it's Gabby. Wanted to tell you I'm home—"

"Oh, hi, Gabby. Uh, could we talk later? Harry Bentley's here and we're in the middle of something."

What? Mr. Bentley was still there? "Oh. Well, sure, I can call

214

back later. Or you can call me. Just wanted to let you know you left your bag here."

"Right. Sorry about that. I thought I'd be back to pick it up. I'll try to get it soon."

"No, no, don't bother. I'll drop it off tomorrow after work. Okay? Bye."

I took the phone off my shoulder and stared at it. Mr. Bentley was *still* at Philip's place? Wasn't he just going to take him home, make sure he got there safely? What was going on?

I flipped the quesadilla, took it out of the pan, made two more, and cut them into wedges—all the while trying to imagine what in the world Harry and Philip would be talking about. Neither one seemed to think much of the other—though Philip *had* thanked our ex-doorman/retired cop for sending aid when Fagan had cornered him in the alley a few weeks ago.

I poured milk and set out a jar of salsa to eat with the quesadillas, then yelled, "Boys! Come and get it!" toward the front of the house. No response. I finally marched into the living room and shut off the TV.

"Mo-om! Can't we eat in here?"

"Nope. Supper's on the kitchen table and you haven't said ten words to me since I got home. Now, skedaddle, before I give your supper to Dandy."

To their credit, the boys cheered up at the sight of food and, once I got them started, talked with their mouths full about the weekend with their father. "Will Nissan came over Friday night." . . . "He was gonna take Dad to a movie, but he brought a DVD of *Pirates of the Caribbean* over here instead." . . . "Yeah, the new one. It was really cool!" . . . "Dad ordered pizza . . ."

Will Nissan again. How come this college kid always seemed to show up on the weekend? He needed to get a life! Though . . . I had to remember he lived with his grandmother. Maybe Philip and the boys were his excuse to get out of the apartment.

I kept prodding. "How did the cross country meet go?"

"Cool! Mr. Josh drove us. It was at the lakefront. Kind of windy. But they let me take Dandy."

"And guess what? Josh's dad came to see me run too! We picked him up when we dropped off Gracie with her grandma."

Yes, that was the plan, for Josh and Denny to hang out with Philip just in case Fagan's goons followed him with mischief in mind.

"Did Lane Tech qualify for State?"

"Nah. But Dad said I ran great." The smile in P.J.'s eyes told me that was as good, maybe better, than going to State.

According to the boys, "the guys" hung around the lakefront till mid-afternoon, then went back to the Baxters' house and grilled steaks in the backyard. I'd seen that backyard. About as big as a postage stamp, but the boys talked about the cookout like it was the greatest thing since the Xbox. Guess it was the company that mattered.

"So you came back here Saturday evening and . . . ?"

Paul shrugged. "Nothin' much. We just watched TV. Dad talked to Nana and Granddad on the phone. Dad seemed upset about somethin', but he didn't say what. But Mr. Josh offered to take us to SouledOut in the morning and invited Dad too."

"Yeah. Tell you the truth, Mom," P.J. said, stuffing his mouth with another wedge of quesadilla, "I didn't think he'd come. But he did. He seemed kinda surprised when we got there. It's not much like Nana and Granddad's church back in Petersburg, you know, meeting in that store in the mall and everything. But he was impressed that I got to work the soundboard by myself."

"That's great, honey. What did Dad say about, you know, the worship service?"

Both boys shrugged. "I dunno," Paul said. "Didn't really say anything. But Josh's parents invited us back to their house for lunch, and Mr. Harry and Miss Estelle came too. Dad said he didn't want to impose, but P.J. and me wanted to go, so he kinda gave in. It was fun. We played Monopoly with Dad and Mr. Harry all afternoon."

"Yeah, but never again with *those* two." P.J. shook his head. "They, like, took it so seriously! Like they were playing for real money or something."

I almost snorted. *Out of the mouth of babes.* "Who won?" I asked.

"Dad did." P.J. got up, his plate empty. "Can we go finish our video game now?"

I let them go, but before I took care of the supper dishes, I got the Manna House staff phone list and dialed another number. Delores Enriquez, the nurse who came to the shelter one morning a week, listened to my tale of woe about Lucy's twisted ankle but interrupted when I said Lucy didn't want to see a doctor. "Sister Gabby, take that stubborn old woman to the clinic first thing tomorrow morning. Tell her I said so! She needs to have that ankle x-rayed. Broken or sprained, doesn't matter. It needs to be treated. At her age, an injury like that could set her back permanently. And, Gabby—call an ambulance if she won't go!"

We didn't have to call an ambulance to get Lucy to the clinic, but it did take Mabel and me and Estelle, and even Tina Torres and a few of the other shelter residents, to convince her on Monday morning that she needed to see a doctor. I'd brought Dandy to work with me and that cheered Lucy some, and finally she let several of us help her out the door and into Moby Van. It meant missing staff meeting, but Mabel told me to just go!

Unfortunately, a visit to the walk-in clinic at Stroger Hospital, Cook County's state-of-the-art new hospital, still meant waiting. I found a machine that dispensed coffee and snacks, and finally Lucy's name was called around two o'clock.

I insisted on going with her while she was processed.

"What is your full name, ma'am?" The intake staffer was politely professional.

"It's 'miss,' not 'ma'am,'" Lucy sniffed. "I ain't married."

"All right. Your full name?"

"Lucinda Tucker."

"Age?"

Lucy frowned. "Kinda lost track."

"Well, your birthdate then."

Lucy pursed her lips. Finally she said, "November three, nineteen hunnerd an' twenty-something . . . um, slips my mind right now. Twenty-six, I think." My ears perked up. Did she actually give a birth date? I quickly figured in my head. If Lucy hadn't just pulled a date out of the air, that made her eighty years old. Or would, on November third, which was . . .

Oh my goodness! Lucy's birthday is next Friday!

I was so amazed at this bit of information that I didn't pay much attention to the rest of the intake process—blood pressure, temp, and more questions about her general health, raising Lucy's aggravation—though they didn't try to put her on the scale because of her injured foot. But I stuck with her when they took her for x-rays, then we waited in the small examining room for the results.

My cell phone rang as the minutes ticked by. *Estelle Williams.* She knew I was at the clinic with Lucy—was something wrong? I went out into the hallway to take the call.

"Thought you'd want to know," Estelle said. "Just got a call from Harry. The jury came back with a verdict. Guilty! Matty Fagan's goin' away for a long time."

"Oh, Estelle! That's such good news. I want to hear all about it—but I just saw one of the radiologists go into Lucy's room. Talk to you later!"

I closed the phone. *Hallelujah!* Couldn't wait to tell Philip. But I hustled back into the small room in time to hear the youngish doctor say, ". . . a severe sprain." A week on crutches, six weeks with an air cast, and maybe six months for the ankle to fully heal. "Too bad you didn't break it," he joked. "Might've healed faster."

Oh great. Real funny.

Lucy's foot was expertly wrapped and she was given a prescription for pain meds and a pair of crutches to be returned when she came back in a week. We practiced with the crutches down one of the hospital's wide hallways, though Lucy kept muttering, "How'm I 'sposed to pull my cart around if I gotta hol' on to these things with both hands?"

She wasn't the only one with questions about how she was going to manage. Once we got back to Manna House about four thirty and got Lucy resettled in Shepherd's Fold with her foot elevated, Mabel called an emergency staff meeting. Not many of us were around at that time of day, but Estelle had just finished her sewing class, and she, Angela, and I crowded into Mabel's office.

"What Lucy needs is a nursing home!" Angela was adamant. "She's in her seventies, for heaven's sake! She can't live out on the street like this."

"Seventy-nine to be exact," I put in. "Her birthday's Friday."

"See? My point exactly!"

"I don't think a nursing home will take her, because she's theoretically ambulatory," Mabel pointed out. "I guess she could stay here for a week or so if she'll use the service elevator. Do we have room on the bed list, Angela?"

Angela shook her head. "Full up. Several came in over the weekend while we were on our Fall Getaway—which was great, by the way. Sorry you missed the staff meeting this morning, Gabby. They had to rely on a report from me, and I'm sure I don't know the half of it. You and Edesa did most of the planning."

"Yes, we want to hear Gabby's report," Mabel said impatiently, "but right now we need to decide what to do about Lucy. Estelle? Any ideas?"

Estelle shook her head. "Wish I could take care of her. Home care for the elderly is what I'm trained for, but that's presuming the elderly person has a home." She wagged her head. "Can't take her in at my place. Stu and I live on the second floor."

My place? I thought. *I'm on the first floor.* But I'd have to kick P.J. out of his room, which didn't seem a good idea at this point. No, my family life was complicated enough as it was. Even the empty apartment at the House of Hope—empty for another five days, that is—was on the second floor. And no elevator.

I sighed. "Well, I can solve one problem. I'll keep Dandy until

Lucy's off those crutches. If she stays here, I can bring him to work with me like I did before. That ought to keep her somewhat happy, anyway."

We finally decided Lucy could stay at Manna House, on a couch in Shepherd's Fold if need be, and give her the first bed that became available. Estelle would take her on as a "patient" in addition to her other work at the shelter, and Delores could give her weekly checkups between clinic visits. Lucy's precious wire cart would stay under lock and key in Mabel's office. Dandy would stay with me.

"Oh, one more thing," I said, stealing Mabel's usual line. Angela and Estelle both snickered. Guess I wasn't the only one she used it on. Grinning, I said, "Found out today that Lucy's birthday is next Friday. What do you say we plan a surprise party for her? I mean, a *really big* surprise party. It may be the first birthday party she's had since she ran away from home as a teenager."

The others thought that was a great idea.

"Banana cake," I added. "Her birthday cake has to be banana. She says it's her favorite."

But I was in the car an hour later on the way to Richmond Towers with Philip's leather bag—after taking Paul and Dandy home—when something I'd said in Mabel's office niggled at my brain.

"*. . . since she ran away from home as a teenager.*"

Where had I heard that recently? Not from Lucy. Somebody else . . .

chapter 25

A flicker of anxiety took over my thoughts as I pulled into a Visitor parking space alongside Richmond Towers. My eyes swept the park between the Towers and Lake Shore Drive. Was one of those thugs still lurking around? How would I feel if I were Philip, still living here after being attacked so viciously in the pedestrian tunnel, the one I could see from my parking space?

I'd be terrified.

So why did he come back here last night?

Well, duh, Gabby. You weren't about to let him stay at your apartment after this weekend. What else could he do?

Taking a deep breath, I grabbed Philip's bag, locked my car, and hustled into the building through the revolving doors. "*Hola, Señor* Gomez!" I called out, using the little Spanish I knew, to the square-built man who used to be the night doorman when I lived here at Richmond Towers "How is the wife and family?"

"*Buenos tardes, Señora* Fairbanks. *Muy bueno, gracias*. Oh, do you want me to let you in?" the man said, seeing me head for the security door into the elevator bank.

I shook my head and waved my security key card. "I still have my key—just don't tell Mr. Martin." I laughed and gave a head jerk in the direction of the building manager's office. "But would you call up to the penthouse and let Mr. Fairbanks know I'm coming?"

Mr. Gomez chuckled as I disappeared into the elevator foyer. Rising steadily upward to the thirty-second floor—a height I tried not to think about—I realized I missed seeing Mr. Bentley there in the lobby as Top Dog Doorman in his blue uniform and cap. The towering glass building with its luxury penthouse had always made me nervous from day one when we'd moved in early last spring— but Harry Bentley, my "first best friend" in Chicago, had been down to earth, a comforting presence who seemed to bring sanity into my discombobulated existence during the months I'd lived here.

And Mr. B had stood by me even when my husband kicked me out, though at the time I had no idea the doorman was a retired cop involved in all sorts of dangerous intrigues within the Chicago Police Department. Or that he was raising a grandson he'd only recently discovered existed. Or that my fellow staffer at Manna House would fall in love with the man.

I smiled to myself as the elevator door dinged open on 32. "Thank You, God, for Harry Bentley," I murmured, "for bringing that beautiful man into my life—" My smile faded and I added, "And please don't let Estelle throw that man away! He's the best thing that ever happened to her!"

Philip opened the door before I even had time to ring the door-bell. "Gabby—Gomez rang me, said you were on the way up." He seemed distracted, even upset, hardly noticed when I handed him his leather overnight bag. "Do you have a minute? I need to talk to you."

I'd intended to stay awhile because I wanted to hear from him how the weekend had gone—but something told me whatever Philip needed to talk to me about wasn't P.J.'s cross country meet or his visit to SouledOut Community Church. Was I going to regret this?

Still, I followed him as he led the way through the gallery into the living room. Even though Philip's hair was growing back, I still wasn't used to how short it was. And the jagged scar still visible in his scalp and the cast on his broken arm had certainly taken the edge off his polished look. At least the facial bruises had faded and he didn't look so scary.

But it wasn't only the change in his appearance. Other things, too, left me not quite knowing how to react. Ever since the accident, he'd started calling me Gabby again instead of Gabrielle, the familiar over the formal, the endearing rather than the distant. And then there was the elegant dining room set that fit so beautifully in the penthouse. He'd given it up. For me.

It all made me feel a bit off balance, a feeling that stayed with me as I settled on one end of the L-shaped couch and glanced at the wraparound glass windows overlooking Lake Michigan. The view was still breathtaking, provided I didn't get too close and look down. Philip didn't sit, but paced, running a hand over the dark stubble on his head.

"Philip? What's wrong?"

"This." He picked up a business envelope from an end table and handed it to me. Then he sank onto the other section of the couch, head in his hands.

I looked at the return address: *Macromber, Fitz, and Morgan.* Sounded like a legal firm. I pulled out a single sheet of paper, unfolded it, and scanned the letter. My eyes widened. "Matty Fagan is *suing* you for breach of contract? But I just heard today— a few hours ago, in fact—that Fagan's been found *guilty* of all the charges that Internal Affairs brought against him. I mean, Mr. B told me the man was charged with fraud, intimidation, assault, illegal distribution of weapons and controlled substances—and that's *before* he got caught threatening you with a pistol in that alley! He was a rogue cop, Philip! And now he's on his way to prison. How can he *sue* you?"

Philip threw out his hands. "I don't know. I guess because I signed a loan and took his money and haven't repaid it. This was mailed"—he looked at the postmark—"last Friday."

"*Humph.* That money was probably drug money he lifted off some drug dealers anyway."

"Oh, great. Thanks a lot. Now I'm implicated in how he got the money?"

"You couldn't have known that! You thought he was legit—right?"

Philip slumped back against the cushions. "I just wanted the money quickly, didn't *want* to know where it came from." He shook his head slowly. "I've been a fool, Gabby. Unfortunately, that's not all." Philip picked up another envelope and handed it to me. "This came last week. Fenchel's making good on his threat too. You heard him—the time you took me to the office right after I got out of the hospital. *He's* suing me too."

I didn't even look at the letter. "Oh, Philip. I'm so sorry." I didn't know what else to say. We sat in silence for several minutes on opposite sides of the L-shaped couch.

Then Philip sighed. "My back's against the wall, Gabby. It's my fault, I know. The gambling—I never meant for it to get out of control. It was fun. I was good at cards. It was no big deal—you know, you lose some, you win some. You come out about even. But I kept raising the stakes, just for the thrill of it, and then I lost a big one. At first I didn't worry, I'd just keep playing and win big. But I didn't. Still couldn't quit, just got more desperate. Kept digging myself deeper into a hole. Maxed out my own bank accounts, decided to borrow from the business." He shook his head. "Didn't think I was really doing anything wrong. After all, half the business belongs to me, right? And besides, once I won, I'd pay everything back. No big deal . . ."

He sank into another silence. I didn't say anything. Didn't know what to say, though Philip hadn't been this honest with me since I didn't know how long. Months. Maybe years. I didn't want to break the spell.

He made a funny sound in his throat, almost a bitter laugh. "*Huh*. Actually felt some hope yesterday after talking with Harry Bentley. Have to admit, I misjudged the man. Hard to think of him as anything but the doorman downstairs. But as you know, the guy saved my butt a few weeks ago—at least saved me from getting my knees shot out. Still . . ." He fell into that silence again, as if he wasn't quite aware that he'd quit talking, as if his thoughts had taken over the conversation.

"You said you felt some hope yesterday?" I prodded.

"Right. Bentley gave me a ride home from the Baxters. We'd been there all afternoon, the boys wanted to . . . anyway, he came all the way up to the penthouse with me. I think he was taking that threat from Fagan's people seriously—I noticed he was wearing his service revolver under his coat. When we got up here, he said he wanted to talk to me about something, so I said okay. But he kind of surprised me, started talking about himself, how things got real tough in the police force and he started drinking. The drinking got so bad, he lost his wife, lost his kid, almost got tossed from the force. Finally admitted to himself he was an alcoholic—an addict, you know. What saved his hide—those are his words"—Philip let slip a small smile—"was going to AA, admitting he had a problem, and having someone hold him accountable."

Harry, an alcoholic? I'd never seen him drink anything stronger than a soda. But if that's why he lost his family, that would explain why he didn't even know he had a grandson till recently.

"Said he almost fell off the wagon not long ago—guess he's had some serious problems with his eyes and he was scared."

Harry was telling Philip this? Of course I knew about his eye problems, but Estelle never said anything about Harry *drinking*.

"I guess he still goes to AA meetings from time to time, but he said he ended up telling 'the brothers' in his men's group—his words again—when he was tempted to turn back to the bottle. I think Denny Baxter is one of the guys in this Bible study, or whatever it is. He said they prayed with him about it and held him accountable, just like his AA sponsor."

Philip took a deep breath and blew it out. "Anyway, he said he was telling me all this to say he knows an addict when he sees one. He got pretty blunt, told me as far as he's concerned, I'm a gambling addict and I need to go to Gamblers Anonymous. And he'd be my sponsor if I wanted one."

Now my mouth fell open. I could hardly believe what I was hearing! With everything Harry Bentley knew about my jerk husband, about how he'd treated me, about his annoying arrogance and selfish ambition . . . Harry had offered to be Philip's *sponsor* if he'd go to Gamblers Anonymous?

Philip looked at me sideways, obviously embarrassed. "I don't think your Mr. Bentley said that because he's fond of me—though he's been decent enough whenever we've been in the same room. He even played Monopoly with me and the boys yesterday. Vicious player, though. Still, I think he talked to me and made that offer because he cares about you. And the boys."

I had to blink quickly to keep the tears back. Finally found my voice. "You said you felt hopeful after talking to Harry?"

My husband nodded. "Yeah. Guess . . . guess it sounded like a place to start, going to GA or whatever they call it. And when Bentley said he was willing to put himself on the line by being my sponsor, someone I could talk to, well, crazy as it sounds, I felt hopeful for the first time since this whole mess started to unravel." He shook his head. "But . . ."

Silence swallowed his words again.

"But, what?"

He didn't answer.

"Philip?"

Philip finally looked at me, his eyes tortured. He pointed to the two envelopes laying on the couch cushions between us. "That was yesterday—before I got those. I don't know what I'm going to do, Gabby. They'll ruin me."

chapter 26

An awkward silence stretched between us, filled only by the ticking of the heirloom clock in the corner. What could I say? I certainly didn't have any answers. Part of me felt bad for him—it was hard to see him hurting so much—and part of me felt vindicated. Served him right. He'd screwed up my life and my plans—now his life was screwed up. But everything I thought of saying—*"You're the one who got yourself into this mess!"* or *"It'll work out somehow, Philip"*—sounded either unkind or pathetic.

The grandfather clock chimed six times. I stood up and reached for my jacket. "Philip, I'm so sorry this is happening. And unfortunately, I've got to go. I still have to make supper for the boys. Do you have anything to eat? You should eat."

Philip was still leaning forward, forearms on his knees, hands clasped, staring at the floor. He didn't look at me, just nodded. "I know. You need to go. I'm okay. Got some leftovers in the fridge." His voice was low, barely audible.

"All right. Take care. I'll, uh, call you tomorrow, okay?"

He nodded.

But when I got to the front door, I hesitated. Philip was crying out for help. True, I didn't have any answers. But when I had come to the end of my rope and cried out for help, my friends at Manna House had taken my case before the Almighty and prayed on my behalf, even before I knew how to pray.

Couldn't I do at least that much for Philip?

I turned and went back into the living room. Suddenly I felt a deep well of compassion for this man who had been my husband for sixteen years—some of them good years—and who was still the father of my sons. Reaching out, I touched him on the shoulder. "Philip?"

Startled, his head turned and he looked up at me with those dark eyes, so full of despair.

"I . . . I know this is going to sound super-spiritual or something, but . . . I'd like to pray for you. God has answered some desperate prayers from me and turned things around when I didn't see any way to go."

He looked away. I waited, but expected any moment to hear him say, *"That's okay. Thanks, anyway, but I'll be all right."* But he didn't say anything. And after a few long moments, he nodded.

He was going to let me pray? I was so surprised, my mouth suddenly felt full of dry cotton. But I sank down on the arm of the couch, swallowed, and took a deep breath. "Dear God . . ." The words came out all hoarse and whispery. I cleared my throat and tried again. "Dear God, Philip is hurting right now. He's made some big mistakes and now he doesn't know which way to turn. Lord, I'm asking You to give him some wisdom—wisdom that comes from You. That verse in Proverbs says that if we trust in You instead of our own understanding about things, You will show us the right path. So I'm praying for Philip right now, that he will trust You to show him the way, and that You will answer our prayer. Amen."

Only then did I realize I'd left my hand touching his shoulder during the prayer. I withdrew my hand, slid off the arm of the couch, and started once more for the gallery. Behind me I heard him murmur, "Thanks, Gabby," but without replying I slipped out the front door and closed it behind me.

Dandy wiggled all over when I brought him to work the next morning to spend time with Lucy, so I left the two buddies together and went downstairs, eager to talk to Estelle, who'd come in early to care for any needs Lucy might have. "Heard you and Harry had lunch with Philip and the boys at the Baxters' on Sunday!" I blurted, leaning on the kitchen counter. I didn't say so, but I was presuming she hadn't broken off her engagement with Harry over the weekend if they'd had Sunday dinner together at the Baxters'.

"Mm-hm." She handed me a potato peeler, a potato, and one of the ugly kitchen hairnets. Estelle believed in putting people to work who wanted to talk to her while she was cooking in the Manna House kitchen. "Harry and I moved Leroy into the nursing home on Saturday, so Jodi figured neither of us had any time to cook. I appreciated it. Sure did."

"Oh, Estelle! I'm sorry, I didn't even ask about Leroy yesterday. I was so rattled about getting Lucy to the doctor and finding a place for her to stay while her ankle heals that—"

"Stop, Gabby." Estelle held up the big knife she was using to chop potatoes. "We all got stuff goin' on. It's all right. Leroy's in a safe place for now. Insurance will pay for a month. Then we'll have to figure something else out."

Huh. Maybe I better keep on praying that "something else" wouldn't mean something foolish like giving Harry his ring back. "Did, um . . . did Harry tell you about his talk with Philip when he drove him back to the penthouse Sunday evening?"

"Mm-hm." She glared at me. "Are you going to peel that potato or not?"

"Oh, right." I peeled furiously for thirty seconds. "Did he really offer to be Philip's sponsor if Philip started going to GA?"

"That's what he said." Estelle handed me a couple more potatoes. "But if that's what you're concerned about, you should just call Harry and talk to him directly." Then she eyed me. "How did you know that? Did Philip tell you?"

I nodded. "He said Mr. B talked to him straight about his gambling addiction, just like alcohol or drugs or anything else."

"Hm. Surprised he told you. Maybe he's serious about dealing with it."

"Yeah, surprised me too. He said it made him hopeful—but that lasted about two seconds." I told her about the letter that had arrived Monday notifying Philip he was being sued by Matty Fagan—loan shark, crook, and felon. "And that's the second one. His business partner is suing him too. Philip was a basket case last night, Estelle! I had no idea what to say to him. He's caught like a fly in a spider web. But—I did pray with him."

Estelle's chopping knife stopped in midair, a smile spreading on her face. "You go, girl! That's the *only* thing goin' to give that man some hope, if he just give the whole mess to

God—including his own messed-up self—and let God work a few miracles."

She pushed a bag of potatoes across the counter to me, but I pushed it back, along with the peeler. "I need to get back to work. We're trying to expand the afterschool program, starting next week. Got a few interns from some of the city colleges looking for work. But I've only got a week to pull it together."

I took off the hairnet and started to leave—then turned back. "Oh! Lucy's birthday. I was thinking—we *could* do a lunchtime thing on Friday here at Manna House like we sometimes do. But if we did something Friday evening or over the weekend, maybe some other folks would be able to come, we could make it a real big deal. A surprise. But either way, would you be willing to make a banana cake?"

Expanding the afterschool program wasn't the only thing hanging over my head. Shawanda Dixon and Celia Jones were supposed to move into the House of Hope this weekend, and neither one of them had any household furnishings. I spent the rest of the day sending out urgent e-mails to the list of churches that supported Manna House financially and the many volunteers who cooked suppers and donated supplies, attaching a list of household items ranging from bedroom furniture and bedding to pots and pans and dishes. Hopefully we'd collect the essentials, at least.

For some reason, I'd totally forgotten this was the last day of October—Halloween. Trick-or-treaters were already out in full force when I dragged myself wearily up the steps of the six-flat after work with Paul and Dandy. Tanya and Sammy were set up in the foyer with bags of candy to give out, both of them dressed in black tights, turtlenecks, and construction paper pointy ears to look—sort of—like black cats.

I thought P.J. would be home already now that cross country practice was over, but the apartment was empty. No book bag, no note. Nothing to indicate he'd been home and gone out somewhere. *Huh.* Should've talked about new expectations before this. Well, we'd do it tonight. And maybe it was time to get P.J. a cell phone so I could contact him—something I'd been putting off until it was absolutely necessary.

Paul had just taken Dandy outside for a short run when I realized the light was blinking on the answering machine. *Oh, good. Maybe P.J. had left a message.* But the caller ID on the handset said *Philip Fairbanks.* Oh dear. I'd said I'd call him today—but frankly, I still didn't know what to say. I hoped he wasn't upset that I hadn't called yet. Only one way to find out.

I pushed Play. *"Hi, Gabby. Just want you to know P.J.'s here. He showed up after school, but I didn't want you to worry. Will Nissan will bring him home by six. Also, wanted to let you know that I'm giving up the penthouse. Talked to Martin today, should work out. He has some foreign guy—Japanese, I think—doing business in Chicago for a few months who wants to sublet. Guy wants it this weekend. But I also talked to my lawyer today. If I can get the money to pay off my loans, I might be able to avoid these lawsuits. I have an idea, but—well, guess you can pray it works out. All right, talk to you later."* Click.

What? I pushed Play and listened to Philip's message again. How did P.J. get all the way up to Richmond Towers? Bus or El, probably. He just hadn't ever done that before. And what was Will

Nissan doing there again? He and Philip sure were getting tight. Nice kid, but—

Wait a minute. *Will Nissan. He's* the one who said something about someone—his Great-Aunt Cindy, I remembered—running away when she was a teenager! So Lucy wasn't the only one back then who struck out on her own, before they had shelters like Manna House. I shuddered. Wonder what happened to his great-aunt? At least Lucy survived—but there were probably a lot who didn't.

I headed down the hall toward the kitchen, my thoughts returning to Philip's phone message. *Well, good riddance to the penthouse.* I was surprised Philip kept it as long as he had. He could find a decent one-bedroom for a fraction of what the penthouse cost! Maybe a two-bedroom, since he'd need room for the boys.

I pulled a frozen pizza from the refrigerator. Didn't feel like cooking tonight. Besides, I was gone all weekend and didn't have time to shop. Well, I'd tell Philip he was making a good decision to cut his expenses. A step in the right direction. But what did he mean about avoiding the lawsuits if he could pay off the loans? Where would he get the money to—?

The house phone was ringing at the other end of the apartment. I sprinted back down the hall and snatched it up. "Gabby here."

"Hey. How's my favorite redhead? You sound out of breath."

My heart tripped a beat and I leaned weakly against the wall. *Lee Boyer.* "I really need an extension in the kitchen, that's what. Um, how are you?"

"Missing you. But I'm wondering if I could fix that. Are you free Friday evening? I found a new Thai restaurant I'd like to try, but I don't like eating out alone. Don't like eating alone, period."

My mouth went dry. A night out with Lee sounded like so much fun. But we hadn't talked about where things stood with "us" since he'd walked away from our relationship that day in the hospital after Philip got hurt. Now he was acting as if it never happened.

"Gabby? You there?"

"Oh. I'm sorry, Lee, just . . . checking my calendar." I squeezed my eyes shut and tried to think about the upcoming weekend. *First weekend in November . . . Lucy's birthday, which we haven't planned yet . . . Shawanda and Celia moving in . . . and seems like there's something else.* I scooted down the hall and eyeballed the wall calendar in the kitchen. I'd written *HOH potluck* on Saturday evening. Oh, right. We'd decided to have a House of Hope potluck the first Saturday of each month. "Um, it doesn't look good, Lee." *Drat.* "We're celebrating Lucy's birthday on Friday evening, a couple of moms and their kids are moving in on Saturday, and that night we're having a potluck meal here for the House of Hope residents."

He barely skipped a beat. "How about Sunday, then? Sounds like you could use some time away from all those high-octane activities. We'll be low key, I promise."

Stop being a wimp, Gabby Fairbanks. Be straight with the man. "Uh, Lee. Dinner sounds wonderful. But to tell you the truth, I feel a little awkward going out on a date. Remember what happened at the hospital? You were forcing me to choose between you and Philip at an impossible moment. Then you walked out of my life like a movie rolling the last credits, and now suddenly, here you are again in the middle of the movie, as if nothing ever happened."

Lee cleared his throat. "Point well taken. What do you say we talk about it—over dinner on Sunday?"

chapter 27

Why I said yes to Lee for Sunday, I wasn't sure. Except . . . I wanted to. It would be something to look forward to after a busy, work-related weekend. And he agreed to talk. That was important. I was tired of playing games, juggling the relationships in my life like so many slippery balls.

P.J. shrugged when I asked why he'd gone to his father's place after school. "Just wanted to see if he was okay. You know, those threats and stuff. He's my dad, Mom! I was glad Will came by to check on him too. Dad shouldn't be living by himself!" P.J. threw his arms out, his eyes angry. "I just wish—never mind. I got homework to do." He grabbed his backpack and headed for his bedroom.

I didn't ask what he wished. Was pretty sure I knew, and I didn't want to get into a discussion about his dad and me—though I wondered if he'd been as worried about me after his dad kicked me out and took the boys to Virginia. But I shook off the thought and followed P.J. to his room. "Okay, I understand. You were worried about your dad. But I was worried about *you*. I didn't know where you were. So let's get this straight. Cross country's over. Lacrosse doesn't start till spring. We need to come up with a new afterschool plan. You want to try out for basketball? A school club?"

He shrugged again. "Not really. Can we talk about this later? I got, you know, work to do." He dumped out his schoolbooks and flopped on the bed.

I waited one second . . . two. "All right. But for now you've got two options. Either come right home from school and call me when you get here, or call me to let me know your plans and where you'll be. Agreed?"

P.J. rolled his eyes. "*Call* you? How am I supposed to—?" And then he must have seen me grinning. Because he jumped up and threw his arms around my neck. "Mom! Are you really going to get me a cell phone? Awriiiight!"

Well, I thought, as I headed for the kitchen, *that hug was worth the price of a cell phone.* Maybe I'd get an extension for the house phone while I was at it, so I didn't have to keep running down the hall to the phone table by the front door—like now, because the phone was ringing. Again.

"Hi, Mrs. Fairbanks. It's Josh. I was wondering—"

"My mother-in-law isn't here, Josh."

"Your who? Oh, right. I get it." Josh Baxter laughed nervously. "All right, start over. Hi, Miss Gabby. Josh here. I was wondering if you'd like to come up to 2A and see how the work's coming along. To tell you the truth, I could use some help painting, and I was wondering if there's any chance we could put everyone to work tomorrow evening instead of having our household meeting."

"I think that's a great idea, Josh. We've all got the evening carved out of our schedules anyway. There are a few things we need to talk about, but I think we can put in a couple hours of painting and do that too. Do you want to call Precious and Tanya, or should I?"

I shanghaied both my sons to our "painting party" Wednesday evening, telling them they needed to get their homework done before supper—sweetening the deal by presenting P.J. with the promised cell phone. Pregnant Sabrina was only too happy to babysit Gracie Baxter instead of painting, as long as she could put the toddler to bed in their apartment on the first floor and not have to haul her big tummy up to the third. However, Tanya's Sammy was not willing to be "babysat" while everyone else was having fun and begged Josh to let him help paint too.

Hm. An eight-year-old with a paintbrush? I left that one to Josh to figure out.

Josh had already painted the three bedrooms and the kitchen—nice, basic colors such as Eggshell, Robin's Egg Blue, and Summer Mist. We decided to work from six thirty to nine, and then the adults would take a half hour for "household business." At six thirty Josh had everything ready to go, putting all three boys to work on the long hallway, Precious and me on the living room, and Edesa and Tanya in the bathroom while he worked on trim.

We didn't get done by nine o'clock, but we stopped anyway and sent the boys to get themselves a snack and off to bed. "Thanks a lot, everyone," Josh said after we'd washed our brushes and rollers, tapped the lids closed on the cans of paint, and settled on the floor of the freshly painted living room in 2A. "I ought to be able to get most of the rest done before Saturday. I can finish the trim after the new ladies move in."

I'd told Mabel not to come to our meeting tonight since we were going to paint, but I suggested we ask her to come back next week since we'd have new residents, just to go over the partnership with Manna House, which was handling the social services for House of Hope residents, as well as to reiterate the house rules for all concerned. "That way we're not focusing just on Shawanda and Celia, but making it clear these are the guidelines and rules for everyone." *And*, I thought, *taking the pressure off me to be the "bad guy."*

"*Humph*," Tanya sniffed. "I'm thinkin' we gonna need to go over them rules at every household meeting. At Manna House, Shawanda was always sayin', 'Since when was *that* a rule?'—like she didn't know it'd been that way ever since Adam."

After spending three days with Shawanda at the Fall Getaway, I felt what the young mother needed was a basic daily structure with some free time built in for herself, away from the kids—maybe one evening out each week, plus a couple mornings of preschool for her little ones. I'd already told Celia Jones that I'd meet with her and Shawanda to help work out housekeeping chores, schedules, and basic responsibilities of sharing an apartment—but that didn't need to be done at a household meeting where everyone else was present.

Next item of business: We'd already agreed to have a potluck supper on the first Saturday of each month. This time it would also function as a "Welcome to the House of Hope" for Shawanda and Celia. After asking who could bring what, I added, "I know it's already a busy weekend with the move and all, but I just found out it's Lucy Tucker's birthday on Friday. What would you guys think of having a birthday party here Friday night—maybe the first birthday party she's had for decades. Estelle said she'd make a banana cake."

"Why not invite her to the potluck and just add the cake?" Tanya wanted to know. "Presto! Party!"

"I know. That makes a lot of sense," I admitted. "Except that will also be our welcome meal for Shawanda and her babies and Celia and her granddaughter. I'd kind of like to do something special just for Lucy."

"*Sí*, I agree." Edesa smiled at me. "A real surprise, just for Lucy."

Precious jumped in. "Why not at Manna House, though? She can't get around that good right now anyway. Take the party to her instead of having it here."

"Well, sure, we probably could. Except—" Why was I pushing beyond the obvious? It'd be more work to have the party here. "I guess I'd like to do it someplace besides the shelter to . . . I don't know . . . to make it more personal and homey. She's been bouncing between the streets and the homeless shelter most of her life. I want more for Lucy—even at this late stage."

Tanya rolled her eyes. "It's just a *party*. Ain't gonna change Lucy's lifestyle. Once that ankle heals, she'll be right back out on the street. But"—she shrugged—"fine. I ain't got nothin' else goin' on Friday night."

Precious nodded. "Yeah. Makes for a full weekend—but no big deal. I ain't complainin'. Whatchu want me to do?"

Once we'd decided to throw the party, Precious, Tanya, and Edesa really got into it, brainstorming ideas to make it fun. Who to invite was a little sticky, since we couldn't invite all the residents at Manna House. We finally decided to ask all the residents to sign a colorful poster card, which could be presented to her the following day, but keep the actual party to staff and their families. Well, Mr. B and DaShawn weren't exactly Estelle's family *yet*, but close enough.

I was half tempted to invite Philip to the party—ha!—since Lucy had played a big role in "upsetting the apple cart" of our lives after that day in the park when I'd tripped over her in the rain and ended up bringing the bedraggled bag lady up to the penthouse. *Oh, you are so bad, Gabby*, I chastened myself. But it was kind of funny—in a weird, sad way—to remember the look on Philip's face and the dropped mouths of Henry Fenchel and his snooty wife, Mona, whom Philip had been trying to impress.

But I did call Philip on Thursday morning, just to see how he was doing and to ask if he'd had any luck apartment hunting. I got the answering machine on his house phone. No answer on his cell phone either, so I left a voice mail. Should I be concerned? I decided, *nah*, he'd probably gone into the office, which he still insisted on doing two or three times a week in spite of Henry's lawsuit—or maybe to spite Henry *because* of the lawsuit. I'd try again later.

Which I did after lunch. Still no answer on either phone. *Odd*. But it was Harry's phone call that evening that put me over the edge.

"Hey there, Firecracker. Do you happen to know where Philip is? He agreed to go with me to a GA meeting tonight, so I stopped by to pick him up—but Gomez at the desk said he hadn't seen him. Gomez called the penthouse, but no answer. He's not answering his cell phone either."

My heart thudded. "Something's happened," I whispered hoarsely. "Do you think we ought to call the police?"

"Maybe, given the threats he's been getting. But he'd have to be missing a lot longer than twelve hours for the police to take it seriously."

"I'm scared, Mr. B."

"Hey, hey, don't get worried yet. He probably just forgot—or got chicken. He'll turn up. You'll see. I'll ask Gomez to let me into the parking garage, see if his car is there. If not, he's probably just out somewhere. He's been driving with that broken arm, hasn't he?"

But I was worried. This wasn't like Philip—at least not recently. *God, please don't let Philip be hurt. Protect him, Jesus. You've started to do a work in his heart—and he needs You, Lord, whether he knows it or not!*

I wandered into P.J.'s room, where my oldest was doing home-work on his bed, plugged into his iPod. "P.J.?" I had to raise my voice to get his attention. "P.J.!"

"What?" He pulled the earbuds out and looked at me.

I sat down on the edge of his bed. "Honey, I'm trying to call your dad but haven't been able to get hold of him. Did he say anything on Monday when you were over there about going somewhere this week?"

P.J. shook his head. "Just that he was going to look for another apartment."

"Did he say anything else? Did he seem worried about work? You said he talked to his folks over the weekend and seemed upset about something."

"Yeah, but that was the weekend. He talked to Nana on Tuesday while I was there, and Dad seemed real happy then."

Philip's mother had called . . . Philip seemed real happy . . .

I suddenly felt lightheaded, as if a whirlwind had picked me up and spun me around. "Uh, P.J., do you remember whether he talked to Nana *before* or *after* he called me to let me know where you were?"

"Why would *that* matter? But . . . had to be before because he was talking to Nana when I got there and he called you later." P.J. gave me a funny look. "Is Dad okay?"

"I'm sure he is, honey. Just trying to figure out how to reach him, is all. Sorry I bothered you. You want a snack or anything?"

P.J. shook his head and stuck the earbuds into his ears. I slipped out of his room and closed the door behind me. Something Philip said in his phone message Tuesday niggled at me. Was it still on the machine? Or had I erased it?

I scurried to the house phone and pressed the Play button. *Whew*. Still there. I listened carefully—there. That part. I replayed it again: *"Also, talked to my lawyer today. If I can get the money to pay off my loans, I might be able to avoid these lawsuits. I have an idea, but— well, guess you can pray it works out."*

What idea? Pay off his loans? Get money where?

And suddenly I knew. *Marlene Fairbanks probably cashed in some stocks or something and bailed out her son.* But I had a bad feeling about it.

Just then the phone rang twelve inches from me, making me jump. I snatched up the handset, glanced at the caller ID, and pressed Talk. "Harry? Is Philip's car there?"

"No, but—"

"Then I think I know where he might be. I'm sure his mother

sent him some money, but I'm guessing he hasn't used it to pay down his debts."

"I know."

"What do you mean, *you know*?"

"Philip just called me five minutes ago. He's down at the Horseshoe Casino in Indiana. That much money was just too big a temptation. He's already lost some of it—so he called, sounding desperate, asking if I'd come drag him out of there before he loses it all."

Having my suspicion confirmed sent me over the edge. "He's at the *Horseshoe*? The spineless jerk! I don't believe this!"

"Gabby girl, wait. This is good. Yeah, he went to the Horseshoe. But he called me. Don't you realize what a big deal that is?"

"No. Well, maybe. I don't know. I guess. But if he realizes what he's doing, why doesn't he just leave? He has his car."

"You gotta understand addiction, Gabby. This is *huge*. He knows he doesn't have the willpower to leave on his own, so he did the next best thing. Called for help. I'm on my way to pick up Denny Baxter right now, so one of us can drive his car home. Hang in there, Firecracker. Talk to you later." *Click*.

The phone went dead in my ear.

chapter 28

I leaned against the wall, then slid to the floor, my head on my knees. My emotions ricocheted like a steel pinball—from relief that Philip wasn't lying dead in an alley somewhere, to fury that Marlene Fairbanks would just *give* her perfect-son-who-can-do-no-wrong a large wad of cash, to disgust that my oh-so-smart-husband would actually go back to the casino, thinking he'd solve his money problems with one big win. And finally, deep, aching disappointment that Philip hadn't changed after all.

Except . . . Harry said this was good. Said it was huge.

Oh God, I groaned. *I'm so confused. Are You really in control here? I'm trying to trust You, Lord, but I don't see any way out of this mess.*

I didn't even know what to pray next. Maybe I should call Jodi. This was when I needed a prayer partner—someone who knew how to pray—and if Denny was driving down to Indiana with Mr. B to pick up Philip, she had to know *something* about what was going on.

I picked up the phone—but at least I had the presence of mind to take it into my bedroom before making the call. The boys didn't need to hear me rehashing what I'd just heard from Harry Bentley. Not yet, anyway.

I woke up before my alarm Friday morning, surprised to see daylight peeking through the slats of my blinds. Ah, yes, thanks to the end of Daylight Saving Time last weekend, the sun now rose an hour earlier, and for a few more weeks before the dark days of winter set in, I could enjoy sunlight in the early morning.

But in spite of dawn's welcome light, something felt wrong. It took a moment or two before I realized what it was.

I still hadn't heard back from Harry Bentley.

Throwing back the covers, I shivered in the chilly air until I'd pulled on my cozy fleece robe and stuck my feet in a pair of slipper mocs, then padded out to the kitchen to make coffee. *Should I call Harry?* It was only ten after six—too early. But had they found Philip at the Horseshoe? Had he gambled away all his mother's money before Harry and Denny got there? Did he go home with them—or did he have just enough luck by the time they arrived that he'd changed his mind and refused, dying to try his luck again.

Dying is right.

Glancing at the clock once more, I realized I still had half an hour before I had to get the boys up. Coffee in hand, I headed for the sunroom, but on the way down the hall I realized Dandy was whining inside Paul's bedroom door, so I took him outside briefly to pee, shivering in my robe and slippers. *Yi yi yi,* it was cold this morning, sun or no sun! What were Lucy and Dandy going to do when it got even colder? I shook away the thought. Couldn't deal with the Lucy-and-Dandy Problem right now.

Back inside, I curled up on the window seat with my Bible, swathing myself in one of my mother's afghans while the geriatric furnace in the basement chugged and wheezed, attempting to summon enough heat to bring the apartment to a livable temperature. Dandy settled down on the floor with a sigh, nose on his paws.

Praying with Jodi had helped the night before—but the same troubling questions crowded into my mind again this morning. Philip had told me he was subletting the penthouse and getting a cheaper apartment, but as far as I knew, he hadn't found anything yet. That Japanese businessman was supposedly taking over the penthouse this weekend—and today was Friday! Which meant Philip would be homeless in twenty-four hours.

Homeless and broke.

Huh. I should be laughing with glee. Talk about poetic justice!

But knowing my husband was on the cusp of finding himself in the same position he'd put *me* in a few months ago didn't give me any satisfaction. I felt sad. And angry. Angry and sad.

In spite of what Harry said, Philip taking his mother's money to the casino seemed like a betrayal of all the promises he'd made in the past few weeks, all the good steps he'd taken, all the positive signs of a changed man—

"How *could* you, Philip Fairbanks?!" I hissed through gritted teeth. Only after the words were out did I realize I'd spoken aloud. I listened. *Whew.* No noise from the boys' bedrooms.

Wasn't sure why I was so upset. It wasn't like he'd used *my* money. And right now, what happened with Philip's money, or his business, or with those lawsuits, didn't affect me directly. I had my own bank account—modest, but adequate. My own apartment—not fancy, but nice enough *and* on the first floor. My own job—not very prestigious or high-paying, but work that was meaningful to me. So why . . . ?

Had I gotten my hopes up? Had I allowed for the possibility that we could *maybe* one day be a real family again? That my husband would care for me? Hold me and kiss away my tears and fears? Be a real, everyday dad for the boys—not just a weekend father? The four of us, sitting down for supper, sharing chores, planning our summer vacation, just an ordinary family, facing the ups and downs of life together?

At that, tears slid down my face and fell on the cover of my Bible. I wiped off the wet splotches. What were those verses Jodi told me to look up last night? I'd told her this whole situation with Philip made me feel like a lost cat, out in the rain, no place to go, nobody to take me in. Which made no sense, really. Maybe four months ago, when those things were literally true, but not now. And yet . . .

Shelter. She'd told me to look up the word *shelter* in my concordance at the back of my Bible and see what I found. I still had ten minutes before getting the boys up, so I flipped to the back of the Bible. A few moments later I was in Psalm 61, underlining the words of the psalmist who seemed to know exactly how I felt: "Hear my cry, O God; listen to my prayer . . . as my heart grows faint. Lead me to the rock that is higher than I. For you have been my refuge . . . I long to dwell in your tent forever and take refuge in the shelter of your wings."

"Lead me to the rock that is higher than I." I smiled. That was like the gospel song that had become "my song" the past few months,

the one that asked, *"Where do I go when the storms of life are raging?"* and answered, *"I go to the Rock!"* Yeah. But then the image changed. The psalmist said he longed to take refuge *"in the shelter of your wings."* Nice.

Psalm 91 was next: "He who dwells in the shelter of the Most High will rest in the shadow of the Almighty. I will say of the Lord, 'He is my refuge and my fortress, my God, in whom I trust.' . . . He will cover you with his feathers, and under his wings you will find refuge."

Another image of taking shelter under the wings of God. I thought about that, imagining a baby bird snuggling under the wings of its parent while those amazing, resilient feathers kept out the wind and rain and cold. Not an impersonal shelter of boards and nails, but a shelter close to the mama or daddy bird's beating heart.

As I read and reread these verses, a sense of peace soothed the ruffles in my spirit, even though all the unanswered questions were still there. God had certainly been my shelter in the past few months, in more ways than one. I just needed to flee there again when the storms came. Stay there. Rest there . . .

Oh God, my heart cried. *If only Philip could find that shelter too!*

I got the boys up, fed, and off to school before I called Harry Bentley, but I got his voice mail. *Rats.* He was probably taking DaShawn to school. I left a message for him to call me at Manna House ASAP and tried to concentrate on what I had to do that day. Two student interns were coming from one of the city colleges today to observe our bare-bones afterschool program and talk with

Carolyn about our proposed expansion and how they could plug in. I was also scheduled to meet with Shawanda Dixon and Celia Jones after lunch to talk about their move into the House of Hope tomorrow, and help them map out a workable arrangement for sharing the apartment, cooking and cleaning responsibilities, and expectations about child care and behavior issues, among other things.

And then there was Lucy's party—tonight!

It was hard not to call out, "Happy birthday, Lucy!" when I got to work, bringing Dandy with me to spend the day with her. But I pretended it was just an ordinary day, asked how the ankle was coming along, and disappeared downstairs. At least she couldn't come down to the dining room where Estelle would be making her cake. Hopefully she couldn't smell the bananas either.

I had invited most of the staff yesterday, swearing them to secrecy. Tanya and Precious were shopping for paper goods, ice cream, and punch, and decorating my apartment. Edesa and Josh were in charge of planning a few games, like a real birthday party.

But in spite of the distractions, I dived for my office phone when it rang. *Finally!* "Harry! Are you guys back? Did you find Philip? Is he—what's happening?"

"Whoa. Slow down, Firecracker." Harry's calm voice felt like a gentle hand on my shoulder, encouraging me to sit back down. "We found Philip. In fact, he was pacing back and forth in the foyer just outside that big room with all the slot machines. The moment we got there, he handed us a big roll of bills and a stack of chips— asked us to pocket the money and cash in the chips, to get them out of his hands."

"Chips? What's that mean? Did he win them?" I knew next to nothing about gambling.

"Don't think he won anything. You have to buy the poker chips and use them instead of cash. Anyway, he gave us what was left. We cashed them in, found his car, and left right away. I drove Philip's Lexus—that's a real nice ride, by the way"—Harry chuckled in my ear—"and Denny drove my RAV4 back. Philip was rattled, Gabby. It was late by the time we got to Richmond Towers, but we saw him up to the penthouse and stayed awhile to talk."

"Did he tell you he's subletting the penthouse and has to be out this weekend?"

"Yeah. He needs to pack and get out, so Denny said Philip could stay at their place for a few days, give him some time to look for an apartment. We're—"

"You're kidding. He's going to stay with Jodi and Denny Baxter?"

"Think so. He seemed open to it, for a few days anyway. He got to know them a bit last weekend while you were out of town, you know, kinda broke the ice. I tell ya, Firecracker, now's a good time to pray. The man's at the end of his rope—an' if he don't hang himself with it, he might just let God use it to pull him outta the hole he's in."

Philip and God? I wished. Mr. B sounded a lot more hopeful than I felt.

Harry didn't seem to notice that I'd gone quiet. "Look, I gotta go. I'm supposed to be gettin' a few guys together to move his stuff tomorrow. Philip said that kid, Will Nissan, volunteered to help too. But he'll need some place to store it till he finds an apartment. Baxters don't have any room." The older man's voice took on a fatherly tone. "Now, don't get too bent out of shape by this, Firecracker. You probably don't know, but I fell off the wagon not too long ago, tried to drown one of my problems with a couple hours in a bar.

Then I did what I should've done in the first place—told my Bible study brothers. See, it's what you do when you know you can't do it on your own that counts. Philip called me, remember? Keep that in mind—and keep your chin up." The line went dead.

I sat at my desk a long time, thinking about Harry's phone call. My fingers itched to pick up the phone and call Philip myself. Okay, I'd try not to get "bent out of shape," but as far as I was concerned, he had a lot of explaining to do. He was still stuck at square one with a truckload of debt and two lawsuits hanging over his head. Oh yeah, *and* a pocketful of money from his mother. So what was he going to do? How was he supposed to be a decent father to his boys while he was tangled up in this mess?

He needed a plan, and he needed it *now*.

I reached for the phone—but was interrupted by two raps on my office door, followed immediately by Shawanda sticking her head in. "Hey, Miz Gabby. Bam-Bam was fallin' apart so I put him down for his nap early. Any chance you, me, and Miz Celia could talk now 'stead of after lunch—while he sleepin'? 'Cause when he wake up, I gotta run out, get some female necessaries—"

My hand pulled back from the phone like it was a hot potato. "All right, Shawanda, if that works for Celia too. Meet you in the TV room in five minutes."

Gathering up my clipboard and notes, I shook my head at the timely interruption. Guess God knew I didn't need to be calling Philip right now. Give him a few days to pack, get out of the penthouse, and find himself an apartment. Give *myself* a few days to get "unbent" and my emotions back on *terra firma* so we could have a decent conversation.

But we *were* going to talk. No more pussyfooting around.

chapter 29

I'd already told P.J. and Paul their dad would be moving this weekend so they couldn't have their regular sleepover, but hosting Lucy's birthday party at our house helped fill the gap. I heated up some leftover chili for a quick supper while Precious drafted the boys to finish decorating with yellow and orange crepe paper streamers—though their contributions made it look like someone had TP'd the place. Paul got creative and even made a "ruff" out of crepe paper to put around Dandy's neck, which made the dog look as if he'd just escaped from the circus. Sammy couldn't stop laughing, but Dandy pranced around happily like he was the star of the show.

The "Baby Baxters" came downstairs to help, and our other guests began to arrive at six thirty so we'd all be there when Sarge showed up with Lucy a half hour later. We'd chosen our no-nonsense night manager for this task, figuring the former female army sergeant was the only one who could go nose-to-nose with Lucy if she got stubborn. What excuse she was going to use to get Lucy into her car and over here, I had no idea, but knowing Sarge,

I had no doubt she'd have Lucy at our door at seven o'clock, even if she had to carry her piggyback.

I assigned Paul to be the doorman as the stream of people arrived. "Mm-*mm!* Who's that *fine* dude Angela's got with her?" Precious murmured as our Manna House receptionist entered, laughing and coy on the arm of a slender young Asian man who seemed smitten.

"His name's Jin," I whispered. "Check him out, be sure he's worthy of our Angela." Then I hurried forward with a big smile. "Welcome, welcome!"—just as Estelle Williams swept in bearing a large, honest-to-goodness banana-shaped cake with bright yellow frosting—and still wearing her ring, I noticed—followed by a puffing Harry Bentley and his grandson, DaShawn, carrying a couple of plastic grocery bags with ice cream.

When Mabel Turner and her nephew arrived, I heard Paul shout, "Mom! Jermaine brought his keyboard! Can we play some music tonight?" The two boys disappeared into Paul's bedroom to cook up a concert.

So much for my faithful doorman.

The buzzer rang a few more times. I was excited when Delores Enriquez, the volunteer nurse who came on Wednesdays, showed up, especially since I knew she had a shift that started at eleven. And, at the last minute, Reverend Liz Handley and Stephanie Cooper, board members who also served as the shelter's case managers, squeaked in after stopping to pick up Carolyn, our former-resident-turned-volunteer who'd been handling the after-school program practically by herself.

"They're here!" Carolyn hissed, her pale, round face devoid of any makeup as usual. "Just saw Sarge's Jeep turn the corner."

She handed a small gift bag to Edesa, who was collecting gifts on the hearth in front of the gas fireplace. *Sweet*, I thought, knowing Carolyn didn't have much money.

We turned out most of the lights and tried to keep from laughing as Tanya, peeking out the sunroom windows, gave us a blow-by-blow commentary on Sarge's efforts to pry Lucy out of the car, prop her up on her crutches, and convince her of the best way to hop up the front steps of the six-flat. I was supposed to go out to the foyer when the buzzer rang and act surprised to see them—but I'd no sooner opened the foyer door when Dandy, hearing Lucy's familiar gravely voice, escaped from the apartment and darted between my legs, jumping up on his mistress and nearly knocking her over.

At which point, the birthday guests crowded into the hallway, calling out, "Happy birthday!"—though most of them were as startled as I was at the unfamiliar version of Lucy standing in front of us. Lucy's normally frowzy gray hair had been braided into a couple dozen tiny braids sticking out all over her head, and her rather stubby nails had been painted a bright fuchsia pink.

"Whatchu starin' at?" Lucy growled at the lot of us. "Hannah say she needed some practice doin' whatever she do up at that beauty salon she work at. I was just helpin' the girl out." She looked around. "So, whose party we at?" She turned an accusing glare at Sarge. "Why didn't ya tell me we was comin' to a party? I woulda wore a party dress or somethin'."

That cracked me up. Lucy in a party dress? It was easier to imagine Sarge tap-dancing in a tutu.

"It's *your* party, Lucy." I grinned. "Come on now, everybody!" And we sang the birthday song right there in the hallway, though I wasn't the only one who got a bit teary-eyed when we sang, "Happy birthday, dear Lucy . . ." because the old lady suddenly went fishing in her pockets for a big red bandana handkerchief to blow her nose.

As the song died away, Edesa and Precious ushered Lucy into the living room and sat her down in the wingback rocker, propped her wrapped foot on the hassock, and placed a construction paper crown on her head. "*Mi amiga*, you are now Queen for a Day!" Edesa declared as everyone clapped. "And now I will turn it over to my husband, Josh, still a *muchacho* at heart, who has planned some party games!"

Which was true. The first game was Pin the Tie on the Mayor. How Josh got a poster-sized photo of Mayor Daley to stick onto the painted bricks of the fireplace, I'll never know. He and Edesa had made "ties" out of construction paper, and he let the kids— Sammy, DaShawn, and Paul—go first. When one-year-old Gracie saw what fun the boys were having, she cried, "Me! Me!" and wanted to be blindfolded too. Jermaine was next and stuck the tie on the mayor's nose, to much hooting and hollering, but P.J. and Sabrina declined, both of them no doubt thinking themselves too "grown-up" for such foolishness.

Most of the adults gave it a try, but it was Mr. Bentley who won—a bag of Garrett Gourmet Caramel and Cheese Popcorn, a Chicago specialty. "Ohh," he groaned. "Who told you my weakness?"

"Don't worry, I can hep ya out with that!" Lucy smirked.

We were in the middle of playing Truth or Dare when I saw Harry answer his cell phone, then pull Josh aside and talk earnestly for a few moments. Then both men looked at me. "What?" I asked, joining them.

Harry waved his cell phone. "It's Denny Baxter about Philip's move tomorrow. We've lined up several guys from the Bible study plus that Nissan kid, so that's good. But Fairbanks checked out some storage places, and for the size he needs to store the whole kaboodle, it's mega bucks for one month minimum—"

"—and I was thinking," Josh picked up, "why not here in the basement? Should only be a week max till he finds an apartment, and there's quite a bit of room down there." He raised his eyebrows like question marks, looking like a kid asking for his allowance.

"We've already got a move going on here tomorrow. I was expecting you to help with that move, Josh."

"Don't worry, I am. Already told my dad that. But you gotta admit, Miss Celia and Shawanda don't have all that much. We can do most of it with Moby Van. I'd be glad to help move Mr. Fairbanks's stuff into the basement, once we're done here."

Truth or Dare had moved to Lucy's chair. I heard her say, "Awright, awright, guess I gotta do Truth, 'cause ain't likely I can do one o' your Dares with this bum ankle."

The other players huddled and whispered, then Precious announced, "Okay, Lucy, Truth. How old are you?"

This I had to hear! "Okay, okay," I whispered to Harry and Josh. "Tell Philip one week, max." I hustled back to the larger group.

Lucy screwed up her face and studied the ceiling as if looking for the answer. "Hm, don't know if I can rightly say. I was born in 1926. How many is that?"

"Wow!" Paul's eyes got big. "That makes you eighty years old, Miss Lucy!" He roughhoused Dandy's ears. "Whaddya think of that, Dandy? That's practically as old as you in dog years."

Everyone laughed, but Estelle held up her hands for quiet. As usual, when she wasn't wearing her big white apron and kitchen hairnet at Manna House, she was dressed in one of her handmade caftans and head wraps, this one royal blue and silver, like a moon-lit night. "Well then, this is a mighty special birthday, the big 8-0 for Miss Lucy. That means it's time for cake and ice cream, you all think?"

Because of Lucy's sprained ankle, we set up a card table for the refreshments in the living room and told Lucy to close her eyes while we brought out the banana-shaped cake, aflame with candles—not eighty, but as many as we'd been able to stick on there. When told to look, her rheumy eyes opened wide under the baggy folds of skin at the sight of the cake. "What's this? A banana cake? For me?" Her shoulders started to shake with laughter. "*Hee hee!* My mama always made me a banana cake back in the day, but never one that *looked* like a giant banana!" She threw her head back, *hee-hee-heeing* until tears ran down her cheeks.

I crawled into bed later that evening, my whole body feeling like a big smile at the success of Lucy's birthday party. While guests were still eating cake and ice cream, Paul and Jermaine had played a duet of Bach's "Jesu, Joy of Man's Desiring," which had brought tears to more than one set of eyes. Even the gifts were a big hit. Lucy's face had turned all red and mottled when she pulled out a brand-new, multicolored wool sweater that the five of us at the House of Hope had chipped in together to get her. The other gifts were just as practical—warm socks, hand cream, earmuffs, gloves. All things that could easily fit into Lucy's wire cart.

As for the banana cake, I had to admit it was scrumptious. Even Dandy got a piece. Couldn't believe there was still some left—but not enough to share with the other residents at Manna House, so Lucy had insisted it stay here. "'Less it start a fight back at the shelter." The old woman had taken my face in both hands just before she hobbled out the door. "Ain't never gonna forget this birthday, Fuzz Top. Takes me back, it does. Sometimes I wish . . ." But she didn't finish. Shaking her head she thumped out the door behind Sarge.

But even though I'd gotten to bed late, I fell out of bed the next morning when the alarm rang to be ready for Shawanda's and Celia's move into the House of Hope. So far we'd been able to collect secondhand beds, mattresses, and bedding for both adults and all three children through donations to the shelter, which Josh was able to bring over from the Manna House storeroom in Moby Van, once he'd removed all the seats. We brought up the sawhorses and large piece of plywood from the basement that I'd used for a table and set it up in the dining room of 2A, and I donated a tablecloth to cover it. The storeroom of donated items at Manna House had also coughed up an assortment of dishes, utensils, and pots and pans—even a toaster oven and small microwave—to get them started. Nothing matched, but both Celia and Shawanda seemed excited as they unpacked the boxes and put things in drawers and cupboards.

In our talk on Friday, Shawanda had wanted all three kids to share a room so she could have her own bedroom, but both Celia and I insisted that was too much responsibility for ten-year-old Keisha, especially since two-year-old Bam-Bam still woke up at night and sometimes wet the bed. Shawanda finally agreed to keep Bam-Bam in her room if three-year-old Dessa could share a room with Keisha. The girls seemed excited when they saw their beds in the same room and promptly started playing "house." Probably feeling grateful to be the one who got her own bedroom, Celia graciously offered to babysit one weekend night per week so Shawanda could go out.

The move was basically over by noon, so after saying we'd meet up again for the potluck that evening in the Baxters' apartment on the third floor, I gratefully disappeared into my apartment for a few hours of downtime before putting together the lasagna I'd planned for the potluck. A nap . . . that's what I needed.

But I'd no sooner laid down for a snooze when Paul burst into my bedroom. "Mom! The truck's here with Dad's stuff. Can we go out and help them move it in?"

My eyes flew open. I'd almost forgotten I'd agreed to let Philip store his stuff in the basement. Wished I'd had more time to think it through—but too late now for second thoughts. Oh well, it was only for a week.

"Sure, hon." Hearing both boys clatter out the back door, I peeked through the blinds. Sure enough, I could see Josh motioning directions as a U-Haul truck backed up behind the six-flat in the alley. Once the truck was in position and the doors opened, I saw Philip—his arm still in its cast—and Will Nissan, Denny Baxter, Mr. B, Peter Douglass, Carl Hickman, and an older man I didn't recognize who had a yarmulke pinned to his white hair swarm around the back of the truck and begin hauling out furniture and boxes. *Huh? A yarmulke? How did a Jewish guy end up helping Philip with his move?*

A nap seemed fruitless, so I got up and started the lasagna.

The guys worked hard, and I could hear good-natured banter and shouts as they carefully shoehorned Philip's good furniture down the narrow basement steps. I peeked out from time to time, watching the men as they laughed and talked. Was Philip connecting with these guys? It felt strange, like separate worlds bumping into each other.

Seeing they'd almost emptied the truck, I fixed a pitcher of lemonade, set out the remains of Lucy's banana cake, then opened the door and called out, "You guys want some lemonade? Cake too! Come and get it!" I didn't have to call twice. Soon all eight of them had crowded into my kitchen, downing lemonade in copious amounts and demolishing the cake.

Philip pulled me aside. "I appreciate you letting me store my stuff in the basement, Gabby. Helps a lot financially. But I'll try to get it out of here as soon as I find an apartment next week."

He seemed uneasy. Did he know I knew about his backsliding trip to the casino? The money from his mother? I had to admit it was only a gut knowledge, but I was pretty sure that's where he got it.

"It's fine, Philip. But we need to talk," I said crisply. I'd confront him about that money when we had time to get some things straight. "You need a plan."

"I know. Maybe we can talk tomorrow. I'll be staying at the Baxters' a few days."

Tomorrow. Sunday. I had a date with Lee.

"Okay. Depends on what time, though. I'm busy in the evening."

He nodded. "Okay. Monday at the latest. I'll call you—oh, hi, Will." Philip nodded at Will Nissan, who joined us. "Appreciate you coming by to help today."

"No problem, Mr. Philip. Glad to do it." The young college student turned to me, holding out his paper plate with the piece of cake. He'd taken one bite out of it. "Did you make this banana cake, Mrs. Fairbanks?"

I shook my head. "No, a friend did. It was for one of our residents at the shelter. Her eightieth birthday."

"Man, it's good! Would you mind if I took a piece to my Nana? She asked me to make her a banana cake for her last birthday, so I used a box mix, but she acted insulted. Said it wasn't anything like the banana cake her mom used to make when she was a kid."

I stared at Will. What was with that generation and banana cake? But I suddenly had a funny feeling. "Yeah, same for this lady," I said slowly. "Will, your great-aunt that went missing. What was her name again?"

"Cindy. Well, that's what Nana calls her. Her real name was Lucinda—or *is*, if she's still alive."

Goose bumps crept up my arms and down my backbone. *Lucinda* . . . that was Lucy's given name on her medical file down at the clinic! Could she be—?

chapter 30

Will wandered away while my mouth was still hanging open. *No, no. Too much like some soap opera plot.* Lucinda was doubtless a popular name back then. Still . . . Will's grandmother *and* Lucy both said their mothers made *banana cake* for their birthdays. Another coincidence?

Should I say something to Will? It might be worth checking out, asking a few more questions. But Josh Baxter had already snagged him and the two university students were talking about getting together for coffee on Chicago's Circle Campus. Maybe just as well. I needed to be careful. Didn't want to raise Will's hopes if it turned out to be another dead end.

But seeing Josh and Will together gave me an idea. That evening, while all the residents of the House of Hope gathered in Josh and Edesa's apartment for our "Welcome Potluck," I pulled Josh aside and said I had a favor to ask him. "Overheard you asking Will Nissan about getting together for coffee on campus. Anytime soon?"

"Think so. We both have classes on Tuesday. What's up?"

Josh looked hungrily at his paper plate piled high with my lasagna, Edesa's homemade burritos, seven-layer salad from apartment 1A, and some fried chicken from Celia Jones, even though we'd told the newbies they didn't need to bring anything this time since they'd just moved in.

I didn't tell him my suspicions, just asked him to get some more details about Will's long-lost great-aunt. "You know, her birth date, family name, stuff like that. Also his grandmother's first name. He always just calls her Nana."

Josh looked at me funny. "I dunno. That might be kind of weird, asking him all that personal stuff."

I smiled. "You can do it. You're one of the most diplomatic people I know, Josh. You could get me to stand on my head and think it was my idea."

He looked interested. "You can stand on your head, Miss Gabby?"

"Oh, shoo! You'll never know!" Laughing, I moved away to fill my own plate from the Baxters' kitchen counter and join the warm bodies in the front room, where Josh had wisely rolled up their bright Aztec-colored rug to accommodate the little ones who were apt to spill. It was good to see Bam-Bam sitting on Tanya's lap and Dessa's meal being supervised by Sabrina, allowing Shawanda and Celia to sit together on the couch, enjoying their full plates in relative peace. But soon the little ones—Gracie, Bam-Bam, and Dessa—were being led on a merry chase up and down the long hallway of the apartment by Celia's granddaughter, Keisha, while P.J., Paul, and Sammy huddled off by themselves on the window seats of the sunroom talking boy stuff.

I watched the noisy activity, smiling to myself. This was the House of Hope—a place to live and belong for single moms who otherwise would be homeless. But there were still two apartments to go before we had a full house—which meant three or four more moms plus kids. What would our potlucks be like *then*?

I wondered if Philip would come to SouledOut the next morning with Denny and Jodi, but I didn't see him when we walked into the large, open storefront-turned-church-sanctuary in the Howard Street Shopping Center. "He's looking at a couple apartments this morning," Jodi said, pulling me aside. "But be praying, Gabby. Denny and Harry plan to meet with Philip this afternoon for some man-talk. Didn't really give Philip a choice about it. I mean, Denny put it real nice, you know, a chance to brainstorm stuff about how to get out from under this gambling debt, what to do about the lawsuits, and stuff. But"—a small smile played at the corners of her mouth—"if I know Denny and Harry, they've got more up their sleeves, and don't plan on playing softball."

I stared at Jodi. "What do you mean?"

She brushed her longish brown bangs aside. "Ever since Denny had a chance to hang out with Philip and the boys last weekend while you were gone, he's been praying for a time to talk with Philip—man-to-man—about all the stuff that happened between you two. Feels like that's gotten swept under the rug ever since Philip got beat up and landed in the hospital. You know, the 'urgent' eclipsing the 'important.' And then this week, out of the blue, Harry calls up Denny to go with him to pick up Philip from the casino, and Philip's gotta move and needs a place to stay, and suddenly here he is, in our house! Denny sees it as an answer to his prayer."

I nodded slowly. "Which I couldn't imagine happening even a week ago." I was trying to process what Jodi was saying. I'd been assuming that Philip running down to the casino the first time he had money in his pocket was the ultimate bad news. But was it possible God was actually *using* it to move Philip into a place where it'd be a natural thing for Denny and Harry—two men I respected greatly—to talk to Philip? God-talk? Man-to-man talk?

The possibility so blew me away I hardly paid attention to the service that morning, letting the worship swirl around me, wrapping me in a protective cocoon that shut out everything else around me. Even the sermon, delivered by Pastor Clark in his gentle way, felt like silk threads tying up the loose ends around my cocoon. I was still in a kind of stupor on the way home from church, half praying in fits and starts, my thoughts bouncing around like popcorn, when P.J. broke into my mental jumble.

"Mom? . . . Mom! Did you hear me? You wanted to go bike riding on your birthday weekend and it rained. But it's pretty nice today. You wanna go on a bike ride somewhere?"

It took a few moments to reenter reality. Had Lee and I set a time for our date? Not really, so there should be plenty of time to go for a bike ride this afternoon and still go out with Lee this evening. I'd told Philip I wanted to talk—but it didn't sound like he was going to be available this afternoon. "Sure, kiddo.

Sounds like fun. Wanna eat lunch first or pack a picnic and eat somewhere?"

I hadn't been on my "borrowed" bike since Lee had given it to me on my birthday, so it took awhile to get used to the gears and brakes again, but by the time we were sailing down the bike path along Lake Michigan, I was enjoying the brisk wind and sun on my face and hearing the laughter and shouts of P.J. and Paul behind me. The "high" for that day was only in the fifties, but I'd dressed in warm layers and the brilliant blue sky and sunshine tempered the chill in the air.

We rode the few miles to the Lincoln Park Zoo, locked up our bikes, and ate our lunch watching the seals poke their noses up out of the surface of their pool, snuffle at their visitors, and disappear once more. We spent another hour at the zoo, mostly watching the big apes grooming each other and the smaller monkeys swinging from rope to rope in their habitat. A bag of popcorn and a couple of Slushies from one of the zoo vendors tanked us up for the ride home—this time against the wind—and we arrived back at the six-flat with tired legs, red cheeks, and cold noses. But I could tell the boys had had a good time, and hopefully they'd cut me some slack when I told them I was going out that evening while they stayed home to do their homework.

The red light was flashing on the answering machine. *Philip?* Was he ready to talk? If so, maybe I needed to cancel my date with Lee. Didn't really want to, but I was the one who'd said we needed to talk ASAP.

I waited until the boys were out of earshot before hitting Play. But it wasn't Philip. *"Hi, Gabby, it's Lee. We're still getting together this evening, right? Is seven okay? Could be a bit nippy once the sun goes down, so dress warmly. Thought we'd go to that Thai restaurant I told you about. Should be able to talk there."*

I winced. That's right. I'd told *Lee* we needed to talk too.

Argh. I didn't need "complicated." Part of me just wanted to take a good long soak in a hot bubble bath, get into my winter jammies, and chill out in front of a mushy Hallmark special with some popcorn and hot chocolate.

But another part of me felt a tingle of excitement at spending the evening with Lee. A Thai restaurant? Sounded nice. Lee always picked a place with good food. With one eye on the clock, I took a hot shower, washed and blow-dried my mane of curls, and dressed carefully in a clean pair of boot-cut jeans, a forest-green mock-turtleneck sweater and matching corduroy jacket, and a pair of comfy leather clogs. I smiled in the mirror as I hooked simple gold loops into my earlobes. Casual but not too casual. Lee would like the red-gold highlights that shone in my hair tonight—if the restaurant wasn't too dark, that is.

Strange that I hadn't heard from Philip. I'd told him I wasn't available this evening, and he'd said, *"Monday at the latest,"* so guess we were still good. I couldn't help being curious whether Denny and Harry had managed to have their man-to-man talk. It wasn't exactly the kind of thing Philip would tell me about, even if they had.

"Lord, help him to come up with a plan to get his life straightened out," I breathed as the door buzzer rattled the intercom. Shrugging into my burgundy raincoat with the cozy zip-in liner and hood, I called out, "P.J.? Paul? I'm leaving now! Josh and Edesa know you're here alone, so if you need anything, just call upstairs, okay?"

The Spoon Thai Restaurant on Western Avenue wasn't large, but it had a warm décor with lots of wood paneling, mostly pine, and bamboo trim. There were no booths, but a long wooden bench ran along each wall, facing a row of small tables on each side, each of which seated two with a chair on the side opposite the wooden bench. Another row of tables ran down the middle of the room, a round-backed wooden chair on each side. For larger parties, tables could be pushed together.

The lighting was neither bright nor dim, just pleasant. The restaurant was populated but not overly crowded, and Lee chose a table beside the front window. He looked good—smooth shaven, a hint of a woodsy aftershave, and wearing a cream-colored cable-knit cotton sweater over a pair of jeans with a light-blue shirt collar sticking out of the neck. His round wire rims and shock of brown hair falling over half his forehead gave him the same boyish look that had captivated me the day I'd first met him in the Legal Aid office.

"I'm not real hungry," I said, scanning the menu. "Maybe just a couple of appetizers—got any recommendations?"

"I might do that, too, but tell you what. Why don't we each get two appetizers and share them, plus we'll get an order of fried rice. That should be plenty. Sound good?"

I smiled to myself. That's what I liked about Lee. We had the

same tastes and enjoyed keeping things simple. I ordered the vegetable egg rolls and something called Kanom Buang Yuan, which
the menu described as a "Thin omelet stuffed with shredded coco-
nut, ground peanuts, shrimp, bean sprouts, tofu, and served with
a cucumber salad."

"Ah ha. Living dangerously," he teased, then ordered Hoi
Tod—"Stir-fried mussels served with hot sauce"—and Satay
Chicken, thin slices of chicken marinated in a light curry sauce
and served with a peanut sauce and the cucumber salad. At least
the Satay was one of my favorites.

After the young Asian waiter took our order, Lee reached
across the table and took my hand. "So what's been happening at
the House of Hope since your birthday two weeks ago?"

Was it only two weeks ago? I let my hand rest in his. "Well, I took
a group of women from Manna House to Wisconsin to see the
fall colors, and Lucy sprained her ankle real bad, so we're keeping Dandy with us for a while. And two more moms and their
kids—well, one's a grandmother and granddaughter—moved into
the second-floor apartment at the House of Hope this weekend,
so that leaves only two more of the original tenants to move out
before we'll have a full house."

I deliberately avoided any mention of Philip and the lawsuits
against him, or the expensive dining room table he'd sent for my
birthday, or even the fact that he was moving out of the penthouse. "Oh, and the boys and I went for a bike ride this afternoon,
down to the Lincoln Park Zoo." I smiled at him. "Thanks again for
the loan of your sister's bike."

Lee lifted an eyebrow and returned a tolerant smile. "It's yours
if you want it, Gabby. You know that."

I slid my hand out of his and sighed. "I know that, Lee. It's just—"

"It's just that you can't take such a big gift from me right now, until we figure out what our relationship is, right?" He eyed me intensely.

I flushed. "Something like that." I took a sip of my water.

"Well, I agree. You're right, we haven't really talked since that night at the hospital when I . . . when I said some things in the heat of the moment that I didn't mean. I was just so angry that—" He stopped himself, his jaw muscles working, then laughed self-consciously. "Okay, Boyer, start over. What I'm trying to say, Gabby, is—"

The waiter appeared, arms laden with dishes. "Shrimp fried rice . . . Kanom Buang Yuan . . ." He named off each dish in his Thai-accented English as he set them down on the table between us, along with two warmed plates, a tea pot, tea cups with no handles, and extra napkins. "You like anything else? More ice water?"

Lee shook his head. "No, no, we're good. Thanks." He dished up half of the appetizers onto one of the plates and handed it to me, then served himself. "Sorry about that. Go ahead, enjoy while the food's hot. Maybe we can talk after we eat, okay?"

I nodded, and for the next half hour we kept the conversation light as we tried the different dishes. The Hoi Tod mussels with hot sauce were a bit too exotic for me, but I enjoyed everything else. As we ate, Lee said he'd had to cut his Legal Aid work back to one day a week, as new cases piled up at his firm. I filled him in on the story of how Lucy sprained her ankle—he roared at the image of our favorite bag lady pretending to be a circus tightrope walker—and described her eightieth birthday party, complete with Pin the Tie on the Mayor, which got a big chuckle from Lee.

Finally the waiter cleared away our dishes, but by now the restaurant had filled up with more patrons and the noise level had risen. "Do you—would you like to walk a bit? There's something I'd like to show you," he said. "If you won't get too cold."

"I'm fine. Got a couple of layers on here."

We put on our coats, and I pulled the hood of my raincoat over my head. Lee grabbed an umbrella from his car because the sky had clouded up and it looked like it might rain. I held on to his arm and we walked a couple of blocks south on Western and turned west on Montrose as he tried to pick up on our "talk" from earlier that evening.

"All I want to say, Gabby, is that I didn't mean to push you away that night. You were in a tough spot, and I should have been more understanding. It was overhearing your jerk of a husband asking you to forgive him that . . . well, it pushed me over the edge. The man doesn't deserve to be forgiven! What he did—"

"Lee—"

"Okay, okay. I know. Let's not talk about Philip. He's your kids' father, and for that reason alone, I guess you'll always have to deal with him. I just want you to know, Gabby, that I care for you a great deal. I behaved badly that night. But I don't want to lose you. Can you forgive *me*?"

I squeezed his arm with the hand I'd tucked into the crook of it. "Yes, of course I forgive you, Lee. And I care about you too. But it's not that simp—"

"Gabby, look." He slowed. "This is what I wanted to show you."

We had started to walk over a two-lane bridge that crossed the Chicago River. I looked around. Classic, old-fashioned streetlights lined the bridge and cast their light on clumps of trees below still clinging to their leaves. A misty fog seemed to be settling down over the river and the bridge. "It's like a fairy park!" I breathed with delight.

"It *is* a park right here. The river is narrow at this point and runs south through Homer Park before it heads through the city. It's pretty in the daytime too."

We stopped in the middle of the bridge, leaning against the decorative iron railings. I picked up what I'd been trying to say. "I do care about you, Lee. You've been a good friend and . . . and I'd like to keep being your friend. But more than that? I don't know. It's not that simple."

He tipped up my chin with a gentle finger. "Why not? You just said you care about me. And I've never met anyone quite like you." His finger traced the side of my face, my mouth . . .

Desire rose in my body like a sweet hunger. My heart was beating so fast I was sure he could feel it. But I pulled back slightly and turned my head away, watching the streetlights sparkle on the water below, trying to recover so I could say what I wanted to say. "I . . . I've got a lot of things to figure out right now, Lee. I'm still married, you know—" I heard a brief snort from Lee and knew he was probably rolling his eyes. "Let me finish, okay?"

"Okay. Sorry."

"The family thing—me, Philip, and the boys—it's complicated right now." I knew Lee didn't understand that. As far as he was concerned, divorce was the only option, the sooner the better, and I had all the cards in my favor. Scratch Philip from the picture. Done. Move on. But funny thing, Philip and I had never once talked about divorce. Maybe we would've by now, if the crisis about his gambling debts, shady loans, and physical threats hadn't overwhelmed the situation.

"But that's not all." I turned to face him. "Something new has been happening in my life, Lee. I grew up in church but let my faith drift for most of my adult life, for several reasons. But God has become an important part of my life again. Not just God, but Jesus. The whole Christian thing. Reading the Bible, praying. Church too. I need to be with other Christians so I don't drift away again." My eyes searched his face. "Can you understand that, Lee? I can't be part of a relationship where God's not the main thing—"

"Gabby . . . Gabby." Lee smiled, laugh lines crinkling beside his light brown eyes. "It's fine! It's all good. I would never stand in the way of something so personal as your faith. Just because God and I aren't on chummy terms, there's no reason why—uh-oh, here it comes!"

Large raindrops plopped onto the hood of my raincoat and the end of my nose. Lee laughed, popped open his big umbrella, and pulled me beneath its shelter, his arm holding me close. And the next thing I knew he was kissing my eyes, the tip of my wet nose, my mouth . . .

Oh, it felt so good to be wanted! *To be loved*. Letting go, I leaned into his embrace, kissing him back.

chapter 31

Oh, dear Lord, what have I done?

Lee and I barely talked on the way home. I'm sure my actions confused him, but I kept my face turned toward the passenger-side window, streaming with rain, as if the heavens were shedding the tears bottled up inside me. When we got to the six-flat, Lee didn't ask to come in, just walked me up the steps and into the foyer, brushed his lips on my cheek and murmured, "I'll call you," before darting through the rain back to his car.

I kept myself together long enough to check on the boys. Dandy didn't even raise his head when I peeked into the room, probably hoping I wouldn't notice he was lying *on* Paul's bed, not beside it. I ignored dog-on-bed and went through the motions of getting ready for bed. But later, alone in my bedroom at the back of the apartment, the sobs finally convulsed my body, wetting the pillow with a torrent of tears. *Oh God!* My heart cried out into the darkness of my room. *I just need . . . I want someone to love me! And I want someone to love! Is that so wrong? Is it that important not to be "unequally yoked," as the Bible puts it? Lee said he'd never stand in the way of my faith . . . he's kind and thoughtful . . . maybe we could make it work . . .*

As my sobs subsided, my mind started sorting through the rational possibilities. If Lee and I were a couple, maybe he'd start coming to church with me. I could be a good influence on him, bring him to God. But of course I'd have to divorce Philip first . . . give the boys time to get used to another man in my life . . .

But even as I toyed with the possibilities, I found it hard to put them into a prayer. *Argh!* Grabbing my pillow, I threw it across the room with such force it knocked something off my dresser, which fell to the floor with a crash.

Uh-oh. Turning on the lamp on the nightstand, I got out of bed, retrieved my pillow, and reached for the object on the floor.

The framed photo I'd taken from Philip's study when I'd moved my things out of the penthouse. *Philip and me on our fifth wedding anniversary, cake smudges on our noses, me tossing my halo of red-gold curls as I laughed up at him mischievously.* Unbroken.

Bringing the picture closer to the light, I gazed at it a long time. In the photo, Philip was looking at me with the same look of adoration Lee had had on his face tonight. Loving me, laughing with me, enjoying me.

I gently set the picture down on the nightstand again, turned out the light, and crawled back under the covers, clutching the pillow. My heart twisted. *Oh God, I want Philip back! I want to be a whole family again! We loved each other once—couldn't we love each other that way again?*

And then I started to laugh aloud—a mirthless laugh with no humor, my shoulders shaking at the irony of it. Even God would

have a hard time sorting through my prayers tonight. *I want Lee . . .*
I want Philip . . . Lee . . . Philip . . . I want . . . I need . . . me, me, me . . .

My mind and emotions finally wrung themselves out, and
as I drifted toward sleep, exhausted, the scripture I'd taped to the
kitchen cabinet and underlined in my Bible rose to the top of my
thoughts and wrapped itself around my confusion. *"Trust in the*
Lord with all my heart . . . don't lean on my own understanding . . . In all
my ways acknowledge Him, and He will direct my paths."

"Okay, God," I murmured into my damp and wrinkled pillow.
"Guess I don't know what I want. Or need. So I'm just gonna love
You first and trust You to figure it out."

The call from Philip came the next morning before I even left for
work. "Gabby? I need to talk to you. Any chance we could have
lunch today?"

For some reason, hearing his voice startled me. I felt like a
deer caught in the headlights. I'd had dinner with Lee last night,
and we'd kissed—and now my husband wanted to meet for lunch.
Would my double life be written all over my face?

Still, I'd told Philip we needed to talk, and he was agreeing.
"Lunch?" I grabbed the appointment book I'd been using lately to
keep my schedule from getting all snarled up. *Monday, November*
6 . . . 10:00 Staff mtg . . . 11:00 Lucy clinic checkup ankle . . .

"I'm sorry, Philip, I don't think I can do lunch. I've got a staff
meeting this morning, and then I'm supposed to take Lucy to the
clinic to check on her ankle, and it's never in-and-out at the county
hospital. Don't know how long it will take. Um, what about this

evening?" I hated to be gone from the boys two evenings in a row, but this *was* important.

"Tonight? That's later than I'd like. There are some urgent things I need to talk over with you and I was hoping—but, all right. Can you call me when you're back from the clinic in case we can get together earlier?"

"Okay, call you later." *Huh.* Later than he'd like? What could be so important that a few hours made a difference?

But my day changed when I walked into Manna House with Dandy on his leash and signed in. A sign written in magic marker was taped to the glass windows of Angela's reception cubby: "No Staff Mtg Today." I pointed to the sign. "What's up?"

The receptionist blew a stray lock of glossy black hair off her face. "Mabel's sick. Sounded like the flu. I'm glad she's staying home—*I* don't want to get sick." She grinned impishly. "Jin is taking me out to dinner tonight."

"Ah, Jin." I grinned. "I'm glad you brought him to the party the other night. He seems like a nice guy—a good sport, too, playing Josh's crazy games, even though he didn't know the rest of us."

Angela made a face and rolled her eyes. "Yeah, even when he chose Dare and they dared him to kiss a girl in the room—*knowing* he'd kiss *me*. In front of you all!"

Laughing, I pushed through the double doors into Shepherd's Fold with Dandy clicking along at my heels. As soon as he spotted Lucy propped up on one of the couches, the dog pulled the leash out of my hand and made a beeline for the old lady. I gave the dog a chance to whimper his joy and lick her face, then said, "Hey, Lucy. You have a checkup at the clinic this morning. Staff meeting just got canceled, so . . . you up for going now? We might get out of there earlier."

"*Today?* Oh, all right." Lucy sounded as if I'd asked her to down a spoonful of cod liver oil, but she struggled to get up from the soft cushions.

It took us a good twenty minutes to get Lucy into her winter coat and down the outside steps—slick with the drizzling rain that had started last night—and into my Subaru. Might've taken longer except Angela left her post and helped Lucy with the steps while I got the car. But soon we were heading south on Lake Shore Drive, the windshield wipers *thump thump*ing as they chased raindrops back and forth.

It occurred to me that Lucy was my captive audience for the next twenty minutes until we got to the clinic. If there was any connection between this elderly street person and Will's grandmother, now would be the time to fish for it. "You still sleeping on the couch in Shepherd's Fold?" I asked, wanting to get her talking.

"Nah. A bed came up empty so I been goin' up an' down that box they call an elevator. Ain't so bad once I got used to it. But if it ever stops 'tween floors? I'm gonna yell bloody murder so loud they gonna hear me clear down at city hall."

I chuckled. "Don't blame you. Glad you got a bed. Have you been able to put any weight on that foot yet?"

"Yeah, some. Sure will be glad to get rid o' them crutches. What a pain! Worse'n the ankle."

"Well, here's hoping the doctors agree." I drove a few more minutes, the *thump, thump, thump* of the wipers and the warmth of the heaters creating a cozy cocoon in the car. Then I subtly shifted conversational gears. "Did you ever twist your ankle or break a bone when you were a kid?"

"Oh sure. Lotsa times. Sprained my ankle, I mean. Never broke anything. But I was always climbin' trees an' jumpin' creeks an' stuff. My ma said I was a bad influence on the other kids, 'cause I was the oldest an' the younger ones was always wantin' ta do what I did."

Oh my goodness. What a perfect segue. "You have many other brothers and sisters?"

"Ha. Too many, if ya ask me. But that's the way it was with migrant families—we needed all the hep we could get pickin', so had to grow 'em ourselves. Leastwise, that's what my paw used ta say."

I was so excited the speedometer had crept upward without me realizing it. *Whoa, slow down, Gabby.* Didn't want an accident. The Drive was slick with rain. Tapping the brake, I let the needle fall below the speed limit. "So tell me some of their names."

"Well, lessee. Maggie was next ta me, then came Tom an' Willy an' George, one after t'other . . ." She drifted into a silence.

"So there were five of you?" I prompted.

She shook her head. "Nah. My ma got sick an' lost a few—two, I think. But then came the babies. Betty an' John, I think." She wagged her head. "Not real sure about them last two. I left home when they was real small." Her voice faded. "Been a long time now."

Seven kids. Whew. I needed to tread carefully here. "Have you been in touch with any of your family? Your, um, next closest sister, for instance?"

"Who, Maggie? Nah. I knew she'd be mad at me fer leavin',

'cause she'd hafta to pick up all the chores an' stuff families put on the oldest kid. Can't blame her. But I had to leave. Had my reasons."

By this time, I'd turned off the Drive and was headed west on the Eisenhower Expressway. But our exit was coming up fast. *"Had to leave?"* I glanced at Lucy in the passenger seat. "Thought you told my mother you ran off with a boy."

"Yeah, well, I did. But let's just say it was complicated. Besides, when them two babies came, it was jus' too many mouths ta feed. None o' the rest of them was old enough ta fend for themselves. Had to be me."

I was so astonished at this bit of news, I almost missed our exit, but I made it up the ramp at the last minute.

Lucy had left home so her family would have one less mouth to feed?

I could hardly breathe. From what Will had shared, it sounded as if the rest of the kids had done all right. At least his grand-mother had gotten married and raised a family, and *her* daughter had married and raised a family—including a brilliant young man named Will who was going to college at the University of Illinois Circle Campus, studying architecture and business.

If Lucy was his grandmother's long-lost sister, that is. Could all be just a coincidence. I'd know better after Josh got together with Will this week.

We only had to wait an hour before Lucy's name was called this time. Her ankle was plenty black and blue when the young intern unwrapped it, but after gently manipulating the foot, he said the ankle was coming along nicely and told Lucy she could begin to put weight on her foot, whatever she could tolerate. "But keep those crutches awhile longer and use them when you need to," the doctor advised.

He replaced the elastic bandage with a padded air cast—all plastic and Velcro—and gave Lucy an appointment card for next week.

We were back at Manna House by twelve. When I realized we'd be back a lot sooner than I'd anticipated, I called Philip on his cell and said I could do lunch after all. Did he want me to pick up some takeout and meet him at the penthouse?

Philip gave a short laugh. "Uh, a certain Japanese businessman might be surprised if you walked into the penthouse today. I'm staying at the Baxters', remember?"

Duh. Of course. "Right. Just slipped my mind for a minute."

"But I'm actually downtown right now—had a doctor's appointment today and, uh; some other business. I've got my car, so let's meet somewhere. You name it, I'll be there. Someplace we can talk, okay? And thanks. I appreciate you making it earlier, Gabby."

We agreed to meet at Baker's Square on Western Avenue at one thirty. The lunch crowd probably would've thinned by then and they had booths—they'd be fairly private.

I signed Lucy in, took Dandy out for a short walk in the relentless drizzle so he could do his "business," apologized to Estelle for skipping out on lunch without advance warning, and signed myself out again.

But at the last minute, I scribbled a note, ran it back downstairs to the dining room, and handed it to Estelle. The note said: *Pray, okay? Philip wants to talk. He needs a plan NOW. Hope that's what this is about!*

chapter 32

Philip's Lexus was already there when I pulled into the wet parking lot at Baker's Square—and it was only one twenty. The old feeling of being "a day late and a dollar short" no matter what I did got my defenses up, but Philip smiled a greeting when I slid into the booth. "Looks like we're both early. I just got here."

Okay, Gabby, back off, start over, cool your jets.

We ordered quickly—a chicken fajita for Philip and Asian chicken salad for me—then faced each other across the Formica-topped table with hot cups of coffee. Two creams each. Had Philip and I always doctored our coffee the same way? I looked him over, puzzled. Something was different about Philip today. His hair? It'd grown back almost an inch, the same dark brown like fresh-roasted coffee, and nearly covered the long scar in his scalp, but I'd already noticed that two days ago when he was moving stuff into my basement. Something else—

"Your arm!" I pointed, eyes wide. "You got the cast off!"

Philip grinned and moved his right arm this way and that. "Yep. This morning. I think maybe this is what Pinocchio felt like turning from a puppet into a real boy—except my arm still feels kind of wooden. Might need some physical therapy."

"I'm glad. You're starting to look like a real person again." *Ouch. What a stupid thing to say.*

But Philip just nodded. "I'm starting to *feel* like a real person again—but not just because of getting the cast off." He leaned forward, arms on the table, his brow suddenly wrinkled in serious concentration. "Gabby, you said I needed to come up with a plan, to stop flailing about like some rag doll caught in the washing machine."

I allowed a grin. "Well, at least the part about coming up with a plan."

"But you were right." He sat back against the padded booth, drew in a deep breath, and blew it out again. "I've decided to take Henry Fenchel up on his offer. To buy me out of the company, I mean."

I nearly spilled my coffee. "You're serious?" Of all the plans I'd imagined, I never thought Philip would consider giving up the company he'd started.

"Dead serious. In fact, that's where I went after my doctor's appointment today. Told Henry if he'd withdraw his lawsuit, he could buy me out, take my name off the door, the whole kaboodle. It'll take several days to draw up the papers, but then it'll be a done deal."

"But . . . when . . . why . . . how did you . . . ?" I hardly knew what to ask.

"Okay, to be honest, I had some help thinking things through," he admitted. "You know I'm staying at the Baxters' a few days until I can find an apartment. Had some time to talk to Denny this weekend—yesterday, as a matter of fact. He and, uh, our mutual friend, Harry Bentley." Philip shrugged. "Figured he'd earned a right to mess with my business after saving my skin that Sunday when Fagan caught me in the alley."

I said nothing, not trusting myself to speak.

"Anyway, they asked me what I thought my options were. Have to admit most of my options sounded rather far-fetched, but I did mention Fenchel had offered to drop his lawsuit if I let him buy out my half of the business—along with half a dozen reasons why I wouldn't even consider it. But Baxter asked me to imagine what would happen if I pursued each of my various options—even the buyout. So, okay, I thought, I'll play along. But as I imagined the implications of accepting Henry's offer, I realized it made a lot of sense! With the buyout, even after paying back the money I owed the company—with interest—I'd have enough to pay off Fagan, which would take care of both major debts. Done. Fagan's lawsuit goes away. No more threats. I'd have a nest egg to rent an apartment and pay my bills until . . ." He spread out his hands. ". . . well, until I figure out what I'm going to do next, I guess."

Our food arrived, and we were busy for the next several minutes getting fresh coffee, extra butter for the hot bread that came with the salad, water refills. Then came that awkward moment. *Dig in? Bless the food? Silent prayer?* But Philip arched an eyebrow at me. "Do you, uh, want to say a table grace or something?"

Surprised, I nodded. What was going on here? Was Philip buttering me up or something, being so agreeable? But I bowed my head and kept it simple. "Father, thank You for Your goodness to us today. Thanks for the food and for Philip's amazing news. Amen."

"Nice," he murmured before taking a dripping bite of his fat fajita.

We ate in silence for several minutes, then I cleared my throat. "Have to admit I never expected you to let Henry buy you out, Philip. But it sounds like a good plan. Makes a lot of sense, clears away a lot of the mess you've gotten yourself into. Lets you start over. I just . . . just want to say I'm sorry it turned out this way. You had a dream, it was a good dream, and you're good at what you do. I wish it had worked out for you."

Philip seemed to have trouble swallowing. But he murmured, "Thanks, Gabby. That means a lot."

I leaned forward and searched his face. "But I do have a few questions. The money you took down to the casino last week—where did it come from? Was it a loan from your parents? A gift? And what are you going to do with it once Henry buys you out?"

Philip sighed and took a sip of his water. "So you know about that. I—"

"Don't know. Just a guess."

"Oh. Well, good guess." His mouth twisted slightly. "My mother gave it to me as a bridge. Wasn't a loan. Don't know where she got it—savings, cashed in some stocks, whatever. But I shouldn't have taken it. I'm pretty sure she did it behind my father's back. And I'm tired of that game, Gabby. I don't want her money. But until I get an actual check from Fenchel, I guess I'll need to use it to line up an apartment and buy a plane ticket, but then I'm going to pay it back. All of it."

It took a moment for what he said to sink in. "Did you say a plane ticket?"

He nodded. "As soon as I wrap up this buyout with Fenchel,

I'm going back to Petersburg to consult with my father. I talked to him on the phone last night . . . had to eat crow, listen to a lot of 'I told you so,' as you can imagine. But I told him I'm selling out, going to make a fresh start. And he's agreed to meet with me and help me think through what I'm going to do next. Map out a new business plan, so to speak." Philip's wry expression seemed to have become a permanent fixture. "I think that was going to be your next question: 'What are you going to do for a job?' Right?"

I nodded and looked down at my half-eaten salad. I pushed it away, suddenly not hungry anymore. I could hardly wrap my mind around the things Philip was saying—selling out his interest in the commercial development company he'd started, paying his mother back for the money she'd given him, actually going back to Virginia to face his father . . .

On one hand, I felt a huge relief. He'd come up with a real plan for untangling the mess he'd gotten himself into.

But . . . not a word about us.

"The boys will miss you," I murmured, avoiding his eyes. "How long will you be gone?"

"I don't know. A week, maybe two. I need to get away, put some distance between myself and too-easy access to the Horseshoe. Bentley made me promise I'd check into a GA group the same day I arrive. I'm guessing he'll be checking on me."

I nodded, still not able to face him. "Okay. Just keep us posted, I guess. Me and the boys."

Digging into my purse, I brought out a couple of fives to cover my salad and coffee and started to slide out of the booth with my jacket, but felt Philip's hand reach out and grab my arm.

"Gabby, wait. There's something else I need to talk to you about. It's important. Please?"

I stopped, his hand holding me back. After two long seconds I slid back into the booth, set down my jacket and purse, and finally looked up without saying anything.

"This isn't the place, but"—he tipped his chin toward the foggy windows of the restaurant—"it's not exactly a great day to walk and talk outside. So I, uh, wrote you a letter." Philip reached inside his sport coat and drew out a long envelope. "This is actually what I wanted to talk to you about, but I realized you wouldn't be able to hear it until I'd made some practical plans to deal with, well, the whole gambling debt mess. I'm sorry to say the consequences of that have overshadowed everything else that's important. Like our marriage. You and me. Our family. The boys." He slid the envelope toward me. "Will you read it before you go?"

I looked at the envelope for several long moments before putting out a tentative finger and drawing it toward me. But I didn't pick it up. Probably a divorce notice. Or a legal separation. What else would he put in an envelope? I shook my head, my heart thumping, loose curls sticking to my damp forehead. "I . . . I'll take it with me and read it later." I picked it up and stuffed it into my purse, once again gathering my things.

Philip reached out his hand again. "Gabby, *please*. Read it now, because there are some things I need to say after you read it." He glanced around. "We're pretty much alone now."

Breathe, Gabby, breathe. Reluctantly I took the envelope out of my purse, lifted the flap, and slid out the single sheet of folded paper.

"More coffee?" The waitress stood over us with a full pot. She must have sensed the unfinished conversation hanging in the air. "Don't worry, take your time."

I licked my dry lips. "Yes, coffee, please." I waited until my cup was full, opened two more of the individual creamers and poured them in, then took a long sip of the hot liquid before unfolding the sheet of paper.

Dear Gabby,

I hardly know how to begin, there's so much I need to say. But the first thing is . . . I'm sorry. Sorry for the pain I've caused you. Sorry for kicking you out of the house. Sorry for everything. I thought I had good reasons, thought you needed a wake-up call—but I'm just now beginning to see that it was all about me. What I wanted. What I thought I needed. We were going in different directions and needed help to get our marriage back on track. But I took matters into my own hands.

I was wrong.

The paper in my hand shook, and my other hand gripped the edge of the table with white-knuckled fingers. I took a deep breath to steady myself and kept reading.

I don't know if you can forgive me. I've hurt you deeply, I know that. I hope you can—but even then I don't know what that would mean. You've picked yourself up, you've moved on, you've made a new life for yourself. I don't know if there's any room in your new life for "us."

If not, I have no one to blame but myself.

Where do we go from here? I don't know. I'm only now getting a grip on how I got into such a mess—thanks to the shakedown I got yesterday from two unlikely "brothers." Still hard to admit I'm a gambling "addict." Hard to admit I ruined my own dream of making it big here in Chicago. Harder still to admit I'm the reason our marriage failed.

But it's all true. I know I need help—just not sure where to get it.

There's a lot more I need to say. Want to say. But the one thing I desperately want you to know is . . . I'm sorry.

The letter was just signed *"Philip."*

Tears stung my eyes and spilled down my cheeks. I hastily brushed them away and used a napkin to blow my nose, staring at the letter. Oh, how I'd wanted Philip to admit he was wrong! To say he was sorry for all the pain he'd caused in my life! To beg for my forgiveness!

But now that he had—in writing, no less, in black and white, in his own handwriting, with his own signature—I had no idea what to feel. Or say.

"Gabby?"

I could hear the question in his voice. But he'd had time to think about what he wanted to say. I needed time too.

Refolding the letter, I slid it back into the envelope, put it in my purse, and took a deep breath to steady my ragged breathing. "I . . . can't respond right now, Philip. I'm sorry."

Gathering my things, I slid out of the booth and started to leave. Then I hesitated—and for the first time since he'd given me the letter, I lifted my eyes and met his troubled gaze. Then I walked out of the restaurant.

chapter 33

By the time I stumbled through the rain to my car, I was a blubbery mess and wanted to sit for a while and have a good cry. But I knew Philip would come out of the restaurant any minute and see my car still sitting there, so I pulled myself together long enough to turn on the wipers and head back to the Wrigleyville North neighborhood.

There was no way I could go back to work. I'd have people in my face asking, "What's wrong? Are you okay? What happened?" and I didn't want to talk to anybody right then.

Taking advantage of a long red light, I called Manna House on my cell and told Angela I wasn't feeling well—*I wasn't! I was a wreck!*—and was going to head home. "Tell Paul when he arrives after school to go ahead and do his homework in the schoolroom with Carolyn, and I'll pick him up at five. Oh yeah, and Dandy."

"Not you too!" Angela wailed. "I hope I didn't catch anything from you this morning! Jin and I are—"

"Uh, gotta go, Angela—green light." I clicked the phone off and waved apologetically to the car behind me as I headed through the rain-soaked intersection. Fifteen minutes later I pulled up in front of the House of Hope, eager to disappear inside, make myself some hot tea, and reread Philip's letter. I had at least an hour before P.J. got home, two before I had to pick up Paul. Blessed peace and quiet.

But even before I got out my house keys, I could see several moms and kids hanging out in the hallway through the glass-paneled door of the foyer. I groaned. I'd temporarily forgotten that *none* of the House of Hope residents had day jobs—not counting my leftover tenants in 2B and 3B—and we had three preschoolers in the building, two of whom were hanging on Shawanda right now and hollering for attention.

Shawanda pulled the door open. "Didn't know you got home this early, Miss Gabby! Tanya an' me was just talkin' about this cute kitty Dessa found under the back porch this mornin'. It was all wet and shivery, poor thing."

"*My* kitty!" Dessa yelled, peeking around her mother's skinny jeans.

"We didn't talk about pets, yet, did we, Miss Gabby," Tanya said, frowning. "I'm kind of allergic—"

"But Miss Gabby's got Lucy's dog here, ain't that right?" Shawanda shot back.

A stabbing headache started at the base of my skull. "Sorry, girls," I mumbled, "I'm not feeling very well, that's why I came home. Maybe we can talk about this later." I fumbled for my house key, let myself in my apartment, and shut the door quickly behind me. *Rats.* Now Tanya would tell Precious and Precious would tell Edesa, and pretty soon I'd hear a well-meaning knock at my door, asking if I'm okay and can they do anything for me?

This community-living, everybody-knows-everybody's-business definitely had its downside.

I decided to be proactive. Pulling open the door again, I said, "I need some quiet right now, might take a nap. Headache, you know. If you girls don't mind?" They took the hint and faded into Tanya's apartment, and I was able to make a pot of hot tea and sink into my mom's wingback rocker undisturbed.

Now . . . *now* I could digest Philip's letter. At first I'd been annoyed that he'd given me a letter to read—of all things!—instead of just talking to me. But maybe I should be grateful he'd written it down rather than trying to remember what he'd said.

I pulled the envelope out of my purse and read the letter again. *". . . the one thing I desperately want you to know is—I'm sorry."* Had to admit he sounded truly remorseful. But was it enough? A general "I'm sorry" that covered everything?

A protest rose up inside me, wanting a detailed list of every offense he'd committed against me! *"I'm sorry for making you feel like your job was just a hobby, nothing important. I'm sorry for not making your mother feel welcome when you brought her here from North Dakota. I'm sorry for stealing our sons and taking them to my parents without your permission. I'm sorry for this . . . and this . . . and this . . ."* Tears and groveling wouldn't hurt either.

I scanned the letter again, pausing at the place where he owned the fact that I'd not only survived the breakup, but I'd moved on and made a new life for myself. That felt good. As for himself, he actually admitted his gambling was an addiction, that he'd ruined his chances to make a success of his business, and even admitted *he* was the reason our marriage had failed. He also confessed it was hard to admit these things, but he *did* say they were true.

Strange, he didn't directly ask me to forgive him, didn't ask if I had room in my new life for him. Rather, it was as if he'd spilled his doubts and fears onto the page. *"I don't know if you can forgive me . . . I don't know if there's any room in your new life for 'us' . . . I don't know where we go from here . . . I know I need help, I just don't know where to get it . . ."*

And there were a few other things I never thought I'd hear from Philip Fairbanks. He said he'd hurt me deeply. Said he was wrong. Said he had no one to blame but himself that our marriage had failed.

Never before in our entire life together had Philip been that vulnerable! Did it have something to do with the "shakedown" he'd mentioned from "two unlikely brothers"? What in the world had Denny and Harry said to him?

I sat in the wingback rocker a long time, staring at the letter. My tea got cold. At one point my cell phone rang—P.J., saying he was hanging out at the school gym with some friends watching girls' basketball intramurals, but he'd be home by supper. I said, "Fine," and hung up, my mind elsewhere.

Something bothered me about the letter. Something missing.

And then I realized what it was. Philip didn't say he loved me. Didn't even sign it, *"Love, Philip."*

I did get a knock at the door later that evening, but it was Maddox Campbell from 3B. "Speak to yuh, Missy?"

"Of course, Mr. Campbell." I opened the door wider and left it open, moving back a step or two so the Jamaican tenant could come in out of the hallway. The tall dark-skinned man was wearing a jean jacket and a different green-gold-and-black knitted "Rasta" tam than I'd seen before, dreadlocks hanging down his back, as if he'd just come in—or was leaving.

He pulled off the knitted tam, as if his mother had taught him to remove his hat indoors or in the presence of women, and played with it nervously. "Mi tink mi found an apartment for de t'ree of us. Mi a-go see it nex' day. But, mi wanting to be sure, no penalty if we move early? Don't want me wife an' mada getting demselves all excited if it not be workin' out."

"Yes, yes, Mr. Campbell. I put that in the letter I gave you. You may leave before the end of your lease without any penalty. When would you move?"

Now the tam seemed to spin around his nervous hands. "Well . . . if me wife an' mada like de place, maybe dis weekend—"

"This weekend!" That meant two Saturdays in a row with movers going up and down the back stairs all day—or front stairs if it was raining. And another apartment for Josh Baxter to renovate after just finishing the last one.

"—if dat be no problem."

"No, no, it's fine, whatever works out best for you." It did feel sudden, but I was the one who'd told him I wasn't renewing his lease in January, and he'd need to find another apartment. "Thank you for letting me know, Mr. Campbell. I hope the new apartment works out for you and your family. Tell me if you need a reference, okay?"

Nodding and smiling, he backed out of the doorway, smashed the knitted tam back on his head, and headed up the stairs two at a time. I slowly shut the door and leaned against it. A tsunami of emotions twisted my gut. *It's too much . . . I can't do this. Philip . . . Lee . . . dealing with petty problems in the building. Now an empty apartment—and Mabel and I haven't even talked about who's next on the list for the House of Hope. And I can't afford an empty apartment for long.*

I took Philip's letter with me to work the next day but didn't call him to talk about it, and he didn't call me—unless he called the house and left a message on the machine. Had to admit I felt bad not responding in *some* way. I hadn't even stayed to hear what else he'd wanted to say. But at least he was respecting my need to take some time before getting back to him.

Still, I should find out when he was going to Virginia. Definitely needed to respond to his letter before then. One way or the other, I'd need to call him.

Oh God! I slumped at my desk in the windowless basement office. *What does this mean? Philip's saying he's truly sorry for the way he treated me. But even he said he doesn't know if I can forgive him—or what it would mean even if I did! Me too, Jesus. Forgiveness is a big deal. I don't want to say it if I don't mean it. And forgiveness is one thing—but trust? Can I ever trust him again after what he's done? Oh God, I don't know what to do.*

Tears threatened to spill over, but I pressed my fingers to my eyes, trying to push the tears in again. *Oh God, I'm so tired of crying over Philip! So tired of feeling confused. What should I do? Forgive him but move on? Divorce as amicably as possible? Or forgive him and try to make a go of our marriage again?*

I finally shook myself out of my funk and tried to focus on the work at hand. Mabel Turner was still out with the flu, but I did call her at home to tell her I was going to have another empty apartment at the House of Hope. And if she was feeling better by Wednesday, we'd like her to come to our weekly household meeting and go over the rules and expectations for everybody so we'd all be on the same page. Though "everybody" meant mostly Shawanda.

Mabel had a coughing fit, an ugly, raspy cough, and finally came back on the phone. "Uhnn . . . talk to you tomorrow, Gabby. Brain's not working right now." She sounded terrible. I felt a little like Angela. Wasn't sure I wanted Mabel back until she was definitely over whatever nasty thing she had going on, even if it meant not having her at the House of Hope household meeting. We'd just have to wing it without her.

Carolyn poked her head into my office to say three new volunteers from the city colleges had shown up yesterday to help with the expanded afterschool program, along with five new students from the neighborhood whose parents had put them on our waiting list. "It was fantastic!" The former shelter resident had a spark in her eye I'd never seen before. "Always wanted to be a teacher but didn't think I had the personality for it—which is why I got my degree in library science." The middle-aged white woman shrugged, still smiling. "Maybe just as well. Wouldn't have wanted to have my mental breakdown in a classroom full of students. But now—I feel as if God is giving me a second chance at life."

I got up from my desk and gave the rather pudgy woman a big hug. "Carolyn, it's women like you who make this one of the best jobs in the world! But I wanted to ask . . . is it still okay if Paul does his homework with you all in the schoolroom? He does need help with his math—not my best subject."

"Okay? Better than okay! Yesterday he was helping some of the younger ones with their reading and *their* math. It was like having another volunteer." Carolyn flipped her stringy brown-and-gray ponytail over her shoulder and pulled open the door. "Well, gotta go. The board chairman's wife—you know, Mrs. Douglass, the principal up at Bethune Elementary—sent over two big boxes of used science curriculum I need to sort through. Looks like some good stuff."

Ah yes. Avis Douglass. Between her and Jodi Baxter, who "just happened" to be a third-grade teacher at that school, they'd supplied a lot of the materials Carolyn was using to organize the Manna House afterschool program.

As Carolyn left, I heard a good deal of clattering going on in the kitchen. Poking my head out the door, I saw Estelle banging utensils and pots around in the kitchen like a one-woman band on a street corner. Not a good sign. Usually meant she was upset about something. A couple of women I didn't recognize—who'd probably come off the street yesterday or over the weekend, both of whom had bad teeth and ill-cut ratty hair—eyed Estelle warily as they dumped heaps of sugar and creamer into their coffee at the counter. Muttering to themselves, they took their cups to the far corner of the dining room where they slouched and guffawed over some private joke.

Picking up Philip's letter, I cautiously approached the pass-through counter between the kitchen and dining room. "Estelle? You okay?"

Bang! went another pot onto the industrial-size stove, into which she dumped the contents of several zip-lock gallon bags. Looked like half-frozen vegetable soup to me.

"Estelle Williams, you need to *slow down*. Time for coffee." I poured the last two cups from the Mr. Coffee pot, doctored mine with cream and hers with sugar, and carried them to the closest table in the dining room. "Estelle!" I ordered again. "Come sit!" To my surprise, she actually came out of the kitchen and lowered herself with a *whomph* into a folding chair. I reached out and touched her hand. "What's going on?" I kept my voice low so as not to be overheard by the duo in the far corner.

She wrapped her hands around the steaming coffee cup and heaved a big sigh. "Leroy, of course. Visited him at the nursing home Sunday afternoon—went by myself 'cause Harry and Denny had some 'man thing' they were doin'—and the medical staff is plannin' on releasing him the end of next week."

"But that's good, isn't it? Means he's getting better."

"And then? Where's he goin' to go, Gabby? He still needs lookin' after. Even the docs there said he shouldn't live alone." Estelle wagged her head slowly, and I could almost see her sorting through the options tumbling around in her head under the hairnet cap. "They sayin' Leroy needs some kind of residential care. Gave me a list of places to look into. But I've made up my mind, Gabby. I need to find an apartment where I can take care of my son. Maybe a house, once the insurance from the fire comes through. I left him on his own once—and look what happened. Ain't gonna do that again, no ma'am. Gonna do what a mama should do." She drew herself up, lips pressed together, looking at me as if daring me to disagree. "So. It's done."

"What? What's done, Estelle?" I suddenly had a horrible thought, and my eyes darted to her left hand. Her ring finger was bare. "Oh no, Estelle! You didn't!"

"I did." For just a nanosecond, Estelle's lip trembled and she blinked back a puddle of moisture in her eyes. But her tone stayed resolute. "Harry don't understand right now, but he'll thank me. No way I can saddle him and that precious grandson of his with what it'd take to live with Leroy."

chapter 34

I was speechless. This couldn't be right. Harry and Estelle were perfect for each other! Hadn't God brought them together in the first place? Harry often said God had given him a second chance at love—not to mention another chance to be the kind of father he should've been to his son. And DaShawn was more excited than anybody that his grandpa was getting married to "Miss Estelle." And why shouldn't he be? The little boy was enjoying being a real kid with a real family for the first time in his life, instead of trying to hold life together for his drug-addled mama with his daddy in jail.

"You can close your mouth, Gabby." Estelle dabbed at her eyes with a stray napkin. "I know everything you're thinkin', so you don't need to say it. It's just . . . sometimes a mother's gotta do what a mother's gotta do." She started to rise—and then her glance went to the envelope I was holding. "What's that? You wanted to tell me somethin'?"

I shook my head and stood up. "That's okay. It can wait. You've got enough on your plate."

"Now *you* siddown. What's goin' on?"

I gave her a half-hearted smile, relieved to see the "koffee-klatch duo" in the corner leaving for the main floor upstairs. *Where to start? Breathe, Gabby.* "Well, you know that 'man thing' Denny and Harry were doing Sunday afternoon? I think they had a man-to-man talk with Philip—at least that's what Jodi said Denny planned to do, taking advantage of the fact that he's staying at their house this week. That's all I know, except yesterday Philip called and said he wanted to talk to me real bad, so we met over lunch—and he gave me this." I handed her the envelope.

Estelle pulled out the letter. I watched her face as she read. Big frown between her eyes . . . replaced by a raised eyebrow . . . followed by several grunts and "Lord, Lord." Finally she let out a low whistle and looked up. "Gabby girl, let me get this straight. Philip says he wants to talk with you, you get together for lunch, then he hands you a letter and wants you to read it while he's sittin' there, instead of tellin' you this himself? Did you two *talk* about this?" She waggled the paper in the air.

I squirmed. "Well, he said he had more he wanted to say after I read the letter, but I was so taken aback after reading it, I said I couldn't respond right then. And I just left."

Estelle's eyebrow went up again. "Mm-hm. You got up and walked on out of there after he'd just spilled his guts all over that paper?"

I squirmed. "Well, yeah." Then added hastily, "I know I need to respond, Estelle, but I don't even know how I *feel* about what he's saying. I need some time." I looked at her anxiously. "What do you think it means? How should I respond?"

Estelle pursed her lips and was quiet for several moments.

"Don't know what it means down the road. That's somethin' you gotta figure out between you an' God an' your husband. But since you're askin'—whatever those two 'unlikely brothers' said to him"—she chuckled at the thought—"I think God's got your man by the ear and he might actually be listenin'. An' somethin' else." She nailed me with one of her Looks. "If Philip handed God this letter with 'I'm sorry' all over it, what do you think God would say?"

My gaze fell and I studied my lap for a full minute. Oh yeah, I knew the "right" answer. But it wasn't that easy and I wasn't going to say it if I didn't mean it. I finally raised my head and met her eye to eye. "Okay, sure, God would probably say, 'I forgive you.' But it's not that easy—and trust is something else, Estelle. I'm *not God*."

Estelle's little self-righteous "test" made me mad. I knew she was right—in my head. But my feelings were so tied in knots, I wasn't sure I knew how to untangle them. Mostly I didn't know what forgiving Philip might mean—or even what *he'd* think I meant if I said, "I forgive you." So I pushed the letter to the back of my mind and busied myself at work, making sure I talked to the new names on the bed list about the classes available to them—typing, cooking, sewing, English as a second language—and trying to assess how many could make use of GED preparation and money management, the next "life skills" classes I wanted to add to our roster of activities.

I still hadn't had the courage to pick up the phone and call Philip by the time I headed home from work that evening with Paul and Dandy in the car. *Please, God, I need some help here. I know*

Jesus told Peter we should forgive someone who wrongs us seventy times
seven, or some horrendous number. But it's not that simple! I mean, how
can I trust Philip after what he's done? If I forgive him, maybe he'll
assume I want to get back together, and—

"Mom! Where're you going? You just passed our street!"

"Oh! Sorry, kiddo. Wasn't thinking." I drove around the block,
which meant parking on the opposite side of the street. Rolling
his eyes at his absentminded mother, Paul took Dandy for a "dog
duty" walk while it was still light, giving me a chance to say hi to
P.J. and check the answering machine as I came into the apartment.

Nothing from Philip. *Hm.* Over twenty-four hours since he'd
given me the letter and he still hadn't called. Well, that was good.
No way did I want him bugging me. I still needed some time to
think and pray about this.

Someone knocked at the front door as I was preparing supper,
and P.J. yelled, "Mom! It's Josh! He wants to talk to you!"

"Tell him to come on back!" I needed to tell him about
Maddox Campbell moving out of 3B. Another apartment to paint
and renovate.

Moments later Josh Baxter sauntered into the kitchen, Gracie
in his arms. The little girl held out her arms to me, nearly falling
out of her daddy's grip. I caught her just in time and swung her
around as she squealed. "Hey, wanna trade?" I teased Josh. "My
two boys for your sweetie-pie here. We can trade back when she
turns thirteen."

Gracie grabbed two fistfuls of my hair and pulled, squealing
again. "Ouch! On second thought, we can trade back now."

Laughing, Josh untangled the toddler's fingers from my curly
mop and sat down with her at the kitchen table. "Got any raisins?

That'll keep her busy. We can't stay long anyway, just wanted to report on my talk with Will Nissan about his missing great-aunt."

I'd almost forgotten I'd asked Josh to do some sleuthing for me. Plopping some raisins in a dish for Gracie, I sat down across from them. "So what'd you find out?"

"Will says he doesn't know all that much about his grandmother's sister. Her real name was Lucinda, but they called her Cindy. He couldn't remember her exact birth date, just November something. Said he has it written down at home somewhere, used it when they were doing some Internet searches. But I did find out his grandmother's name—Margaret Simple."

November birthday? A tickle of excitement made me grin. *Margaret?* Lucy had said her sister's name was Maggie. *Could it be . . . ?* "Wait. You said his grandmother's last name is Simple? Maiden name or married name?"

Josh looked blank. "Uh, I don't know. Didn't think to ask."

"Josh!" I threw up my hands. "What kind of sleuth are you? But it's got to be her married name, right? I mean, Will's her grandson, so she was probably married, and that generation of women always took the husband's name." I frowned. "What we need to know is her maiden name—"

"More!" screeched Gracie, banging the plastic bowl I'd given her, empty now.

Josh pried the bowl from her fingers and jiggled the toddler in his arms. "Guess I should get Gracie home—she hasn't had supper yet." He stood up from the table.

"Okay. Thanks for the info, Josh."

We walked together toward the front of the apartment, and I remembered at the last minute to tell him about the tenants in

3B moving out that weekend. "That means more work for you, I know. Repairs, redoing floors, that kind of thing."

But as I opened the front door for him, I realized he was still stuck on our other conversation. "The name thing," he said. "Does it matter? Maybe the missing sister got married and has a different name now, too, which is why they can't find her."

I scowled. Possibly, but if so, it was less likely that Lucy was the missing sister, since I'd never heard her say *anything* about a husband.

Josh jiggled the impatient Gracie. "Mind telling me what this is all about? Will wanted to know why I was asking, and since I didn't *know* why you wanted to know, I just said Manna House sees a lot of people and maybe we could ask around. But it sounded kind of lame."

I grinned at him. "Good answer, though."

"Uh-huh." He looked at me funny. "I think you know something." Then he sniffed. "Uh, is something burning?"

"Oh no!" I tore down the hall and jerked the scorched pan of rice and beans off the stove. *Now* what was I going to do for supper?

Mabel Turner was in her office with a wad of tissues when I got to Manna House Wednesday morning with Dandy. "Glad to see you back, lady." I leaned into her doorway, not wanting to get too close, but Dandy pulled on his leash, whining. "Just a sec." I unsnapped the leash and let the dog into Shepherd's Fold, even though I didn't see Lucy anywhere in the big room. "Go on, find

Lucy," I urged the dog, then went back to Mabel's office. "You feel up to coming to our household meeting tonight?"

Mabel blew her nose. "Maybe. Not promising, though. Everything okay with you?" Poor woman sounded all stuffed up.

"Um, we're all healthy."

"Uh-huh. And?"

I rolled my eyes. Mabel was too perceptive. "Oh, just more drama going on with Philip." I stepped into her office, closed the door, and leaned against it. "Not sure you're going to believe this." I tried to bring her up to date on everything that had happened in the past few days—Philip moving out of the penthouse, staying with the Baxters while he looked for a cheaper apartment, his plan to pay off his debts and settle the lawsuits out of court by selling his half of his business to his partner.

Mabel's eyes had widened. "Whoa. That's major! Good news, right?"

I nodded. "No kidding. Never thought he'd ever agree to give up the business. But seems like he's finally dealing with the whole mess. And, well, another thing." I hadn't really planned on telling her about Philip's letter of apology, not yet anyway, but it just came blurting out.

"My goodness, Gabby! Are we talking about the same man? The guy who kicked you out of house and home and all that? What happened?!"

Funny, Mabel's astonishment made me feel as if I'd stepped outside myself, listening to what I'd been saying through her ears—and it *was* amazing. *What happened? Good question!* But something Estelle said when I'd shown her the letter suddenly echoed in my head: *"I think God's got your man by the ear and he might actually be listenin'."*

chapter 35

Mabel did show up for the household meeting at House of Hope that evening, bringing Jermaine with her, much to Paul's delight. The boys immediately began setting up Paul's electronic keyboard to do some "jammin'."

"Mom!" P.J. hissed at me as I gathered up my folders and notebook. "Why do they get to take over the living room on your meeting nights? I can't study in my room when they're making all that racket!"

I touched P.J.'s cheek gently with the back of my hand. "I'm sorry, hon. I know it doesn't seem fair. But I don't think they'll bother you if you study in my bedroom in the back. This won't happen often. Ms. Turner won't be coming every Wednesday night, she's just helping us get started. Okay?"

P.J. shrugged off my hand. "Well . . . okay." But as he lumbered off down the hall dragging his book bag, he gave me a half smile, as if he'd just needed reassurance that I understood *he* was the one having to make a sacrifice.

The door to 1A was open across the hall as I came out my

door, and somewhere inside I heard Sabrina raising a fuss about why she had to babysit Bam-Bam and Dessa as well as Sammy and Keisha on Wednesday nights. "Why can't Shawanda get 'em to bed by eight o'clock like little Gracie? I got homework to do, too, you know!"

"Uh-huh," I heard Precious snap back. "Girl, you been on the phone since you got home from school—and *now* you wanna do your homework?" Precious flounced into the hallway in a huff, but then stuck her head back into the apartment. "Besides! Sammy an' Keisha are big enough to help amuse the little ones. You just keep an eye out an' make sure they play together peaceful-like."

Precious pulled the door shut behind her, muttering as we walked up to the third floor together. *"Humph.* Maybe that girl learnin' a thing or two about gettin' babies into bed at a decent hour. Makes me wanna scream when I see little kids outside at all hours of the night or gettin' trundled about till one or two in the mornin', just 'cause they stupid mom or dad wanna go party somewhere."

As we walked into 3A everyone else affiliated with the House of Hope had already gathered in Edesa and Josh's front room—Tanya, Shawanda, and Celia Jones, as well as Mabel Turner—snacking on yogurt-covered peanuts and helping themselves to the tray of hot tea Edesa had prepared. But since we were all there, I asked Edesa to start us off with a prayer and then we got down to business. "Mabel, why don't you review our list of Rules and Expectations? Everyone's read and agreed to them, but this would be the time if anyone has questions or additions we need to make."

Mabel had barely got through the list when Shawanda waved

her arm in the air. "How come we can't have mens in the apartment after ten o'clock on weekends? You guys treatin' us like little kids."

"You signed these rules and expectations, Shawanda," I reminded her.

"Well, yeah. But you said we could ask questions. I'm just *askin'*."

Mabel explained the reasons: for general safety in a building with mostly women and children, courtesy to their apartmentmate. "And because we're a Christian facility, Shawanda, and want to conduct the House of Hope in accordance with biblical principles. You're all single women and we don't want men coming and going at all hours of the night."

My cheeks felt a little hot. *Oh Lord.* How close I'd come—more than once—to inviting Lee into the apartment "for coffee" after a date. I'd had my own reasons for not inviting him in—but I hadn't even thought about needing to be an example for the other single women in the building.

Shawanda wasn't finished. "Can we get us a kitty? Don't say nothin' in here 'bout pets. Dessa wanted ta keep that poor kitty she found under the back porch on Monday. Now it's gone an' she all heartbroken."

I doubted the three-year-old even remembered Monday. But we opened the topic for discussion. The list of concerns got lengthy: residents with allergies; ability to pay for shots, food, and litter for cats; scooping poops for dogs; obnoxious barking; damage to furniture or floors from ill-behaved dogs or cats.

"Yeah," Shawanda muttered, "but Miss Gabby here already got her a dog. Don't know what we need to keep talkin' 'bout."

"Shawanda, taking in a feral cat is *not* the same thing as Dandy staying here. Besides, he's temporary," I reminded her tersely. "Lucy sprained her ankle, remember?"

Mabel finally tabled the discussion "to be continued," suggesting we form a small committee of staff and residents. *Humph*, I thought. *We also better get clear what rules are for residents and what rules are for staff*. Personally, I thought a dog or two owned by staff might be good security for the building, but allowing pets willynilly could get out of hand.

I reported that the tenants in 3B might be moving out this weekend, adding to our House of Hope apartments. But the apartment would also need renovation and repairs. We agreed to schedule another painting party on one of our household meeting nights soon. No, we didn't know who'd be moving in yet.

Just before we closed the meeting—we were still trying to keep them to one hour—Edesa said she had a proposal. "Some of you know I'm part of a women's prayer group we call Yada Yada, which meets every other Sunday evening. Estelle Williams is part of that group, too, and Jodi Baxter, Josh's mom, and Avis Douglass, the wife of the Manna House board chairman. Well . . ." The black Honduran woman beamed her infectious smile around the circle. "I was thinking it would be so *bueno* to start another Yada Yada Prayer Group right here at the House of Hope—on the *other* Sunday nights."

"You givin' up the other one? Or gonna be part of both Ya Ya prayer groups?" Precious asked.

Edesa laughed. "Not Ya Ya . . . *Yada Yada*. It's actually a Hebrew word that's found in the Bible hundreds of times! It means 'to know and be known intimately'—or something close to that. The way God knows us in Psalm 139. And yes, I'd like to be part of both groups. If God blesses this one as much as He has the original, well . . . none of us will be the same."

Shawanda looked dubious. "Ya mean we'd hafta go? I ain't all that religious, ya know."

Edesa shook her head. "No. Entirely voluntary. For anyone who would like time to pray together with other sisters." She eyed her husband. "*Hombres* not allowed."

Josh threw up his hands. "*No problemo*. I've got my own men's prayer group."

"*Sí*, the Yada Yada Brothers." Edesa laughed and gave her husband a hug.

Celia Jones spoke up for the first time during the entire meeting. "I'd like that very much. My kids are all grown, and there's not much I can do about some of the poor choices they've made. Keisha's mother, well, some would call my daughter a lost cause, which is why I have custody of my granddaughter right now. But I do know there's one thing I *can* do—an' that's *pray*."

"*Sí! Sí!*" Edesa cried. The others of us readily agreed. What was there to decide, anyway, if it was optional? But Edesa was so excited, she had tears in her eyes. "Oh, *mi amigas*, if you only knew how prayer can change the lives of all the women and children who come to live at the House of Hope! This may be the most important decision we ever make in this meeting!"

I thought the meeting had gone well. So far, Shawanda seemed to be settling in all right, though I wanted to check in with Celia privately to see how things were working out with sharing chores and Shawanda living up to her end of the responsibilities.

After saying good-bye to Mabel and Jermaine, I sent Paul to his room to finish his homework and knocked on the door of my bedroom to check on P.J. No answer, so I opened the door slowly. "P.J.? It's me."

My oldest son was propped up on my bed, staring at a picture frame he held in his hands. I shot a quick glance at the bedside table. The photo of Philip and me was gone.

"Dad called," he said.

I sat down on the foot of the bed. Shouldn't be surprised Philip had finally called. I still hadn't responded to his letter. He had to be wondering what I was thinking. I'd call him tomorrow. I owed him that much.

"What'd he say?"

"He said he's flying to Petersburg on Friday to talk with Granddad about some business stuff. But he wants to know if he can come over tomorrow night to see Paul and me. Wants you to call him."

I nodded. "Of course he can. Would you like him to come for supper?"

P.J. shrugged. "I guess." He stared at the picture some more, then turned it around and showed it to me. "Do you still love Dad?"

His question caught me off guard. *Did I?* Love had certainly taken a beating in the last six or seven months—maybe longer. I looked away, wondering what to say. But P.J. was a product of our love. He deserved an answer. I took a deep breath. "There's a way I'll always care for your dad, P.J. He's your father, and we both love you very—"

"That's not what I asked!" P.J. snapped. "Do *you* love *him*? Like this?" He stabbed a finger at the photo and held it in front of my face.

We stared at each other a long moment. Mother and son, both desperate to know the answer. Finally I sighed. "To be honest, P.J., I don't know. I don't know if he loves me anymore either. That's something we're trying to figure out. But some good things have happened recently, hopeful things—"

"Never *mind*." P.J. tossed the photo frame aside, vaulted off the bed, and strode out of the room, slamming the bedroom door behind him.

I called Philip that night, saying of course he could come by the apartment to say good-bye to the boys and stay for supper too.

"Thanks," he said. "Sorry to invite myself over. I haven't had a chance to tell the boys the decisions I've made, and I'd like to do it in person. I'd ask them to come to my place but, uh, I don't have one yet." He laughed a bit nervously.

"It's all right. What's happened with Henry Fenchel?"

"I'm going into the office tomorrow to sign the papers. Henry had his lawyer draw them up, and my lawyer's going over them. I have Henry's word that he's dropping the lawsuit. Hopefully Fagan's lawyer will do the same when I give them a cashier's check tomorrow to pay off that loan."

I snorted in his ear. "*Humph*. The money he loaned you was probably illegal drug money to begin with."

"Don't rub it in, Gabby. I should've been more careful. But at this point, I'm just trying to take care of my business. Put an end to it."

"I'm sorry. You're right." We let silence hang between us for a moment or two. Working up my courage, I said, "I know I haven't responded to your letter yet. I—"

"That's okay," he cut in. "I understand."

"No, I want to. I shouldn't have left you hanging this long. Maybe tomorrow night we can find some time to talk. Before you leave for Virginia."

"All right. Just want you to know, I didn't mean the letter to stand by itself. There's more I wanted to say. More I *need* to say."

"Okay. Well, see you tomorrow then."

Thursday passed in a blur. The temperature actually hiked up into the low seventies, but I spent most of the day cooped up in my tiny office, one thought occupying my mind: *What was I going to say to Philip when he came over tonight?*

I kept hearing Estelle saying it seemed to her that God had got Philip's attention, and he was actually listening. No way did I want to get in the way of what God might be doing with Philip Fairbanks—though it seemed to *me* God had a mighty long way to go.

At the same time, God had brought me a mighty long way too. From a different place, maybe. But what must God think of a girl who'd been brought up knowing the Bible, who'd sat in church and heard the gospel, who'd said she believed—and then chucked the whole thing? Not much different than the prodigal son who'd said, "Bye-bye, I can make it on my own!" I, too, had left the shelter of family and faith for the glitter of a romantic encounter in France, a Southern marriage, and all the comforts old money could buy.

As for Philip, he'd never pretended to be "born again," and he didn't have very good role models when it came to his parents. *Their* marriage was a constant contest of who could one-up whom.

If God was working on Philip, he wasn't a "prodigal son," but an adoptee with issues.

All these thoughts tumbled around in my head as the clock inched its way through the day. I caught a glimpse of Lucy at lunch, hobbling around a bit better with the air boot, but I couldn't deal with that whole business about Will Nissan's missing relative right now. Another time. Estelle seemed to be avoiding *me*—and maybe everyone else—after giving Harry his ring back. Well, I couldn't deal with that right now either.

Paul poked his head into my office after walking Sammy and Keisha to the shelter after school, an arrangement that'd been working well since school started. "Mom? Where's Dandy? I can't find him anywhere—or Lucy either."

I smiled at the oh-so-serious expression on my youngest son. "Oh, I'm sure they're around. I brought Dandy with me this morning and I saw Lucy at lunch. Maybe they're outside. It's such a nice day today—practically Indian Summer." Not that I'd taken advantage of it.

"But *I'm* supposed to take him for a walk after school. Lucy said!"

"Well, she can't be far with that sprained ankle. Why don't you go ask Angela at the front desk. Maybe she knows."

Paul was back two minutes later, damp curls plastered on the worry lines in his forehead. "Mo-om! Miss Angela said Lucy went out with Dandy about an hour ago!"

"Well, see? It was probably just too nice a day to stay inside. They'll be back soon." I couldn't imagine Lucy could walk very far, even with the air boot.

"No-oo! You don't understand! Angela said she took her cart with her too!"

chapter 36

It was true. Lucy's cart was gone. I couldn't believe the old woman had just taken off without saying anything. But she still wasn't back by the time five o'clock rolled around and I had to leave with Paul, Sammy, and Keisha.

Paul threw himself into the front seat of the Subaru and slammed the car door. "Lucy's so *mean*, Mom! We've been taking care of Dandy ever since she hurt her foot. He's been sleeping on my bed and everything! Why'd she just go off with Dandy without saying anything? It's so *unfair*."

I decided not to remind him he wasn't old enough to sit in the front seat yet. It was only a mile to the six-flat. Glancing in the rearview mirror at Sammy and Keisha, I said, "Seatbelts, everybody!" Then I turned to Paul. "Honey, maybe she hasn't really left. She just might be outside enjoying the day and hasn't realized the time. After all, she's been cooped up inside for a couple weeks. She's not used to that." But frankly, I had a sinking feeling Paul might be right—Lucy had just up and gone back to the streets, dog and cart in tow.

Argh! It might be weeks before we saw her again! And this Indian Summer weather would definitely not last.

But at the moment I was more worried about Paul than I was about Lucy. His dad was coming over to talk to the boys and I didn't want Paul all upset and distracted by the disappearance of the old bag lady and my mother's dog. Those two had created enough drama in the past several months to last a lifetime—and I sure didn't want this new wrinkle to overshadow our evening just before Philip left town.

But I did my best to cheer up the atmosphere at home, setting the Belfort Signature table with my mother's wedding china with the tiny bluebells around the edges—a bit faded and slightly chipped here and there, but still special. I used royal-blue cloth napkins and arranged several pillar candles of different sizes on a round, etched mirror in the center. Maybe a bit fancy for lemon-baked chicken and roasted potatoes, but it was one of Philip's favorite meals.

He arrived at six thirty on the dot, and I could hear the boys screeching. "You got the cast off, Dad! How come you didn't tell us?" They dragged him down the hall to the dining room. "Mom! Did you know Dad got the cast off?"

I just smiled and nodded. He was looking healthier by the day, except for the pallor of his skin, still pale and drawn.

Philip lifted the aluminum foil off the hot dish I set on the table. "Is that what I think it is? Mm, lemon chicken and roasted potatoes." He winked at the boys. "Your mom's got a good memory."

I set the rest of the food on the table—apple-walnut salad and green beans—and lit the candles, which cast a lot of reflected light in the mirror. Philip and P.J. sat on one side of the table, Paul and I on the other. And now . . . the Awkward Moment. But at my gesture, we joined hands and I offered a short prayer of thanks for the food and asked God to bless Philip's journey back to Petersburg.

When I opened my eyes, he was grinning self-consciously. "The Baxters are training me well. They hold hands and pray at mealtimes too."

As the food was passed around, Philip tried to ask the boys what was going on at school, but P.J. cut to the chase. "How come you're going back to Virginia? When are you coming back? Can we go back too?"

Philip glanced at me, then put down his fork and wiped his mouth with the cloth napkin. "Fair enough. But first I'd like to back up and tell you boys something important. I didn't mean to do this during supper, but first things first."

My mouth suddenly went dry. What now? I thought he was just going to tell them about selling his share of the business, paying off his debts, and going to Virginia to consult with his dad about "starting over."

The two boys stared at their father. "What?" P.J. said.

Philip cleared his throat and blew out a breath. "Five months ago I did something very wrong. Your mom and I were, well, having some problems, and I got angry. A lot of things felt as if they weren't working out after moving to Chicago. Your summer camp fell through, which was supposed to keep you busy last summer, the penthouse felt overcrowded when Grandma Shepherd and her dog came back with you from your vacation to North Dakota. I was trying to get my commercial development business started, your mom had a new job that just seemed to complicate things, we weren't communicating very well, and I lost it. I decided things weren't working for us. So I took you boys back to Virginia to stay with your grandparents, and I—"

His face suddenly flushed and his jaw muscles tightened. P.J.'s stony face was unreadable, and Paul picked at his food. I had stopped eating, too, my stomach in a knot.

Philip took a deep breath. "It's hard to say it, but I basically kicked your mother and your grandmother out of the penthouse. I thought we needed a big shakeup around the Fairbanks household, that if I took drastic measures, I could get rid of all the distractions, get my business off the ground, and pick up the pieces later."

I stared at Philip in total shock as the words poured out of his mouth. *Get rid of all the distractions? That's what we were? And just pick up the pieces later?*

"But what I did was wrong," he continued. "Very wrong. I didn't even tell your mother that I'd taken you back to Virginia. I—"

"You told us we had to go so Mom could take care of Grandma Shep!" Paul blurted.

Philip nodded. "Like I said, I was angry, I didn't do things the way I should've. Most of all, I hurt your mother very much." For the first time since he'd started, Philip glanced at me, held my gaze for a long moment, and then looked back at his sons. "I've told her I'm sorry. Desperately sorry. And I want to tell the two of you I'm sorry too."

Silence descended over the room. The food on our plates was growing cold. Paul shifted uncomfortably in his chair. "Okay, I guess."

But P.J. stood up so vehemently his chair fell over. "Sorry isn't good enough! You hurt us, too, Dad! We've been jerked back and forth between you guys and the grandparents all summer long—no, ever since you up and moved here! Even now, we get jerked back and forth between 'mom's house' and 'dad's house.' Where's *our* house? Huh? Have you ever thought about *that*?"

P.J. started to bolt from the room, but Philip stood up quickly and put a hand on his shoulder. "P.J., wait. Please. You have a right to be angry. But you asked me a question awhile ago and I want to answer it. Please—sit down."

Breathing heavily, P.J. just stood there for several moments, then picked up his chair and sat down in it. "All right. What?"

Again, Philip took a deep breath and blew it out. "Obviously, things didn't get better living on my own. I spent too much time at the Horseshoe Casino, gambling with money I couldn't afford to lose. You know most of this part—that I got over my head in debt and took some loans to pay it off that got me in trouble. Big trouble. Kept gambling, thinking my luck would turn. It didn't. Couldn't pay back the loans. Ended up making some enemies who put me in the hospital."

Paul's lip trembled. "I was really scared, Dad."

"I know, son. Scared me too. I've put you boys through a lot of trauma, and I'm truly sorry about that too. But I had a lot of time to think in the hospital. To take a long, hard look at the choices I'd been making, the direction I was going. For a while I thought I could patch it up, fix it, make it work. Figure out a way to pay off the debts, hold on to my business, and patch up our family too. But I couldn't. I'd made a mess of things and didn't know how to get out of it."

My astonishment knew no bounds. Fairbanks men didn't admit defeat, didn't say they were wrong. Didn't cry, "Uncle!" But

Philip was not only admitting his failure to his sons but doing so in my presence. Or—was I really the one he was speaking to?

"Funny thing," Philip said, "the first time I felt some real hope is when a couple of guys told me hitting bottom is a good thing, because the only way to go is up. But it means starting over. Not fix the old stuff, but start over, do it right. So that's what I'm trying to do."

The boys listened intently as Philip told them he'd sold out his share of the commercial development business to Henry Fenchel, paid off his gambling debts, and got rid of the lawsuits hanging over his head. "But that's only the first step," he said. "I've had to face the fact that I'm a gambling addict, so I'll be going to Gamblers Anonymous for a long while. Our old friend, Mr. Bentley, the doorman at Richmond Towers, has agreed to be my sponsor. But Bentley used to be a cop—did you guys know that? So I think he'll be breathing heavy down my neck."

Paul giggled and even the corners of P.J.'s lips twitched.

"So, guys, I'm out of a job. That's why I'm going back to Virginia, to talk with your granddad and your Great-Uncle Matt, see if they can help me put together a new business plan. Start over. Soon as I know what step two is, you guys will be the first to know."

We all just sat and looked at each other. Then P.J. nodded, a bit grudgingly. "Okay." He picked up his half-eaten plate of food and pushed back his chair. "Can I heat this up in the microwave, Mom? C'mon, Paul. Let's go play that video game we started. Maybe Mom and Dad need to talk."

Philip and I watched in silence as the boys headed into the kitchen with their plates, then two minutes later disappeared down the hallway toward the living room and their video game. Philip raised an eyebrow. "Either he's a good escape artist or extremely diplomatic for his age. Uh . . . do you want your food warmed up too?"

I let him take my plate, suddenly feeling exhausted. We did need to talk, but I was glad for a few minutes to sort through my thoughts. There was something I needed to say too—something I hadn't wanted to think about, much less put into words. But it had been festering in my subconscious for weeks, ever since Mabel Turner had said she'd been concerned about our relationship from the first time she'd interviewed me for the job. *Is this the time, God? If so, You've gotta help me!*

When Philip returned with our plates of microwaved food and sat down across from me, I was the one who spoke first. "Philip, I"—*Oh Lord, I want to say the right thing here*—"I appreciate you telling the boys yourself that you were wrong to kick me out of the penthouse. Out of our marriage. Out of your life." He winced, but I went on. "And I've been thinking about the letter you gave me last Monday. Thinking about it a lot. And I believe you. Believe that you're sorry."

"Oh, Gabby. I am! If you only knew—"

I held up my hand. "Don't. It's my turn now." I needed to keep going or I'd lose my courage. "This isn't easy for me to say, because you're right, Philip, you hurt me a lot. You hurt our family, you hurt our sons, and—you've hurt yourself."

"I know." The words came out strangled.

"But I've been praying a lot this week, struggling with how to respond to your letter. I didn't want to forgive you, because I don't know what forgiveness means. I don't even know what forgiveness feels like. I don't know what it means for us—for you and me—for the future. And to be honest, I still don't. Don't have a clue. But there is one thing I know. God has forgiven *me*, forgave me even before I got my life together. So I know I have only one option— and that's to forgive you. So I do. I forgive you, Philip."

He struggled for words. "Gabby, I . . . I don't deserve—"

Again I held up my hand. "Wait. There's something else I need to say." *Huh.* He thought *that* was the hard part. But the hardest part was still to come. The lump in my throat was so big I could hardly push the words past it. "You . . . you didn't ruin our marriage all by yourself, Philip. God has shown me—through a few say-it-straight sisters, just like the brothers God brought into your life recently—that there are some things I need to take responsibility for too. Especially—"

The lump got bigger. Oh, how easy it would be to talk myself out of saying this! To tell myself *anything* I'd done paled in comparison to the horror he'd heaped on me. But suddenly I realized that for Philip to truly be able to start over was to wipe the slate clean. I needed to own up to my failures and mistakes too. Put them on the table and let the blood of Jesus cover them all with forgiveness.

The lump seemed to dissolve with my resolve. "Especially the fact that I went ahead and did things behind your back, made decisions about things that affected *us* without talking with you about them ahead of time. Taking the job at Manna House. Bringing my mom and Dandy back from North Dakota without consulting you, even though I felt I had lots of good reasons. I was afraid you'd say no to everything I wanted to do. But . . . it still wasn't right. As a wise woman told me, no marriage can function that way for long, pulling in different directions."

Philip stared at me. He seemed to be in shock. He shook his head, but no words came. And then his shoulders started to shake. Silent sobs racked his body from somewhere deep. I didn't know what to do, but something in my spirit said, *Touch*.

I reached across the table, took his hand, and just held it while he wept.

chapter 37

A loud crack of thunder made me bolt upright in bed. Rain washed against my bedroom windows, which were letting in a faint light. What time was it anyway? I reached for my digital alarm so I could see the lighted numbers—six fifteen. Almost time to get up anyway. I'd probably have to give P.J. a ride to school or he'd get soaked waiting for the city bus.

Swathed in my cozy fleece robe and waiting for the coffee to drip, I wondered if the storm would delay Philip's flight that morning. Hopefully they'd hold the flight if there was any danger. Didn't actually know what time his flight was due to leave. I'd asked him last night if he needed a ride to the airport, but he said Will Nissan had offered to give him a ride as far as the UIC campus, and he'd just take the Blue Line from there to the airport. A straight shot, and a lot cheaper than a taxi.

We hadn't said much after my confession and Philip's emotional reaction—just let the weight of the whole evening sit there with no conclusion. I sensed we both understood "it was what it was." Significant but unfinished. Neither of us knew what it meant for the future. But I'd gone to bed feeling a strange sense of peace. After Philip's honest confession to his sons, I'd obeyed the prompting from the Holy Spirit to own up to my own failings in the marriage. "It's in Your lap now, Jesus," I'd murmured as I turned out the light.

But the early morning thunder must've awakened Paul, too, because he padded into the kitchen in a mismatched pair of pajamas and bare feet and went straight to the back door, peering out the square window. "Mom! What if Lucy and Dandy are out in all this rain?"

The thought had crossed my mind too. Nighttime temperatures had fallen to low fifties. Not too bad, could be worse, but still.

I pulled Paul into a fleece-warm hug. "Betcha anything they came back last night and are snug as a bug in a rug at the shelter. But even if not"—I held Paul away from me and looked into his hazel eyes—"Lucy probably found shelter somewhere. She's smart that way."

Well, maybe. The first time I'd "met" Lucy, she was camped under a bush, supposedly out of the rain, swathed in plastic garbage bags that didn't do much as far as keeping her dry.

"Go on, drag your brother out of bed," I told Paul. "I'll give both of you rides to school today. What do you want for breakfast?"

Frankly, I didn't want to worry about Lucy until I had to, which turned out to be as soon as I got to work at Manna House after dropping off the boys.

"Lucy here?" I asked Angela at the front desk, shaking the rain off my umbrella.

"Haven't seen her." She pointed to the sign-in book. "And she hasn't signed in since she signed out yesterday afternoon."

I glanced at Lucy's wobbly signature. Even though the old woman could barely read or write, Carolyn had helped her learn to sign her name. "Oh, okay. So, how's Jin?"

The phone rang and Angela picked up. "Manna House Women's Shelter." She covered the mouthpiece and gave me a sly grin. "He's coming to dinner at my parents' house this weekend!" Then into the phone: "I'm sorry. Who was it you wanted?"

I headed for my office, realizing I missed bringing Dandy to work and seeing the happy reunion between Lucy and the dog each morning. And I'd been so distracted this whole week with the most recent melodrama concerning Philip that I'd put off doing anything about my concerns for Lucy and Dandy with cold weather coming on, much less following up my suspicions about Lucy's identity—and now she was gone. And who knew when she'd show up again. Next week? Next year?

The cracks of thunder were coming closer together and the lights in the building blinked off and on several times. The storm was getting worse. I dialed Philip's cell but only got to leave a message. "Just wondering if you got off okay. Give me a call when you get to Petersburg. The boys will want to know you got there safely." *Me too*, I almost added, but didn't.

Estelle Williams poked her hairnet-covered head into my office at five to ten. "Come on outta that hole, girl. We're goin' to Edesa's Bible study. You an' me both been pushin' people away all week, not wantin' to talk about all the angst we feelin' 'bout the men in our lives. But we can't push away the Man Upstairs. So c'mon." She actually grabbed me by the hand and pulled me out of my office and up the stairs to Shepherd's Fold. She had me laughing by the time we got to the circle of couches and chairs that had been pushed together for Edesa's weekly Bible study.

More people than usual had gathered, probably because of the rain keeping people inside. Edesa, looking a bit damp herself, raindrops still sparkling on her tight corkscrew curls, grinned at our presence. "*Buenos dias*, everyone! Looks as if the rain is blessing us with a good group to study God's Word today. Sister Naomi, will you pass out the Bibles? If you want a Spanish translation, we have those too . . . all right. As soon as you get a Bible, turn to the Psalms, chapter sixty-one. Will someone please read the first four verses?"

Monique, our fountain of religious clichés, waved her hand. "Praise Jesus, I'll read it. I just love the Psalms! I read one ever' mornin' an—"

"Just read dis one, Monique," Wanda growled, rolling her eyes.

"I was just *sayin'* . . . oh, all right." Standing up, Monique read in a preachy voice: "'Hear my cry, O God! Attend to my prayer. From the end of the earth I will cry to You, when my heart is overwhelmed. Lead me to the rock that is higher than I'—oh, yes, Jesus!—'For You have been a shelter for me, a strong tower from the enemy. I will abide in Your tabernacle forever. I will trust in the shelter of Your wings.' The readin' of the Word, amen." She sat down, beaming.

In spite of Monique's pontificating, I recognized the same psalm Jodi had encouraged me to read when I was all upset about Philip heading for the casino last week. Edesa's smile looked a little strained, but she said, "Let's pray before we talk about this important scripture." And in her quiet, lilting Spanish accent, she thanked *El Señor* for hearing the cries of our hearts and comforting us with His promises. After her "Amen," she asked, "How many of you are feeling overwhelmed right now?"

Hands all around me went up. *Well, that's me too*. I raised my hand. Estelle too.

Edesa nodded at the sea of hands. "There are a lot of reasons we feel overwhelmed—probably as many reasons as there are women in this room. At these times we just need something—or Someone—we can count on to hold on to . . . or to hold on to us. That's what this prayer of David is all about. He had a lot of stress in his life, and even though he was a *king*, the most powerful person in the country, he cried out to God to be his rock, to be his shelter from the storms of life swirling all around him."

Heads were nodding all around the room, along with "You got that right" and "Mm-hm, say it."

Edesa swept her hand around the room. "Sometimes we need a physical shelter, like Manna House here, to put a roof over our head and food in our mouths, so we don't have to be out in the cold and wet, like today . . ."

I winced. Except Lucy and Dandy *were* somewhere out there in the cold and wet. What kind of shelter had they found?

"And sometimes we need a shelter like this—" Edesa turned and looked up at the mural painted on the wall of Jesus cradling a small lamb in His arms. "Someone to love us and care for us, to make us feel safe. But I think I can safely say all of us have been let down by people who should've been that kind of rock, that kind of shelter."

Now the nods and bursts of agreement got more vigorous.

"But this psalm tells us that there is a Rock, a Shelter, a Strong

Tower that will always be there for us. And that is Jesus. Here, listen to this song . . . Sister Gabby, I think you will recognize this one." Edesa cast a warm smile in my direction and pushed a button on a CD player plugged into the wall. The gospel song her young husband had once recorded for me filled the room. I listened, squeezing Estelle's hand beside me—or was she squeezing mine?

Where do I go . . . when there's no one else to turn to?
Who do I talk to . . . when nobody wants to listen?
Who do I lean on . . . when there's no foundation stable? . . .
When I need a shelter, when I need a friend
I go to the Rock . . .

Edesa's Bible study and the Dottie Rambo song stayed with me the rest of the workday, and I used up most of my box of tissues. *Huh!* I could be the poster child for a woman who'd been let down by the men in my life who should've been my protector, my shelter. I'd thought the well-connected Philip Fairbanks was the rock I needed after my ill-fated marriage to Damien Spencer right out of high school. But Philip had abandoned me too. Like many of the women here, Manna House had been a lifesaving shelter for me this year in more ways than one. But I'd also found my real Shelter when I'd renewed my faith in Jesus, the solid Rock who never moved even when I'd moved away from Him. The One who'd never stopped loving me and carrying me—even now. Even with Philip reaching out to me, and Lee Boyer pulling me away from him.

Obviously I couldn't have it both ways. In fact, I had to face the possibility I might lose both men. But whatever happened, I knew I still had Solid Rock beneath my feet.

"Thank You, Jesus," I breathed for the hundredth time that day. Glancing up at the clock, I realized it was almost time for Sunnyside Magnet School to be out. I could still hear thunder rumbling overhead and was just deciding I should probably pick up Paul at school when my phone rang. "There's someone here to see you, Gabby," Angela said.

Lucy and Dandy? I scurried up the stairs and burst through the double doors into the foyer—and stopped. "Will?" Will Nissan stood in the foyer, glancing up at the stained glass windows that made Manna House look like a church from the outside, and peeking beyond me at the wall mural he'd glimpsed when I'd come through the double doors. "What are you doing here?"

The young college student grinned at me. "Hi, Mrs. Fairbanks. I, uh . . . well, here." He handed me a square card envelope that looked a little worse for wear. "I gave Mr. Philip a ride as far as Circle Campus this morning, and he asked if I'd give this to you on my way home from classes. I think he wanted you to get it today rather than put it in the mail. Told me where you worked."

"Thanks, Will." I took the envelope. But Will showing up on the shelter's doorstep, today of all days, was giving me an idea.

He was still looking around, curious as usual. "I knew you worked at a women's shelter, but I've never actually seen one. Do you, uh, give tours?" He smiled that engaging grin of his.

"I'd love to—another time," I said. "But right now, I have a huge favor to ask of you. Angela? Sign me out, will you? I'm going to pick up the kids from school and then I've got an errand to do. Will, come with me."

Maybe because he was young and adventurous, Will waited good-naturedly while I got my raincoat and bag, then we hopped into my car without much of an explanation from me. I didn't want to say anything until after I'd picked up Paul and the other two kids and deposited them at the House of Hope. Fortunately, most of the House of Hope adults were home because of the constant rain, and Precious said she'd keep an eye on Paul until I got back.

"You okay?" She eyed me suspiciously.

"I'm fine. I owe you." I ran back out to the car and jumped into the driver's seat just as the skies let loose another downpour. "Drat! I think Chicago's gonna float away if this keeps up." I hoped Josh was checking the basement for flooding—especially with Philip's good furniture down there.

"So what's up?" Will still had that amused, curious look on his face.

I started the car and turned on the wipers and defroster. "Okay, here's the deal. We've got a missing person from the shelter—Lucy, the old woman I told you about?—and I need someone to help me find her."

"The banana cake lady?" Will was grinning. "Still haven't met her."

· "That's the one. She's got my mother's dog and I'm, you know, worried about them." But that's all I said. I still hesitated to tell Will my suspicions—not until the three of us could sit down and talk together. But we had to find Lucy first.

But where to look? I drove back toward Manna House and we circled the streets in the Wrigleyville North neighborhood for a while, even stopping from time to time to ask passersby if they'd seen an old lady with a dog and a wire cart. No . . . no . . . no.

"She's probably not out on the street—not in weather like this," Will pointed out reasonably.

"I know!" I hit the steering wheel. "She could be anywhere!" I groaned aloud.

Pray, Gabby.

The Voice in my spirit was so strong, I pulled over and stopped the car. *Duh!* What was wrong with me? Jodi Baxter was always telling me, *"Pray first, Gabby."*

"Will, hope you don't mind, but I'm going to pray." And I prayed aloud, a simple prayer that the rain would stop, that we'd know where to look, that God would help us find Lucy. Then I started the car again.

Will had laughter in his voice. "My grandmother would like you. She's *always* praying."

I grinned at him. "Well, I hope I get to meet her sometime. I could use some praying lessons."

Will rode in silence as I turned north on Sheridan Road. "So, where are you going?"

Where *was* I going? "I know this sounds a little silly, but I'm going to the park up by Richmond Towers. That's where I first ran into Lucy last spring. Might as well start at the beginning. She used to hang out there a lot."

I pulled into a parking space on the frontage road, realizing that the rain had slowed to a drizzle. *Thank You, Lord!* With Will being a good sport, I headed down the path and turned off at the bush where I'd first tripped over Lucy's cart. Maybe . . .

But no one was there. I looked around. The pedestrian tunnel! That could provide shelter.

But the tunnel under Lake Shore Drive was empty. And not

that dry either. We sloshed through the puddles that had gathered in the tunnel, and I had to admit I was glad Will was with me. The place was eerie, with only about a third of the lights working, casting strange shadows as we passed.

Coming out on the other side, the lake was gray and wild, tossing up white caps everywhere and sending waves smashing against the rocks. Not really knowing what I was doing, I headed toward the only other shelter within sight—the Foster Avenue Beach House. The sand was soggy, and I wondered why I hadn't grabbed my gym shoes when I had the chance back at the six-flat. My leather ankle-boots were going to be a mess.

The beach house was shuttered and locked. Even the restrooms were locked for the winter. But between the men's and women's changing rooms was a wide walkthrough that housed a concession stand in summer. I pointed it out to Will. "Let's go through there."

I thought I heard voices as we came close to the walkthrough and I hesitated. No telling *who* was in there. Drug dealers or gang-bangers for all I knew. I put out my hand to stop Will and strained to listen, but it was hard to hear anything with the constant splashing of waves against the shore. Will held up his hand, as if he understood the necessity to be careful and inched closer under the eaves that led into the walkway. I followed. We stopped again and listened as the voice—voices?—grew louder.

The sound was low-pitched and gravelly, almost sing-songy. Will and I crept a few steps closer. Man? Woman? Was the person drunk? It was hard to tell.

A few more steps, and we could make out the words.

"An' bless this house, oh Lord we pray. Make it safe by night an' day. Bless these walls, so firm and stout, keepin' want and trouble out. See, Dandy? We gonna be fine. Someone'll come. Don't worry. Bless the roof an' chimney tall, let Thy peace lie over all . . ."

My heart practically leaped into my throat. "Lucy!" I shouted. I grabbed Will's coat sleeve. "C'mon! That's Lucy!"

But Will didn't move, his eyes wide, his skin pale. "That . . . that prayer. That's my grandmother's prayer!"

chapter 38

I didn't have time to explain to Will what was going on. I rushed into the walkthrough, making out a couple of shadowy lumps bunched against the closed concession stand. "Lucy? Lucy, it's me, Gabby! And a friend."

The smaller lump moved and a dog's snout poked out of a cocoon of ragged towels, whining. "Dandy, it's just me . . . good boy . . . good dog. Lucy, are you okay?"

The other lump moved, and as my eyes adjusted to the dim interior, Lucy's wrinkled face appeared from a similar cocoon. "That you, Fuzz Top? Heh heh, see there, Dandy? What'd I tell ya. Told ya somebody would come sooner or later . . . *oof*. Gimme a hand here, will ya?"

"Will! Can you help Lucy stand up? Calm down, Dandy. Easy boy . . ." Dandy was whining constantly and trying to lick my hand. I unwrapped the towels and other rags and realized the dog was soaking wet and shivering. Beside me, Will was undertaking a similar operation, untangling the old lady from layers constructed of blankets and odd pieces of clothing and then helping her to her feet.

"Lucy! Why is Dandy so wet? Are you soaked too?" I used one

of the damp, ragged towels to rub the dog all over, realizing I was getting myself muddy and wet in the process.

"Nah, I'm okay. But he chased a seagull into the lake as we was headin' for the beach house, got hisself all wet. Glad ya came, though—I twisted this bum ankle again tryin' to stop him. Maybe ya can take us back to the shelter to get dry." She squinted at the young man who was trying to help her into a one-legged stand. "Who'd ya say this here kid is?"

Will finally recovered his voice. "My name's Will. I'm a friend of the Fairbanks. Your name's Lucy? Can you walk, Lucy? It's a ways to the car."

"Well, I can if ya give me a hand. Stupid ankle . . . was doin' fine till ever'thing got all wet an' slippery—hey! Can't leave my cart. Need all them towels an' stuff too."

The light outside was fading fast. Rolling my eyes in frustration, I gathered up the damp, muddy towels, blankets, and odd bits of clothing and stuffed them into the wire cart. Everything in there was going to need a thorough washing back at Manna House. At least the heavy rain had stopped. We inched our way out of the beach house walkthrough—Lucy leaning heavily on Will and half hopping on her one good foot, me pulling her rickety cart and holding Dandy's leash—and made our way across the soggy beach to the jogging path, heading for the pedestrian tunnel and my car on the other side.

It took us a good forty-five minutes just to get back to the car, and another fifteen to drive to Manna House and get Lucy up the steps and inside. The office and reception desk were closed, but Sarge was on duty and said Lucy's bed hadn't been reassigned. She'd make sure the old lady got into something dry and had supper, which was being served up that night by the Silver Sneakers, a group of charming retirees from the Jewish Center.

"She should get that ankle elevated and maybe packed in ice again," I told Sarge on the side. "And tell Lucy I'm taking Dandy home with me to get a bath. I'll bring him back tomorrow. Just gonna get this stuff"—I jerked a thumb at Lucy's wire cart—"into the washing machine first."

As soon as Sarge disappeared into the service elevator with Lucy, I called P.J. on his new cell phone, told him I'd be late and could he get something to eat for himself and Paul? "Yes, you can order a pizza . . . *yes*, I'll pay you back. Be sure to tip the delivery guy. And tell Paul . . . uh, tell Paul that Lucy and Dandy came back to the shelter and they're fine, okay?" I rolled my eyes at Will as I flipped my cell closed. "One of these days I need to teach those boys how to cook!"

I realized the sandy-haired young man had said very little since we'd found Lucy and Dandy, though he'd been very helpful getting her back to the car and into the shelter. Now, kneeling beside Dandy, where he'd busied himself rubbing the dog dry, he looked up at me. "Uh, Mrs. Fairbanks, can we talk? You know, about . . ." He jerked his head toward the doorway where Sarge and Lucy had disappeared.

"Sure. I want to talk to you too. Just let me get these things started in the wash—you mind helping me get this cart downstairs?"

We stuffed everything washable in Lucy's cart into the two

washing machines in the small laundry room on the lower level. Ten minutes later we were back in Shepherd's Fold, which we now had to ourselves since everyone had gone to supper. Dandy was still shivering, so Will actually sat on the floor and let Dandy curl up close to him, head in his lap.

"Mrs. Fairbanks, that banana cake you made last weekend—that was for Miss Lucy's birthday?"

I nodded. "November third. Born in 1926. Turned eighty last week."

"And that prayer she was saying out in the beach house . . ."

I nodded again. "She told me her mother said that prayer every time they moved into 'new digs,' as she called them, which was sometimes every few months. A migrant family, following the crops."

Will stared at me. "And her name, Lucy . . ."

"Real name Lucinda. Lucinda Tucker. Does that last name ring a bell with you?"

He practically gasped. "That's the family name! I used it in my Internet searches. And Nana has a couple of brothers, my great-uncles. Their last name is Tucker." He looked at me in wonder. "So this Lucy . . . Lucinda . . . you think—?"

"I think she could well be your grandmother's missing sister. Maybe she changed her name from Cindy to Lucy . . . Lucinda could be either."

Will wagged his head slowly. "Unbelievable! To think she's been here all this time." He stroked Dandy's still matted and muddied fur for several long moments. Then he looked up at me again. "Does she know? Have you said anything?"

"Nope. Didn't even suspect it until you said that thing about the banana cake last weekend. I asked Josh to find out a little bit more about your missing great-aunt when you two had coffee together the other day, but he wasn't a very good sleuth. Except you did tell him your Great-Aunt Cindy had a November birthday. So then I started adding all the bits together. Wanted to tell you—and then Lucy up and did a disappearing act yesterday! I thought I'd lost my chance. So when you showed up today . . ." I shrugged.

"I've got to tell my grandmother!" Will scrambled to his feet, startling Dandy. "What do you think, Mrs. Fairbanks? What should we do? How should we get them together? Do you think Lucy would go with me to meet my grandmother?"

I shook my head. "Not likely. Besides, she's had a setback with that ankle of hers." I thought a moment. "Do you think your grand-mother would come here? I could talk to Lucy first, kind of prepare her."

"Tomorrow? Could we do this tomorrow?" Will was agitated, excited. "As long as Nana has looked for her sister, I don't want to wait another day!"

Paul was excited to see Dandy when I got home, but glared at me when he saw how muddy and matted he was. "You said he was fine, Mom. He's not fine! Look how he's shivering. I'm gonna give him a bath."

"Fine." I grinned. "Just give me a chance to hop in the shower first to get all this mud off *me*. Then you can have the tub—if you clean it afterward!"

P.J. said his dad had called and left a message that he'd arrived safely. Wrapped in my robe and warm slippers after my shower, I punched Play on the answering machine and listened to Philip's short message saying he'd call tomorrow to talk to the boys. But hearing his voice reminded me of the note Will Nissan had brought me—before all the drama of hunting for Lucy had crowded everything else from my mind.

Chewing a piece of leftover pizza at the kitchen table, along with a cup of hot tea, I opened the note. It was dated *Thursday, 10:00 p.m.* Last night.

> *Dear Gabby,*
>
> *I want you to get this note sooner rather than later, so I'm hoping Will can deliver it tomorrow. First, I want to say thank you for saying you forgive me for all the pain I've caused you. It's more than I deserve and it can't have been easy. But it means more to me than I know how to put into words. I hope to earn that forgiveness by being a better man than I've been in the past.*

Earn my forgiveness? Didn't Philip realize none of us can *earn* forgiveness? At least, the only way I'd been able to forgive *him* was realizing that Jesus forgave all of us "while we were still sinners"—there was a Bible verse that said that somewhere. I was glad he wanted to become a better man. But he'd soon realize that wasn't going to happen without a lot of help. God's help.

I pushed the cold pizza away, wrapped my hands around the warm mug of tea, and continued reading.

> *. . . Also, you caught me off guard when you said the breakdown in our marriage wasn't all my fault. I wasn't expecting that. The decisions you made without telling me and the lack of*

communication did upset me a lot, so I deeply appreciate what you said. But one thing you said hit me hard. You said you didn't talk to me because you were afraid I'd say no to everything you wanted to do. That's what hit home. I didn't see it, couldn't hear it—until now. But staying with the Baxters this past week opened my eyes to a lot of things. Denny's a YES man! Everything Jodi suggests, he tries to make it happen. Never seen anything like it! She's the same way. It's like they bend over backward to keep the other one happy. Doesn't always work out, but the fact that they know the other person tried seems to make it OK.

Made me realize I never saw that in my home growing up. I'm so sorry, Gabby. Sorry for all the NOs I've thrown at you if it didn't suit me. Guess I've been a pretty selfish guy. Wish I could do it all over, things might be different now.

Better go. It's getting late. At least I don't have to pack since I'm basically living out of my suitcase anyway!

Once again the note was just signed, *"Philip."*

I'd been so absorbed reading Philip's note that I didn't realize the house phone had been ringing until I heard the answering machine click on. Jumping up from the kitchen table, I ran through the dining room and down the hallway to catch the call—but stopped when I heard Lee's voice leaving a message.

". . . on your cell but you must not have gotten my message. Would like to see you this weekend sometime. Call me, okay? Talk to you soon."

I could have snatched up the phone and caught him before he hung up—but something stopped me. My emotions were too stretched and thin to talk to Lee right now. I let the machine click off and headed back down the hall. I'd call Lee later. Tomorrow maybe. Or . . . maybe not.

chapter 39

I woke up Saturday to the familiar sound of loud thumps going down the outside stairs in back of the six-flat as Maddox Campbell moved out of 3B. Clouds still covered the city, but at least it wasn't raining on the movers. I ran upstairs at one point to say good-bye to his wife and mother, but no women were to be seen—just a sweaty crew of dark-skinned men, mostly Jamaican, lugging out boxes and furniture. It was obvious the women had been at work, though. Boxes were stacked neatly in each room, the kitchen appliances had been scrubbed—even the inside of the refrigerator—and the old, scratched wooden floors looked as if they'd been waxed and shined.

I did catch Maddox as he came back for more boxes, his dreads caught back in a thick ponytail, and shook his hand. "Best wishes to you, Mr. Campbell. I'm sorry I couldn't renew your lease. But if I *was* going to rent out these apartments, I would want to have good tenants like you."

The man nodded soberly. "Tank you, Miss Fairbanks. You a good woman. Good heart. Good head—under all dem crazy red curly-Qs." He grinned. "But why you not have a man? If you interested, I got two or t'ree who be good men. Hard workers. No gangbangers or Rastas."

It was hard not to giggle, but I was saved by my cell phone, which rang just then. So I just smiled at Mr. Campbell, thanked him for the compliment, and flipped open the phone as I scurried back down the two flights of stairs. *Huh!* Just what I needed right now—a matchmaker with dreadlocks!

The call was from Will, saying he could bring his grandmother by Manna House around two o'clock, which meant I needed to get over there earlier than that to talk to Lucy. I'd also promised her I'd bring Dandy back today, much to Paul's dismay. He'd not only given the dog a bath the night before but had brushed Dandy's yellow coat until it lay silky and smooth.

"Good job, kiddo. He looks like a different dog," I said, giving Paul a hug. I wanted to tell my tenderhearted son I was going to confront Lucy about her inability to take care of herself and Dandy on the street in the winter, but I didn't want to get his hopes up about taking care of the dog. And who knew what was going to happen when Will and his grandmother met Lucy?

Right after lunch I changed into slacks and a sweater, left the boys with a list of chores to do and a promise we'd go see a movie later, and showed up at Manna House with Dandy while lunch cleanup was still going on. Several residents were playing cards and board games in Shepherd's Fold, a few were reading old magazines, and others were just sitting. I could hear the TV blaring all the way from the TV room.

Lucy, however, was snoring on a couch in a corner of the main room, her left foot propped up on a stack of pillows, the ankle wrapped once again with an elastic bandage until the new swelling went down. I hesitated to wake her, but Dandy had no such qualms, putting his paws up on the couch cushions and licking her face.

"Umph . . . uh . . . wha—?" Lucy woke, startled. "Oh, heh heh, hey there, Dandy." She tried to sit up, but fell back. "Dagnabit! These old muscles don't bounce back like they used to."

"That's okay. You take it easy." I found a few more throw pillows and propped her up with a little help—hindrance was more like it—from Dandy.

"Say, now, don't you look fancy," Lucy murmured, stroking the dog's head. "That Paul, he sure does know how to purty you up."

I sat down on the other end of the couch, taking care not to jostle her foot. "Something I want to talk to you about, Lucy. About you and Dandy—"

"I know, I *know!*" The old lady threw up a hand. "Been thinkin' 'bout it all night. Dandy just couldn't stop shiverin' after he took a dunk in th' lake. Tell you the truth, Fuzz Top, I was skeered—skeered he was gonna get pneumony if somebody didn't come along an' find us purty soon. Woulda walked him back here myself if I hadn't twisted my ankle again." She leaned over and waggled the dog's ears with both hands. "Guess I been an old fool, Dandy, thinkin' you an' me could make it out on the streets this winter." Her voice drifted and she looked away, almost as if she'd forgotten I was there. "But he's good company, ya know? Gets mighty lonely sometimes."

This wasn't going to be easy. I cleared my throat. "I know. You've been good company for Dandy, too, Lucy. He was lonely after my mom died, and he loves you, plain to see that. But sometimes we have to do what's best for those we love, not just what we want, and I think we need a new plan."

"Yeah, yeah," she growled. "I know whatcha gonna say. Was gonna say th' same thing. Ya think Paul would mind watchin' Dandy over the winter, at least till this bum ankle heals and the weather gets warm again?"

I wanted to laugh. *Mind?* Not for a minute. Though I'd actually been going to ask if she'd be willing to *give* Dandy to Paul to be his own dog, not just take care of him for Lucy. But I didn't. It was going to be hard for Lucy to part with the dog, period. Maybe it was easier for her to think about it in stages.

"But it's not just Dandy I'm worried about," I said. "You're eighty years old. It's not safe for you to still be out on the street in this kind of weather, Lucy—especially not with your ankle still weak. And it's only going to get worse, you know that. But I have good news." I took a deep breath. "Someone's been looking for you—and I think he's found you. Someone who doesn't want you to have to live on the street anymore."

Lucy squinted her rheumy eyes at me. "What in tarnation you talkin' 'bout? You not makin' any sense a'tall, Gabby Fairbanks."

I scooted closer on the couch. "You know that nice young man who was with me when we found you yesterday?"

"Yeah. So?"

"His name is Will Nissan. He's Maggie Simple's grandson—"

"Maggie *who*? Don't know nobody named Simple. What kinda name is that?"

"Simple's her married name. But growing up her name was Maggie Tucker."

I waited for this news to sink in, but Lucy just scowled and pinched her lips.

"Lucy?" I said gently. "I'm talking about Maggie Tucker,

your *sister*. She's been looking for you for a long time—she and her grandson, Will. They're coming here to see you in about—" I looked at my watch. 2:05. "Well, any time now."

As if I'd just spoken biblical prophecy, I heard the front door buzzer. "That might be them now. I'll go let them in." I stood up and headed for the foyer, thanking God for Lucy's bum ankle. The way she was acting, I wouldn't have been surprised if she'd try to disappear in the two minutes I was out of the room.

I opened the big oak door. Sure enough, Will Nissan stood on the steps of Manna House holding the elbow of an elderly woman in a brown coat, wisps of gray hair framing her rather square face under a brown-and-tan knit hat.

"Please, come in!" I ushered them into the foyer. "Mrs. Simple? I'm Gabby Fairbanks, program director here at Manna House." I held out my hand. "I'm so delighted to finally meet you. Your grandson has been a helpful friend to my, uh, husband."

Maggie Simple shook my hand. Her skin was cool, soft. "Yes. Will told me about the gentleman who's been helping him with his architecture classes." Her voice was polite but tentative. "Is . . . Cindy here?"

"Well, we know her as Lucy, but her given name is Lucinda. Yes, she's here. Sprained her ankle a couple weeks ago, though. In here." I led the way through the double doors, wishing we had a private room where this at-long-last meeting could take place. The chapel? But moving Lucy anywhere would be an ordeal, so I tossed that idea. We'd just have to make do.

Mrs. Simple approached slowly, clinging to Will's arm. I quickly brought a chair next to Lucy's couch, and the elderly woman sat down on the edge. Lucy's face was expressionless, her eyes focused somewhere else. Dandy started to get up and sniff at the newcomers, but Lucy's hand gripped his collar and held him back. He whined and sat back down, as if confused.

Make that two of us. What was going to happen here?

But oh my goodness. It was like looking at aging twins—or would be if Lucy's hair had a wash and a good cut. Same squarish, wrinkled face, same hazel eyes and heavy lids, same body build. Lucy's skin, however, was rough and leathery from years on the streets, while Maggie's had the soft, natural pink of a healthy woman in her seventies.

"Cindy? Is that you?" Mrs. Simple's voice wavered.

"Name's Lucy," Lucy muttered. "Don't nobody call me Cindy."

Will spoke up. "Lucy, you remember me from last night, right? My name's Will Nissan, and this is my grandmother, Maggie Simple. She's been looking for her sister, Lucinda Tucker, for a long, long time. We think we've found her."

Lucy said nothing for several moments, then growled, "Don't got no family."

"But it's me—Maggie! Your sister!" Tears had started to puddle in Mrs. Simple's eyes. She fished for an embroidered handkerchief tucked up her sleeve and dabbed her eyes. "You've got a lot of family! Brothers and sisters, nieces and nephews. Ma and Pa, they've been gone now, oh, twenty years. But most of us children got married, had a passel of kids and grandkids—like Will here." She looked up into her grandson's face and smiled through the tears.

Lucy's lip seemed to tremble, just for a moment, but she still didn't look Maggie Simple in the face.

Will's grandmother wagged her head. "Things were bad back then, Cindy. I know that. But all that's past. No one thinks about . . . about what happened. Tucker family's doin' well now. 'Cept for one thing—our missing sister. Everybody thinks you're dead. But not me. I knew one day we'd find you. Will and me, we come to Chicago to look for you, and here you are."

No one spoke. But women around the room were looking curiously our way and starting to make comments. I slipped away from the reunion and moved from group to group. "Lucy's got visitors and needs some privacy. Just leave them alone right now, all right? Thanks."

I returned to Lucy's couch just in time to hear Lucy mutter, "Been a long time. Too long. Can't nothin' be different now."

"But—" Maggie Simple started to say, but Will stopped her with a hand on her shoulder.

"I think maybe we should leave now. Maybe we can come back soon." He helped his grandmother to her feet. But then he stepped forward and squatted down beside Dandy, taking the dog's face in his hands. "Thanks for looking after my Great-Aunt Cindy, Dandy. Tell her it's a big job for a dog, though. Tell her we'd like to help you out, look after her now. Tell her we want to bring her home. Can you do that, fella?"

Without another word, he stood and walked his grandmother out into the foyer. Maggie kept looking back, as if she was afraid to leave, afraid the sister she'd just found would be lost again. But she clung to Will's arm as I followed and opened the front door for them. As they stepped outside, Will turned back and gave me a lopsided grin. "That went well for the first visit, don't you think?"

chapter 40

Lucy refused to talk to me about her visitors. I wanted to tick off all the clues that led Will and me to realize she was his missing great-aunt, or . . . or shake her, the stubborn old fool! Didn't she realize what an amazing miracle this was?! That her family had not only found her but wanted to provide a home for her?

But after a few tries that got me nowhere, I gave up and decided to leave her alone. Maybe she was in shock.

Paul was ecstatic when I brought Dandy back home with me. True to her word, Lucy had let me take the dog home with a message for Paul, asking if he'd take care of him for her this winter. *"Jus' bring him ta see me when ya come ta work, promise?"* she'd fussed at me. *"When I'm here, that is."*

I'd promised, thanking God I worked in a place that let me bring a dog to work—well, *this* dog, anyway, who'd become the Manna House mascot after saving Sarge that night from a knife-wielding intruder. But it bothered me when Lucy said, *"When I'm here, that is."* She obviously wasn't planning to change her come-and-go lifestyle anytime soon.

Well, we'd see about that.

When I got back to the House of Hope, Josh Baxter was already at work prepping walls in 3B, and Celia Jones stopped by to let me know she and her granddaughter were going to spend the rest of the weekend on the South Side with her brother's family, giving Keisha a chance to spend a little time with her mom who lived nearby. "We babysat Bam-Bam and Dessa last night so Shawanda could have a night out, didn't we, Keisha? So she should do all right while we're gone."

"How about you?" I asked. "You doing okay sharing the apartment with Shawanda? You need to let me or Mabel know if you have any problems."

Celia shrugged and smiled. "We're doing all right. And I'm sure it'll get better. Shawanda's still young. She just needs some stability."

Philip had called while I was out and talked to both boys. I was sorry I'd missed his call, but decided to wait until his next call to ask how his business consultation with his father and uncle was going. He hadn't directly answered P.J.'s question the other night about whether he was going to move back to Virginia for good, but I had my own suspicions about what might happen. Either he'd come back here and start up a new company, which would be in direct competition with Henry Fenchel, or he'd hop back into the family business there in Petersburg. Both options would affect me and the boys—but right now, I needed to take things one day at a time.

I hadn't called Lee back either. But P.J. and Paul were both antsy to get out of the house for our movie-and-pizza date, and by the time we got back, I was so pooped, I couldn't wait to take a long soak in the tub and fall into bed.

Tomorrow. I'd call Lee tomorrow.

A loud clatter woke me several hours later. I sat up in bed, my heart pounding. What was that? Sounded like something tumbling down the outside back stairs and breaking. I squinted at the glowing numbers on my digital clock. 2:12. Fumbling in the dark, I found my robe, pulled it around me, and peeked though the blinds on my bedroom window overlooking the back porch. A shadowy figure was bent over on my landing, picking up the pieces of . . . something.

Feeling my way, I moved quickly into the kitchen, sidled up to the back door, and moved the curtain on the window an inch. The hunched figure was a man. Could it be Josh? The tenant still in 2B coming home late? Or had Maddox Campbell come back for something? Not likely. He'd given the apartment keys back to Josh before he left.

Just then the man straightened and looked back up the stairs. By now my eyes had adjusted to the glow coming from the alley light. Youngish, slender, dark skin, shaved head—whoever it was, I didn't recognize him. *Drat!* Why hadn't I grabbed my cell phone? I should be calling 9-1-1 and reporting a stranger on my property! I was just about to run for the phone in the hallway when I heard footsteps coming down the back stairs and another figure appeared on my landing. What in the world?

Shawanda!

The two young people giggled surreptitiously, and I heard the word "flowerpot." They kissed, then the young man hustled down the last few steps to the walk that led to the alley, tossed something into the dumpster, and the girl ran back upstairs.

Of all the nerve! Shawanda had snuck a *man* into her apartment tonight while Celia was gone.

I shuffled back to my bed. Good thing I hadn't called 9-1-1. But Shawanda would have to face *me* tomorrow, and as far as she was concerned, that might be even worse.

The next morning I was out at the dumpster before breakfast, picking out pieces of the flowerpot Lover Boy had knocked over as he snuck out last night. Thank goodness trash didn't get picked up on the weekend. Fortunately, the broken pot sat on top of the numerous bags of trash Maddox Campbell's moving crew had tossed. If the dumpster had been empty or even half full, I'd never have been able to reach the bottom.

Pieces in hand, I marched up the back stairs and knocked loudly on the kitchen door of 2A. I had to pound on the door two or three minutes before Shawanda peeked through the curtain, hair wrap knotted on her head, eyes bleary. She opened the door two inches. "Miss Gabby? Uh . . . whatchu want? Ain't it kinda early?"

I held up the pieces of the broken flowerpot. "We need to talk."

The door opened another couple of inches, and she pulled her thin robe around her body. "Oh, sorry 'bout that. Was it yours? I, uh, knocked it off the porch rail last night by accident."

"Cut the crap, Shawanda," I snapped. "I don't care about the pot. Wasn't mine, might be Celia's. What I do care about is the young man who left your apartment shortly after two this morning—the one who knocked this over and woke me up."

She squirmed. "Oh, uh . . . sorry that woke you up. He, uh, he's just a friend, came by to drop somethin' off for me, an' I *told* him it was too late, but—"

"Shawanda." *No sense getting angry*, I told myself. *Speak calmly.* "Look, don't make this any worse by lying about it. You know the rule: no men in the apartments after ten p.m. The first time Celia's gone overnight, you broke the rule. That's serious."

Shivering in the doorway, Shawanda's face morphed into a pout. "Don't see why it's anybody's bizness. Celia and Keisha, they gone, we didn't bother them none."

"It's the rule, Shawanda. You signed an agreement to live by the rules here at the House of Hope."

"But you treatin' us like little kids! I'm grown! What I do shouldn't make no difference to you."

I realized this was getting us nowhere. And now I was shivering in the damp morning air. "I'm not going to argue with you, Shawanda. We'll talk about the consequences later. But I'm disappointed. I was hoping this arrangement would work out for you and the kids." I shoved the pieces of flowerpot into her hand. "Better let Celia know she's minus a flowerpot when she gets back." I turned and started down the stairs.

"Wait!" Shawanda came out the door and leaned over the railing as I descended. "You not gonna kick us out, are you, Miss Gabby?" Her voice had lost the pout and was shrill with anxiety. "You can't do that! No way can I go back to the shelter!"

But I just slipped back into my apartment and shut the door.

"I told her the truth," I said to Jodi Baxter after the worship service at SouledOut later that morning. "I *am* disappointed. I was hoping the House of Hope could be a turning point for Shawanda." I hadn't seen or talked to Jodi since the previous Sunday when she'd told me her husband and Harry were planning a gutsy talk with Philip, so we'd grabbed a couple cups of coffee and were huddling in a corner, trying to catch up with each other.

"Is that it? Break one rule and she's out?" Jodi seemed surprised.

I sighed. "I don't know. We didn't say definitely. But Shawanda's the kind of person if you give her an inch, she takes a mile. Poster kid for the cliché." I smiled wanly. "Don't worry, I'll talk with Mabel and the Baby Baxters before I—what?"

Jodi looked shocked, then she burst out laughing. "The Baby Baxters? Is that what you call Josh and Edesa?"

"Oops. Did I say that?" Now I was laughing. "Uh, that's what Precious calls them. Guess it kinda stuck. *Anyway* . . ." I took another sip of weak coffee, made a face, and set it aside. "I don't want to talk about Shawanda. You probably know what's going on with Philip, since he was staying at your house before he left for Virginia—"

Jodi nodded. "Pretty much. He and Denny talked a couple more times last week, and I know he decided to sell out his share of the business and pay off the debts and everything. It's amazing. But Denny kind of hinted that Philip's had a couple of serious talks with you, right?" She raised an eyebrow. "Anything you want to tell me?"

I brought out the two notes Philip had written to me, trying to fill her in on the roller coaster of emotions I'd been through that week. We talked a long time, so long that Denny finally gave P.J. and Paul a ride back to the House of Hope along with Josh, Edesa, and Gracie, while Jodi and I ended up at The Coffee Cup for a couple of lattes and oversize cranberry-nut muffins so I could also bring her up to date on the drama going on with Lucy and her long-lost family.

"It's a miracle, Jodi! Think about it. Philip meets Will his last day in the hospital, Philip agrees to mentor Will in some of his classes, Will casually mentions his grandmother is looking for her long-lost sister—who turns out to be Lucy Tucker, of all people! After sixty-plus years! But Lucy's being weird about it. Almost as if she didn't want to be found. Or doesn't want to give up her independence—or *something*."

"Well, like you said earlier, maybe she's just in shock."

I shook my head. "I don't know, Jodi. Lucy's the most stubborn woman I've ever met."

She snorted. "Except maybe Estelle. You know she gave Harry his ring back."

I rolled my eyes. "Oh yeah. And I noticed they didn't even sit together in church this morning. How silly is that? They're crazy about each other! But Estelle's got this notion in her head that it's either Harry or Leroy."

Jodi shook her head, glanced at her watch, and sighed. "I know we better go, but if you've got a few more minutes, Gabby, I think we should pray. Let's put the whole kaboddle in God's lap and let Him sort it out!"

After dropping Jodi off at her house, I thought, *Should've told Jodi about Lee too*. I still needed to return his call. Just thinking about all the tangled relationships in my life was a recipe for a sure-fire headache—but after my long talk and prayer time with Jodi, I felt more at peace than I had all week.

Shawanda was at my door Sunday evening, all penitent,

begging for another chance. I told her breaking the rule about no men at night was a serious matter and I had to talk to Mabel Turner about whether she'd disqualified herself for housing at House of Hope. She ran upstairs in tears and slammed the door. For two seconds my resolve to be "fair but firm" wavered and I almost followed her, wanting to say, *Okay, okay, we'll give you another chance*—which we might, but I made myself close my door and stick to my guns about talking to Mabel before I did anything. Besides, it wouldn't hurt for Shawanda to feel a little holy fear for a while.

Philip called while I was making supper and I was the one who answered the phone. "Oh, good, you're home tonight," he said. "I wanted to talk to you too."

I tensed a little. "Well, how's it going? Have you talked with your dad and uncle about a new business plan?"

"Not yet. Dad set up a meeting with Uncle Matt tomorrow morning. Not sure how long I can stay here at the house with the folks, though—it's kind of tense with my mother. She got all bent out of shape when I returned the money she'd given me. She's also mad that I sold out my half of the business to Fenchel, even though I explained it was the only way to get the lawsuits and the debt monkey off my back. She can't understand that, told me she could've bailed me out and I'd still have the business."

I bit my lip, determined not to say anything. But Marlene Fairbanks's response didn't surprise me one iota. Then it just slipped out. "Proud of you for sticking to your guns, Philip. Time to move out of the nest."

"Ouch. That's what I was trying to do by moving to Chicago. Thought it was Dad wanting to run my life, because Mom championed the move, you know. Don't know why it took me so long to realize *why* she was always taking my side against Dad—almost like divide and conquer. I got out from under Dad's thumb, but she still had her hooks in me. Always wanting to throw me a safety net." He chuckled in my ear. "Wish you could've seen her face when I gave her money back—with interest. It wasn't pretty."

I couldn't help it. I laughed aloud. "Oh dear. I better let you talk to the boys before I get myself in trouble . . . P.J.! Paul! It's your dad!"

"Gabby, wait. There's something else I wanted to tell you."

"Oh. Okay." I scrunched the phone under my ear and resumed work on the chicken wraps I'd been making with leftover chicken and large flour tortillas. Paul poked his head into the kitchen, but I waved him away again.

"I went to church this morning."

I nearly dropped the phone. "You—what? Went to church? Where?"

"Same one we used to attend from time to time. Briarwood Lutheran. But it seemed . . . different this time."

"What do you mean?"

"Well, the boys probably told you I went to SouledOut that Sunday you were out of town and I was staying at your place. They wanted to go, so—"

"Yeah, they told me. I was glad you took them. But you didn't say anything about it, and you didn't come last Sunday when you were staying with the Baxters. So I figured it probably wasn't your thing."

"Well, SouledOut was certainly different than anything I was used to. A bit loud. But I could see why the boys liked it—and why *you* like it. Everybody was so into it—the singing, everything. Not an audience with performers up front doing the religious stuff, but everybody participating. Like it was the greatest thing to spend Sunday morning with God and each other. I've thought about it several times since then—and this morning I just decided to go to church. Not sure exactly why . . . okay, it was partly to get out of this house since my mother is barely speaking to me. But—"

I could hear several clicks in my ear. Another call coming through.

"Gabby? Do you need to get that call?"

I pulled the phone away from my ear and looked at the caller ID.

Lee Boyer.

chapter 41

I felt torn. Lee was going to think I was avoiding him! But . . . no, this was important. "It's all right," I told Philip. "I can call them back. You were saying?"

"Okay. Anyway, the pastor's sermon was really good. Something about how we are created in God's image, but that image has been broken by sin and evil in the world, and it's our job to let God heal the brokenness and rediscover God's image in our lives—His qualities, His character, stuff like that."

I had stopped rolling up the chicken wraps, astonished to hear Philip talking like this. "It does sound like a good sermon."

"Yeah. Kind of hit me between the eyes. A lot of things in my life feel broken right now—our marriage primarily, but a lot of other stuff too. But the pastor said God wants to restore the stamp of His image on our lives. Gave me some hope that maybe it's not too late for me. To get things right, I mean."

A long silence hung in the air. Coming from Philip, what he was saying sounded like a foreign language. At the same time, it reminded me of the strong sense I'd had not long ago, that it was God holding my broken heart together.

"Gabby? You still there?"

I found my voice. "Yes . . . yes, still here. Just thinking about what you said. I don't think it's ever too late, Philip. Not from God's point of view, anyway. But that brokenness you mentioned? That's not something we can fix on our own. Gotta let God do it. It's the only way."

I called Lee back later that evening. Had to apologize several times for not getting back to him. Told him I'd spent Friday evening hunting for Lucy . . . Saturday overseeing a reunion between the streetwise old lady and her long-lost family . . . not to mention another tenant moving out and Shawanda already breaking the house rules. "It's just been a hectic weekend, Lee." And that was without saying anything about the major moves in Philip's life that affected me and the boys.

"Okay. I understand, I guess. Just feels as if there's a lot going on in your life I only find out about after the fact. I would've been glad to help you look for Lucy when she went missing. Just call me, Gabby! I'm here for you, you know."

"I know, Lee. I appreciate it."

He wanted to set a date to see each other next weekend, but I hesitated. There was so much up in the air! Not knowing when—or if—Philip would return from Virginia. What it would mean if Lucy accepted the invitation to go live with her sister. Estelle maybe moving into an apartment with her son. Work on the newly empty apartment. Next weekend already felt like a zoo.

Not to mention the real question. Should I even be seeing Lee right now?

Wimp that I was, I put him off, telling him I'd know better what my weekend would look like later in the week, but I could tell he wasn't a happy camper.

Monday turned out to be another dreary, rainy, chilly November day—but at least the weather upped the odds that Lucy would still be at Manna House when I showed up for work. Will had said he would try to bring his grandmother again after his Monday classes. I met with Mabel first thing, bringing her up to date on the whole amazing story of Maggie Tucker Simple finding her long-lost sister by a series of almost miraculous clues pointing to our own Lucy.

Mabel's smile grew with the story. "That's God, Gabby. Has to be God."

"Yeah, but I'm sure God knows that was the easy part. Convincing Lucy to accept her sister's invitation to come live with her—*that's* going to be the hard part." We both laughed in agreement. "Okay, change of subject?"

I told her about Shawanda and her nighttime visitor. Good ol' Mabel. She said I ought to talk to Celia Jones and get *her* advice about whether this infraction was a deal-breaker, or whether the situation called for grace and a second chance. After all, she said, Celia was closer to Shawanda's situation than any of us, even though she'd been away that night. I was impressed that the director of the shelter was willing to defer to the advice of one of our "clients." But that was Mabel. Treated our residents as individuals who just happened to be homeless, not a class of down-and-out women who had nothing to offer.

Paul stuck his head into my office after school to say the rain had stopped and he was taking Dandy for a walk around the block—and by the way, Will and his grandmother were upstairs in Shepherd's Fold talking to Lucy. Curious, I followed Paul and Dandy up to the main level as they headed for the front door. But Maggie and Lucy actually seemed to be talking to each other on the far side of the big room—or at least Lucy seemed to be listening as Maggie and Will talked to her, grunting and nodding from time to time. So I turned around and went back to my office—and when I got there, I closed the door and actually got down on my knees by my desk chair.

"Jesus," I murmured aloud, "like they say at SouledOut, You've brought us too far to leave us now! Soften Lucy's heart, Lord. Help her to see *You* are the one who brought Maggie and Will to Chicago, to find her after all these years so she wouldn't be alone and out on the street in her final years." Remembering how Jodi often prayed, I added, "Thank You, Lord, for everything You've done so far, and for everything You're *going* to do!"

I managed to catch Celia that evening as she came in the front door with groceries and asked if I could talk to her privately. After listening to the tale of Shawanda's nighttime visitor, the middle-aged grandmother pursed her lips and was quiet for a few minutes, as if digesting the information and trying to decide which options were healthy choices or empty calories.

Finally she spoke. "Shawanda's kind of at a crossroads. If we send her packing, not sure what would happen to her. She might not have the motivation to clean up her life and learn how to be a responsible mom. If she stays, well, we still have some influence on her, bringing some order into her mothering and personal life." She smiled. "Was just reading the gospel of Luke where Jesus and His disciples were going through a Samaritan town, and the townspeople weren't very hospitable to the travelers. The disciples asked Jesus if they could call down fire from heaven and wipe them out!"

"Really?" My eyes widened. "I don't remember that."

"Chapter nine. You can look it up. Anyway, Jesus told the disciples to let it go, because He came to bring life, not death, to people." She shrugged. "Maybe that's how we should respond to Shawanda this first time. Don't bring down the consequences on her head. Give her another chance at life. But you can always say if it happens again, she'll have to move out."

I was amazed by the woman's wisdom. I ran the whole thing by Edesa and Josh, as the other House of Hope staff members, and they both affirmed Celia's suggestion. "But why don't we tell her privately instead of bringing it up at the household meeting tomorrow," Edesa suggested. "No sense embarrassing her unnecessarily."

Which we did. Edesa and I sat down with Shawanda and Celia that evening and laid it out for her, so by the time we all got together for the weekly household meeting on Wednesday, Shawanda was falling all over herself being cooperative with everything.

However, the incident helped us realize we needed a specific plan to deal with violations of the rules that everyone understood. What we'd just done had seemed wise—so we presented a plan that when a rule was broken, the consequences for a first-time offense would be decided by at least two House of Hope staff plus one of the residents. A second offense would mean a meeting with the director of Manna House. "Participation in the House of Hope is a privilege, not a right," I said. "Cooperation with one another and with the rules we've all agreed to are essential to our success."

No one mentioned Shawanda's violation as the impetus for the new plan, but by the look Tanya gave Precious, I think they had a pretty good idea.

"Hey, Thanksgivin' is next week," Precious reminded the group. "If y'all don't have other plans for feastin', I got me an idea." We all looked at her curiously. "Why don't we have a House of Hope Thanksgivin', with ever'body inviting any family members they got 'round here—well, within reason. Two or three extra folks per, know what I'm sayin'?"

"But we don't have any space in this building big enough for a sit-down Thanksgiving meal," I protested.

"Jus' hold on, I ain't done yet. We could do it like one o' them progressive dinners I've heard about. Y'know, serve salad in one apartment, turkey in another, dessert in another. See what I'm sayin'?"

The idea caught on—and soon everybody was talking at once about whom to invite and how if everybody brought something, the food wouldn't be a big strain on anybody. "And if I'm far enough along getting 3B painted," Josh added, pointing across the hall from 3A where we were meeting, "maybe we could do some games with the kids or something in there. No furniture!" He grinned.

As we were leaving, Edesa said, "Don't forget, we're going to have our first House of Hope Yada Yada Prayer Group this Sunday evening. Is five o'clock okay?"

By the time I got back to my own apartment, I was feeling buoyant. We'd dealt with our first major problem in a positive way, we'd come up with a reasonable plan to deal with future problems, we were starting a prayer group for the ladies, and everyone was excited about celebrating a holiday together.

"God is good . . . all the time . . . all the time . . . God is good," I hummed as I peeked in on the boys, who were still doing homework in their respective rooms, earbuds to their iPods plugged into their ears. A few telltale dishes sitting on their desks with puddles of ice cream in the bottom gave away the latest raid on the kitchen.

I resisted gathering up the dirty dishes—snack dishes were supposed to be returned to the kitchen by the snackee—and headed for my bedroom, hoping to crawl into bed early and read till I got sleepy. But I was interrupted by my cell phone. I looked at the caller ID. *What? Philip?* He'd been calling on the home phone so he could talk to the boys each evening. Why my cell? I flipped it open. "Hey."

"Hi, Gabby. Hope you don't mind me calling your cell, but I need to talk to you, not the boys."

"O-kaay." This was it. The Big Plan. I plumped up my pillows and leaned against them on the bed.

"My dad and uncle made me an offer today. Very decent of them, given how badly I messed up in Chicago. They're willing to take me back into the firm as a manager of one of their divisions—sort of a mid-level position, decent salary. If I behave myself for five years"—he gave a half laugh—"they'll consider making me a partner."

For some reason, my chest went tight. Had I been afraid of

this all along? That Philip's trip to Virginia would result in him moving back there? What had I been hoping for? Something, but not this. Even though we were separated, at least the boys got to be with their dad every weekend. They were moving into their teen years! The time when boys needed their—

"Gabby? Are you still there?"

I tried to find my voice. "Yes. Still here. Just trying to digest this news. Thinking about the boys especially. This is going to be hard on them."

"I know. I've been thinking about the boys too. And you. Which is why I'm going way out on a limb here and ask you something . . ." I heard him clear his throat several times. "Gabby, uh, would you consider moving back here to Petersburg with the boys—not now, of course, but maybe at the end of the boys' semester? Between Christmas and New Year's or something like that? Or if not then, at the end of the school year? Maybe we could start over, give our family another chance."

Now I could hardly breathe. How dare he ask that of me! He'd pulled me away from our home in Virginia to come here, which meant giving up a job I loved there, then dumped me. Now I'd started over, made a home for our sons, found another job I loved, even developed the House of Hope, which was giving hope to homeless moms, maybe for the first time in their lives.

As for "us"—Philip and me—we hadn't even talked about our future! Why would I move a thousand miles to be "together" again when I had no guarantees—none!—that we could put our family back together again? Admittedly, things had been better between us, downright decent in fact, for the past several weeks. And I was proud of the tough decisions he'd made recently to own up to his gambling addiction, sell out his partnership, pay off the debts he'd accrued, be willing to start over . . . but that didn't answer any of the questions about *us*.

I took a deep breath and blew it out. And said simply, "No, Philip. I'm not moving back to Petersburg."

I heard him chuckle. "Didn't think so. That's why I told my dad and uncle I couldn't accept their offer. So tell the boys I'll see them in a day or two. Just got to wind up a few things here, then I'll catch a flight back to Chicago."

"What?" I thought I was over being shocked. "Wait . . . Philip. But what about that job offer? It's really generous, would help you get back on your feet, and put you back into the commercial development business. That's what you love doing, right? I mean, why would you turn it down?"

He didn't answer for a moment or two. And then . . . "Why? Because it took some hard knocks to make me realize what's most important in my life—and it's not the business. It's my family. You and P.J. and Paul. I need to give myself every opportunity to do right by my family. Put it back together if I can, but at least *be there* for you all—and I can't do that from Petersburg."

chapter 42

It took me a long time to fall asleep after the phone call with Philip. I could hardly believe it! His father had offered him a decent way to get back into the commercial development business—not a bailout, like his mother had been ready to do, but a chance to prove himself over a period of time, a chance to rectify his mistakes and start over. And he'd *turned it down*?

Guilt nagged at my spirit. Maybe I should've been willing to at least *consider* moving back to Petersburg so he could've taken them up on the offer.

Funny thing, though. The guilt trip didn't come from Philip. Even though he asked if I'd consider moving back to Petersburg, he wasn't surprised by my no. In fact, he said he'd *already* turned down the offer, realizing it wasn't realistic to expect the boys and me to drop everything and move back there.

No, *he* was making a choice. Putting his family first.

It was so . . . so incredibly amazing, I hardly knew what to do with myself. I finally threw off the covers, got up, and put a load of laundry into the machine in the basement, then scrubbed the stovetop, which had needed it for at least a week. I checked on the boys—both of them asleep, Paul with an arm flung over Dandy, who was curled up on his bed, P.J. splayed out on the bed still in his clothes, desk light on. "Your father really does love you," I whispered to each one as I kissed their cheeks and turned out the lights.

But I still didn't know the answer to the next question.

Did I still love Philip?

Did Philip love *me*?

The boys were ecstatic when I told them the next morning that their dad would be back in a few days. But I was still in shock when I arrived at work. And worried. Did Philip have a Plan B? What was he going to do for a place to live? Even more critical, what was he going to do for a *job*?

Estelle came in late that morning, bustling around the shelter kitchen like a banshee on the loose, trying to put lunch together on time. I came out of my office and leaned on the counter. "You okay? Need some help?" To be honest, I was so distracted that morning I figured I'd be more productive chopping vegetables than pushing my computer mouse around anyway.

She snapped up my offer in a nanosecond, handing me a potato peeler and a ten-pound bag of Idaho potatoes, while she peeled onions for a vegetable soup, fussing the whole time. "Was s'posed to look at a couple apartments this morning. First one, the so-called bedrooms were 'bout as big as your broom-closet there"—she pointed a knife at my office off the dining room—"and the next one, landlord never showed. Lord, have mercy! If I don't find an apartment soon, don't know what I'm gonna do. Leroy s'posed to get released from the nursing center this weekend." Her knife flew so fast chopping the peeled onions, I was afraid a couple of her fingers might end up in the soup.

"Can't you ask them for an extension? I mean, they can't release him if he doesn't have a place to go, right?"

"That's what I'm gonna do, ask 'em for another week at least! Got a meeting with the staff there tomorrow mornin' at ten. Maybe you all can pray for me during Edesa's Bible study."

"Mrs. Fairbanks?" The male voice made me jump. Will Nissan appeared out of the stairwell and headed toward the kitchen. "My Thursday classes got cancelled, so Nana and I came a little earlier today—oh, hi, Miss Williams. I'm Will, Lucy Tucker's great-nephew." He held a hand across the counter toward Estelle.

"Mm-mm. Whoever you are, son, I like your manners." Estelle shook his hand. "Whatchu need . . . coffee? Got some left-over sweet rolls from this mornin'."

"I'm fine, thanks. Just wanted to tell Mrs. Fairbanks here that I think we're making some progress. Lucy says she's willing to go visit the condo where my grandmother lives—you know, give her an idea of what it'd be like to live there with her sister. Would tomorrow afternoon about three be okay?"

"That's fantastic, Will! I'll make sure Lucy's ready to go." I looked at him quizzically. "If Lucy does move in with your grand-mother, what about you? Is the apartment big enough for all three of you?"

He ran a hand through his sandy hair. "Not really. It's only a two-bedroom. I'll have to move out to make room for Aunt

Cindy—Lucy, I mean. I put my name in for student housing at UIC, but they don't have anything available 'til semester break. So, yeah, it's a little tricky. I need to find something temporary for six weeks, maybe eight. But"—he shrugged—"it'll work out. In fact, I'm looking forward to living near campus. I'd like to get involved in more stuff than just going to classes. Oh, been meaning to ask. Have you heard anything from Mr. Philip? I was wondering if he's going to stay in Virginia or come back to Chicago."

I smiled. "Last I heard he's coming back here. In a day or two, in fact."

"Hey, that's great. He's been a real help to me on some of my architecture projects. Could use some more of his advice. Well . . ." The young man grinned and lifted a hand in a wave. "Guess I better get back to my girls." He laughed and disappeared up the stairs.

We watched him go. "That there is a nice young man," Estelle murmured. "Hope Lucy knows how lucky she is to have family like that." Then she eyed me with a lifted eyebrow. "So Philip's coming back to Chicago. How come I think there's more to the story than that?"

Philip called again that night to say he was arriving at O'Hare the following afternoon—Friday—and the Baxters had said he was welcome to use them as home base until he found an apartment. "I hate to ask, Gabby, but could I leave my stuff in your basement for a few more days? Another week at most. I'm sorry it's been this long."

Another week. But so far nobody in the building had complained. "I guess so. But you did say one week and it's already been two."

"I know. Guess I should have rented a storage locker. But at this point, I'd like to avoid moving it twice."

An awkward silence hung between us for a few moments. I was just about to push him on whether he had a Plan B for a job when he said, "I've got some good news, though. My father has been surprisingly supportive of my decision to return to Chicago—Uncle Matt too. Told me I'd made the right choice to put family first. Not only that, they're calling a board meeting to talk about creating a division of Fairbanks Commercial Development in the Midwest, probably Chicago. If so, they'd want me to head it up."

Furniture in my basement seemed a piddly concern compared to this news. "That's great, Philip! . . . I think. I mean, how do you feel about that? When you were working for your dad and uncle before, you were chafing at their traditional designs, feeling like they were stuck in the past."

"Yeah, well, the old 'if it ain't broke, don't fix it' mentality. You're right. It would be a challenge to work under the old Fairbanks business model. But I have to admit, it doesn't seem as important now to do my own thing. I had to eat crow just coming back here, admitting I'd messed up, asking their advice. But it wasn't so bad. It's hard to explain, Gabby, but there's a certain freedom in not having to be right all the time."

I hardly knew what to say. My entire experience with Fairbanks men had been they were right and it was up to you to admit it. Not just the men—his mother too. It infected the whole family. If

Philip could break *that* generational curse, I really would believe in miracles.

"—maybe teach some day," Philip was saying.

"What? I'm sorry, Philip. What were you saying? I didn't catch that."

"I asked if you'd heard anything from Will Nissan lately. Because I've enjoyed helping him with some of his student projects, and it made me think, maybe I'd like to try teaching at the college level some day. Architecture, maybe business . . . use my experience to develop a new generation of bright minds who are interested in city planning, commercial development, stuff like that."

"That's . . . that's a fantastic idea, Philip. But you mentioning Will made me realize I haven't told you something amazing that's happened since you left. Will found his missing great-aunt!"

"Really? You're kidding me. I mean, how long has she been missing . . . sixty years? I would've bet the farm it was impossible. So tell me where they found her."

By this time I was laughing. "Are you sitting down?"

I wish I could've seen Philip's face when I told him Will's missing great-aunt was none other than our own Lucy Tucker. I had to go over the various clues we'd pieced together before he believed me—and then all he could say was, "Unbelievable!"

Couldn't wait to tell Estelle about the latest revelations in Philip's reality show broadcasting from Virginia either. She'd wagged her head in serious disbelief on Thursday when I told her he'd turned down a generous job offer from his father and uncle because he wanted to "put family first." "Might just change my mind about that man," she'd murmured as we'd thrown the last of the vegetables into the soup pot.

But when she hadn't arrived at Manna House by mid-morning on Friday, I remembered she had a ten o'clock appointment to ask about extending Leroy's stay at the psychiatric nursing facility until she was able to find an apartment or house where she could take care of her son.

And she'd asked us to pray!

I scurried upstairs to catch Edesa before she started her Bible study, and the group of ten or so women who'd gathered took the request seriously. One called on Jehovah Jireh, God our Provider, to "make a way out of no way!" Another said, "An' we ast ya, Lord, to meet every need, known and unknown, for this poor boy an' his mama." Monique prayed on task, asking God to give Estelle favor when she asked for more time to find an apartment. "An' lead Estelle to the exact apartment You've prepared for her and Leroy—not tomorrow, not next week, but *today*, Lord Jesus, because you *said* where two or three are gathered together in *Your* name, there You are in the *midst!*"

I squirmed a bit. Had to wonder how God felt about Monique telling Him exactly how our prayers should be answered.

Edesa's prayer was almost the flip side of Monique's, praying that Estelle would not "lean on her own understanding" in this situation but would trust *El Señor* to care not only for her son but for herself and Harry—"that precious couple," she called them—as well.

Hoo boy. I wondered what Estelle would think if she knew

we were throwing prayers for her and Harry into the same pot with her request to bless the path she'd chosen for herself and Leroy.

An hour later the Bible study was disbanding and I was talking to Lucy—who hadn't exactly joined the Bible study circle but sat close enough to listen—about maybe getting a shower and into some fresh clothes before her sister and nephew arrived for their excursion that afternoon, when Estelle dragged in. Several of the residents said, "We prayed for ya, Miss Estelle," and asked, "How's that boy of yours doin' today?" But she just shook her head, shrugged off her coat, and sank into one of the overstuffed couches in the big room. I excused myself to Lucy and sat down with Estelle. Edesa joined us a moment later.

"How'd it go?" I asked. Our diva cook didn't look too happy.

Estelle frowned darkly. "That Leroy! Unpredictable as ever. Told me he didn't *want* to live with me. 'Stop treatin' me like a baby, Mama!' he said—right in front of the doctor an' two social workers! How is wantin' to do my duty as his mama, takin' care of my baby proper-like, and makin' sure no druggies or free-loaders take advantage of him, treatin' that boy like a baby?"

I repressed a smile. "He doesn't want to live with you? What does he want to do?"

"*Humph*. Told those social workers he wants to go live at that halfway house—the Lighthouse Care Center or whatever they call it—for folks with mental health issues. He said it'll be a peer group, people like himself who take care of each other. *Humph*. What do *they* know about what my baby needs? And those social workers didn't help a'tall! They nodded an' smiled an' said he was showin' good decision making." She glowered at no one in particular. "Good decision making, my big toe. Sounded to me like he was just parroting things those social workers told him to say."

"So what's going to happen?" I prodded.

"Well, he *thinks* he's movin' out of the nursing center tomorrow into that Lighthouse place. But all I need is a few more days, a week maybe, to find us a place to live. Then he'll change his mind, you'll see."

Edesa and I looked at each other. The answer to our prayers was taking shape right before our eyes—and Estelle didn't see it.

"*Mi amiga*," Edesa said softly, laying her hand on top of Estelle's. "Why are you insisting on finding an apartment for you and Leroy to live together?"

Estelle frowned. "Why? Because I need to take care of him, that's why. I wasn't there for him when he needed me, and look what happened! I won't do that again. Lord, forgive me!"

"But, Estelle, don't you see? God has provided a ram in the bush, just like He did for Abraham in the Bible! God tested Abraham, asked him to do something very hard. But God knew Abraham's heart and at the last minute provided a new plan—one that gave life to his son!"

I saw where Edesa was going and eagerly jumped in. I took Estelle's other hand. "God knows your heart, too, Estelle. He knows you'd do anything to help Leroy right now—even give up your engagement to Harry! But God is providing another plan for Leroy—a plan where Leroy will be taken care of properly, not living alone, but as an adult among peers. And He has a good plan for you too." I couldn't help the smile that was spreading on my face. "God brought a good man into your life, Estelle. His name is Harry Bentley. And I, for one, do not believe God has taken him away from you."

Estelle sat perfectly still on the couch, blinking from time to time as if trying to process what we were saying. I hardly dared to breathe, but after a minute or two I broke the silence. "Go to him, Estelle. Go to Harry now. I'll . . . I'll even do lunch for you."

At the word *lunch*, Estelle looked at me with a start, as if the word had broken the spell. "Then you better get started, girl! What are you just sittin' there for?" She struggled up off the couch, grabbed her coat, and stuffed her arms into the sleeves. Heading for the double doors into the foyer like a runaway steam locomotive, she called over her shoulder, "Ham! Cheese! Sandwiches! Chips! Pudding! It's all in the fridge!"

And she was gone.

chapter 43

The weekend seemed to speed by like the El during rush hour, in spite of gray clouds, chilly temperatures, and occasional heavy rains, which were getting a bit dreary as far as I was concerned. Lucy wasn't back from her visit to Maggie Simple's condo by the time I left work Friday evening, which I hoped meant the visit was going well. Then Philip stopped by to see the boys early Friday evening on his way in from the airport, bringing gifts to P.J. and Paul from their grandparents.

I studied him as the boys eagerly opened their gifts—waterproof sport watches with features that included a timer, a chronometer, alarms, the works. Philip's dark-brown hair had grown back, and the scar on his head was nearly invisible now except for the inch that started on his forehead. All in all he was looking great. Even the desperate look in his eyes had given way to a kind of . . . peace.

"Oh yes, got something for you, too, Gabby." Philip handed me a rectangular package wrapped in gold foil and ribbon.

I shook it. It rattled slightly. "Oh, ho! Bet I know what this is." The ribbon and foil wrap came off in seconds. "Yay! Gourmet goodies!" I danced around with the package, which contained three jars of Virginia's finest cashews, roasted peanuts, and black-berry jam. Philip was grinning at me. "Mm, thanks," I said. "You remembered my favorite snacks." I felt I should offer something in return. "Do you want to stay for supper?"

He shook his head. "I better get going. I told the taxi to wait. C'mere, guys, give your ol' dad a hug. Wish we could do something tomorrow, but I need to get an early start looking for an apartment."

I followed him out into the foyer. "Philip? We're having a Thanksgiving dinner here at the House of Hope on Thursday. Everybody's inviting family members. I know the boys would like to have you here. Can you come?"

For a few seconds Philip glanced away as if to get his emotions under control. Then he nodded. "I'll be here," he said, hustling down the steps to the waiting cab.

Saturday was a blur with a lot of the usual on my to-do list: shopping for groceries, cleaning the apartment, folding laundry, and phoning my sisters for our weekly gabfest. I gave the boys a choice of cleaning their rooms or helping Josh Baxter start paint-ing in 3B. *Ha.* So much for getting their rooms cleaned. I could hear their music blasting all the way down the stairwell to the first floor.

Precious knocked on my door just as I was leaving for the gro-cery store, holding up a jar with slips of paper in it. "Draw one. That'll be your Thanksgiving food assignment."

I fished out a slip of paper. "What? Macaroni and cheese? What kind of Thanksgiving food is that? And greens? I don't know how to cook greens."

She looked at me funny. "Girl, ain't no Thanksgivin' dinner without mac-an-cheese. If you wanna throw in somethin' the cowboys eat in North Dakota, too, feel free."

"Who's doing turkey? I'll trade."

Precious snatched the paper from me. "Oh, gimme that. Here. You can have Tanya's and my slip of paper, which has turkey an' cornbread dressing on it. We'll do the mac-an-cheese an' greens." She flounced across the hall muttering something about "white folks' food," but I didn't let it bother me. Turkey I could do.

I didn't hear from Philip Saturday or Sunday, and he didn't come with Jodi and Denny to SouledOut Sunday morning either. Not that I expected he would. Hoped, maybe. After all, he'd gone to church last week while he was in Petersburg.

"Just thank God for whatever baby steps you see, Gabby," Jodi encouraged me after worship. "Right now, he's concentrating on one thing—finding an apartment big enough so he can have the boys sleep over on weekends, but not too big or too expensive."

"Okay, fine." I started toward the coffee pot. Not sure why I felt a little snitty.

"Gabby, wait," Jodi said. "I wanted to ask you something. That whole business about Will Nissan needing to move out of his grandmother's condo so Lucy can move in—Estelle told me he needs someplace to stay till something opens up in student housing at semester break. What do you think about us offering to let him stay with us after Philip moves out? Amanda will be coming home for Thanksgiving and Christmas, but there's Josh's old room—where Philip is staying now."

My little snit about Philip not coming to church dissolved. "Oh, Jodi. That's a fabulous idea. He's such a nice kid—I know he wouldn't be any problem." I gave her a hug. "You and Denny are angels, did you know that?"

"Or selfish." She grinned. "We might be the ones 'entertaining angels unawares'—like the Bible says. And speaking of angels . . ." She jerked her eyes in the direction of Harry and Estelle, who were busy serving coffee to a cluster of nosy folks who clustered around them, probably wanting to confirm that the engagement ring was back on her finger. "Methinks a few angels were working overtime on Estelle and Harry's case this weekend."

We laughed—and then she pulled me into a "prayer hug," whispering a blessing into my ear for our first-ever House of Hope Yada Yada Prayer Group that evening. "You can't imagine how excited we Yada Yadas are about our new offspring." She giggled.

Edesa had suggested we meet in Precious and Tanya's apartment, since we'd been meeting at their apartment for the weekly household meeting, and meeting in Celia and Shawanda's apartment might feel like pressure on Shawanda, when she'd sounded iffy about whether she wanted to come or not. Of course, there was the matter of who's-gonna-watch-the-kids-and-where. We finally all chipped in to pay Sabrina ten bucks to watch the under-ten crowd in my apartment—much to P.J.'s dismay—but it worked out because they put in an old video of *A Bug's Life*, which kept them all entertained for the duration.

Shawanda did come with Celia, saying she'd try it out but not promise anything. "Let us worship *El Señor* as we begin," Edesa encouraged as the six of us women gathered. And she simply began to pray aloud, thanking God for His salvation, for His faithfulness, for His constant watchcare. Precious and Celia both joined in, praying aloud, while I prayed silently—I still wasn't used to this everybody-praying-at-once form of worship. To transition, Edesa led us in a simple chorus of "Oh, How I Love Jesus," which most of us knew.

Then it was time for sharing prayer requests. "Gotta pray for Sabrina," Precious said. "She 'bout ready to pop that baby. Was hoping he would wait till winter break so she wouldn't miss the last few weeks of school, but he actin' like he want outta there."

"So it's a boy?" Shawanda wanted to know. "Sabrina got a name yet?"

"We can talk names another time," Edesa said. "Right now, let's hear from everyone about what we need to pray for."

Tanya was concerned that Sammy didn't have a daddy—and she had no brothers to be active uncles. "He needs somebody to teach him how to be a man—a good man," she said, getting teary.

Celia asked prayer for her daughter, that she'd get drug-free and be the mother she was supposed to be for Keisha. Shawanda passed, saying things were "fine." Edesa asked prayer for Gracie's adoption, which still hadn't been finalized. I didn't know how much to say about Philip, since only Edesa and Precious knew anything more than that we were separated. So I just said, "I want to thank God for answering a lot of prayers for my boys' dad, but ask you all to keep praying for him. He's looking for an apartment and needs a job."

And then we prayed, simple prayers for one another. Celia prayed for Shawanda, too, even though she hadn't asked for anything, and the girl seemed touched by it. And I added, "Lord, thank You for Josh and all the hard work he's doing on 3B, and for the way he keeps this building ship-shape. And, Father, show us who is the next homeless mom to move into the House of Hope when that apartment is ready, because You are creating a family here. Give us open arms to love and serve our new sisters, whoever they may be."

Our prayer meeting lasted only an hour, less time than the movie playing in my apartment, but since it was only sixish, I said the kids could stay and finish. Turning down the volume on the TV set, I stopped by the phone to listen to a couple of messages. The first was from a telemarketer, which I cut off in mid-sentence, and then let it go to the second message.

"Gabby? What's going on?" Oh no! Lee! I'd forgotten to call him again! *"You were going to call me and let me know when we could see each other this weekend. If you don't want to see me, I wish you'd call and tell me, rather than just giving me the silent treatment. So . . . ball's in your court. But, Gabby"*—his voice actually got tender on the answering machine—*"let's not ruin a good thing. You and me."*

I leaned my forehead against the wall. "Oh God," I groaned, "what am I going to do?"

To my relief, when I finally did call Lee, I got his voice mail. Once again I apologized, told him I hadn't intentionally not called him, but I was up to my eyeballs dealing with things at Manna House and the House of Hope and, I admitted, with issues surrounding Philip's recovery. "Please be patient with me, Lee. I don't mean to ignore you. But I've got a lot of things to figure out. Don't call me right now—but I will call you sometime soon. I promise."

I felt better after that, being honest with Lee and putting him "on hold" for the time being, rather than setting up expectations and letting him down.

But I got another surprise when Dandy and I got to work on Monday: Cordelia Soto and her kids were back on the bed list. "Dandy!" screeched Trina and Rufino, her first and second graders, like twin trumpets. "Miss Lucy tol' us you were comin'!"

While the two dark-haired children fell all over the dog, I gave Cordelia a hug and gasped, "What happened? I thought you'd moved back to Little Village, with your brother or something!"

The Latina mother nodded, tears immediately puddling in her dark eyes. "*Sí*, I did. And *mi hermano* was good, wanted me to stay. He said *la familia ayuda a la familia*—you know, family helps family. But he's got a new girlfriend, Norwegian or something, one of those real blondes with white lashes, ever seen that? Anyway, she was all in my face about crowding the apartment, always saying, 'Shut up' to the kids . . ." Cordelia shook her head. "Couldn't take it anymore, Miss Gabby. I don't want to stay where I'm not wanted."

"Well, I want you," I said firmly. "Let's go talk."

"What do you mean?"

I grinned at her. "We've got another apartment open at the House of Hope. And just last night we were praying about who God wanted to move in. See? You're our answer to prayer!"

I started Cordelia on the necessary paperwork the city required, making sure she understood the apartment wasn't ready yet—a week or two at the most—and then went to check in with Lucy before staff meeting. When I asked how the visit to her sister Maggie's condo went, she shrugged. "Nice place. Ain't no room for me there, though. The kid's livin' with her—ain't right to kick him out."

"Oh, Lucy, don't worry about that. He's a college student, he even said he'd like to live near campus. I think he was only living with his grandmother so she wouldn't be alone. But if you live with her, she won't be alone! That's what Maggie wants."

Lucy just shrugged again. "Can't have no dogs, neither. Building rules."

My exasperation level upped a few notches. "Well, you can't take care of Dandy on the street either. Either way, he's doing just fine with Paul." Then my tone softened. "It'll all work out for the best, Lucy. You'll see."

The next time Will and Maggie came to see Lucy, I pulled Will aside. "How did the visit go last week? Any progress in Lucy accepting Maggie's invitation to move in?"

"I think so." He grinned. "We invited her for Thanksgiving dinner. By then I hope to have my stuff moved out of the bedroom so she'll know Nana really wants her to stay—oh! Did you know that the Baxters invited me to hang my socks up at their place till student housing opens up? Soon as Mr. Philip finds a place." The young man laughed. "Kind of like musical chairs."

Musical chairs. I smiled at the analogy as he rejoined his grandmother and Lucy. Except, I thought, when God's providing the music, everyone gets a chair.

Philip called Tuesday night to tell me he'd found an apartment— a two-bedroom with a sun porch that he could use for an office. "I can move in right after Thanksgiving, so I'll get that stuff out of your basement either Friday or Saturday."

"I'm glad, Philip—that you found an apartment, I mean. And work? Have you heard anything from your dad?"

"Funny you should ask. No, haven't heard anything about a Chicago division of the Fairbanks business—but then again, I didn't expect to. Those wheels will grind slowly, knowing the old codgers who sit on the board." He snorted a little. "But you know Peter Douglass—guess he's on the board there at Manna House, and he's also a good friend of Denny Baxter and Harry Bentley. Anyway, Denny says he's looking for someone to manage his new products division at Software Symphony. Looking for someone with business experience, not so much software development. Denny said he'd put in a good word for me. What do you think?"

What did *I* think? I blinked back a few tears. Philip asking me what *I* thought about a job possibility was like a gully gusher after a long drought—*that's* what I thought.

chapter 44

Thanksgiving . . .

When I peeked out the front windows of the sunroom Thursday morning, it looked like just another cloudy day in Chicago with periods of rain. But as the day progressed, the temperature hit the upper fifties and the sun poked through from time to time. Not too bad for the end of November.

I got up early to make the cornbread dressing and stick the turkey in the oven—basted with butter and rosemary and covered with cheesecloth, just like my mother used to season it—and had some quiet time curled up on the window seat with my prayer journal and coffee before the boys got up and House of Hope family guests started to arrive.

We'd agreed to start our progressive dinner around two o'clock, but the front door buzzer was ringing by noon, with the senior Baxters and Josh's sister, Amanda, arriving, carrying pies and various snacking treats as their contribution to the feast. Philip came with the Baxters and showed up with flowers—brilliant yellow, orange, and rust-colored mums—not just for me, but four bouquets, which he delivered to each household. "Nice touch," I teased. "Flowers will buy you dinner."

Celia's daughter showed up, sober as far as I could tell, and ten-year-old Keisha clung to her mother like an extra appendage, preening like a peacock every time she introduced her to someone else. "This my mama, her name is Cissy." Cissy seemed embarrassed, but at the same time pleased to be included as part of the family holiday. From what Celia had said, it'd been many years since they'd spent a holiday together.

The only family member who showed up at Shawanda's request was a cousin . . . male. I gave him a good once-over to make sure he wasn't her midnight visitor masquerading as a relative, but DeWayne Dixon seemed legit, even brought a couple gallons of fruit punch to go with the molded Jell-O salads and Celia's homemade dinner rolls that apartment 2A was providing. It was good to see him playing around with Bam-Bam and Dessa, who clung to his legs like leeches and kept demanding piggyback rides.

Precious didn't have any family in Chicago, so we made an exception and let her invite a girlfriend. "She been more a sister to me than my own family anyway," Precious had sniffed. "Sabrina been callin' her Auntie Kim ever since she a baby."

Tanya had invited an aunt and uncle who were supposed to come on the El from the South Side. When they hadn't appeared by the time we were ready to start our progressive dinner, Josh and DeWayne Dixon offered to walk to the nearest El stop to see if they'd gotten lost, but Tanya snapped, "Don't bother. Auntie Mae's always late to everything. If she and Uncle Dee show up—fine. If they don't show up—fine. I don't care."

I felt bad for Tanya. It was obvious she did care. How could we be the family she so desperately wanted—and needed—for herself and Sammy? Made me realize the House of Hope couldn't fill all the empty spaces in the lives of our homeless moms. Sending up a quickie prayer—*Bring her Auntie Mae and Uncle Dee today, Jesus! Let her know You care!*—I headed for the kitchen to baste the turkey one last time.

My cell phone rang as I pulled the turkey out of the oven. I flipped the phone open. The caller ID said *Will Nissan*. "Will? What's up?" I had to stick a finger in my ear to cut out all the noise in the next room.

"Sorry to bother you, Mrs. Fairbanks, but I came to Manna House to pick up Lucy, you know, for Thanksgiving dinner at our place, and she's not here!"

"What? Are you sure? Maybe she's up in her room, or . . . or down in the dining room. Maybe she got confused and is having turkey dinner there at Manna House."

"She's nowhere in the building. Miss Williams and Mr. Bentley are both here, hosting the dinner for the residents, and they helped me look. Nobody's seen her today. And another thing—her cart is gone."

I closed my eyes and groaned. Lucy took off? Disappeared? *Oh God, not now!*

"Will, I don't know what to say. I am so sorry. She probably got scared. Someone from her family showing up after so many years, the whole idea of coming off the streets and living in an actual apartment . . . it's probably overwhelming to her."

Will was silent for several moments. Then he said, "Yeah, I know. I just hate . . . hate having to go back to the condo and telling Nana that her sister's disappeared again. She's been cooking for two days. It's going to break her heart."

"Oh, Will." My own heart felt like it was breaking for them. But I took a deep breath. "Will, listen to me. Are you listening? *Don't give up*. Keep looking for her. I can't help you look for her right now, but we'll find her. Or she'll show up. She always does, eventually. If anything, I know one thing is true. *Lucy needs you*. She may not know it. But God does. He's the one who helped you find her, and He's not going to let you down."

I was rattled by the news about Lucy, but it was already two thirty and the kids were clamoring to eat. So we all crowded into Celia and Shawanda's apartment on the second floor to begin our progressive Thanksgiving meal with salad and bread—everyone except big-bellied Sabrina, that is, who refused to climb *any* stairs.

Holding hands in one big mob that only slightly resembled a circle, Josh welcomed everyone to the First Annual House of Hope Thanksgiving Dinner, joking that he was being allowed to say the blessing on the food, since as the lone adult male living in a building full of females and kids, it was the only time he got a word in edgewise. As the laughter died down, Josh gave thanks to our heavenly Father ". . . for the House of Hope, for the moms and kids, present and future, who will find a home here, and for our families, who give us the support we all need to make it through."

"Don't forget the food!" Sammy shouted.

"Amen!" we all added amid laughter and a few teary faces.

After taking the edge off our appetites with Shawanda's

layered Jell-O salads and Celia's hot rolls with apple butter, Precious herded everybody down to the first floor, where we'd decided to open up both apartments at the same time, since we had the main course dishes—turkey and dressing in my apartment, side dishes in theirs. "Don't save your paper plates," Precious admonished. "We got new plates for each course—just like in them fancy buffets, 'cept ours is paper."

I shanghaied Philip to carve the turkey, and he seemed grateful to have something to do as he wasn't too comfortable with small talk. He served it elegantly from the beautiful mahogany table, even though our plates were Chinet, not china. The idea was for people to get their turkey and dressing in this apartment, then go across the hall to get their mac-an-cheese and greens. I had just helped Sammy and Keisha with their plates and was ushering them over to the other apartment when we ran into Sabrina standing stock still in the hallway holding her plate and a large plastic cup of fruit punch, staring in horror at a puddle at her feet.

"Ha ha, Sabrina spilled her punch!" Sammy sing-songed and dashed into the open doorway beyond her. Keisha giggled and followed.

"Oh, honey, it's not a prob—" I started to say. And then I read the expression on her face. "Sabrina! Your water broke?"

The teenage girl nodded frantically. I quickly took her plate of food and cup, set them on the stairs, and guided Sabrina into her own apartment. "It's going to be fine, honey. Just relax. We have time . . ." I ran into their bathroom, grabbed a towel, spread it on a chair, and helped her sit down. Then I ran back into my apartment. "Precious! Somebody get Precious!" I hollered. "We're having a baby here!"

Josh and Edesa volunteered to accompany Sabrina and Precious to the hospital, so I gave them my keys to the Subaru, and Grandma Jodi said of course she'd stay with Gracie until they got back home. As Josh and Precious were helping Sabrina down the steps of the six-flat, they passed a bewildered middle-aged black couple who looked as if they'd come to the wrong address.

"Are you Tanya Smith's aunt and uncle?" I asked from the doorway. When they nodded, I said, "Come in! Come in! We just had a little bit of excitement, that's all. Baby's deciding to come into the world on Thanksgiving Day." I laughed and beckoned them inside. "But I know Tanya will be happy to see you. There's still plenty of food left."

It was hard to concentrate on food and guests and cleanup knowing Sabrina was at the hospital having her baby and Lucy was still unaccounted for, but we managed to do justice to the pies the two Baxter families had baked for the party—pumpkin and apple and banana cream and mock mince.

Finally, at seven thirty that evening, we got the call. "Baby boy!" Precious crowed into my ear. "Six pounds, seven ounces. Looks just like me, I think. An' Sabrina doin' fine—though she screamed bloody murder pushin' him out."

"His name, Precious! What's his name?"

"Sabrina still deciding. But right now, given the day he picked to make his grand entrance into the world"—she snickered—"we callin' him Lil' Turkey."

Jodi and Denny and their college daughter, Amanda, were the last to leave, waiting until Josh and Edesa finally came home from the hospital. Which meant Philip, who'd come with them, also stayed into the evening, playing video games with the boys and talking to Denny.

When Josh and Edesa came home around nine—Precious was spending the night at the hospital with Sabrina and "Lil' Turkey"—we all gathered in the Baxter apartment on the third floor to hear a play-by-play recount of the birth. But at one point Philip beckoned me aside. "Mind if I go down to the basement and take a look at the stuff I've got stored there? The apartment I'm renting is a lot smaller than the penthouse, and I want to get an idea of what's going to fit where."

"No problem. I'll go with you." I led him out the Baxters' back door and down the outside stairs to the basement, pulling the light chains after unlocking the door.

Philip walked among the boxes, desk, chairs, china cabinet, bedroom and living room furniture stacked on wooden pallets, then turned to me. "No way all this is going to fit into the apartment I've rented. But maybe you can use some of it here. You should take what you want, Gabby—like the china and china cabinet. The cabinet is really a set with the dining room table. And you've got two more apartments to furnish here at the House of Hope, don't you? Those ladies could probably use anything you don't want or need."

I stared at him. Philip was offering some of this expensive furniture and furnishings to homeless moms like Cordelia Soto? "Are you sure, Philip?"

He nodded. "I'll take my desk and personal stuff, but I certainly don't need three TVs." He gently kicked a box marked "Bedroom TV" and grinned, looking like the teasing twenty-five-year-old who'd swept me off my feet that summer beside the Fountain of Three Graces in Montpellier, France.

"I'm sure we can use it somehow . . . though I don't know about the, um, king-size bed. That won't fit in these apartments either." My face suddenly felt aflame. *Our marriage bed.*

Philip didn't say anything for a few moments. Then, "You know what day tomorrow is, don't you, Gabby?"

I nodded but couldn't speak. November 24, 1990 . . . our wedding day sixteen years ago. I'd been trying *not* to think about it.

He stuffed both hands in his pant pockets—gray Dockers with a casual gray-and-black pullover sweater—and leaned against the king-size bed frame. "Feels weird to be moving into my own apartment on our sixteenth anniversary. But . . ." He shrugged. "I've accepted that's how it is right now. Still, I was wondering, would you be willing to go out to dinner with me tomorrow night for our anniversary? After the move, I mean. I'd like that."

I almost gasped at the bizarre scenario. Six months ago our marriage had crashed and burned . . . I'd ended up in a homeless shelter . . . he'd ended up a casino junkie and victim of a beating by a ruthless loan shark. But here we were, standing in the basement of a vintage Chicago six-flat where *I* lived and that had become a House of Hope for several homeless moms and their kids, surrounded by the boxes and furniture of our old "penthouse life" together, with plans for him to move into an ordinary apartment where *he* was going to live . . . asking me to go out to dinner because it was our sixteenth wedding anniversary.

I was close to laughter—or tears. Wasn't sure which. But I nodded. "Yes. I'd like that."

chapter 45

I wasn't scheduled to work at Manna House on Friday because of the holiday weekend, but I did promise Will I'd help him look for Lucy for a while. Another moderate day in Chicago—some clouds, some sunshine, a sprinkle now and then, upper fifties—which meant she could be anywhere.

And this time she was alone, without Dandy. An old bag lady with a yellow dog was easily remembered—but an old bag lady alone tended to be invisible. Realizing she didn't have Dandy also sapped some of my confidence that she'd show up back at Manna House sooner rather than later. As long as she had the dog, I knew she'd be back to refill her bucket of dog food every week or so from the Hero Dog stash we still had at the shelter.

"I'm so sorry, Will," I said when we finally came back to Manna House without finding her. "Some miracles take a little more time than others. I'll get in touch with you the moment I know anything."

He shrugged. "Yeah. Except, now I don't know whether I should move my stuff up to the Baxters' in Rogers Park or not.

I'd planned to do that today, but now . . . don't want to leave Nana alone if we don't find Lucy."

I didn't know what to tell him. "Just don't give up hope, Will. One of these days she'll realize she needs shelter and she'll be back." *Oh please, God.*

A trip to Weiss Memorial maternity ward that afternoon to see our new House of Hope baby, however, lifted my spirit. Sabrina looked so young lying in the hospital bed, worn out from the delivery, her creamy chocolate skin and black braided hair a stark contrast to the white sheets. But her eyes shone as I peeked into the Plexiglass bassinet beside the hospital bed where "Lil' Turkey" slept, swathed in a receiving blanket cocoon, a knitted blue cap perched on his tiny head. "Oh, Sabrina, he's beautiful," I breathed.

Precious came back just then, carrying a large coffee and bag of doughnuts. "Gabby Fairbanks! Whatchu think? Ain't he beautiful? You want to hold him?"

I'd been too shy to ask. But she practically pushed me into the recliner in the corner of the room and placed the baby in my arms, a small warm bundle that snuggled against my chest, his tiny bow-shaped mouth sucking in his sleep. "Have you named him yet?" I asked Sabrina, touching the soft black hair that escaped from the little blue cap and curled onto his smooth brown forehead.

"His daddy's name be Dontrell, an' I was thinkin' he could be a Junior, but Mama, she don't want no part of him." Sabrina stuck her lip out in a pout, using a tiny mirror to apply lipstick to her pretty face.

"*My* daddy's name is Otis—Sabrina's granddaddy. If she wantin' a family name, Otis would be fine with *me*." Precious sounded just as petulant.

I decided to stay out of this one. One way or another, the baby would have to have a name for his birth certificate.

As I laid the baby back in the bassinet, I kissed Sabrina good-bye and said, "You remember Carolyn at Manna House? She's heading up our afterschool program now. But I think if you asked, she'd be willing to tutor you so you can keep up with your studies and graduate with your class next year. What do you think?"

Sabrina brightened. "Really? Yeah . . . yeah. I wanna graduate high school and maybe go on to community college. Don't wanna just pop out babies." Then she grinned. "Though Lil' Turkey's pretty special, don't you think?"

I shook a finger at her. "You watch out, young lady, or that name'll stick."

Laughing, Precious walked me to the elevator. As the door dinged open, I suddenly turned to her and said, "Today's our sixteenth anniversary."

"Anniversary? Whose—yours an' Philip's?"

I nodded. "And he wants to take me to dinner. And I said yes." I stepped into the elevator and turned around just in time to see Precious's eyes pop and her mouth drop before the door closed between us. *Good.* I wanted somebody to feel as shocked as I did.

Philip had made dinner reservations for seven that night at the Café Bernard, a French bistro on Halstead. But he showed up at my door at six thirty a bit flustered, asking if he could shave in our bathroom. "Somehow my shaver got lost in the move," he said sheepishly. "Had to stop at a drug store and buy a cheap razor."

He'd picked up Paul and P.J. that afternoon when he'd come by with his moving crew—Denny Baxter and some of his Bible study guys—to get his personal things out of the House of Hope basement, then brought the boys back when he came to pick me up. The boys thought losing the shaver was hilarious, but once shaved, Philip looked as handsome as ever in black slacks, an open-necked white shirt, and a blue-gray sport coat. "Just be glad I'm not showing up in sweats," he said. "I was afraid I wouldn't be able to find any of my clothes after Denny's crew got done moving me in."

He seemed pleased at the turquoise two-piece I'd chosen, one of the better colors that complimented my hair—a belted rayon tunic with a boatneck and flared pants that hung in soft folds like a long skirt. I kissed both boys good-bye with reminders about the leftover turkey in the fridge and that Josh Baxter would be checking in on them. "And don't walk Dandy by yourself before bed," I told Paul, smoothing an unruly curl on top of his head. "I'll take him out when I get home."

"Glad you're going out with Dad instead of that other guy," P.J. muttered to me as we headed out the door. I glanced anxiously at Philip, who was holding the foyer door for me, wondering if he'd heard, but he didn't say anything on the way to the restaurant.

The French café was nice, with cloth-covered tables and romantic, recessed lighting, though somewhat crowded. I ordered a beef tenderloin salad and Philip had a steak, adding a nice bottle of red wine because it was a special occasion. We chatted about this and that—Sabrina's baby, Lucy going missing again, where Philip might go to school to be able to teach brilliant young minds like Will Nissan's—but the evening felt a bit schizophrenic. Here we were, celebrating our sixteenth wedding anniversary when we'd been separated for six months and had had no discussion about our future.

As the waiter cleared our entrée dishes and brought dessert and coffee, my cell phone rang with a strange ringtone, and a text message appeared in the little window—something I hardly ever used. I glanced at it in case it had something to do with the boys, but it was from Jodi Baxter, and it just said, "Come 2 church Sunday. Important."

"Everything okay?" Philip asked.

I showed it to him and shrugged. "Have no idea what it's about. Guess I'll find out." I turned the phone off and put it away. No more interruptions.

When I looked up again, I realized Philip was watching me. He suddenly leaned forward and looked into my eyes. "Gabby, I—I want to ask you something—something important."

O-kaay. I lifted my cup of coffee and sipped. Waiting.

"I would like your permission to court you."

My cup jerked and coffee slopped onto the cloth tablecloth. I nervously mopped up the spill with my napkin. "What—what exactly do you mean, 'court' me?"

He laughed self-consciously. "Not exactly a word used in today's dating scene, I realize. But . . . if there's going to be any hope for us, for you and me, I know I need to start all over again. At the beginning. So I'd like your permission to court you—to take you out, to spend time together, getting to know each other all over again. Not rushing it, going as slow as would be comfortable for you. But I'm not talking about just dating for kicks. I'd like to court you with the hope of one day renewing our marriage vows. The vows we made sixteen years ago."

I was so taken aback, I couldn't speak for several long minutes. But I finally found my voice. "But why, Philip? Why do you want to court me?"

I knew he might misunderstand my question, might just repeat what he'd said about hoping we could renew our marriage vows down the road. But there was something I needed to hear— desperately needed to hear before I could say yes.

But he didn't misunderstand. "Why?" His brown eyes softened. "Because I love you, Gabby Shepherd Fairbanks. I had no idea how much I loved you until I lost you. And I want a chance to win your love back."

Tears crowded into my eyes and slid down my cheeks, and for a few moments I was too choked up to do anything but mop my face with the now-mangled napkin. But finally I smiled through the tears and reached across the candlelit table, taking his hand. "Yes," I whispered. "You may court me, Philip Fairbanks. From the beginning."

The smile on his face was one of the most beautiful things I'd ever seen.

We sat in silence for a few minutes, just holding hands, absorbing the immensity of the decision we'd just made. Then, knowing I risked spoiling the sweetness of the moment, I cleared my throat. "We need marriage counseling, too, Philip. Which will mean work. *Work* . . . not just wine and roses. Are you willing to do that?"

He nodded soberly. "Whatever it takes."

One of the wait staff came by with a fresh pot of coffee, and our hands slid apart as he filled our cups. We both sipped the fragrant coffee in silence, gazing at each other over the rims of our cups, hugging our private thoughts. It occurred to me with sudden clarity that when I got home that evening, I needed to make an important phone call. Or maybe a letter would be better. A "Dear John" letter to Lee Boyer. *"Dear Lee . . ."*

I finally put down my coffee. "Can I tell you where I'd like the beginning of our courtship to start?"

Philip looked at me curiously. "Well, sure. Your call, Mop Top."

I smiled at the familiar nickname. "Come to church with me on Sunday. Come to SouledOut with me and the boys."

He nodded. "All right. I will. When should I pick you up?"

The hospital released Sabrina and the baby on Saturday afternoon. I picked them up, bringing one of the infant car seats donated to Manna House. "His name's Timothy," Sabrina said proudly as she strapped the tiny little boy into the car seat. "It's from the Bible. So Mama's happy. But I like it too."

"What about a middle name?"

"Gonna let him choose that himself when he get old enough."

I winced. If it didn't devolve into "Lil' Timmy Turkey" before then.

True to his word, Philip picked us up in his Lexus SUV at nine Sunday morning. Since we had a ride, I let the Baby Baxters use my Subaru to get to church. They brought Tanya and Sammy too. Nice. Maybe Tanya would find the extended family she needed at SouledOut.

All four of us Fairbankses walked in together and sat in the same row, Philip on one side of Paul and P.J., me on the other. I knew eyebrows were raising, but people just greeted us with handshakes, hugs, and smiles. Before the service started, Josh motioned to P.J. and asked if he could man the soundboard that morning since they were short a man. Now only Paul sat between us.

Jodi came by before the service started and asked about Sabrina's baby. "They finally gave him a name," I said. "Timothy."

She beamed. "Great name! Timothy means 'One who honors God'! Tell Sabrina that, okay? This little boy might be a blessing, just like the biblical Timothy."

I grabbed her hand before she left to find her own seat. "What's so important about today? The text message you sent, I mean."

Jodi just grinned. "You'll see."

Avis Douglass was worship leader that morning on the theme of "Give thanks!" and the scriptures and songs of praise and thanksgiving wove together like a tapestry. We sang "Awesome God" and "We Bring a Sacrifice of Praise" and "Give Thanks with a Grateful Heart," lifting the music with such heartfelt joy that passersby shopping the mall all around us started peeking in the windows and the door. Philip did not know the songs, but I saw his fingers tapping in time to the music on the back of the chair in front of us.

As the worship band wound down the music, Pastor Joe Cobbs practically bounced up to the front, followed by the older and more sedate Pastor Clark. I loved seeing the black and white pastors together, though they did make a funny pair. Pastor Cobbs was short and energetic, Pastor Clark taller, thin, and his shoulders tended to hunch over like a tree bending in the wind.

Facing us, Pastor Cobbs said, "On this Thanksgiving weekend, we have a very special occasion to celebrate—two people who have every reason to give God thanks for bringing them together. Will the musicians come forward?"

"'Scuse me," Paul said, and climbed over Philip and walked to the electric keyboard up front. Philip and I looked at each other. *What in the world—?* And then we saw Jermaine Turner, Mabel's nephew, join Paul at the electric keyboard. I swiveled my head—there was Mabel in a row behind us. What was going on? She was a member at Salem Baptist down on the South Side. I gave her a questioning look, but she just smiled. And I turned back as Paul and Jermaine began playing a duet that I recognized as Bach's "Jesu, Joy of Man's Desiring," the same one they'd played at Lucy's birthday party.

"Will everyone stand in honor of the bride and groom?" said Pastor Cobbs over the music.

What—? Bride and groom? With everyone else, my head swiveled toward the double doors that led into the back rooms of SouledOut—and saw Estelle Williams and Harry Bentley walk out together holding hands, both of them dressed in beautiful African dress. Estelle was wearing a cream-colored caftan and head wrap with huge gold swirls that seemed to sparkle under the fluorescent lights, and she was carrying a white rose. Harry was wearing a man's tunic of the same material, looking a bit shy and embarrassed. But one side glance at the woman beside him, and he strode down the middle aisle with her, beaming.

I strained my neck looking for Jodi and gave her a *why-didn't-you-tell-me!* glare when I caught her eye, but she just grinned back.

Estelle and Harry stopped when they reached the two pastors standing on the six-inch platform at the front of the room, and the music faded. Pastor Cobbs had to take a step or two to the side to be seen by the congregation. "You all may be wondering why we are having a wedding in the middle of a worship service here at

SouledOut. Well, why not? Estelle Williams and Harry Bentley, who are members here, decided they're not getting any younger— and they told Pastor Clark and me they wanted to put their time and energy into building a good marriage, not a big shindig wedding that would last one day and run them into debt."

Laughter rippled through the congregation.

"And second, what better time to say vows to each other and before God than in a service dedicated to God, in the presence of their brothers and sisters in Christ?"

Now spontaneous clapping erupted around the room. I was so excited, I could hardly sit still. Harry and Estelle were actually getting married! I might even forgive them for not telling me ahead of time.

Pastor Cobbs held up his hand for silence. "This won't take long, but I have a word for the bride and groom. Estelle, God has not only given you a talent for the traditional gifts of sewing and cooking that used to keep a woman at home—but He has also given you a compassionate heart, and you have used those gifts to make a home for homeless women at the Manna House Women's Shelter—not to mention dressing up this ex-cop so fine that he's barely recognizable."

Again we all laughed as Harry ducked.

"Harry, you've been a police officer most of your life and seen a good many rough things go down. But you always tried to protect the innocent and do what is right. You've even taken your grandson, DaShawn, into your life and your home, and given him love and shelter. Now, God is giving you a good woman—a woman who has lost her home and, in a sense, her family. Be her shelter, Harry Bentley, the way God is our shelter and covers us with His wings."

"Amen!" . . . "Say it, pastor!" rang out all over the room.

"Pastor Clark will now lead Harry and Estelle as they exchange their vows. Can we have the rings?"

DaShawn, dressed in a white shirt and bow tie, stood up and, with a big smile on his face, fished in his pants pocket and pulled out two gold bands, handing them to Pastor Clark.

As SouledOut's copastor started the brief ceremony, Philip scooted into Paul's empty seat between us. He leaned close to my ear and whispered, "Gabby, I want to learn how to be that for you—a shelter, not the storm."

Turning my face toward him, I saw the sincerity in his eyes. Maybe God *was* doing a new thing in Philip's life . . . and mine. It would take awhile. We had a lot of rebuilding to do, a lot of trust to regain, a lot of old patterns to change. If it were going to work, we'd both need God at the center this time. Maybe we could change the words to my favorite gospel song . . .

When we *need a shelter, when* we *need a friend*
We *go to the Rock.*

As Harry and Estelle, bless them, said their vows with the whole church as their witnesses, I reached out, put my hand in Philip's, and whispered back, "I've got a song I want to share with you . . ."

reading group guide

1. If you've read the previous novels in the House of Hope series, what were the questions or situations you hoped might be resolved in *Who Is My Shelter*? Did you have expectations for how things would (should) turn out with Philip? With Lee? For Lucy? For Gabby? Were you disappointed? Surprised? Pleased? In what ways?

2. Philip Fairbanks seems to be the "jerk husband we all love to hate." At what point did you begin to have some empathy for him as a person, even with all his faults? If not, what factors stood in your way?

3. Will Nissan is a new character in this novel who befriends Philip. In what way(s) does his friendship with Philip complicate things for Gabby? In what way(s) is his friendship a gift to Philip?

4. In chapter 4, Gabby admits she resents having to deal with all the mess Philip's in—just when the fledgling House of Hope needs her time and attention to get up and running on a solid footing. Have you experienced a crunch between family needs and ministry needs that pulled you in different directions? How can we tell when Satan's just distracting us from doing the Lord's work, versus needing to reset or readjust our priorities?

5. The House of Hope residents decide a regular house meeting is important to deal with kinks that need to get worked out,

relationship issues, and infractions of the rules—as well as to plan celebrations and give encouragement. Some families schedule a regular family meeting for the same reasons! If you've tried something like that in your family, what were the benefits? How might family meetings help solve some of the everyday problems in *your* family?

6. As things get more complicated with Philip—he's in debt, he's in trouble, he's in danger—Gabby struggles with what it would mean to forgive him (see chapters 4, 16, 17, 18). If you had had a chance to counsel Gabby, what cautions would you give her? Advice? Encouragement? Scriptures? What experience with forgiveness could you share with her from your own life and relationships?

7. Even though Gabby found physical shelter at Manna House when she was homeless and now has a home of her own, emotionally she "still needed a shelter, a safe place for my broken heart to be mended"—a longing for "a man's arms around me . . . making me feel he would protect me from any storm . . ." (see chapter 18). Many of us can identify with that natural longing, that human need. And yet, why do you think the Voice [the Holy Spirit] in her spirit said, *"Wait, Gabby. Let Me be your everything"*?

8. Gabby and Edesa use Jodi Baxter's idea of the *meaning of names* to bless the shelter women on their Fall Getaway. Do you know the meaning of your name? Check out these scriptures to learn just how important our names are to God: Isaiah 43:1; Isaiah 49:1; and Isaiah 49:14–16—especially if you put both the NIV and NLT translations of verse 16 together.

9. Throughout the House of Hope series, Gabby has been learning

that *God* is the One we can go to when we have no place to go. *God* is the One we can talk to when no one else seems to be listening. *God* is the One we can lean on when even well-meaning people fail us. *God* is the unmovable ROCK of our salvation, the shelter we need when the storms of life rage around us. And yet . . . God uses *people*, too, to be His hands, His feet, His ears, His presence. In chapter 20, when the Baxter family surrounded Philip and the boys with their presence and protection so Gabby could take the shelter ladies on their Fall Getaway, Gabby thought, "God's peace in skin is what it felt like." Has someone been "God's peace in skin" for you lately? Is there someone for whom *you* could be "God's peace in skin" this week?

10. Feeling caught between the two men in her life, and not even sure *what* she really wants or needs or feels (see chapter 31), Gabby turns often to the verses in Proverbs 3:5–6: "Trust in the Lord with all your heart and lean not on your own understanding; in all your ways submit to him, and he will make your paths straight" (NIV). How do these verses help Gabby navigate her relationship with Lee Boyer? With Philip? Do you think the outcome would have been different if she'd followed her "natural" inclinations? Why or why not? For better or worse?

11. What does it mean to *you* to "trust God with all your heart" instead of trusting (leaning on) your own understanding of things? What does it mean to "submit to Him" in *all* your ways? Are you facing a situation in your own life where you need to apply this scripture and claim its promise?

12. Why do you think Gabby had a hard time responding to Philip's letter, even though he admitted he had hurt her deeply, that he was wrong, and wanted her to know he was "desperately sorry" (chapter 32)? What made a difference at their

family dinner before Philip left for Virginia that allowed Gabby to finally respond, to finally forgive (chapter 36)? Do you think it was a good thing for Gabby to ask Philip to forgive her as well for her failings in the marriage? Or did that stick in your craw, like comparing a chilly breeze to a raging hurricane? Explain your reaction to that conversation.

13. Why do you think Lucy disappeared *again* on Thanksgiving Day—just when it looked as if she would have a chance to be reconciled with her family and finally get off the street? If you were going to write Lucy's life story, what in her past do you think triggers her disappearing acts? (Have fun with this! No wrong answers. In fact, maybe there's a book idea here!)

14. In the last chapter, Philip asked Gabby if he could "court" her as a way of starting over. Does that seem like a promising concept to you after the ugly breakdown in their marriage? Why or why not? What pitfalls might be ahead? What would be the benefits?

Has God been nudging you, your prayer group, or your church to ask, "How can *we* make a difference for homeless men and women in our community?" If so, a great resource is a new book, *The Invisible: What the Church Can Do to Find and Serve the Least of These*, by Arloa Sutter, director of Breakthrough Ministries. (Breakthrough's shelters for homeless men and women in Chicago were the inspiration for the Yada Yada House of Hope series.) Check it out on our website: www.daveneta.com.

Author to Author Interview

The Thomas Nelson Fiction team invited our authors to interview any other Thomas Nelson Fiction author in an unplugged Q&A session. They could ask any questions about any topic they wanted to know more about. What we love most about these conversations is that they reveal just as much about the ones asking the questions as they do the authors who are responding. So sit back and enjoy the discussion. Maybe you'll even be intrigued enough to pick up one of Kim's novels and discover a new favorite writer in the process.

NETA JACKSON: Kim, I'm so excited to meet a new, promising author on the Thomas Nelson fiction team! And it was so fun to meet you in person at the ICRS convention in St. Louis. Tell my readers a little bit about yourself. (You could pass for a college kid. Are you really only 19???)

KIM CASH TATE: Oh, you flatter me, Neta! You know I turned 22 this year! Okay, my teenager's giving me the eye, so I'd better 'fess up. I've been married to my husband, Bill, for 18 years, and we have a teenage son and soon-to-be teenage daughter—in other words, we're in the no-drama super fun season! *grin* I'm originally from Maryland, but we've lived in St. Louis for almost a decade. Oh, and I had a little stint as a practicing attorney—well, 8 years—but somewhere in there I gave my life to Christ and He kind of let me know that practicing law was *my* plan, not His. Who knew He had a plan for my life? That still blows me away.

NJ: Okay, okay, so you're a full-fledged, card-carrying, happily married adult—with kids! In your recent novel, *Faithful*, you tackle a touchy subject: infidelity. You really peel away the layers of lies and self-deception that usually mask the true nature of unfaithfulness. What prompted you to write this novel?

KCT: I had friends who'd been married for decades, strong Christians I looked up to as role models in marriage, and their marriage ended because of an affair. I was so rocked by it. I remember asking God, "If *their* marriage could end like that, whose is safe? What hope do we have?"

Over time, that situation and others began to bubble into a story. I wanted to explore real life trials and real life responses to those trials—the questioning, the doubt, the fear, the weariness—as we try to hang on and trust God. The back of the book asks, "Will they trust God's faithfulness . . . and find the strength to be faithful to Him?" That's really what it's about—that two-sided dynamic. God is always faithful, but will we trust that, and will we be faithful to Him? In a very real sense, whether we're married or single, He's the One to whom we pledge to be true.

NJ: Let's get real. Someone reading *Faithful* might feel your characters could maybe-kinda-sorta be excused for "fudging" a bit on the faithfulness scorecard. I mean . . . A wife finding her husband with another woman in *her* bed? A believing wife "unequally yoked" to an unbelieving husband—and then she meets a wonderful Christian man who shares her faith? (Is this the man she should have married?) And their friend who's forty and still single? (That clock is ticking!) What would you say to someone who thinks you haven't allowed any "wiggle room" for certain "understandable" circumstances?

KCT: Ahh, yes, the perfect storm for each of them! It would've been too easy otherwise. (smile) These are Christian women who would tell you in a heartbeat that they love God and want to honor Him in every area of life. But when those storms blow in, they're challenged to step back and assess whether they'll *really* trust Him. A wife finding her husband in bed with another woman is the deepest of betrayals. Without divulging the outcome, I wanted to show that even through the unthinkable, God is with us. He's our strength, our peace, and our guide. Of all the characters, she's the one who could respond in a number of ways, and we wouldn't blame her. But staying faithful to God in the storm is our saving grace.

Phyllis is the believing wife with the unbelieving husband. She actually became a believer during the marriage, and rather than join her, her husband has grown more and more hostile toward her new faith. In her wildest dreams, she'd never think she could be unfaithful. But she finds herself drawn to another man *because* he's a strong Christian, the very thing she wants her husband to be. Understandable wiggle room? She'd like to think so!

And Cyd, the friend who's single and turning forty—and forced to ring in her fortieth as maid of honor at her younger sister's wedding. I love Cyd. She knows exactly the kind of Christian man she's waiting for, and she will not compromise her principles . . . until she meets the playboy best man who just happens to sweep her off her feet. Oh yes, that clock is ticking . . . but she knows she's about to borrow a whole lot of trouble if she doesn't "wiggle" out of this one fast!

NJ: *Faithful* is your first novel with Thomas Nelson—but not your first novel. Tell us about your previous books—one of which is a very personal memoir, I understand.

KCT: The memoir was my first book, published in 1999. Had no plans to write a book. I was on maternity leave with my firstborn and felt

God tugging on my heart to leave the firm. Got my own new plan and started researching home-based businesses. But one day at church, I heard clearly in my heart that He wanted me to write about my spiritual journey. Even had the title—*More Christian than African-American*—before I left the service. Seems a little crazy that God would move me to write about my spiritual journey so early in my spiritual walk. But a huge part of my identity—okay, basically *all* of my identity—was in who I was as a black person. I like to say I lived, moved, and had my being in blackness. But God let me know I had been bought with a price—I needed to live, move, and have my being in Him. That was a jarring adjustment! The book tells the before and after of my spiritual journey, touching on many other ways in which Jesus turned my life upside down.

Fiction hadn't been on my radar screen either. After the memoir, I thought I'd write more nonfiction—then, with two toddlers, I thought I'd never write again! But years later, a story began forming in my mind, which became my first novel, *Heavenly Places*. It's about a woman whose mother had always treated her in an inferior manner. She has little self-worth, and her attempt to find it in a career was successful—until that career was gone. The reader goes on a journey with her as her sister coaxes her into a small group Bible study, where they decide to study Ephesians. Slowly, and with lots of bumps along the way, she begins to learn who she is in Christ. Her views of herself, her husband and children—and even her mother—are transformed. The greatest blessing has been hearing from women who've read the novel alongside the book of Ephesians, some reading Ephesians for the first time. Hearing that they've been inspired to see themselves and their circumstances through God's eyes—and even to start their own Bible studies!—has been pretty amazing too.

NJ: Did you have a passion to write as a young girl? Who (or what) influenced you the most to become a novelist?

KCT: I was one of those girls who always had a notebook and pens at the ready, writing little poems, journaling, even taking a stab at song lyrics. But as I said, writing novels never entered my imagination. Total and complete God-thing. When He began piecing *Heavenly Places* together in my mind, I cocked my head, and said, "Huh. Really? You want me to write fiction? How in the world do I write fiction?" Didn't know a single fiction author, had never read a writing blog or been to a writing conference—nothing. He led me through the entire process, from books I should read (both novels and books about the craft), to the actual writing. And you'd better believe I was hanging on to Him every step of the way!

NJ: What are some of your other passions and interests? Any secret wishes—something you'd love to do that you haven't done yet? (You've got time, girl!)

KCT: I've still got some time? Cool! Let me grab another sip of coffee. When I think "passions and interests," the Bible comes to mind immediately. I knew next to nothing about the Bible when I became a believer at 27. But once I started digging in, I was totally captivated . . . and my world completely changed—attitudes, beliefs, opinions, actions, everything. Now, I have a passion to help others understand and be changed by the truths of the Bible. I love that I can do that through fiction, and I've also done weekly devotions and small group Bible studies. Given the way God likes to surprise me, I'm looking forward to seeing what else He might do with this passion.

But wait . . . can't leave "passions and interests" without mentioning Hawaii! That's right, it's my dream to move there one day, to bask by the ocean, in the shadow of majestic mountains, daily soaking in warm sun. That's my ultimate secret wish!

NJ: And now . . . you've recently joined Women of Faith as one of their speakers! Wow! That's fantastic! Tell us how that came about and what God is teaching you through that experience.

KCT: Oh, God has taught me tons, from the moment I became aware that I was being considered for Women of Faith. The Thomas Nelson Fiction team threw my name into the mix, and I thought it was nice but it wouldn't go anywhere. Me? Speaking in front of thousands of women in an arena? The most I'd done was speak to a couple hundred in a church setting. But God had already been nudging me about "upping" my faith, so He kept whispering to my heart, *Believe.* I was flown to a conference and had an opportunity to meet the Women of Faith leadership, as well as speakers and others on the team. It was fabulous—yet, I still struggled to believe it could actually happen. Soon after, though, I was offered an opportunity to speak at four events in 2010. In 2011, I'll be speaking at all fourteen events on the Women of Faith Imagine tour. When I think of the way it unfolded, I'm still in awe of God. He's teaching me, yes, to believe that He is able to accomplish His plans and purposes—regardless of our own limited abilities or experiences. But He's teaching me so much more. Doesn't matter how many are in the audience. I have an audience of One, and I need to keep my eyes fixed on Jesus.

NJ: As you know, there haven't been that many African American novelists published in the Christian market, so I'm delighted the evangelical world is discovering this rich resource. Since each part of the Body of Christ is important and has something crucial to contribute to the kingdom of God, what would you say African American Christians have to bring to "Christian fiction" that's unique?

KCT: Whew . . . do I still have time? Can I pour a fresh cup of java? It's interesting . . . African Americans, like everyone else, come from so many different walks of life. What anyone brings to fiction will depend on background, denomination, and his or her personal walk with God, among other influences. For example, many African American Christians grew up in the church, whereas I didn't belong to a church until my late twenties.

But absolutely, I do believe we bring a unique voice to the genre. We're able to infuse our culture, aspects of our unique history in America, and perspectives that others in the Body of Christ may have never considered or experienced. For example, in *Heavenly Places*, the main character has a darker skin complexion, and her mother has always openly favored her sister, who has lighter skin. Many outside of the African American community have told me they had no idea that that sort of favoritism or dynamic existed.

I also think the "something crucial" we bring is simply awareness that we exist as part of this Body. As you stated, there haven't been many African American novelists published in the Christian market. If someone picks up a "Christian fiction" book, the chances are great that it won't even contain African American characters (which is why I admire your books so much!). In essence, just as we have our separate places of worship, we have our separate segments of the publishing market. But Jesus prayed that we would be one, as He and the Father are one. I think our voice in "Christian fiction" helps to bridge the greater gap that exists. It's my prayer that many Christian authors, regardless of color, will begin to diversify their characters, to show through story how we ought to live in life, as living, breathing parts of the Body fitted together.

NJ: Who are some of your favorite authors? Any recent discoveries you'd like to recommend?

KCT: Because I've homeschooled a number of years and have read lots of books with my kids, my list of favs might seem a tad unusual. But I just love Homer's *The Iliad* and *The Odyssey*. Such great fun reading those with my son! Another fav is J.R.R. Tolkien's *The Lord of the Rings*. Hmm . . . I see I have a love affair going with the epic story. But I do have present-day favorites as well! Can't claim you as a "discovery"—not in front of your readers anyway—but I can't let the interview end without saying how much I love you! I've told you before and have to say openly that you are my hero. I love your heart for the Body of Christ and love that you write stories that reflect the diversity of the Body. And you're just a plain good storyteller as well (smile). It's very obvious that your walk with God spills out on paper. Thank you for being you!

NJ: Kim, I know readers who are captivated by *Faithful* will be looking forward to your next novel. Any hints what that will be, and when it will be coming out?

KCT: I'd love to give some hints! My next novel is *Cherished*, and it releases in fall of 2011. It features many of the same characters in *Faithful*, but will focus on two new main characters, one of whom is "the other woman" who was involved in the affair in *Faithful*. The heart of this book is the lavishness of God's grace and mercy to cover the shame and guilt of the past. I'm praying that many women will find healing and strength through the story.

NJ: Thanks so much, Kim! You certainly have your plate full with raising children, writing novels, and speaking for Women of Faith. Whew! We don't want you to burn out—but we *are* looking forward to the ways God intends to use you to bless the rest of us in the Body of Christ. Shalom, dear sister!

To learn more about Kim Cash Tate and her novels,
visit her website at KimCashTate.com.

Party with the
Yada Yada Prayer Group!

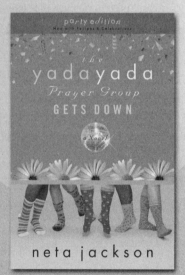

Each novel
includes
numerous pages
of celebration
ideas and
recipes that flow
from the story

An excerpt from

The Yada Yada Prayer Group

The lobby of the embassy suites hotel in Chicago's northwest suburbs was packed with women. An intense hum ros and fell, like a tree full of cicadas. "Girl! I didn't know you werecoming!" . . . "Where's Shirlese? I'm supposed to be roomin' with her." . . . "Look at you! That outfit is fine!" . . . "Pool? Not after spending forty-five dollars at the salon this morning, honey.Who you kiddin'?"

Avis and I wiggled our Mutt and Jeff selves through the throng of perfumed bodies and presented our reservations at the desk.

"Jodi Baxter? And . . . Avis Johnson. You're in Suite 206." The clerk handed over two plastic key cards. "If you're here for the Chicago Women's Conference"—she added with a knowing smile—"you can pick up your registration packet at that table right over there."

Avis let me forge a path back through the cicada convention to a long table with boxes of packets marked A–D, E–H, all the way to W–Z. As we were handed our packets emblazoned with CWC in curlicue calligraphy, I noticed a bright gold sticker in the right-hand corner of mine with the number 26 written in black marker. I glanced at the packet being given to the woman standing next to me at the A–D box who gave her name as "Adams, Paulette"—but her gold sticker had the number 12.

"What's this?" I asked the plump girl behind the registration table, pointing to the number.

"Oh, that." Miss Helpful smiled sweetly. "They'll explain the numbers at the first session. Don't worry about it . . . Can I help you?" She turned to the next person in line.

Humph. I didn't want to wait till the first session. I was nervous enough surrounded by women who seemed as comfortable in a crowd of strangers as if it were Thanksgiving at Grandma's. I didn't want any "surprises." Avis waved her packet at me over the heads of five women crowding up to the table between us and nodded toward the elevators. We met just as the door to Elevator Two pinged open, and we wheeled our suitcases inside.

"What number did you get?"

"Number?"

"On your packet, right-hand corner, gold sticker."

"Oh." Avis turned over the packet she was clutching in one hand, along with her plastic key card, purse strap, and travel-pack of tissues. "Twenty-six. What's it for?"

I smiled big and relaxed. "I don't know. They'll tell us the first session." Whatever it was, I was with Avis.

As it turned out, we didn't need our key cards. The door to Suite 206 stood ajar. Avis and I looked at each other and stole inside like the Three Bears coming home after their walk in the woods. The sitting room part of the suite was empty. However, through the French doors leading into the bedroom, we could see "Goldilocks" sitting on the king-size bed painting her toenails while WGCI gospel music blared from the bedside radio.

The stranger looked up. "Oh, hi!" She waved the tiny polish brush in our direction. "Don't mind me. Make yourselves at home."

an excerpt from *The Yada Yada Prayer Group*

We stood and stared. The woman was average height, dark-skinned, and lean, with a crown of little black braids sporting a rainbow of beads falling down all around her head. Thirties, maybe forties; it was hard to tell. Her smile revealed a row of perfect teeth, but a scar down the side of her face belied an easy life.

Avis was braver than I was and said what I was thinking. "Uh, are we in the right room? We didn't know we had another roommate."

The woman cocked her head. "Oh! They didn't tell you at registration? Suite 206, right?" She capped the nail polish and bounced off the bed. "Florida Hickman—call me Flo." She stuck out her hand. "Avis and Jodi, right? That's what they tol' me downstairs. Anyway, I was going to room with this sister, see, but she had to cancel, and I didn't want to pay for a whole suite all by myself. Had to sell the kids just to get here as it is." She laughed heartily. Then her smile faded and she cocked her head. "You don't mind, do you? I mean . . . I don't need this whole king-size football field to myself. Unless . . ." Her forehead wrinkled. "You want me to sleep on the fold-out couch?"

My good-girl training rushed to my mouth before I knew what I was saying. "Oh, no, no, that's okay. We don't mind." Do we, Avis? I was afraid to look in Avis's direction. We had pretty much agreed driving out that since it was a suite, we could each have a "room" to ourselves. Avis was definitely not the stay-up-late, sleepover type.

"Oh. Well, sure," Avis said. "It's just that no one told us." I didn't know Avis all that well, but that wasn't enthusiasm in her voice. "I'll sleep on the fold-out," she added, wheeling her suitcase over to the luggage stand.

I noticed that she didn't say "we." I stood uncertainly. But our new friend had generously offered the other side of the mammoth

426

bed, so I dragged my suitcase into the bedroom and plopped it on the floor on the other side of Florida's nail salon.

Well, this was going to be interesting. I had thought it would be quite an adventure to get to know Avis as my roommate for the weekend. As members of the same church, this was a chance to get beyond the niceties of Sunday morning and brush our teeth in the same sink. But I hadn't counted on a third party. God knows I wanted to broaden my horizons, but this was moving a little faster than I felt ready for.

As I hung up the dress I hoped would pass for "after five" in the narrow closet, I suddenly had a thought. "Florida, what number is on your registration packet?"

Florida finished her big toe and looked at it critically. "Number? . . . Oh, you mean that gold sticker thing on the front?" She looked over the side of the bed where she'd dumped her things. "Um . . . twenty-six. Why?"

about the author

Neta Jackson's award-winning Yada books have sold roughly 700,000 copies and are spawning prayer groups across the country. She and her husband, Dave, are also an award-winning writing team, best known for the Trailblazer Books—a 40-volume series of historical fiction about great Christian heroes with 1.5 million in sales—and *Hero Tales: A Family Treasury of True Stories from the Lives of Christian Heroes* (vols. 1–4). They live in the Chicago metropolitan area, where the Yada stories are set.